RYAN BARTLETT

THE
LAST
OF THE
DREAMERS

Kingdom of Athus
Westharvest
Athus
Modalphia
Anchorsfell
Ergman Island
Morvena
Archmagi
Refuge
N

The Origin
Alysand
Fyrin
Celara
Kingdom
Broich
Olthar
Prixia

The Last of the Dreamers

Copyright © 2021 by Ryan Bartlett

Cover art and design by Ryan Bartlett
using Midjourney and Adobe® Photoshop.

Edited by Stephanie Slagle
www.stephanieslagle.com

Map art and design by Angel Perez and Ryan Bartlett.
Check out Angel Perez's Simple Fantasy Maps at
www.fiverr.com/s/gzLWja

ISBN: 979-8-9890225-1-9

ABOUT THE AUTHOR

Ryan Bartlett

Follow me on social media to stay up to date on my writing.

Website: RyanBartlettBooks.com
Email: contact@raynbartlettbooks.com
Twitter: @ryan.bartlett.author
TikTok: @AuthorRBartlett
facebook.com/RyanBartlettAuthor
instagram.com/AuthorRBartlett

THE
LAST
OF THE
DREAMERS

By
Ryan Bartlett

TABLE OF CONTENTS

1

The Nightmare Begins

Sihera's hand trembled as she peered down at the dagger clenched within her fist, her heart aching. She never knew where her dreams would take her, but this dream frightened her the most.

Why? she thought to herself. Her eyes turned forward to the teenage boy standing with his back toward her—oblivious to the danger he was in. *Why does he have to die?*

Sihera was sixteen years old, but her brown, still youthfully wide eyes swelled with tears from behind the black curls of her hair.

"Sihera!" A man's voice rang out through her mind.

She woke with a gasp, her eyes blinking wildly. She glanced around the room, trying to recall where she was.

Large stone walls and oak shelves lined with books surrounded her; she was in the study hall of the Archmagi Refuge, sitting on a meditation mat, wearing her mage's robe. Laval, her grey-haired and thin-framed mentor, was beside her shaking her shoulders. His face was normally flat and emotionless, but this time there was panic in his eyes.

The words flew from his mouth. "Sihera, we have to go! The refuge is under attack!"

Her brow tightened in confusion as her head reared back. "What?" she asked, gently pawing Laval's hand off her shoulder. "What are you talking about?"

"We're evacuating the city. I must get you to a safe—"

Evacuating? But what happened to the boy in her dream? Sihera locked her arms out, pressing her palms against Laval's chest. "Wait! I have to see him!" She clamped her eyes shut and focused on recovering her dream. A cloudy image of the boy began to appear, but before she could clear the fog, she was ripped awake again.

A grunt was forced from her lungs as Laval hoisted her over his shoulder, his boney collar digging into her stomach.

"There isn't time!" Laval cried, flinging the door open as he rushed outside.

Wincing at the burst of sunlight, Sihera shielded her eyes. A barrage of cries and calamity flooded her ears as people ran frantically about. Families scrambled for their belongings, and women called for their children. A group of Archmagi guards—knights in full plate—pushed through the crowd. In the distance, the outer city wall began to crack and crumble. Her eyes widened. Laval was right; this was serious.

As the wall collapsed, a wave of creatures clambered over the debris. They were aiko. Those thin, gangly frames. Their large, black, deep-set eyes. The sleek, rubbery texture of their charcoal-colored hide. And worst of all, those razor-sharp talons for hands.

As a swell of aiko flowed over the wall, the wail of their shrieks—a sound akin to a terrible, high-pitched hiss—filled the air.

The aiko had breached the city walls. She knew it wouldn't be long before the creatures ravaged the entire city and everyone inside it.

Laval turned and sprinted toward the docks, Sihera bouncing along on his shoulder.

Why was there suddenly so much suffering and death around her? She struggled to make sense of it. All Sihera ever wanted was to protect the people she cared about.

An image of the boy from her dream flashed before her eyes.

The boy! What had happened to him? As Laval waded through the mayhem, Sihera conjured up all of her will and concentrated.

Closing her eyes and focusing on her breathing, she forced the chaos surrounding her from her mind. Slowly, the noises faded, and the image of the boy came to the forefront of her consciousness.

When her dream came back into focus, something had changed. She let out a sigh of relief to see the boy walking safely in front of her, leading her down a winding, cavernous hall. Moonbeams poured in through cracks in the ceiling, creating beautiful drapes of white light along the rocks.

The boy held her hand as he walked. His skin was soft and warm, and her heart gave a pleasant flutter as the heat rose into her round cheeks.

Sihera cared for this boy. She didn't know his name, but she had dreamt of him before. He was like her, a Dreamer—a person born with the gift of magic.

"Where are we going?" she asked with a smile, but as usual, he didn't reply; he never did. Still, she felt connected to him. Whether he was aware of it or not, they shared a bond. They were two of the few remaining dreamers left in the world—the last of the dreamers.

Most people, even those who knew magic, spent their nights in peaceful sleep—their unconscious minds devoid of any thought. But dreamers, for better or worse, were forced to endure a barrage of dreams and visions whenever their body was at rest.

As they continued down the cavernous hallway, Sihera spotted a washed-out engraving along the wall depicting ancient battles with mages portrayed as heroic figures.

I've dreamt of this place before... she thought curiously.

The boy stopped. In front of them lay a natural pool of water, but the liquid was dark, almost black. It churned, bubbling hot beneath its surface, as if it were alive.

Sihera gasped. *The Origin...*

How did the boy find it? The Origin was sacred ground. Its location had been lost for generations. This was where a person came to be transformed into an Arcane Bearer—the most powerful of magic wielders. Since she was young, Sihera had been told she was destined to become an Arcane Bearer. She had worked diligently most of her life for that sole purpose. Why would the boy have come here? Unless…

It suddenly felt as if a rock had been lodged in her chest. With dread in her eyes, Sihera glanced down at her hand, and her heart sank. In her clutches remained the dagger.

Stop! Sihera cried out inside her head, but she was startled to find she couldn't speak. She tried to move, but her body continued forward as if of its own free will. Her lungs tightened at the realization; this wasn't a dream, this was a vision—a glimpse into the future. In a dream, she could do whatever she wanted, but in a vision, she was merely an observer, watching the tragedy of events yet to come unfold before her eyes.

It terrified her knowing the boy—her fellow Dreamer—was going to be murdered. It tore away at her heart to watch, but she couldn't bring herself to look away. She couldn't just leave him.

Her chest ached, helpless to stop the inevitable. She yearned to hold him in her arms, but her efforts to control this body were in vain.

As if finally giving in to her demands, her left arm reached out and hugged the boy gently. She could feel his warmth. She could smell the scents of his wavy, copper hair—light and airy, like an ocean's summer breeze. She held him there with his back to her chest and, for a moment, she was happy.

Her right arm drew back.

No... she whimpered, but there was nothing she could do to stop it. The dagger thrust deep into his back. *NOOO!!!*

Sihera burst forth from her dream, screaming and flailing her arms. "No! No! No!" Tears poured down her face as she kicked and pounded her fists against Laval's back.

"Sihera!" Laval shouted, thrown off by her suddenly squirming body. "Calm yourself!"

"No! No! No!" she cried.

Laval came to a jolting stop. "Damn it…" he murmured.

Through a watery haze, Sihera peered ahead where a barricade of roughly fifty armored guards and a single line of mages stood, their backs toward her, forming a barrier between her and the ocean.

An eerie stillness hung in the air. The soldiers stood firm, weapons at the ready, their silence heavy with anticipation.

The head of a single aiko emerged from the ocean. Casually, the creature marched up onto the beach. Then another, and another.

Soon, hundreds of aiko were rising out of sea.

Laval's voice fell to a whisper. "We're too late."

Spurred without any warning, each aiko began sprinting forward.

"Here they come!" called one of the armored guards.

"Hold the line!" shouted another.

The aiko horde charged forward in unparalleled unison; individual creatures all moving together as one, rearing back their razor-sharp talons.

"Steady!"

Sihera held her breath. A thunderous crash rang out as the wave of creatures clashed against the armored guards. Sihera watched in horror as an aiko thrust its claws up underneath one man's helmet. Blood—a deep red—shot across the glistening metal of his armor. The guard's limbs went loose, and he crumpled backward to the ground. Rows of armored guards fell lifeless, and the Archmagi ranks began to pull back. This was the signal for the mages to counterattack.

Men and women dressed in leather armor drew their arms back, straining as lightning and fire arched from their hands and cascaded down upon the aiko. These few mages were the pride and elite of the Archmagi military. Sihera had trained with them often. She spotted a familiar face amongst the mages, a woman in her early twenties. *Elehia!* Elehia wasn't a Dreamer, but she was the most powerful mage Sihera had ever seen.

"Let me down," Sihera insisted, the desperate need to help igniting within her.

"No, Sihera," demanded Laval, but Sihera wriggled free, sliding off his shoulder and sprinted toward the beach.

"Elehia!" she cried.

Elehia turned, surprised to see Sihera racing up behind her. "Sihera! What are you doing here?!"

"Tell me what to do. How can I help?"

Despite her surprise, a spark of admiration reflected in Elehia's eyes. As her face turned stern again, Elehia's head panned, searching the docks nearby. "There, at the end of the pier, there's one ship left.

You can still get out of here if you hurry."

Sihera shot a harsh look up at Elehia. "I'm not leaving you."

From behind her, winded and breathing, Laval called out, "Sihera!"

Sihera pressed her lips together and held her defiant gaze.

Elehia's voice was gentle. "Sihera…You can't stay here. You're a Dreamer."

Sihera hated that response. What good was being a Dreamer if she couldn't protect the people who needed her? She had been helpless once before, and she refused to be helpless any longer. The heat churned inside her as her fists tightened. Today she would fight.

"Not today," Elehia said with gentle confidence, as if she had read her thoughts. Sihera's jaw fell open as she looked up at her with surprise. Elehia gave a somber grin. "One day, you'll get your chance…but not today."

A knot formed in Sihera's throat, and a swell of sadness welled up in her chest. She stared up at Elehia with wide, teary eyes.

Elehia gave her a gentle nudge toward Laval. "Now, get going."

Laval wrapped an arm around her shoulders, urging her toward the pier. Sihera stared back in disbelief, her heart heavy, tears streaming down her face. Elehia nodded and smiled at her one last time through a grievous expression, and then turned to face the oncoming horde.

The aiko, like a wave of darkness, charged forward. With a deep breath, Elehia held her arms out in front of her. She gritted her teeth as her arms flexed, and her hands gripped at the air like claws. Lightning arched between her palms, and a loud crackle filled the air. Her limbs shook and the muscles in her back strained as she stretched the electricity wide across her chest.

A torrent of fire erupted from Elehia's eyes as she let out a resounding cry, and the lightning between her hands snapped, collapsing into a singularity. Where there was thunder, now only silence remained.

From that silence came an explosive roar. Like a stampede, an immense shockwave burst forward, kicking up clouds of dirt as it rushed across the land. Sihera gasped at the deafening sound, her heart pounding. The shockwave crashed into the aiko, sending aiko body parts flying in all directions.

Exhausted, Elehia fell to one knee and her head slumped forward. The Archmagi were too few to fend off a full-fledged aiko attack, and the creatures were already driving forward again.

An armored guard hurried to Elehia's side to help her up, but it was too late. An aiko leapt through the air and plowed its claws through Elehia's leather chest piece as they tumbled together to the ground.

A whimper escaped Sihera's lips the last of the Archmagi's defenses were overrun. "Elehia…"

Laval rushed aboard the ship and sat Sihera down on the deck. Numbness engulfed her, spreading from head to toe, weighing her body to the floor. She could do nothing but crumple up beside the ship's railing and weep.

"Is she aboard?" asked the captain. "Is the Dreamer with us?"

"What are you waiting for?" shouted Laval, waving his arms, as if it could move the ship faster. "We've got Sihera! Cast off, already!"

"You heard him! Get this hunk of wood out to sea!"

As the sailors cut the tethers loose and released the sails, the ship began drifting out into the ocean as the aiko overtook the city.

Laval knelt by Sihera's side. She felt hollow inside, as if her body was hovering somewhere between life and death.

"It's all right, you're safe now," Laval said.

But as her tears dried and her head slumped listlessly to one side, she realized the harsh truth: Nothing would be all right—not Elehia, not the Archmagi, not even her Dreamer boy—and there was nothing she could do about it.

2

Unexpected Encounter

The ocean air had grown cold as the sun set on the horizon. Sihera hadn't moved. She sat on the deck, trapped in a mental prison of despair, swaying back and forth with the steady motions of the sea. The billowing smoke was still visible in the distance, rising from the ashes of the Archmagi Refuge, drawing ghostly images across the dim lit sky.

The ship she was on had caught up to and now sailed alongside a dozen other Archmagi vessels, their sails like dark silhouettes painted against an orange and yellow horizon.

A dozen... Sihera sighed. That's all that managed to survive. Her heart ached. There was a hopelessness that engulfed her, deadening her nerves. Once again, everything she held dear had been taken away from her.

"Sihera?" Laval's comforting voice called to her. She gave a short, startled gasp, as she was pulled back to the present. She blinked, searching her surroundings. Laval's hand rested on her shoulder. "How are you doing, my dear?"

Her voice was weak. "Elehia..." she whimpered. "All those people... And I did *nothing*."

"There was nothing *anyone* could have done."

"When I close my eyes, all I see is death. I can't even save the Dreamer boy."

Laval appeared surprised. "What Dreamer boy?"

It was difficult for her to talk about at first, and her eyes turned to the floor. "I—I had a vision...of a boy. A Dreamer..." Gradually she told Laval about her vision: the boy, the cave and the Origin, and the helplessness she felt from her inability to protect him.

As she spoke, Laval massaged his square jaw, and a slight grin appeared on his face.

"What?" she asked.

"You always manage to bring out the silver lining on even the darkest of days, my dear. Don't you see? Your vision is a sign of hope. There is another Dreamer somewhere out there, and we can save him."

Sihera pondered that for a moment. Laval was right, there was one person who still needed her; one life she could still protect. Her eyes opened slowly. Out of the chaos, a beacon of clarity had emerged. Her fists tightened as life once again surged through her. Her voice was soft yet firm. "I can save him."

She stood and looked forward over the bow, a new-found determination coursing through her veins. The salty breeze threw back the dark curls of her hair, and her eyes held a flash of hope. As the sun set over the remains of her old home, a new day would soon be rising, and she would have to do everything she could to rescue him, to protect her Dreamer boy, wherever he may be.

* * *

Many miles away, Jokahn sat alone at a table that was strategically positioned closest to the tavern's exit. With narrowed eyes and his bent forefinger pressed against his lips, he cautiously scanned the room. Having just turned fifteen years old, and with vivid blue eyes and bronze, wavy hair, Jokahn knew he had no rightful business in a tavern.

This tavern was a popular stop for sailors passing through the small harbor town of Anchorsfell. Here, all ranges of men drank and quarreled with each other at their hardwood tables, the bitter, salty smell of ocean and alcohol constant in the air.

Jokahn turned his gaze toward a large, hulking man who steadily distributed drinks from behind the counter, and he was relieved to see the barman was well occupied. Jokahn knew his brown, tattered clothes clearly labeled him for what he was—a peasant and a thief. A skilled thief, but a thief none-the-less.

Teenagers, especially the thieving kind, were not allowed in taverns. However, traveling drunkards with spare coin were too easy to prey on. Confident the barman was oblivious to his presence, Jokahn pushed the rustic waves of his hair back from his eyes and shifted his attention to a nearby table.

There sat a man, alone and staring down into his drink. He was in his late thirties, and wore a loose, gray shirt and a pair of workman's leggings. Across his waist hung a tool belt. The man appeared dead to the world. The only sign of life was the pendulum-like movement of his arm as he drank. On que, his cup rose again, but the man paused. His drink was empty. With a sharp whistle, the man pulled a large coin purse from his toolbelt.

Jokahn's eyes lit up, and his body instinctively edged forward.

The man spoke the common tongue with a harsh dialect, southern peninsula sounding. "Fill'er up, would you, doll?" he said, tossing a coin to the waitress.

"Another one, coming up, Bakta," she replied as the man stuffed the purse back into his tool bag.

Jokahn's eyes narrowed, and his finger again rose to his lips. His foot tapped eagerly against the floor. He knew better than to rush into a situation like this. However, impatient as he was, he didn't remain stationary for long.

As Jokahn rose from his seat, the tavern door swung open, forcing him back down into the chair. At first, no one entered, and the door remained pressed open. Jokahn glared, grinding his teeth as he waited. Then, with a delicate clunk and the small chime of metal, in strode a finely armor-plated boot.

Jokahn's eyes panned upward as the figure entered. Swaying down to their ankle was an elegantly woven gown designed for battle. Holstered on their left hip were two equally grand short swords. Continuing upward was a beautiful, rugged, leather chest piece, which hugged perfectly around the curves of the girl's torso. Her skin was smooth and flawless. Atop her shoulders was the most gorgeous and commanding face Jokahn had ever seen. Her eyes were a bold, emerald green, matching her attire. And her hair, a rich brown, hung slightly in her eyes before being pulled back into a long braid that danced behind her as she walked.

She came to a stop as the door swung closed behind her. The girl was no more than a year older than Jokahn—two at the most—yet there was a presence about her, a poise she carried that was well beyond her years. Standing tall, a full head-length above him at his peak, she placed her hands on her hips and glared into the crowd.

From the looks of her attire, he could only assume she was a royal guard, or perhaps a wealthy warrior from a distant land. Whoever she was, her mere being was awe-inspiring. Along with her beauty, she portrayed an undeniable strength; a power that radiated through the floor around her. It was a force that couldn't be seen, only felt. Just as gravity pulls objects toward its center, Jokahn was drawn toward this girl. He couldn't imagine her presence being any more profound, that is, until she spoke.

"*Baktaaaa!*" the girl roared; her voice strong yet fluid.

Bakta sheltered his head between his shoulders as she scanned the tavern.

The room had fallen silent. Anyone whose attention had not already been drawn to the elegant warrior as she entered was now securely fixated on her. Jokahn held his breath, afraid of drawing unwanted attention in the unexpected silence. Bakta sat frozen, as if trying to hide himself. Finally, her eyes settled on him.

"Quit sulking, Bakta," she demanded. "Drahig has the ship stocked and ready." Jokahn couldn't quite place her accent. It was foreign, with a smooth, velvet feel to it. "We're leaving. It's time to go."

Jokahn shook his head, frightened he might have lost his opportunity to steal Bakta's coin purse before ever having a chance.

Of all the people, why did she have to come for him?

"How'd you find me, Ticahrla?" asked Bakta, still staring down into his drink.

Her eyes narrowed. "I followed the stench of alcohol and

mourning," she said in a sarcastically blunt tone. "Now hurry up."

Jokahn glowered at her. *Ticahrla...* Her name tasted vile on his tongue. While the men swooned at her beauty, Jokahn saw her as nothing but a threat; a snake trying to steal his prey.

"Yeah, yeah. You're right, I'm wrong, as always." Bakta said, skidding his mug across the table. "But dammit, Ticahrla, can't we just relax for once?" He turned to face her, apparently trying to appeal to her sympathetic nature, although Jokahn doubted she possessed such a thing.

Ticahrla shot a fierce stare at Bakta, crossing her arms as she tapped her steel toe on the floor.

"One more drink," she finally said. "Then you meet Drahig and me on the ship. You got that?"

Jokahn exhaled in relief. Everyone in the tavern must have felt the same, as the room once again began to fill with random chatter.

"See, I told you you're a good person, Ticahrla." Bakta nodded and turned back to his drink. "I don't care what the rest of the kingdom says."

Ticahrla glared at him a moment longer. Then, with a disgruntled snort and a shake of her head, she turned and pulled open the tavern door.

Jokahn's mind raced with nothing but the thought of being rid of this irritating girl.

That's right, keep walking, Ticahrla.

Her body stopped with a jolt, and her back stiffened up tall. She stood there frozen—tight and rigid—as if a cold chill had rushed down her spine. Jokahn struggled to decipher the aggravated look on her face. It was something trapped between anger and shock.

Just go already!

But she didn't. She just stood there. Then, with a subtle tilt of her head, Ticahrla turned to glare viciously down at Jokahn.

There was something formidable in her gaze, a kind of contained ferocity. His muscles seized up, and the hair on his arms stood on end. At first, he couldn't help but stare back, gazing deep into her fiery green eyes—eyes that, as he looked closer, became literally engulfed in a rich green flame that lapped at the sides of her face. The hot, emerald vapor poured from her eyes. It was both terrifying and hypnotic, and her gaze pierced through his being like a knife. With some strained effort, Jokahn forced himself to look away.

Had Ticahrla discovered his intentions? Did she somehow realize his plan to steal from Bakta? Jokahn's legs began to tremble. How could she have singled him out from the crowd like that?

A few moments passed before he was able to build up enough courage to face her again. He strained, glanced cautiously from the corner of his eye…

She was gone.

Jokahn sat forward, scanning the tavern, but there was no sign of that evil girl.

Relief spread through him like a wave as he exhaled and slumped back into his chair. He had to get that coin purse, and fast.

Jokahn turned back toward Bakta's table, but it was empty. His breath faltered. He thrust himself up from his chair.

Where'd he go?! He spotted Bakta already strolling toward the side exit. *No!*

Leaping forward, Jokahn sprinted across the room. He only had one chance at this. As he got closer, he focused on the tool bag. Bakta pulled open the door right as Jokahn slammed his shoulder into the man.

"Hey!" cried Bakta as he reared back.

"Sorry!" Jokahn called over his should as he ran by. Bakta glared harshly at him for a moment, rolling out his shoulder, but then continued out the door. Jokahn gave a wicked grin as his run slowed and he made his way to the back exit.

As Jokahn walked out into the tavern's back alley, he looked down at the coin purse in his hand. With two fingers he pried open the purse and snuck a glimpse inside.

Athus coin! Currency from the kingdom of Athus always held a high value in Anchorsfell.

Jokahn smirked as he pocketed the coin purse and strolled down the alleyway, pleased with his haul, when a strange sensation began to wash over him. He paused and his face tightened at the bizarre wave of heat that flowed through him. The feeling was very foreign, but somehow, it almost felt as if someone was watching him.

The image of Ticahrla's flaming green eyes flashed in his mind. He turned and his eyes panned cautiously down the empty alley.

Nothing. No Ticahrla. No one following him.

Soon, the fiery sensation faded away, and Jokahn gave a dissatisfied grunt. It took a while before he convinced himself he wasn't being followed, but eventually, he turned and continued down the way.

What a strange day this has turned out to be.

"Ow." Jokahn winced, surprised by an unexpected pain twisting in his shoulder.

He looked down to see a hand with familiar flawless skin grasping the collar of his shirt.

No! It can't be! Following the hand, his gaze shifted up the arm and to the face he knew would be waiting for him. *Ticahrla!*

3

No Escape

Ticahrla was leaning against the wall, hardly acknowledging Jokahn as she held him at arm's length.

"Who are you?" she asked with that firm yet silky voice.

Jokahn was frozen, too terrified to respond. But as she turned her head to face him, she showed no anger. Her eyes were soft and comforting. He didn't respond, lost in her beauty and the gentle green warmth of her eyes.

Ticahrla's voice hardened. "I asked you a question," she said, pushing off the wall and pulling him in close. "Who are you, boy?"

Wincing at the strain in his collar, Jokahn struggled to pry open her fingers, but Ticahrla's grip held firm. *Wow, she's even stronger than I thought.* A swift kick to her shin caused a loud ping to echo through the alley as a sharp pain shot through his toes. Jokahn clung to his foot in agony, reminded of Ticahrla's armored boots.

Jokahn grimaced as Ticahrla tightened her grip around his collar, and her voice turned demonic. "Listen to me, you little shit!" Her eyes burst into emerald flames.

Fear tightened around his chest. He stared wide-eyed back at her. Ticahrla's eyes, which had appeared so soft a moment ago, had transformed into something monstrous. The heat from the flames singed his face as Ticahrla hissed at him through clenched teeth.

"Do you think I'm playing games, boy?! Answer me, or I swear I will—" Ticahrla broke off mid-sentence, her fiery eyes extinguishing at the sound of footsteps racing down the tavern's back alley.

Bakta stumbled around the corner, breathing heavily. "That little rat! He stole my—" Bakta paused as he saw Ticahrla holding Jokahn captive by the collar.

An awkward silence lingered between the three as they exchanged glances with each other.

Ticahrla sighed, rolling her eyes as she thrust a hand into Jokahn's pocket, retrieving Bakta's coin purse. Jokahn's eyes flickered back and forth between Bakta and Ticahrla. *Now's my chance.*

Clutching her forearm with both hands, Jokahn gritted his teeth and pushed with all his might. His shirt began to rip. *Yes!* The fabric tore free from Ticahrla's grasp, and he fell back hard onto the floor. It hurt, but not enough to slow him down. His heart pounded in his chest. *Just run. Don't look back.*

Scrambling on all fours, Jokahn clawed his way to his feet, sprinting down the alley and quickly rounding the corner.

* * *

Later that night, outside, under the chilled moonlit sky, Jokahn lay sound asleep on a bed of rags. Losing Bakta's coin purse was unfortunate, but he didn't dwell on it; such things were normal in the life of a pickpocket. As he slept, his mind raced with a flurry of thoughts. Some nights he would think of strange places he had never seen before. Other nights he would recall events from the past, or sometimes the future. Wherever his late-night ponderings took him, to Jokahn they were commonplace. He paid little attention to them, as if they were nothing more than the musings of a wandering mind.

A soft hand reached out and caressed Jokahn's forehead, pushing away his unkempt, wavy hair from his eyes. Their hand was warm. He cherished this simple touch, unconsciously turning his head into their palm with a deep, comforting breath.

As he felt the warm touch pull away, his hair fell across his face, tickling his nose. Jokahn flinched and groaned, batting at his frustrating locks.

A voice chuckled nearby.

Jokahn's eyelids began to flutter open. Rubbing them with his fists as he yawned and stretched his shoulders, he strained to distinguish the shadowy figure in front of him.

A familiar voice spoke calmly from the darkness. "Has anyone ever told you that you talk in your sleep?"

Still struggling to wake, he knew he had heard this voice before, but from where? It was a girl's voice, obviously, but it sounded different than before; it sounded soft and almost kind.

Oh, no! Not her!

In a flash, Jokahn was wide-awake and scrambling to his feet.

"No, no, no! Wait!" Ticahrla's voice called out as she leapt forward from the shadows.

With both hands, she grasped Jokahn's shoulders and pinned him against the cobblestone wall. His head slammed against the hard surface, and a sharp pain ran down the back of his skull. He winced, pressing a hand to the nape of his skull as he clamped his eyes shut.

Dazed from the impact, it took him a moment for his thoughts to realign. His head was throbbing. When his sight refocused, Ticahrla's face was in front of him. Her beauty was just as profound in the moonlight.

"It's all right, I'm not going to hurt you," she said gently, though there was an unease in her voice. "I—I just want to talk."

Jokahn's brow came together in a tight, angry point. He didn't want to talk. He loathed this girl. How could she possibly bring him anything but pain? But then something surprised him. It was the way her eyes frantically searched his own, as if they were looking for something. She looked almost…worried.

"Please," Ticahrla added after a moment of silence.

The anger drained from his body, replaced only by a strange and unjustifiable pity. Pity for the flawless girl who held him pinned to a wall against his will. *Stupid* was the only word he could form in his mind. Stupid for knowing this girl was manipulating him but being helpless to resist.

It really was ridiculous to feel pity for Ticahrla. And, although he couldn't bring himself to show it, he actually despised her more for how powerless he was to deny her.

Jokahn nodded, and Ticahrla beamed a glorious smile, the kind of smile mere mortals should never be allowed to obtain. Carefully, she loosened her clasp from his shoulders, allowing him to slide down the wall and onto his bed of rags.

He rolled his shoulders, trying to free them from the ache. Her strength continued to amaze him.

Crossing her legs and lowering herself gracefully to the ground, Ticahrla tucked the edges of her gown beneath her ankles. For a short while she gazed happily at him, examining him, not saying a word. The way she studied him made Jokahn uncomfortable, and he turned his eyes toward the floor.

"So, how should I begin?" Ticahrla thought for a moment. "How about a name?" she asked, but Jokahn didn't reply. "You do have a name, don't you, boy?"

"It's Jokahn," he muttered, still not looking up. He was surprised by how lighthearted she was taking the situation. Something about it felt out of place, almost unnatural.

"*Jokahn.* All right…" Ticahrla chuckled.

Jokahn's eyes snapped up to see why she was laughing at him. "What? You don't like it?" he barked.

Ticahrla shook her head and waved a hand, as if trying to restrain from laughing.

"Well, what kind of a name is Ticahrla, anyway?" Jokahn spat.

"It's a fine name," she said, finally suppressing her laughter. "It stands for elegance and nobility." Then she gave Jokahn's tattered clothing a quick, and vaguely repulsed, glance over. "What is *Jokahn* supposed to stand for?"

Jokahn rolled his eyes and crossed his arms. *Elegance and nobility? Ha!* "It doesn't stand for anything. It's just me. It's just my name."

"So, it is just you then? All by yourself? No family? No friends?"

He had no memory of his family. He never even knew what their faces looked like. "I have friends." Jokahn was quick to correct her, but he could tell the tone in his voice was not as convincing as he had hoped.

Ticahrla cocked her head to the side, taking a moment again to study his reaction.

Why does she keep looking at me like that?

"I saw you talking in your sleep. What were you dreaming about?"

Jokahn didn't answer. *Dreaming?* he cringed. Jokahn had never heard of this word before, but without much thought, he dismissed it.

"Have any *nightmares* lately?" she continued, giving an odd grin and raising an eyebrow.

"What's a nightmare?"

"You know, a nightmare. Something that frightens you while you sleep."

"You mean besides *you?*" The sarcasm flew from Jokahn's lips without any conscious effort.

Ticahrla was quiet for a moment, and he began to wonder if his outburst had upset her. Perhaps he ought to be more careful about what he said. After all, he was still Ticahrla's prisoner in many ways. Jokahn's tongue had a bad habit of getting ahead of him, and it often got him into more trouble than he wanted. To his relief, she chuckled and proceeded with her questioning.

"Dreamers are extraordinarily rare these days. Are there any more around here?"

Jokahn shrugged his shoulders this time, figuring a silent answer would be a safe answer. He couldn't grasp what Ticahrla was trying to get at. Why these questions? Why ask about dreams?

A bright smile encompassed her face. "You really don't know what you are, do you?"

Jokahn looked up at her with a confused expression. Who was this girl? He couldn't decide if she was friend or foe.

"Have you ever heard of an Arcane Bearer?"

Jokahn shook his head.

"Becoming an Arcane Bearer is the one thing I want more than anything. Call it a life-long ambition if you will. You see, Arcane Bearers are the most powerful magic wielders to ever live. But to become an Arcane Bearer, I first need to find a Dreamer—someone born with the gift of magic." Ticahrla pointed a finger at Jokahn and sneered. "I need *you*."

Jokahn gave her a disgruntled frown, not believing a word she said. What could anyone possibly want from him? "But I don't know any magic. Can't you find someone else?"

"I wish." Ticahrla snickered. "Anyone can learn magic, but only a Dreamer can make me an Arcane Bearer, and dreamers are nearly impossible to find these days. Honestly, you're the first one I've come across." She rose gracefully from where she sat, brushing the dirt from her gown. "So, what do you say? Will you come with me?"

He looked up at her reluctantly. "Come with you? Where?"

Ticahrla extended her palm to him. "To the Origin, so you can make me an Arcane Bearer."

He stared suspiciously at her open hand. He didn't fully believe Ticahrla or her elaborate stories. All this talk about dreamers, the Origin, and Arcane Bearers. It sounded made up. Even if it was true, why would he care? What would he get out of it? Was she going to feed or pay him?

"Don't be frightened." She said softly, taking one step closer.

Jokahn shied away. He still wasn't willing to trust her, and for good reason.

"Jokahn." Ticahrla pleaded in an angelic tone, but once again he retracted. In an instant, her expression turned hard. "*Come on, boy,*" she demanded, stomping her foot, and forcing her open hand at him.

Jokahn was shocked by the sudden change in Ticahrla's demeanor. How could someone be composed of such extremes? She was like a majestic mountainside that was ready to explode into a volcano at any moment. The image of her eyes bursting into flames pierced through his mind, and he knew he didn't want to be around when Ticahrla finally erupted.

Ticahrla withdrew her hand and rested it on her hip, taking a deep breath as she stared down at him. "What is it? What do you want?" She started pacing, searching her surroundings, as if the answer to her question could be found somewhere in that alley.

Her body language was growing frantic. He had to get out of there. With her back turned toward him for just an instant, Jokahn saw an opportunity.

As he thrust himself to his feet and sprinted down the alley, Jokahn could hear her voice continue as it grew quieter in the distance.

"Here I am, trying to help you. Trying to—eh…" she stuttered and fell silent.

Turning to glance over his shoulder as he hurried away, it was hard for him to make out anything in the darkness. But as he turned the corner, he saw the spark of two fiery green, anger-filled eyes igniting in the distance.

Jokahn's lungs tightened, and his eyes went wide.

"You can't run forever, boy!" Ticahrla's voice called out, reverberating like a shockwave down the alleyway. The powerful sound sent chills down his spine as he ran. Then her voice whispered like an echo in his mind—calm and sure, almost seductive. "You've got nowhere else to go."

4

Crossing the Threshold

Jokahn raced through the city under the moonlit sky. Through empty markets and roads, he ran to the point of exhaustion and beyond, until his body could do nothing but collapse.

Coming to a stop at the same tavern from before, Jokahn stumbled onto his hands and knees at the side of the road. He stayed there for a moment, his chest heaving, his head spinning. Ticahrla's last words were still circling through his mind. *"You've got nowhere else to go."* For some reason, they stung more deeply than he expected. He looked down at the tattered clothes that hung loose and ragged on him, branding him as the lonely, low-class, *filth of Anchorsfell* that he was.

A solemn pressure began to build in his chest. It was that same heavy, miserable feeling that would slowly work its way up into his shoulders and head until his entire body would ache. It was the feeling of being completely and utterly alone, and Jokahn knew all too well that he was the cause of his own suffering.

Clamping his eyes shut and burying his face in his hands, he cried out inside, *I know I'm worthless! I know everyone hates me! I know I could die right now and no one would care! I know, I know, I know!*

Jokahn keeled forward and pressed his forehead to the ground as he wept, tears running down his face. His limbs were shaking, and the tightness in his chest constricted his breath into short, stuttered gasps. It wasn't often that Jokahn cried like this, but tonight he was helpless to restrain himself. He cried and cried until he finally cried himself to sleep.

* * *

Sihera followed the boy down that same winding cave. She had never had such a consistent and vivid vision before; every detail was so clearly defined. She had spent most of her day scanning her thoughts, searching for any clue that could lead her to her Dreamer boy.

A sharp pain tightened around her skull like a vice, and she winced. An intense heat washed over her. It was a force, a pressure trying to push her out. The vision of her boy began to falter and fade.

What is this?! She had no idea who or what, but something was overpowering her dream. The vision of the boy collapsed in on itself, fading in a cloud of smoke. Sihera fell to her knees in the midst of the empty fog, clutching the sides of her head in agony. Her teeth clenched together. Nothing was said, but in that emptiness, something spoke to her, as if warning her to stay away. Then the pain vanished.

Sihera crumpled to her hands and knees, gasping in relief and grateful for the release.

What could have done that? What had the power to reach through her dreams like that? Before she could think of an answer, the ground beneath her began to morph, revealing a snowy hillside. As her head rose, a large kingdom stood before her, with its large limestone walls. *The kingdom of Athus!* Within those walls was a familiar face. His blue eyes stared back at her, sending her heart racing; it was her Dreamer boy.

Sihera woke with a lurch from the hammock inside her cabin. It was dark in the room. Sihera was panting. "Oh no… Not Athus."

The Archmagi and Athus had a troubled history; their societies had always clashed. The Archmagi viewed magic as a beautiful energy that existed within all life; a natural force, causing growth, death, and the cycles of life. But people from Athus feared magic, preferring large walls, vast armies, and an authoritative monarchy. A Dreamer wouldn't last long in Athus.

Sihera threw herself from her hammock, and hurried down the

dim, candlelit hallways of the ship. She was still dreary from lack of sleep, and the constant sway of the sea didn't help. Walking her hands down the wall, she made her way to the map room where Laval had been spending a lot of his time. Candlelight was shining from beneath the door. She turned the nob and eased it open.

Laval and a circle of his most trusted men huddled over a parchment that lay unfolded on the table, a cluster of maps and insignias scattered haphazardly around it. They conversed in hushed whispers.

Sihera caught the tail end of Laval's sentence before he noticed her. "…anything but the king's compass." Laval stopped to do a double take at her as she lingered in the doorway. Then he smiled. "Sihera, what are you doing up so late?"

Laval's men carefully folded and put away the maps.

"I had another vision. The boy Dreamer, I saw him in Athus."

Laval and his men exchanged surprised glances with each other.

"A dreamer? In Athus?" asked the man to Laval's right.

"Not yet," replied Sihera. "But he will be."

Laval gave Sihera a hardened look. "You're sure the boy Dreamer will be in Athus?" he asked.

Sihera thought back on her vision; certain parts had been a little muddy, but she'd seen him clearly. She looked up at Laval and gave a confident nod.

"Then we go to Athus," he said astutely.

Sihera's brow pressed firmly down over her eyes. "You're joking."

Laval shrugged. "We can't keep sailing forever. We need to settle somewhere, and I can't think of a safer place from the aiko than Athus. Maybe this was meant to be."

Sihera folded her arms across her chest. "Great, the aiko won't kill us, but the people of Athus might."

* * *

It wasn't until well into the morning that Jokahn finally woke.

The streets of Anchorsfell had begun to fill, and the crowds had started to bustle. Jokahn strained and squinted his eyes, stretching his limbs out as he groaned at an awful kink that had developed in his neck.

"Out of the way, you mongrel," an old man shouted, kicking aside Jokahn's outstretched leg.

Jokahn thrust himself to his feet and beat the dust from his clothes. "You're the mongrel, you—you crusty old grouch!" he shouted after he was confident the man was far enough not to hear him.

"What's all this racket?!" a deep, musty voice shouted from behind him.

Before he could turn, a large hand tightened around Jokahn's bicep and spun him around.

"I told you to stay away from my tavern," spat the barman.

Jokahn stood there petrified, wide-eyed and quivering under the barman's shadow, when a familiar voice roared from across the street.

"Let... Him... *Go!*" the girl commanded, striking a strong emphasis on each word.

Jokahn turned and his jaw dropped at what he saw. Ticahrla's fiery green eyes were ablaze, and her hands were curled into tight fists at her sides. With the vibrant orange of the rising sun at her back, Ticahrla managed to look absolutely terrifying and yet stunningly beautiful at the same time. The barman and Jokahn stood frozen in place as they gawked at the furious girl.

"That means *now*," growled Ticahrla.

Instantly, the barman released his grip and Jokahn stumbled free.

Jokahn stood there for a moment, unsure what was happening. Then, looking up at the large, muscular man, Jokahn came to an astounding realization. The barman was trembling. His enormous hands shook as he stared across the road at Ticahrla. Jokahn couldn't believe it. Was she that intimidating, even to this overgrown brute? He had to find out.

With a whip of his leg, Jokahn kicked the barman in the shin and braced for the retaliation. The burly man winced and hobbled backward a step, shooting a confused glare down at Jokahn, but then he straightened up and watched cautiously for a reaction from Ticahrla.

This was amazing. No, it was beyond belief! A snicker unconsciously escaped Jokahn as the corner of his mouth curled with delight. He was beside himself with the freedom he had discovered just for being associated with Ticahrla.

"Come here, boy," called Ticahrla.

He did as he was told. As they turned and walked calmly down the street, Jokahn took one last glimpse back at the barman from over his shoulder. The man appeared as dumbfounded as he was. Jokahn didn't know what to say, so he did the only thing he could think of. He shrugged his shoulders and smiled at the barman as he walked leisurely away.

Once the barman was out of view, Jokahn looked up at the girl who had come to his rescue. The fire in her eyes had dissipated, but an angry scowl remained. They walked together through the busy streets of Anchorsfell, never saying a word, her face permanently tightened into that angry pucker of hers. Until, suddenly, her expression changed.

She stopped dead in her tracks and cocked her head to the side, studying the crowd intently.

"What is it?" asked Jokahn.

She gasped, and her face went pale. "Get down," she said, twirling as she spun her body around Jokahn's and pinned him against a wall.

Jokahn was shaken by the sudden jolt of Ticahrla's movements. Before all his senses could realign, he took something in that his mind didn't fully comprehend at first. It was a pleasant smell. A warm but gentle scent, almost floral, like fresh lavender. Jokahn enjoyed breathing it in. Or, at least until he opened his eyes, only to realize it was the scent of Ticahrla's skin pressed against his face as she held him tight. Jokahn cringed and snorted as he shook his head in disgust, trying to force it from his nose.

"What are you doing?" cried Jokahn.

"Quiet," whispered Ticahrla. "They're looking for you."

"Who is?" he whispered back. It was hard to see anything with the way Ticahrla had coiled herself around him.

"Hush," Ticahrla said, even quieter this time.

Jokahn did as he was told and kept quiet.

"There, the three behind me," she whispered.

Jokahn wriggled around until he could see a sliver of the people in the street beneath Ticahrla's arm. He scanned through the bodies and soon enough came across three tall, lean figures.

At first glance, there was nothing noticeably abnormal about them. They moved about with the flow of the crowd. Then he realized something odd. All three were shrouded from head to toe in clothing that was ever so slightly mismatched. Two of the figures wore tax collector's robes with their rain hoods draped unusually far over their faces for a perfectly sunny day. The third wore a sailor's uniform and—for some reason—a deckhand's sun hat with the brim pulled way down. He couldn't quite put his finger on it, but something was frightfully unnatural about them.

The three figures stopped and turned their heads in chilling unison toward him. His eyes widened as he took in the sleek, shadowy curves of the faces hidden behind their clothes. Deep, black-set eyes and dark, silk-like faces stared cautiously in his direction.

Aiko!

Jokahn sheltered himself behind Ticahrla. Although her back was toward the three creatures, he could tell her senses were on high alert. Every muscle in her body pulsed. Her hand slowly came to rest on the hilt of her sword. Seeing this caused his heart to speed up, and his muscles to tighten. The instinct to run was growing strong, but Ticahrla held him fixed to the wall.

Eventually, the three shrouded figures moved on down the road.

Ticahrla's body relaxed, and her grasp loosened, allowing Jokahn to move freely again.

"What are the aiko doing here in Anchorsfell?" asked Jokahn.

"Isn't it obvious?" Ticahrla replied. "They're doing the same thing I am. Looking for a Dreamer."

That's ridiculous. "Why would the aiko be looking for me?"

Ticahrla's mouth started to open, but her face became strained, and she closed it again. What was she thinking of? She shrugged and continued. "The aiko fear magic wielders. Which means they fear Arcane Bearers more than anything." Ticahrla gave Jokahn a moment to process that.

Still confused, Jokahn awaited further explanation.

"*And*...if there are no dreamers, then there can't be any Arcane Bearers." Ticahrla gestured with her hand, waving Jokahn forward.

Jokahn's eyes shifted to the side quickly and then focused back on Ticahrla. He had no idea where she was going with this.

She let out a long sigh. "If you were dead, they would be much better off. Get it?"

The dread crept onto Jokahn's face as it dawned on him. The aiko were in Anchorsfell for one reason, to kill him. His chest began to rise and fall, slowly at first, then faster.

Ticahrla leaned forward with concern in her eyes. "Listen to me. You're going to be all right. I'm not about to hand you over to those aiko without a fight. I need you, boy."

She needs...me? No one had ever needed him before, or wanted him, for that matter. He could feel his eyes starting to well up. *No, don't cry.*

"I can pay you," Ticahrla continued. "You'll have food and a warm bed. We'll find the Origin together and you can help me become an Arcane Bearer. So, what do you say? Will you come with me?"

Jokahn took a deep breath as he questioned himself. A part of him wanted to go. This was a chance at a new life, something better than living off the streets, but Anchorsfell was all he had ever known. Could there be a life for him outside this decrepit, old city? It was such a foreign idea that he struggled to imagine it. For some reason, that made the thought of leaving all the more frightening. Although, there was something about Ticahrla that urged him forward, something strange pulling at his heart, but could he trust her?

Ticahrla's face became strained with worry in Jokahn's bizarre silence. So much so that he wanted to reach out and comfort her, but it was Ticahrla who spoke first.

"Don't worry," she said. "I'll watch over you."

That did it. He could feel the tears swelling again, just like the night before. But he couldn't cry, not in front of Ticahrla, that would be unthinkable. Yet, here again, he found himself helpless to reel in his emotions. How embarrassing it was to cry so much in such a short period of time.

Jokahn tucked his chin to his chest to hide his face, well aware she was still eagerly awaiting his answer. Though he dared not speak for he was sure his unsteady voice would expose his true feelings. Instead, he simply nodded his lowered head up and down to announce his approval.

Ticahrla chuckled. "Is that a yes?"

Again, he nodded, never taking his eyes off the ground.

Ticahrla stood up and extended a hand toward Jokahn, but he didn't accept it. He stared at her open palm with a puzzled expression on his face, his cheeks freshly painted with tears.

As Ticahrla's hand sat open and waiting before him, he finally realized the significance of this simple gesture. Taking her hand—accepting to go with Ticahrla, entrusting his life to her—this was a threshold he was crossing. He was about to leave behind the only life he had ever known. He had no idea what tomorrow would look like; he couldn't imagine what his future would hold. It was both terrifying and exhilarating at the same time.

How had this happened? Just yesterday, he was a lonely orphan living in an obscure harbor town. Now, within the breadth of a single day, Ticahrla had rescued him twice. Once from the barman and again from the aiko. He was extraordinarily lucky to have found her.

"What's wrong?" she asked.

"Ticahrla…" Jokahn finally said as he glanced up at her with a tear-filled smile. She looked astutely down at him. "I think you might just be the best thing that has ever happened to me."

Ticahrla grinned her glorious smile down at Jokahn. Then she gave him a playful wink. "Come on, boy. Let's go."

Jokahn reached forward and placed his hand in hers.

5

Dangerous Games

Jokahn couldn't believe it. There he was, on a ship with a girl he hardly knew, sailing steadily out to sea.

Ticahrla's ship, the *Nahktaio*, was a masterpiece of craftsmanship. It was a single-mast cutter, small and built for speed, with a dark umber brown hull and sails the color of wheat. It was the only cutter he'd seen with a second deck and a full captain's lodge. The controls were stationed at the helm, atop the upper deck. The ship looked fast just tethered to the dock. Now, out on the open sea with a strong wind at its back, Jokahn could feel the ocean parting beneath him, giving way for such an immaculate vessel.

Jokahn looked back as the only place he had ever called home receded farther into the distance. *Anchorsfell... It looks so different from here. So small.*

Leaning his elbows against the railing and resting his head in his palms, Jokahn noticed something strange in the wake of the ship. Three ripples steadily drawing closer. His brow pressed down over his eyes. It was almost as if something was watching him.

"You won't miss it," Ticahrla said, resting a hand on his shoulder. He jumped slightly, but luckily, she didn't seem to notice. "There was nothing for you in Anchorsfell. Soon, you'll hardly remember it." She smiled at him.

As he gazed up at her, that glorious smile of hers warming his heart, a subtle yet blissful grin stretched across his face. Ticahrla's smile alone could send him into a pleasant daze.

Jokahn looked back out at the calm water behind them, the city of Anchorsfell shrinking into the horizon. What had he been thinking about? He couldn't remember.

"There's the little rat," a man's voice said as someone grabbed his shoulders from behind and shook him. Looking back, he saw Bakta grin with a playful chuckle, but there was a hint of irritation in his voice. "Steal from me, huh? Bet you didn't think you'd see me again so soon."

Jokahn's eyes turned to the floor. He'd forgotten Bakta was part of Ticahrla's crew.

After a heavy pat on Jokahn's back, Bakta rested his elbows against the ship's railing beside Ticahrla.

Ticahrla looked over at Jokahn, and then turned to glare at Bakta. When the man didn't react, she elbowed him in the side of the arm.

"Ow." Bakta glared at her, massaging his arm. "What was that for?"

She chuckled and shook her head. "Are you going to play nice, or am I going to have to sit you in the corner?"

Bakta grumbled, and his face scrunched. "Yeah, well, he started it." He jabbed a finger at Jokahn.

Jokahn's head sank between his shoulders.

"Face it, Bakta," Ticahrla said. "You're just an easy target. How could the boy resist?"

Jokahn looked up at her, surprised to see Ticahrla so quick to come to his defense. Then she smiled at him and winked.

Bakta's brow raised. "Hey, I was just messing around. No need to get so personal." He stood there and stewed for a moment. "Man, I need a drink," he finally said as he walked away, muttering to himself. "When did people get so sensitive these days? Can't even take a joke anymore."

Ticahrla shook her head. "Don't worry about Bakta. He's a good man once you get to know him."

A good man? Jokahn didn't see much good in him. He folded his arms and let out a derisive chuckle. "Yeah, a good man with the charm of soggy cabbage." Jokahn gasped and clasped a hand over his mouth, but it was too late, the words had already escaped him.

Ticahrla gave a warm and hearty laugh. "Oh, I almost forgot. You haven't met Drahig yet."

Drahig? Where had he heard that name before?

Ticahrla gave a sharp whistle and called out, "Drahig, come down here."

The mast shook, and a huge figure plummeted downward. The creature landed hard on all fours, rocking the ship.

Jokahn lurched back, melding himself with the railing. His head craned back as the huge reptilian-like giant slowly rose upright. Jokahn's jaw fell open as the hulking figure towered over him. The muscular lizard wore a uniform resembling the same craftsmanship of Ticahrla's armor, and the yellow glint of his eyes complemented the green and grey patches of his scales.

Ticahrla raised a hand and patted the arm of the oversized reptile. "Meet Drahig."

"My name is Drahig," the giant lizard said in a deep, resonating voice, and nodded respectfully.

Jokahn couldn't speak, but he tried not to think of the words *Could break a man in half* as he gawked at the creature.

"What's wrong?" asked Ticahrla. "Never seen an ergman before?"

Jokahn shook his head. Drahig stood tall in front of him, as if awaiting his next orders.

"Don't worry, boy. Drahig is perfectly tame. I've had him since we were both young."

"He's your pet?!" exclaimed Jokahn.

"He's much more than that. He's my best and most loyal friend."

Ticahrla excused Drahig with a nod. As the ergman meandered over to the other side of the deck, Jokahn slowly peeled himself from the railing.

A best friend. Jokahn had never had a best friend before. It was hard to make friends as a pickpocket. Being alone was easier—safer. No one could hurt you if you were alone. But maybe he didn't have to be alone anymore. He looked up at Ticahrla, hopeful; maybe things would be different now.

He studied her expression as she watched Drahig and Bakta

conversing. She seemed so nice and charming. Those beautiful green eyes could be so alluring, and her smile—that unearthly smile—melted his heart every time he saw it. She was the only person who had ever stood up for him. The small corners of his mouth curled up into a pleasant grin.

But there was another side to Ticahrla, he reminded himself. Jokahn's smile faded. He had seen the anger boil over inside her; he had felt the heat from those fiery eyes. It made him question if her intentions were genuine. Was all that talk about becoming an Arcane Bearer true? Was she actually taking him to the Origin, or was she was planning to sell him off to some slave traders instead? It suddenly worried him that he had so blindly entrusted his life to a girl he knew so little about.

"Ticahrla?" he asked. She turned to him, still smiling. "Can you tell me more about the Origin? I mean, if you need me to help you become an Arcane Bearer, I'd like to know more about it."

Her smile faded slightly, but only slightly. Then her beaming grin returned. "Of course. What do you want to know?"

Jokahn's brow pulled together. "Well, where are we sailing to?"

Ticahrla scoffed, "I told you already. The Origin."

"Yes, but *where* is the Origin?" he clarified. "Actually, *what* is the Origin? You talk about it as if I should know already."

"The Origin is a source of great power. It's been lost for generations now, but I have a good idea of where to find it. It shouldn't take more than a month to get there by sea."

"A month?!"

Ticahrla chuckled. "If it were midsummer, it would only take a few days to sail through the Northern Pass. But seeing as the pass is still thawing this time of year, we're going to have to take the long way around, through at least five of the seven sovereign kingdoms."

"If the Origin has been lost for so long, how do you know where it is?"

Ticahrla tilted her head up rather proudly. "My father taught me. For a while, it was all he obsessed about, finding the Origin."

"Where's your father now? Wouldn't he want to be here when we find it?"

The pride quickly fell from her face. She nodded. "Yes, he would have," she said in a somber tone. "He died. Many years ago."

Jokahn's heart sank. "Oh, I—I'm sorry. I didn't know."

Ticahrla shrugged and then began reciting in a gentle tone, "Feel not sorry for those who have lost, for they are infinitely better for ever having had at all."

Jokahn grimaced. "What was that?"

"You haven't heard that story before?"

How embarrassing for her; stories were for children. Jokahn gave a snide expression. "You like stories, huh?"

"I *love* stories," Ticahrla rebuked rather proudly, her eyes beaming with excitement. Then she leaned over and drew her face in close to his. With a coy smile, she whispered, "Just imagine the stories people will tell about me one day once I become an Arcane Bearer."

Jokahn looked at her in wonder. Talk of magic was rare, especially in Anchorsfell. Many feared it, thinking of it as a dark art—something of a taboo. Yet, Ticahrla was so open and confident about her ambitions. He could already envision the grand tales that would be written about her one day, the legends that would be passed down for generations. She was the kind of person you felt in awe of just standing beside her.

"Tell me about becoming an Arcane Bearer," he insisted. "And about magic. You said anyone can learn it. Do you know magic?"

"Not really. Sometimes, when I'm angry or upset, strange things will happen, but I don't know how to control it. Well, I know a few parlor tricks. Not enough to be dangerous with, though. Not yet at least. That's why I rely on these." Ticahrla patted the two swords on her hip. "But even the most skilled sword is no match against a powerful mage."

"Really?"

Ticahrla nodded. "Trust me."

Now it all made sense. That was why she needed him; that was why she wanted to find the Origin. Ticahrla wanted to become a powerful magic wielder. "That's why you want to become an Arcane Bearer."

"You got it."

Jokahn thought to himself for a moment. "How does it work?"

"Magic? There's nothing all that special about it. It just takes a lot of practice." Ticahrla leaned forward and pressed her hand firmly against his chest. Her voice was soothing. "It starts here. It begins as a warmth—a heat that builds in your core. Do you feel it?"

Her eyes looked deep into his. Jokahn's heartrate elevated. She smiled and his knees weakened.

"Here, let me show you," Ticahrla said. She pulled down the neckline of her chest piece and pressed his hand to her collar.

Her skin was soft and warm. His brow rose and his forehead began to sweat as he felt her chest gingerly rise and fall with each breath.

"Every living thing has energy. It's the same energy that allows you to see, taste, and touch. Magic is simply the act of channeling that energy inside you and exerting it outward."

Ticahrla's skin started to grow noticeably warm, hot to the touch. She brought her free hand up to her line of sight and focused on it. Her fingers strained, forming a claw as a spark crackled from her fingertip. Then another, and another. Jokahn's eyes widened. His jaw fell open. Soon, lightning branched and arced in all directions from her hand.

It was amazing. There was something about Ticahrla that could play with his emotions in a way he had never felt before. For the first time in a long time, he actually felt...*happy.*

Ticahrla glanced out the corner of her eye. Jokahn followed her gaze. Bakta was leaning against a wall with an ale in his hand as his eyes glared at Ticahrla.

"That's enough magic for today," she said. The heat in her chest began to cool and the sparks in her hand died out. She motioned to Jokahn. "Go get some rest. We'll chat again later."

With a warm heart, Jokahn made his way to the stairwell that led below deck to the sleeping quarters. He looked back at her—she was smiling—and waved. Ticahrla raised a subtle hand to wave back.

For a while, he had questioned if leaving Anchorsfell had been a good decision, but as the warmth of her smile filled his heart, he knew he had made the right choice.

* * *

Ticahrla watched intently as Jokahn made his way below deck. She managed to uphold her smile, but something unsettling stirred inside her.

Bakta and Drahig walked over to her side.

"Making friends, are we?" Bakta asked in a low, almost cautious tone.

She shrugged. "Eh, the boy looked like he could use some cheering up."

Bakta's next words were calm but stern with intent. "We're going to kill him, remember?" he said as though it was a deliberate attempt to tromp on her pleasant mood.

It nearly worked. Ticahrla's stomach clenched, and her eyes turned down, but she didn't let it show. "How could I forget? The legend says I have to sacrifice a Dreamer to become an Arcane Bearer." She reached behind her back and unsheathed a large dagger. "The boy has a good heart. Taking his life…it's not going to be easy." Slowly, she twirled the blade in her hand as she thought to herself. "But then again, I suppose doing the right thing rarely is."

Apparently satisfied with her response, Bakta managed to express a level of compassion again. He shook his head. "Terrible shame, isn't it?"

Ticahrla nodded. "I wish there was another way." She holstered the dagger behind her back again. "But I *need* to become an Arcane Bearer. Everything depends on it."

"I know." Bakta placed a firm but comforting hand on her shoulder.

"We all know." Drahig nodded. "It's for the best."

Ticahrla gave her companions a heavy but grateful grin. As much as it weighed on her, she knew it as well. It *was* the right thing to do, sacrificing one boy's life to save an entire kingdom.

She turned toward the sleeping quarters where Jokahn lay happy and oblivious. "Well, we've got plenty of time before any of that happens. Until then, try to have some fun with the boy. No point in making the journey miserable for everyone."

Bakta and Drahig agreed.

"So, are we off to find the Origin now?" asked Bakta. "Off to make you an Arcane Bearer?"

"No." Ticahrla let out a long sigh. "I've got a few stops to make first."

6

Fractured

Sihera was below deck meditating when a loud ruckus caught her attention. Her eyes eased open. She could make out the muffled sound of heated voices clamoring in the distance. She rose and made her way to the upper deck.

As she emerged into the salty evening air, she saw Laval arguing with several irritated mages and their families.

"Athus is just a five-day sail away," pleaded Laval. "We have to at least try."

"Why?" barked one woman as she jabbed a finger at Sihera. "Because *she* had a dream?"

Everyone turned to look at Sihera. Sihera's head reared back with a stern look. What had she done to upset this woman?

One man stood up tall and raised his voice to be heard. "Dreamers like Sihera are the only beacon of hope we have left. If Sihera and Laval say we need to go to Athus, then that's what we should do."

"He's right," said Laval. "Sihera is one of the last remaining dreamers in the world. If there is even a chance that we can save the life of another, then we must take that chance."

A man stepped forward with a furious scowl. "What is so great about dreamers? She hasn't shown herself to be any more capable with magic than the rest of us."

A woman clung to her children. "We are barely surviving as it is. I'm not going to risk my family because of some dream."

Marching forward, a man ignited a fireball in his hand. "If it's us or the dreamers, then I chose us."

Sihera gasped and stutter-stepped backward as the man bared

down on her with rage in his eyes. Laval planted himself between Sihera and the approaching man, lightning crackling from Laval's fists and fire pouring from his eyes. More mages on each side faced off, staring each other down.

Sihera pressed her back against the wall, her heart pounding. She couldn't believe what was happening. How could Archmagi turn against each other?

Laval's voice rang out strong. "Stand down!" The mob paused, and Laval's voice calmed to a simmer. "Or you'll be dead before you can lift a finger."

The enraged man stood there, breathing heavily as he glared at Laval. It was an unnervingly long wait for Sihera before the man answered. When he finally spoke, his voice was calm yet somber. "If you're taking us to Athus, we're as good as dead already."

Sihera's eyes bulged, and her lungs tightened as the man reared back his arm.

The crackling energy within Laval's fists bloomed as he shot his arms forward, casting a bright glow across his hardened face. Lightning whipped across the deck, throttling the man backward and into the railing.

From Sihera's right, a burst of amber hues roared spiraling through the air toward Laval. One of Laval's trusted men cut his arm through the air, creating a deafening shockwave that deflected the fireball, sending embers bursting out over the water.

Sihera watched in horror, her breathing erratic. People who once thought of each other as family had been replaced by a frightened and angry mob. The deck was transformed into a chaotic battlefield, the wood groaning amongst the onslaught. Chaos erupted all around her, each flare of magic that streaked by carved somber trails of darkness in her heart. Her eyes swelled with tears.

She pulled a deep breath into her lungs and shrieked, "*Stop!*" Her voice echoed off the ship's hull and reverberated around her. Everyone froze. All eyes turned towards her, the rage in their expressions dimming. Her heart was like a frantic bird in her chest as the words quivered from her lips. "Haven't enough people died already?"

Laval lowered his arms and his lightning flickered, then died. He straightened his robe, but his breathing remained heavy. "We're going to Athus. If you don't want to, that's fine. Leave now, and abandon what little hope we have left of saving magic in this world."

His words hung in the air as dread washed over everyone's faces, and people exchanged cautious glances. The deck was left eerily quiet.

That night, three ships sailed off into the sunset, dwindling the Archmagi's numbers even further.

Sihera threw herself onto her hammock and stared up at the ceiling, tears running down her cheeks. Her heart constricted as her thoughts veered back to the vision of the boy. If she couldn't even help what was left of the Archmagi, how was she ever going to save her Dreamer boy?

* * *

Jokahn stood high atop a cliffside overlooking the water. The wind rushed through his hair, but he was not cold, nor frightened, nor excited. He was just there, calm, peaceful, and relaxed.

A flush of heat came over him; he could feel her fiery green eyes on him. Jokahn turned to see Ticahrla. She was smiling. She stood there, quietly observing him.

There was something intoxicating about her. Just gazing up at her filled him with joy. He closed his eyes and, for a moment, felt weightless. As his eyes opened again, he realized he was falling headfirst down the cliffside. The wind rushes past him, but he remained calm. As the ground neared, Jokahn casually turned his body upright. His descent slowed and he touched the ground softly, first one foot, then the other.

Jokahn's brow pulled together. He held his hands out in front of him, staring down at his open palms. Something was eerily wrong with this place.

"Where am I?" he murmured. Then it hit him—he was dreaming.

None of this was real. And with that realization, the world around him blew away like dust in the wind.

He gasped. Alone in an empty fog, he hugged his arms around his chest and scanned the vast emptiness surrounding him. The fear crept up from inside him, familiar and heavy in his chest. It was the dread of being completely alone.

The sound of weeping echoed through the air. Jokahn turned, and he was in the hull of a ship. A girl with dark, curly hair sat on the floor, crying. He didn't recognize her face, but she had a kind and gentle look. She was very pretty, and her big brown eyes gave Jokahn a sense that he could trust her.

He cocked his head to the side and walked toward her. Why was she crying? "Are you all right?" he asked, but the girl didn't reply. He brought his face in closer to hers. She sat there whimpering as she stared through him—her gaze occasionally fluttering from side to side, never quite finding a lock on him.

Without thinking about it, Jokahn extended his hand, lacing his fingers through the girl's soft, silky curls as he gently rested his palm against her cheek. His eyes lit up. He could touch her.

The girl's face turned pale, dread overtaking her, as a long gasp was pulled into her lungs. Jokahn glared in confusion at her expression.

Large red flames came roaring to life from her shock-filled eyes, and Jokahn leapt back.

She sprang forward, stretching her arm out toward him in desperation. But as she lunged, her body moved slowly, as if passing through molasses. Even the flames lapping at the sides of her eyes waved gradually through the air.

Jokahn cautiously angled his head, staring at her from the side of his eye. He wasn't sure what to do. Run? Don't run? Moving as slow as she was, she didn't appear to be a threat. And her eyes, although engulfed in flames, appeared frightened.

He stood there watching her hand draw closer, but he didn't shy away. As her fingertips finally pressed against his chest, the girl evaporated into a cloud of smoke.

Jokahn's brow tightened. He searched all around him, but she was gone. Again, he was left alone in a world of fog with nothing but a dissipating grey cloud to remind him of her.

"What is going on?" Jokahn cried out. None of it made any sense. Just as he thought his dream couldn't get any more confusing, a hand touched his shoulder from behind. He let out a yelp and spun around.

It was Ticahrla. Jokahn exhaled sharply in relief. His body keeled forward, his hands on his knees, and his eyes closed. He was panting. This dream was becoming too much for him.

Jokahn rose and peered up at Ticahrla. She was more beautiful and perfect than ever. Her eyes squinted with joy as she cast her glorious smile down at him. There was something unworldly about Ticahrla's smile. Every time he gazed upon it, he could feel its warmth melting through his body. He basked in the ecstasy of it, and his face stretched into a subtle yet gleeful grin.

But then the warmth inside him began to wane. Jokahn eyed her cautiously as he noticed she too was gradually fading from sight.

"No!" Jokahn leapt forward and threw his arms around her. "Don't leave me. Please, I don't want to be alone. I don't want to be scared anymore." He pleaded with her, tears swelling in his eyes, but she didn't respond.

The sound of a roaring fire ignited above him. He turned up to look at her as Ticahrla's emerald, green eyes burned like a raging inferno. As she peered down at him, her once glorious smile was now replaced by a wide, maniacal grin.

Jokahn took a deep breath as he lurched upright in his hammock. He panted heavily, sweat pouring down his face as his eyes panned the dark room of the sleeping quarters. Ticahrla, Bakta, and Drahig were asleep in their hammocks. The world was quiet, but he couldn't escape the horror he felt inside him.

Eventually, Jokahn calmed his breathing. As he laid back down, eyes wide open and fixed on the ceiling, he began to question if being a Dreamer was really such a gift after all.

7

Athus

After four days at sea, Jokahn was beginning to find his rhythm living amongst his new shipmates. Life on the *Nahktaio* was surprisingly devoid of activity for him. Between Ticahrla navigating the controls and Drahig managing the sails, Jokahn was left with little to do outside of mopping and scrubbing. Bakta, in addition to being a handy man, was a skilled chef who spent several hours each day prepping and cooking meals.

With every duty accounted for, there were still plenty of hours left in the day that needed to be occupied. One of the more popular ways for everyone to pass the time was gambling.

Jokahn and Bakta sat downstairs playing a game of chips in the dining quarter. The room was simple, just a large, square table in the center and a long continuous bench along the wall.

Ticahrla, bored and with nothing else to do, sat sprawled out across the bench, watching them play. Of course, they never actually played for real coin, but the games still got very competitive. Ticahrla was especially fierce when it came to winning or losing. Jokahn had yet to beat her at a game of chips—he had yet to beat her at anything, really. Bakta, on the other hand, was a rather "easy target," as Ticahrla had once put it.

Bakta stared intently at his hand of chips as Drahig propped up a small stool in the entryway of the dining area. The ergman wiggled and nestled himself into the seat that was far too small for his body. That was how Drahig always sat at the dinner table. His large frame would have never fit onto one of the benches.

"Hurry up, Bakta," Jokahn groaned, slumping his head into his palm. "This isn't a staring contest."

Bakta scowled, chewing nervously on his finger as his eyes bored through the remaining chips in his hand. He threw two chips onto the table and buried his face in his palms. Ticahrla scoffed and shook her head as she looked away in disappointment.

With a short sigh, Jokahn pulled a chip from his hand and placed it on top of Bakta's two. "Tough luck, Bakta." He swiped up Bakta's two chips from the table. "Looks like you're about to lose again."

"How does he do that?!" exclaimed Bakta. "How does he beat me every time? I even had the high chips this time."

Beating Bakta was almost too easy. Still, he couldn't help but smirk a little. "I know. It's almost impressive how you can ruin such a winning hand." Jokahn snickered, but the strain on Bakta's face put a damper on his heart. Jokahn gave a sigh. "The game is more about tricking your opponent. Don't get so excited when you play. If I know you have high chips in your hand, I just sacrifice my low chips so I come out ahead in the long run."

Bakta pounded the table in frustration and placed his finger back in his mouth to gnaw on. He studied the table but continued to appear dumbfounded. Meanwhile, Ticahrla began to fidget uncontrollably in her seat. The steel toe of her boot tapped frantically against the wood floor as her arms hugged tightly across her chest.

"Oh, for crying out loud!" She threw her hands in the air, wrenching one of Bakta's chips from his hand and slamming it down onto the table. "There!" she shouted, swiping up three of Jokahn's chips and throwing them in Bakta's face. Then she shoved her way past Drahig and stormed out of the room, muttering to herself. "I'm surrounded by *morons!*"

Jokahn's face dropped. It was an excellent play, one that even he hadn't anticipated.

Bakta cheered. "All right, I'm back in the game!"

Jokahn looked furiously down at the board. Thanks to Ticahrla, he was going to have a hard time coming back and winning the game now. Lately, this seemed to be the way of things. She managed to beat him at everything they did. Whether it was playing chips, wining arguments, or even a belching contest, Ticahrla always had to be the best. And she was! It infuriated Jokahn to no end how one person could be so perfect at everything. It wasn't fair.

"Hey, *boys,*" Ticahrla taunted from above deck, "quit messing around and get up here."

One by one, they marched up to the deck. Jokahn was the last to pull himself out into the chilled ocean air.

Not far off was a land of brilliant colors. The rich, blue sea crested against a sheared-off limestone shoreline, as if the rockface had risen straight out of the water. Above that sat a rolling hillside of white and emerald—patches of grass peeking through layers of snow. In the distance was an enormous kingdom. White stone walls shot far into the sky, taller than any structure he had ever seen. Great fortifications wrapped around the city, running straight to the water's edge.

"Here we are." Ticahrla sighed. "Home sweet home. Welcome to Athus."

Jokahn glared resentfully up at Ticahrla. *Of course, she's from Athus.* Of course, Ticahrla came from one of the wealthiest and most powerful nations in the world.

Two gargantuan metal gates sat plunged in the waters, separating the harbor from the ocean. Armed guards in towers stared intently down at them. As the *Nahktaio* surged forward through the waves, a voice called out, "Gates up!"

"Gates up!" repeated another man.

"Raising them up!"

A deep and earthy thud—like a giant's hammer striking the ground—shook through Jokahn's body, shortly followed by a second. The two resulting shockwaves streaked across the ocean surface. A loud, metallic clanking echoed through the air. It was a deafening sound, even from a distance. But, slowly, the two metal gates began to arch up and outward.

The *Nahktaio* passed easily under the enormous metal slabs that hung from above and rained ocean water down upon him. His mouth gaped open, staring up in wonder, as the ship pulled into Athus' heavily fortified harbor.

"Gates down!" shouted one man.

"Bringing them down!" replied another.

Jokahn hurried to the stern of the ship as the clanking began to chime in reverse. The gates lowered into the ocean again and came to a stop with a heavy thump.

Inside the fortress was a bustling harbor. Countless armed guards moved about the massive ships and fortifications. He had heard tales of Athus; he had overheard people speaking of its elegance, grandeur, and military power. Now seeing it for himself—the impenetrable walls, their sizeable army, the beauty of its stone structures—he realized the stories all failed in comparison.

With the help of a few harbor workers, Drahig docked the ship and Ticahrla quickly made her way down the ramp and onto the pier.

"Let's go, boy," she said, not stopping to wait for him.

Caught off guard, Jokahn wasn't sure why Ticahrla wanted him to follow her.

"Hurry up," she commanded, and he hustled off the ship after her.

Jokahn glanced over his shoulder as he kept pace with Ticahrla. Bakta and Drahig waited on the *Nahktaio*. "Where are we going?" he asked.

"The palace, of course," said Ticahrla. "I need to speak with the queen."

Jokahn's face lit up. He had never met royalty before, nor had he ever been inside a palace, and he squirmed with anticipation as they made their way into the city.

The architecture was unlike anything he had ever seen before. Every building was carved out of stone as white as the clouds. Massive rock archways supported aqueducts that channeled water all throughout the kingdom, creating an intricate blue web that fell over the city like a net. Patches of ivy grew along the walls, adding touches of emerald to all the structures. Snow-covered roofs were scattered throughout. In the heart of the city, towering above it all was the palace. Two large waterfalls cascaded down each side of the citadel. Elegant in design, overpowering in size, the palace was awe-inspiring.

That seemed to be a reoccurring theme in Athus. Each person was as remarkably well dressed as the next, although they acted notably peculiar, staring and gossiping as Jokahn and Ticahrla walked through the streets.

He ducked his head shyly between his shoulders as he walked. Did he stand out that obviously as a foreigner? Were his tattered clothes so appalling to these people? Jokahn looked at the horrific stares on their faces and thought it must be true. In a kingdom of such grandeur, he must look like a wild animal. His disheartening thoughts were only reinforced as Ticahrla lead him through the palace and into the queen's throne room.

The throne room was as elaborately decorated as the rest of the palace with ivory furnishings and beautiful drapery. All along the walls hung enormous paintings of previous kings and royal families. At the end of the long room rested two thrones, one of them empty. In the larger of the two sat the queen, dressed in layer upon layer of formal attire. Jokahn was struck by the poise and grace she exuded from merely sitting atop her throne. But at the same time, an immense sense of power and experience showed through the steady firmness in her eyes. Whatever he had imagined a queen would look like, this woman well surpassed it.

The queen was speaking with her advisors, but she quickly dismissed them as Ticahrla and Jokahn strode past several guards to approach her.

Jokahn questioned why the queen was so quick to dismiss her staff, and why the guards appeared so at ease, when a large painting on the wall caught his eye. It depicted a young girl, about half his age, with rich brown hair flowing to her waist. She was dressed in a large, elegant gown, seated upon a throne with her pet lizard coiled up and asleep on her lap. Jokahn recognized the colorful patterns on the reptile and realized the striking resemblance to Ticahrla's pet.

Could it be? Is that Drahig? It looked like Drahig, but the lizard in the painting was so small. Jokahn chuckled to himself at the thought of Drahig, as big as he was now, sleeping on someone's lap.

He wondered, if that was Drahig, then who was the girl? It couldn't be Ticahrla, could it? But the more he thought about it, the more everything began to make sense. Her greedy and self-centered personality, her wealth, her poise. Jokahn's mouth fell open as he gawked at the portrait. It was Ticahrla! Even as a child, she portrayed the same fierceness and beauty that she carried with her now.

He looked up at her in astonishment. Ticahrla was royalty! He couldn't believe it. Just when he thought she couldn't have been any more perfect, just when he thought he couldn't be made to feel any lower, he discovered she was also of noble descent. How was *this* fair?!

Jokahn's heart swelled with hatred for Ticahrla, so much so that his hands to clench into tight fists at his sides, and his eyes burned into the back of her skull.

The queen spoke in a powerful voice. "So, after all this time, I see the spoiled child has finally returned. Yet you still do not bow before your queen. It seems the world has taught you nothing of respect."

"Get over yourself, *Mother*," growled Ticahrla as she approached the throne.

Jokahn gasped and his feet planted. *Mother?!*

The queen shook her head. "I just don't know what to do with you, my dear. To rule the world would be nothing of an accomplishment compared to taming you."

The queen rose from her seat as Ticahrla approached her. They stopped face to face and stared each other down—their eyes like daggers. For a long time neither one of them spoke.

Finally, Ticahrla let out a short breath. "It's good to see you again, Mother," she said, her tone still coarse.

The queen sighed and shook her head as her eyes turned empathetic once more. "And you, my darling." They wrapped their arms warmly around each other in a hug that appeared to be long overdue.

As Jokahn glared at Ticahrla's back, the queen peered over her daughter's shoulder. He jumped to find the queen gazing curiously at him, and the anger quickly fell from his face.

"Who is this young man? Could it be my daughter has finally found a suitor?" the queen asked with playful sarcasm.

"*What?*" Ticahrla pulled away from her mother. She turned to see Jokahn and laughed. "Oh, no. This is just a boy I found recently."

"I see," said the queen with a vibrant smile, her mood snapping from one extreme to the other. Now Jokahn knew where Ticahrla got it from. "Allow me to introduce myself. I am the high ruler of Athus, Queen Mehrabel. And you are?"

"Jokahn," he said, with some reluctance.

"Jokahn! Such a strong name," the queen said, clapping her hands together with enthusiasm. She leaned forward and placed a velvet-soft hand to his cheek. "What a handsome young man. Such beautiful blue eyes." She gazed at him wondrously, and Jokahn began to fidget shyly. He had never paid attention to the color of his eyes—no one had ever seemed to care—but he would surely take more pride in them after this.

Queen Mehrabel scoffed and turned toward her daughter. "Ticahrla, what in the world do you have him wearing?" She examined his clothes with a delicate hand. "No, no, no. This won't do at all. Come, we will get you cleaned up in a hurry." The queen grabbed him by the shoulders and spun him around. He glanced from side to side in confusion as the queen pressed a ginger hand against his back and passed him off to one of the maids. "See to it this boy is cleaned and presentable."

"Yes, Your Majesty." The maid curtsied as she took Jokahn's hand and led him out the throne room.

It had all happened so fast. His mind was spinning. With one last bewildered glance back at Ticahrla, Jokahn was swiftly ushered out the door.

* * *

Ticahrla snickered seeing the boy dragged off like that.

"So…" the queen said, strutting quietly back toward her. "I see you finally found yourself a Dreamer."

Ticahrla gave a cunning grin as she turned her eyes back to her mother. "I was wondering how long it would take you to notice. Not long at all, it seems."

"One tends to develop an eye for such things over the years. But, darling, how did you find him? Dreamers are so rare in this day and age."

"Honestly, it was completely by chance, but the timing couldn't have been more perfect."

The queen released a disheartened sigh. "You're going to try for your father's compass again, aren't you? Never resting until you find that wretched Origin."

Her mother had always despised the legend of the Arcane Bearers, and the way Ticahrla—like her father—obsessed over it. Ticahrla tilted her head down and looked up at her mother through her brow, hoping she would connect to the empathy in her eyes. "I'm close, Mother. I'm so close I can taste it."

The queen's face pursed together as she clenched her eyes shut, pressing her fingers to her forehead. "Ticahrla," she groaned, "how many times must we go through this?"

"I know, I know." She interrupted before her mother could spiral downward into another one of her rants. "But that's not why I came here." She paused and looked gravely at her. "I ran into a scout team of aiko a few days ago."

Queen Mehrabel's face filled with rage and her muscles tightened. "Do not play your games with me, Ticahrla. I don't know what follies you are scheming up this time, but I am in no mood for them!" The queen clutched her gown tightly and stomped back toward her throne.

Ticahrla's jaw slacked open, surprised to see her mother doubted her. "I wouldn't lie to you!" The queen glared viciously over her shoulder as she walked. "Not about this," Ticahrla winced, correcting her statement. "Would I have come back without finding the Origin if it wasn't truly important?"

"The aiko have not threatened our kingdom since well before my time. Why would they surface again now?"

"I don't know, but I saw them! I think they were searching for the boy."

The queen's expression softened, and her walk slowed. She sat delicately down onto her throne, struggling to retain her gracefulness as she did.

"If you are right," the queen said, wringing her hands together, "then there are sure to be grim times ahead. I will do my best to prepare the troops, but Ticahrla, my dear…" Her nervous eyes shifted up to meet Ticahrla's. "I fear this generation may not be ready for the challenges ahead."

"Humans have fought off the aiko before. We can do it again."

"Yes, but times were different back then. Humanity stood together. Today, kingdoms are divided. People care for nothing but their own greed. And worst of all, what may very well be the last of the dreamers is here in this palace."

"*That* may actually be what saves us."

The queen was quiet for a moment as she thought to herself. "Ticahrla, my love," she finally said, "stay here, I beg of you."

"Not this again." Ticahrla moaned. "I can't stay here, Mother. Not when I'm this close."

The queen continued as if Ticahrla hadn't spoken. "You and the boy will be safe here in Athus, where we can weather this storm together. You know how it frightens me to see you go out there alone."

"Mother!" Ticahrla interjected angrily. This time the queen fell silent, and an uneasy pause followed. Forcing her temper under control, Ticahrla calmed her voice. "It's going to be all right. *I'm* going to be all right. Trust me."

A sorrowful smile stretched across her mother's face as tears welled in her eyes. "You always did have your father's strength. I am sorry he was taken from us while you were so young."

Disgruntled, Ticahrla folded her arms across her chest. "Yes, well, I'll be addressing that shortly as well."

"Come now, Ticahrla. Why must you be so morbid? Avenging your father's death will bring you no relief. Nor will that power you seek. Why continue this needless endeavor?"

"I can't stop," Ticahrla said, growing frustrated by her mother's persistent needling.

"Finding the Origin was your father's obsession. Do not make it your own. Let it go."

"I *can't.*" Ticahrla declared through a clenched jaw.

"Why not?"

Ticahrla's eyes burst into flames as she reared up, fists clenched tightly at her sides. "Because I'm nothing without it!"

She panted, glaring at her mother from behind fiery eyes, her knuckles turning white. A pained expression filled her mother's face, and her hand reached out.

Ticahrla slowed her breathing. The fire in her eyes died out, and her muscles relaxed. "I can't because…" Her voice grew soft, and she turned her eyes to the floor. "Because if I give up now—if I don't come back as an Arcane Bearer—then everything they have said about me is true. If I fail, then I truly have abandoned my people. What good am I then?"

The queen gently touched her hand to Ticahrla's face. Ticahrla closed her eyes and relaxed her shoulders, pressing her cheek into her mother's palm. Yet still, Ticahrla's brow was stuck in a frustrated "V" upon her forehead.

"You are my daughter, the princess…" Hearing these words again, Ticahrla let out a disgruntled moan and batted away her mother's hand. "…and the soon to be queen of Athus."

Ticahrla paced back and forth across the floor. "How many times do I have to say it? I'm not taking the throne. I want to *rule* Athus, not become some subservient queen to whatever pigheaded nobleman I am forced to wed."

The queen shook her head and sighed. "Who better to rule a kingdom consumed by greed than you, my dear?"

Ticahrla rolled her eyes. It was astonishing. After all the time she had been away, it took only minutes for their old arguments to pick up right where they had left off.

"Noblemen are not all bad, you know," her mother continued.

"They are a pack of half-witted dogs," Ticahrla snapped. "All strutting around in a pissing contest as a pathetic attempt to claim territory."

"True." The queen laughed. "Oh, how I've missed that sharp tongue of yours, my dear." She reached out her hand and placed it on Ticahrla's shoulder to calm her uneasy stampeding. Ticahrla stopped and looked back at her mother. "But nevertheless, my love, my time to rule is short-lived. You are the only remaining heir to Athus' throne. If you do not choose someone of noble decent to marry soon, the council will gladly assign someone for you."

Ticahrla had no response to that. What her mother said was true, but that was all the more reason why she had to become an Arcane Bearer, and fast. Ticahrla had her own plans for her future, and they were bigger than anything she could ever obtain as the *queen* of Athus.

As an Arcane Bearer, Ticahrla could finally rid Athus of the royal council—old, corrupt men who had plagued her kingdom for generations. If she were to assume the throne without finding the Origin, she would have to marry a nobleman who would become her king, and she would take on the proper role of a queen, bearing children, not ruling a kingdom. The one exception was her mother.

Her mother wanted nothing more than to serve proudly under her king; she had no desire to rule. When Ticahrla's father was murdered, the king's son should have assumed the throne, but Ticahrla was their only child. And so, Queen Mehrabel became the first female ruler of Athus.

"The boy knows nothing of your plans, does he?" asked the queen.

"He knows only what I want him to know. According to the legend, I have to sacrifice a Dreamer in order to become an Arcane Bearer. He would have to be insane to sail with me to the Origin if he knew I was just going to kill him in the end."

"It doesn't bother you knowing his blood will be forever on your hands?"

Ticahrla scoffed. "My hands were stained red a long time ago.

The boy means nothing to me. Even if he can be entertaining at times, he's just some orphaned pickpocket."

"You are wrong, my dear." The queen smiled. "He is a Dreamer. And you know as well as I do exactly what a Dreamer is capable of."

"I know what I'm doing," Ticahrla assured her, crossing her arms against her chest.

"Of that I have no doubt. You have always been bright and headstrong, my dear. No one can deny that. But you think you know this world and what it is capable of. You think you know *yourself*. Well, know this: there will come a day when you are humbled by the realization of how little you truly understand."

Ticahrla shrugged off her mother's warning. "You worry too much. That boy is like putty in my hands. I'll use him to become an Arcane Bearer, and then be done with him."

"Still so manipulative." The queen shook her head. "Everything you do—every touch, every glance, every word—is just a ploy to make that boy to succumb to your every will." It wasn't a question, just an observation.

Her mother was right, of course. Ticahrla was a master at getting whatever she wanted. She knew exactly how to use her words, mind, and body to exploit everyone around her.

"You make it sound so harsh." Ticahrla chuckled. "I do the same as every other person in this world. I simply do it better." She grinned her wicked smile at her mother—the smile that only showed itself when Ticahrla knew she was right. Her mother's jaw dropped in awe. Then Ticahrla turned and strutted away.

As Ticahrla left the room, she heard her mother whisper, "That poor boy."

* * *

That was all Ticahrla could stomach of her mother. Ticahrla strolled through the old, familiar palace corridors. It had been over a year since she'd last walked these halls, but nothing had changed, including her relationship with her mother.

She and her mother had never spent much time together. She preferred to keep a comfortable distance between them whenever possible. It wasn't that she didn't care for her mother. Ticahrla loved her more than any other living human, but her mother wanted such a different life for her. As stubborn as they both were, their conversations would often turn to arguments.

Even though she couldn't stand her mother at times, she still admired her, considering it a bit of cruel fate that their lives were so separated. Under Queen Mehrabel's rule, Athus was one of the few kingdoms these days that was actually flourishing. For being suddenly thrust into a position of power, she was proud of everything her mother had accomplished.

"Oof!" Ticahrla gasped as a man ran into her while turning a corner.

"Pardon me," cried the man as he gathered his footing. He straightened his robe around his enormous belly and, upon realizing who he had run into, gave Ticahrla a disgruntled stare. "Oh, it's you, Princess." The overweight man bowed reluctantly. "I heard news of your unexpected return. Must you still parade around in that ghastly armor of yours?"

Speaking of cruel fate. Ticahrla grimaced. "Apotri, you are looking as old and fat as ever. Must you still be so obviously infatuated with me?"

Apotri glared at first, but then shot a cunning grin at her. "I cannot deny you would look much better out of that armor than in it."

The retch heaved up into the back of her throat. How could someone be so foul? "You're disgusting, even for a councilman."

"Chairman now, actually," Apotri corrected rather snidely.

Ticahrla's eyes grew wide, and her spine straightened. Why would her mother appoint such a pompous, egocentric, womanizing glutton like Apotri as chairman? He was corrupt. Sure, everyone on the council was corrupt, but she loathed Apotri the most.

"It's good to have you back, Princess. Your absence has been causing a great unease."

She turned a hard eye at him. "What do you mean?"

"Has no one told you?"

She shook her head.

A sly grin coiled up in the corner of his mouth, appearing far too pleased for Ticahrla's liking. "Civil war is breaking out in Athus."

Civil war? "And what hand did you play in this?"

"Temper your accusations, Princess. It's *your* reluctance to assume your duties as queen that is causing this kingdom to become divided. Your absence has created a needless fight for succession. Athus needs a king. The council is giving you until your seventeenth birthday to choose a nobleman to wed."

Ticahrla glared at the fat man. She knew him well enough to know he was scheming something. Apotri would take any opportunity to further himself, no matter who he had to step on to do so.

Still, why didn't her mother mention any of this to her? Was Ticahrla truly at fault? The guilt began to weigh heavy on her chest, but she couldn't give up on becoming an Arcane Bearer now. She wasn't about to let some fool become king and run Athus into the ground. "What if I refuse to marry?"

"Then Athus will fall into chaos because of your carelessness."

Ticahrla let out a troubled sigh, and her eyes turned to the floor. "My seventeenth birthday? That's less than two months from now. That isn't enough time. I haven't found the Origin yet."

Apotri clicked his tongue. "Life is full of tough choices."

Ticahrla glare at him through her brow. The rage inside was starting to boil.

"Will you be staying with us long, Princess?" continued Apotri. "Or will you shortly be deserting your people yet again?"

"Don't speak to me that way, you swine," Ticahrla snapped at him. "I don't have to stay here and listen to such insults from the likes of you."

"Obviously not." Apotri bowed slightly and strutted past her. "Good luck on your quest to become an Arcane Bearer," he called out as he walked away. "Word is you might have some competition in that area."

Ticahrla peered over her shoulder with a scowl, and a spark of green flame escaped her eyes. *I really hate that fat, old man.*

What was Apotri talking about? Who else could possibly be searching for the Origin? Its location was unknown to almost everyone. Even Ticahrla didn't know its exact whereabouts, although she had a good idea of where it was and how to find it. Besides, to become an Arcane Bearer, a person needed to sacrifice a Dreamer. Ticahrla had found Jokahn. How many other dreamers were left in the world?

A flush of heat poured over her. It was an intensity—a power—unlike anything she had felt before. With a scowl, Ticahrla slowly turned toward the courtyard.

Walking through the garden was a group of men. Their long red and white robes clearly identified them as members of the Archmagi occult. But these men were not what had grieved Ticahrla so suddenly. It was the black-haired, teenage girl walking in the center of the ring of red robes.

From behind her delicate curls, the girl's eyes focused intently on Ticahrla. The girl grinned, her big brown eyes piercing though Ticahrla's heart. Then, as she turned and walked out of the courtyard, the heat faded.

"No…" gasped Ticahrla. "The Archmagi have…a *Dreamer?!*"

8

Keeping Secrets

Sihera chuckled as she walked down the palace halls, the image of the princess' horrified expression still fresh in her mind.

Princess Ticahrla... Sihera snickered and shook her head. Laval had warned her to stay away from Ticahrla; he probably didn't want his "promising pupil" corrupted by the princess. But what he failed to mention was the immense energy she radiated. There was no denying the princess's strength. Even from a distance, Sihera felt its pull—like a tether—tugging on her bones.

It was a humbling feeling, but then Sihera realized that, just as she could feel the pull from Ticahrla, Ticahrla had felt her. And when she caught a glimpse of the terror in Ticahrla's eyes, Sihera couldn't help but smile.

The quartermaster escorted Sihera and the few high-ranking Archmagi down the hall and introduced them to Athus' royal council. As Laval made his rounds and introductions, Sihera, as usual, followed by his side.

The Archmagi had been allowed to temporarily stay in Athus. It wasn't surprising. Even though there had been tensions between Athus and the Archmagi in the past, how could any decent human turn away a group of people whose home had been destroyed by the aiko?

She followed along as one councilman showed her and Laval the house they would be staying in. As the two men droned on about politics, Sihera's head leaned to one side with a glazed-over look on her face. Her eyes blinked slowly.

It had been an exhausting couple of weeks as she traveled to

Athus. Sleep was a luxury she rarely found thanks to her relentless nightmares and the now recurring vision of her Dreamer boy being stabbed in the back. She had told Laval about her vision in hopes it would provide one night of peaceful sleep, but it did little to ease her mind.

Although not all her dreams were bad. Occasionally she would dream of the boy happy and healthy again. She still didn't know his name, but she was confident she would figure it out. She was making good progress in her dreams; soon he would be able to see and hear her. The link between them was growing stronger. Sometimes it was so strong it felt as though she could reach out and touch him.

Sihera placed her hand on her cheek, remembering the warmth she had felt one night. She had not seen who it was, but something inside her knew it was her Dreamer boy, trying to reach out to her, just as she was trying to reach him.

"So, is this the soon-to-be Arcane Bearer?" the councilor's voice asked.

Her eyes blinked awake, and her head straightened, looking up at the councilman. He was one of the heavier-set councilmen, and he was smiling down at her with a sinister expression. How did he know she was going to be an Arcane Bearer? That was something the Archmagi tried to keep private.

Laval gently moved Sihera behind him. "*She* is none of your concern, Apotri."

Apotri smiled warmly at Laval. "Of course. How inconsiderate of me. It's rude to prod around in other people's business. Don't you agree, *Laval?*" The way he emphasized Laval's name sounded more like an accusation than a question.

Hugging her even closer, Laval replied in a low, cautious voice, "I don't know what you're implying."

Apotri's voice grew stern. "Keep your men on a tight leash. The next time I find them snooping around, you won't be getting them back." Then the overweight man turned and stomped away.

Laval's grip began to relax. "Come," he said, grabbing her wrist and pulling her the opposite direction. Sihera looked back at councilman as she struggled to keep pace with Laval's stride.

"What was that about?" she asked.

"Nothing," he snorted. "Just politicians doing what they do best."

Sihera's brow pulled together as she probed her memory. She recalled Laval talking privately to a few of his trusted men about looking for an old artifact—"the king's compass" he called it. She had heard Laval speaking of this ancient device long before they came to Athus, but he seemed to have a renewed interest in it lately.

"Was the councilman right?" she asked.

Laval's voice was brash. "What?"

"Are you looking for the compass? You were talking about it the other day."

"Don't be ridiculous. I said nothing of the sort."

Sihera's face scrunched, confused by his blatant lie. "But I heard you say—"

Laval stopped and swung her around to face him. "Sihera, please!" he snapped.

Sihera held her breath and pursed her lips. Laval stood in front of her, his jaw clenched, and his hand—shaped like a claw—shaking.

Finally, Laval let out a long sigh and his body relaxed a little. "I—I'm sorry. It's just… This has been a difficult time for everyone. You understand, don't you?"

Sihera didn't understand, but she nodded anyway.

"Good." Laval let out a short breath. "You know, you're probably bored listening to all these old men talking. Why don't you go to the palace library? You would enjoy that, wouldn't you?"

Sihera frowned. She was growing tired of Athus. She wanted to get back to her training, but Laval had forbidden her from using magic in Athus. She wasn't happy about it at first, but she understood. Most people were not as accepting of magic as the Archmagi, many were even fearful of it.

She looked up at Laval and saw his wide smile. Reluctantly, she agreed.

* * *

Laval left her alone to study in the library. She sat there, unable to focus, her mind was spiraling downward with questions.

She tried to justify why Laval would have lied to her. She could understand lying to Apotri—that man was about as trustworthy as he was thin—but Laval had never lied to her or hidden things from her before. What was so special about this artifact that he had to keep it a secret?

She needed answers, but who could she talk to? She couldn't ask Laval. The library was bustling with people, yet she suddenly felt very alone.

Her eyes widened as an idea struck her. She scanned the room, gazing at the volumes of books lining the walls. She had all the answers she needed right in front of her; she just had to find them.

She picked up a book about rare artifacts and flipped open the cover to search for—what was it called again—the King's Compass? Her eyes lit up as she found the page. The compass was an ancient stone, like a jewel, discovered by the late king's men. As she read on, her jaw began to slack open.

Now she knew Laval had lied to her. Of course, he was looking for the King's Compass. Its entire purpose was to lead someone to the Origin. Laval had been searching for the Origin's location for years. He would do anything to get his hands on such a trinket. Why hadn't he been honest with her? She would have understood.

What else wasn't Laval telling her? What else was he hiding?

Sihera rummaged through the library's archives, collecting any book she could find about the Origin or Arcane Bearers. Fanning them out across the table, she traced through the records.

Her hand screeched to a halt as one word jumped from the page: "…sacrifice…" Her mind flashed a vision of her Dreamer boy as the blade pierced through his back.

She couldn't believe what she was seeing. She read on. In order to be granted the power of the Arcane Bearer, a Dreamer must be sacrificed. She glared down at the gruesome text, unable to move.

No. This can't be right. She—a Dreamer—was supposed to

become an Arcane Bearer. But Laval had never said anything about a sacrifice. He had always told her how he would take her the Origin one day and use the sacred waters to transform her into an Arcane Bearer.

A disturbing thought circled through her mind. Was Laval using her? Did he want the power for himself? Was she the sacrifice?

Sihera shook her head. No, Laval would never do that. He was like a father to her. He took her in when she was just a child and raised her as his own. He dedicated years to teaching her everything he knew about magic. Why would he have gone through such trouble if she was nothing more than a sacrifice?

The notion of sacrificing a Dreamer was causing her head to ache. She pressed her face into her palms and let out a groan of frustration. How was she supposed to become an Arcane Bearer if a Dreamer needed to be sacrificed? What did this mean for her vision?

Her heart clenched, and her breath halted at the dreadful thought that came to mind. Her eyes peered through her fingers down at the pages below her.

"No," she exhaled, sitting back in her chair. Then she scoffed—almost a chuckle—at the absurdity of the idea, but then she turned back to scowl at the page. It was ridiculous. How could it be true? She must have misunderstood something. Yet she couldn't force the terrible thought from her mind. She would never…

Was *she* going to sacrifice her Dreamer boy?

9

A Longing to Fly

Ticahrla's mind ached. That bastard Apotri was even more conniving than she remembered. He'd practically left her with no choice but to marry, and now the Archmagi had a Dreamer of their own. What were they even doing in Athus?

The Archmagi were a small cult of idealists, heavy practitioners of magic that sought to return things to "the way they used to be." They envisioned a world where magic was the cornerstone of humanity, bringing peace across the lands.

Ticahrla never believed in such ridiculous ideology. She knew wars raged on even when mages flourished, but she did recognize the Archmagi were serious in their beliefs. If they had already found a Dreamer, it wouldn't be long before they discovered the location of the Origin.

What was she going to do? Give up and get married? She had fought, bled, and clawed her way for this chance. No! She couldn't give up now that the Origin was nearly in her grasp.

Her temper was boiling over. She needed to calm herself. She tried to relax her body, but her fists clenched tighter and tighter.

"Damn it! The Origin is *mine!*"

She breathed heavily as the image of her Dreamer flashed across her mind. It had been a while since she had seen him. Perhaps she should go check on the boy. Her fists began to loosen, and her muscles began to ease. Yes, she would check on Jokahn. After all, she was curious to see how the maid had faired at turning him into a "presentable young man."

* * *

"He's all done, Your Highness," the maid called through the doorway as she gave Jokahn a nudge.

He made his way out of the dressing room where Ticahrla was waiting for him. He caught a glimpse of himself in a mirror and had to do a double take, not recognizing the reflection of the young man mimicking his movements.

His hair was slicked back, and he was dressed in a uniform fit for a prince. The gold buttons glistened against his navy-blue jacket. The tan trimming complemented the dark colors of his coat, black slacks, and polished shoes, but it was uncomfortably snug. It was strange having clothes that hugged his body so precisely. He grimaced and tugged irritably at the sleeves. Ticahrla chuckled.

"It's not funny," he grumbled. "I'm not used to this kind of stuff."

"No, it looks good on you," Ticahrla said in a caring tone.

Jokahn stopped fidgeting with his new clothes. He looked up at her; she was smiling.

"You clean up nicely."

That was the first genuine praise Ticahrla had ever given him. He could feel the heat rising into his cheeks. "Uh, thanks…" he said shyly. He wasn't sure how to respond, so he changed the subject. "Did you talk to your mother? Err…I mean, Queen Mehrabel?"

Ticahrla nodded, but her smile waned and her eyes turned to the floor.

"So, what do we do now?"

She started to shrug her shoulders, but then she paused. Her eyes shifted towards him, and a smug little grin appeared across her face. "Come on, I want to show you something."

Outside the palace walls, she led him to the top of a cliffside overlooking the ocean. Cool, salty winds blew in from the sea. It was peaceful. The only sound was the waves crashing against the base of the cliff far below, and birds calling from the distance.

Ticahrla's voice was soft as she stared out at the sea. "I used to come up here when I was little." Then she chuckled. "Mother always hated it. She used to say it was too dangerous." Ticahrla walked Jokahn to the edge, where the cliff dropped off into a vertical slope, straight down to the water. "Look down there. Isn't it amazing?"

Jokahn's eyes widened, and his stomach clenched. "That's a long drop." He tugged lightly on Ticahrla's hand to signal for her to back away, but she either didn't notice or chose to ignore him.

"Tell me." Her voice was quiet, almost sad. "If a person is willing to give up everything they love and care for, in the end, do you think they'll achieve the one thing they want most in life?"

He glanced up at her with a puzzled expression. "What do you mean?"

"Have you ever heard the story, *The Girl Who Longed to Fly?*" Jokahn shook his head.

"It's the story about a girl who, more than anything, wished she could fly. Over and over, the girl tried everything she could to fly, but she always failed. No matter how badly she wanted it—no matter how much it consumed her—she could not fly. But she knew, deep in her heart, if she was willing to give up *everything*, then one day she would soar."

He could hear the quiver in Ticahrla's voice. She didn't say anything for a while after that. She just stood there, staring down at the ocean. "Ticahrla?" Jokahn asked with concern, but she was lost in thought.

"Come here." Ticahrla snapped back to life, pulling Jokahn a few paces from the ledge. She sat him down on the rocks and tugged at his coat. "Take this off."

"What are you doing?" he asked as Ticahrla pulled his arms free of the jacket.

"Just hurry up and get undressed," she insisted, throwing his coat to the side. She sat down beside him and began to pull off the layers of her armor. Jokahn was startled to see Ticahrla undressing in front of him. His heart began to race, and his face became hot. But Ticahrla was undressing a lot faster than he was, so he hurried to keep pace.

Now, both sitting in nothing but their undergarments, Ticahrla grabbed his hand and yanked him to his feet.

"Come on," Ticahrla grinned. She towed him behind her as she sprinted toward the cliff. They stopped right at the brink, Jokahn's toes dangling off the edge. His stomach lurched up into his throat as he peered down at the perilous drop. "Do you know what happened to the girl who longed to fly?" she asked.

"Huh?" He looked up at Ticahrla with panic in his eyes.

"One day, the girl climbed to the top of the tallest cliff she could find…"

What is she doing?

"…and without hesitation…"

"No, Ticahrla, we're not going to—"

"…she walked to the edge…"

Holy shit, she's going to jump! "Ticahrla! *Stop!*"

Closing her eyes with a glorious smile, Ticahrla whispered, "…and flew."

Jokahn gasped as Ticahrla leapt from the edge, pulling him along with her. Time seemed to slow as his heart seized up and his feet left the earth behind.

They plummeted through the air. He couldn't believe what she had done. At first, he was terrified. His eyes bulged and his lungs clenched together as he stared down at the approaching water. The rush of the wind and a sickening, weightless feeling twisted his stomach into knots. He clung desperately to Ticahrla's hand, but as he glanced over at her, the fear, sickness, and doubt all disappeared.

He watched Ticahrla in amazement. Her hair dancing in the wind, her face glowing with that radiant smile, and her skin flushed with cherry highlights. Jokahn's heart raced. The tips of his face and fingers tingled. He was intoxicated by it. He wasn't sure if it was the adrenaline or Ticahrla that had brought on this feeling. All he knew was he wanted more.

Ticahrla shot through the water the way an arrow passes gracefully through the air. Jokahn slapped, flat on his side, against the ocean's surface. A searing pain tore through his ribs, quickly ridding him of any pleasant feelings.

He floated atop the waves for a moment, like driftwood, then sank to the bottom of the ocean, air bubbling from his mouth.

As his butt came to rest on the sea floor, his lungs began to strain for air. He tried to hold his breath and swim for the surface, but no matter how much he flailed his arms and legs about, his body remained weighted to the ground.

His chest heaved, and the sting of saltwater hit the back of his sinuses. It burned, but more concerning was the liquid filling his lungs. Panic overtook him as he wriggled wildly. Again, a painful gasp of salty ocean was sucked into him.

An arm hooked around his chest, and a jolt thrust him off the ocean bottom. He breached the top of the water, gasping and coughing up liquid. Relief spread through him as he took in a deep breath and once again pulled precious air into his lungs.

"Wh—what were you doing, you idiot?!" Ticahrla scolded as she coughed and spat out water. "Were you just going to sit there and drown?"

Her arm clung around his chest as she treaded water. He shot Ticahrla a vicious glare as he grumbled in his partial state of consciousness. *What was I doing?! She was the one who jumped off the cliff!* Jokahn's thoughts swirled through his mind, but he couldn't find the strength to voice them.

Ticahrla towed him to shore and laid him down on the wet sand with waves lapping at his legs. The pain in his chest was burning, and the glare of the sun was so bright. All he could see through his squinted eyes was a thick, white haze in front of him.

A silhouette eclipsed the bright light. As his eyes adjusted, Ticahrla's glorious face, dripping wet, hovered over him. Her eyes nervously searched his. She was so close and so beautiful.

"Are you all right, boy?"

He wheezed. "You tried to kill me."

Ticahrla chuckled. "*Me?* Grant *you* a quick and merciful death? You think too highly of me," she said jokingly.

A quick and merciful death? "What's that supposed to mean?" Jokahn said as he massaged his forehead.

"You know, a quick death. The preferred death for any true warrior. As opposed to a slow death—a punishment for some wrongdoing."

Jokahn had no idea what she was talking about.

Ticahrla scoffed, shaking her head with a smile. "Never mind. I guess you are not cultured enough to appreciate my wit."

Ticahrla rose to her feet and, with a grunt, hefted Jokahn's weight up off the ground. Jokahn groaned at the ache straining in his ribs as she draped his arm over her shoulder.

"Let's get you back to the palace."

* * *

It wasn't until late that night when the throbbing in Jokahn's chest and head finally subsided. He'd spent most of his time in a palace bedroom, relaxing in an oversized feather bed. Somehow, Queen Mehrabel had gotten wind of—as the queen had said—"the horrendous acts her daughter had done to poor, helpless Jokahn," and hurried to his bedside to nurse him.

"Do not fret over your clothes," said the queen. "I've given Ticahrla a trunk full for you to wear. Here, I had my chefs bake you a warm meal. I wasn't sure if you preferred your meat lean or plump, so I had them make both for you."

Jokahn was stunned by the banquet laid out on platters before him. He wasn't sure what lean or plump meat was, but he was confident he would devour them both. He picked up the closest slab of meat with his hands and tore off a large bite.

"My word!" cried the queen. "No, no, no. Here, like this."

Queen Mehrabel gently pried the meat from Jokahn's mouth and placed it back on the tray. She sliced off a small portion with a prong and knife and scooped it up with a small silver fan for him. Jokahn pulled the meat off gingerly with his teeth—watching the queen to make sure he was doing it right—and swallowed it down.

"Excellent!" she cheered with a loving smile. "Now you try."

Jokahn had never seen anyone eat like this before. It seemed like a lot of pointless work for such a small bite, but he picked up the prong and knife simply to appease her. It didn't take long for him to get the hang of eating with the utensils. He even managed to duplicate the elaborate way the queen held them in her hands.

After his meal, the queen recommended a game. She took two large books from the shelf and handed one to Jokahn.

"We must sit up nice and tall for this. Place the book atop your head. Carefully now. Chin up so as not to let it fall."

Jokahn laughed as he contorted his body in the shape of an awkward crane to balance the book. "Like this?"

"Well, no…" the queen said, straightening him out again. "There, perfect. Now, repeat after me." The queen pushed her shoulder to his and swayed gently from side to side as she sang. "We dance with waves that flow through the night. Back and forth. Back and forth. Keep steady the towers which stand for what's right. Back and forth. Back and forth."

He glanced at the queen from the corner of his eye. Was this what it was like to have a mother? Were they all this eccentric? He wasn't sure, but he liked it.

They chanted together, "We dance with waves that flow through the night. Back and forth. Back and forth."

"Please, no. Not *that* song." Ticahrla grimaced as she entered the room, crossing her arms and leaning against the wall.

"Just because you don't enjoy it doesn't mean we can't," said the queen, placing the book in her lap and turning up her nose.

"Well, we wanted to see how the kid was doing," said Bakta as he and Drahig bowed their heads into the room.

"Drahig, my dear boy!" the queen exclaimed, rising to her feet. Drahig fell to one knee before her. "I didn't think you could grow any larger. I'm going to need a bigger palace if you keep this up."

"It's time for us to go, Mother," Ticahrla interjected sternly.

The queen gawked and took a step back in surprise, pressing her fingers against her chest. "What? But you just arrived. You can't leave."

"Get up, boy." Ticahrla signaled to Jokahn with a nod, ignoring her mother.

He saw Ticahrla was growing irritated, so he cautiously stepped out from under the covers.

"Drahig, Bakta, get the ship ready," ordered Ticahrla.

Bakta and Drahig bowed out of the room and left. The queen's breathing grew heavy as her eyes shifted nervously. "Ticahrla…" she said, but Ticahrla wouldn't look at her.

Ticahrla grabbed Jokahn by the arm to pull him up. In a panic, Queen Mehrabel threw herself onto the bed and latched onto his free arm. Jokahn's eyes widened in fear as he found himself the rope in a deadly game of tug-of-war.

Ticahrla's spine straightened. Her eyes grew large, and her face turned red with anger. "Let go of him, *Mother*." She snarled through gritted teeth.

"Come now, don't be silly. You don't have to leave so soon," said the queen, attempting to mask her worry with a smile.

Jokahn knew the queen wasn't afraid of Ticahrla's temper, at least not in the same way he was, but it was clear she was terrified of losing that which was most precious to her—her daughter.

The queen pleaded, "Please, sit down, my dear. We're having a wonderful time."

"Yeah, Ticahrla," Jokahn said, attempting to calm her fury. "It's a lot of fun."

But hearing him siding with her mother only fueled Ticahrla's rage. "Great! Now you've got him talking nonsense, too!"

"Don't blame me. If the boy wants to stay, let him stay."

"I will not be undermined by my own mother!"

Tears formed in the queen's eyes as she tried to uphold her smile. "Ticahrla, don't be ridiculous. Why would I—"

"Mother, I'm never going to be your 'little princess,' all right?! So just stop it!"

The queen's skin turned pale, and her body went numb.

"The faster you can get that through that thick skull of yours, the faster I can get on with my life!" Ticahrla wrenched Jokahn to his feet and stormed out the door with him in tow.

Jokahn looked back at Queen Mehrabel lying there, stunned, and grief-stricken. Tears streamed down her face. He tried to imagine what it must have felt like to be her at that moment; one of the most powerful people in the world forced to watch helplessly as all that she ever loved was taken away. The sadness in her eyes terrified him.

Despite her attempts, that was the last time Queen Mehrabel ever saw her only daughter.

10

Hope and Betrayal

The *Nahktaio* was clear of Athus' gates and sailing toward Ticahrla's next destination. Jokahn leaned back in the dining quarter, full and content after finishing his meal.

"You shouldn't have left home like that," said Bakta as he sprawled out across the bench.

Ticahrla groaned. She finished the last bite of her food and tossed the empty tray across the table. "You're starting to sound like my mother. There's no way I was going to stay in Athus."

Jokahn couldn't understand why Ticahrla wanted to leave her home. He would have given anything to have her life. She was the princess—and soon to be the queen—of Athus. Why would anyone give up a life of luxury like that?

"Why not?" asked Jokahn with genuine curiosity. "Why not wait in Athus until—what was it called—the Northern Pass thaws? We could go to the Origin then, couldn't we?"

"Because she's running out of time." Bakta snickered. "If the princess here doesn't become an Arcane Bearer in the next month or so, the royal council will force her to marry."

Ticahrla was using her fingernail to dig a piece of food from her teeth.

"What happens when you become an Arcane Bearer?" asked Jokahn. "Won't the council still force you to get married?"

Ticahrla shook her head.

"Why not?"

"Because," she said, flicking the speck of food across the room. She turned to look him dead in the eyes, a confident yet emotionless expression on her face. "I'm going to kill them all."

Jokahn's brow raised as he leaned away. Was she joking? Did Ticahrla actually intend to overthrow her own kingdom?

She continued, "I'll make sure every last councilman suffers a slow and miserable death." Then she leaned in close to him and whispered, "And with the council gone, and me on the throne, I will be the greatest ruler Athus has ever seen."

Her eyes lingered on his, as if staring into his soul. He held his breath, unable to reply.

With a grin and a playful wink, Ticahrla relieved some of the tension that had built up in his shoulders.

"What about the Archmagi?" asked Drahig.

She sat back and kicked her legs up on the table. "Forget about the Archmagi. I realized if they actually knew where the Origin was, they wouldn't be wasting their time in Athus."

Jokahn adjusted the rolled-up sleeves of the tan undershirt the queen had given him. He had decided to ditch the blue overcoat; it was too snug.

"I still don't understand why you don't like my idea," said Bakta.

Ticahrla groaned and she rolled her eyes. "Not this again."

"What? It makes sense, doesn't it?" Bakta refuted. "Queen Mehrabel is ruler of Athus because the king was assassinated. Why can't you do the same? Find some no-good, half-wit nobleman, marry the loser, and then quietly kill him. You would be the unquestioned ruler of Athus, just like your mother. How is that a bad plan?"

Ticahrla sighed. "Bakta, why must you be such an idiot? My first responsibility as queen would be to produce an heir. I'm not about to get impregnated by some drooling moron in the hopes that I off him before having a son. Not to mention, the council would *love* to see me hung for something like that. No, I have to find the Origin. That's the only way I can fix this."

Bakta grumbled. "Yeah, well, that aside, I still think what you did to the kid was cruel."

"The boy is fine." Ticahrla sneered, jabbing a hand toward Jokahn as if to present the evidence for her case. "The fall didn't cause any long-term damage."

"I'm not talking about jumping off a cliff. What I meant was…well… When a boy sees a girl, looking the way you do, strip down to nearly nothing to go for a swim, that kind of thing plays with a young man's mind."

A flush of heat rose into Jokahn's cheeks.

Ticahrla belched out a laugh. "*Him?* He's too innocent. The boy's not perverted like most of you men."

Ticahrla, Bakta, and Drahig all turned to face Jokahn. It was suddenly warm in the cramped room. He huddled his head between his shoulders and his eyes turned down to his plate as he picked at the remaining scraps of food.

"Then again…" Ticahrla said in coy tone. "Tell me, boy," Ticahrla leaned back, stomping her metal boot up on the bench, exposing her thigh. Jokahn's jaw dropped. A wicked half smile coiled up in the corner of her mouth as she ran a sensual finger across the line of her collar. "Do you like girls?"

His heart beat frantically. His mouth salivated, but his throat felt dry as he struggled to swallow. He looked down at his plate, not wanting to stare, but he couldn't stop his eyes from periodically flickering upward at her.

"Cruel, Ticahrla." Bakta shook his head. "Too cruel."

Ticahrla turned to Bakta and bit down on her tongue with a gleeful sneer.

* * *

Back in Athus, Sihera was especially numb and sleep deprived. Dark circles ringed the underside of her eyelids. Every time she closed her eyes, that terrible vision returned. The guilt was wearing on her. How could *she* be her Dreamer boy's killer?

Throughout the day, Laval continued to drag her around from one meeting to another. She didn't know why. It wasn't like she did anything in those meetings. Laval would stick her in a chair in the corner or outside the room, and then practically forget she was there. He still wouldn't allow her to practice her magic, not even in the privacy of her own room, and it was beginning to feel like an itch she couldn't scratch.

Her head slumped forward. She thought back to the way life used to be at the Archmagi Refuge, and a warm but weary glint of a smile appeared on her face. Laval used to devote entire days to her: she had reading and studies in the morning with him, meditation at noon, and then magic practice in the evening with Laval or Elehia and the other mages.

She was just eight years old when Laval had adopted her. Right from the start, he set to teaching her everything there was to know about magic. He had always been reserved, never really one to show affection, but she adored the look of pride in his eyes whenever she learned a new magic skill or improved on her technique. She missed those times when Laval seemed to have nothing to do but dote upon her.

Sihera let out a sigh as she raised her head to see Laval now. He was in the center of three Archmagi men, all of them with their backs toward her. In front of him was a large, standing map. Laval was waving his hand over it with enthusiasm, occasionally jabbing his finger at different locations. They were talking—she could see their lips moving—but the sound of their voices had been turned down by her brain into muffled distortion that played in the background.

Sihera had to do a double take as her eyes caught sight of a familiar rock formation on the map. It was something she had dreamt about every night now for several days, and it stood out clearly against the rest of the geography.

One of the men was drawing a large circle around the map as the sound of their voices came back into focus. "—our resources tell us it must be somewhere in this area, but more than that, we just don't know."

Laval let out a long, drawn-out sigh. "Where are they hiding that *compass*?"

Another man shrugged his shoulders and placed his hands on his hips. "Without it, it's impossible to know where the Origin is."

The words jumped out of her, almost instinctively. "It's there." Sihera pointed a finger at the familiar rocks at the bottom edge of the map.

Laval and his men turned to look over their shoulders at Sihera, appearing surprised to realize there was another person in the room.

It was intimidating to have all their eyes suddenly bearing down on her. She huddled shyly back into her seat for a moment, but she was confident she had seen that formation before. Sihera pointed again. "There. Between those rocks. Near where the river runs into the ocean."

Laval's head tilted slightly as he squinted one eye at her. Then he turned and walked over to her. He placed his hands on her shoulders and knelt to bring his face in close to hers. "Are you sure?" he said in a calm but weighted tone.

The seriousness of his voice sent doubt running through her. She looked nervously through her brow back up at the map. There it was, clear as day. She had seen it many times before. She nodded confidently. "I've seen it. In my dreams."

Laval let out a sigh and turned to look back at his men. One of them shrugged. "Without that compass, it's the best guess we've got."

"All right," Laval said, rising to his feet again. "I think that's enough for today. We'll reconvene tomorrow morning."

* * *

As Sihera slept that night, she knew that terrible vision would return. *Why this dream?* she asked herself. *Always this dream.*

The boy led her down the same damp cave. As he came to a stop near the dark spring of water, her arm reached out. As usual, she hugged him, pulling him in close, his back pressing against her chest. In her free hand, she held the dagger.

Her heart ached. She knew what was coming, and it tore away at her every time she saw it. Was sacrificing her Dreamer boy the price she had to pay to become an Arcane Bearer? Was it worth it? As the dagger drew back, she knew her answer.

No... she whimpered to herself. It wasn't worth it. She could never hurt him. But why then was her vision so clear? Why was it so consistent?

The blade pierced deep into the boy's back. She winced as he struggled in her arms. Gradually, her Dreamer boy stopped fighting, and a warm, pulsing liquid ran down her front.

His arms and head went limp. The full weight of his body fell forward, pulling on her arm. Her body gave the boy one good heft to keep him upright, then she walked him over to the dark water and pushed him in. The boy fell forward and splashed into the water.

Sihera's body wasn't crying, but inside, she wept. As his body sank, something caught her eye on the surface of the water that she hadn't noticed before—a reflection.

Her heart raced. She peered down at the stranger's face that stared back at her. The girl in the reflection looked exhausted, yet there was a hint of relief in the way she tried to slow her breathing. And her eyes—those fierce, green eyes—stared back with anxious anticipation.

Sihera gasped. She knew this girl. The realization created a hollowing pain in her chest, as if someone had sucked the life from her.

Ticahrla. The name resonated in her mind. Athus' princess was her Dreamer boy's murderer.

Panic ran through her, and her breathing grew heavy. She was desperate to wake from this nightmare, but she couldn't move. Her inability to control this body suddenly felt paralyzing, almost claustrophobic.

"Sihera?" Laval's voice called. "Sihera, wake up."

Her eyes shot open as she lurched upright in her bed, panting.

"Take it easy," Laval said, sitting down beside her. "What's wrong?"

She looked up at him with tear-filled eyes. He stared back, stern-faced. It was difficult to talk about at first, but gradually she told

Laval about her vision of the boy: the cave and the origin, the princess who murders him, and her helplessness to protect him.

"…and I know about…the sacrifice," she said cautiously. Sihera looked up at Laval, studying his expression.

Laval's spine straightened and his eyes narrowed, but he didn't say a word. That's when she knew he had lied to her.

"Why didn't you tell me?" she asked in a pained voice.

Laval gave a long sigh. "Sihera, you are like a daughter to me. I—I don't know. I suppose I was trying to protect you. Trying to shield you from the harshness of this world."

"I can't do it," she said calm but assertively. Laval turned his head in confusion. "I can't kill him. I won't become an Arcane Bearer, not if it means I have to sacrifice the boy."

The shift in his expression was slow at first. Laval's brow tightened, his fists clenched, and his eyes bared down at her. "Sihera," he said in quiet, almost quivering voice. "You know how long we've been working toward this."

She could tell he was furious, but she didn't care. She stared back at him, confident in her decision.

The pain showed through his eyes. Laval stuttered, trying to speak, but never managed to form words. His head slumped forward, defeated, almost to the point of tears. "All right," Laval said with a weary grin. "If that is what you truly want."

Sihera's face began to light up. "Really?"

Laval nodded. "We'll start a rescue mission for the boy tomorrow morning."

"You mean, you'll help him?"

Laval looked almost shocked. "Of course!" A snicker escaped him. "We're Archmagi. We must do everything we can to help our fellow magic users."

Sihera smiled, exhaling as if a huge weight had been lifted off her shoulders.

Laval continued, "We'll find the princess. And when we find her, we'll rescue the boy."

Her smile beamed brighter than ever as she looked back at Laval with pride. She had made the right decision to tell Laval about her vision. Soon, her Dreamer boy would be safe.

* * *

The next morning, Sihera woke with eagerness as Laval sent his men searching Athus for the princess. It didn't take long for one of them to come racing back, out of breath and with panic in his voice.

"Laval!" cried the man. "It's about the princess."

Laval appeared confused. "Yes, what is it?"

"The princess. She's gone."

"Gone where?"

"She set sail the other day with a boy. She's headed for the Origin."

Sihera's heart dropped. Were they too late? She looked up at Laval for answers.

Laval's eyes panned quickly back and forth as he massaged his jaw. Then he froze, slowly turning to the messenger with dread. Laval's voice was quiet, but with a furious undertone. "The princess has the compass."

11

Risky Endeavors

Sihera didn't like Laval's idea, but they needed help; Ticahrla had her Dreamer boy and was already heading for the Origin. Laval thought they should get assistance from the royal council, more specifically, from Apotri. She understood the urgency, but she didn't trust the chairman. There was something off about him, something wrong.

Sihera sat in an uncomfortable chair outside Apotri's office, flanked by two of the chairman's personal guards. For some reason, Laval dragged her along wherever he went. Apparently, he wanted to keep her close, but not so close that she could overhear his conversations. It didn't work. Even with the door closed between them, she could make out everything Laval and Apotri were saying.

"Do you know where Princess Ticahrla is?" asked Laval.

Apotri responded with a light and astute tone. "The princess is out of the kingdom at the moment, performing private duties."

"Looking for the Origin," Laval corrected bluntly.

Apotri paused. This time his voice was low and candid. "What do you want, Laval?"

Laval gave a long sigh. "Well, I don't know how to put this lightly, so I guess I'll just come out and say it. I need to get to the Origin before the princess does."

Sihera heard the wood creak as Apotri leaned back in his chair. "The princess of Athus beating the Archmagi in a race to the Origin." Apotri clicked his tongue. "I understand your predicament, Laval, I truly do."

Laval's voice was disheartened. "But you can't help us."

Apotri was quick to respond. "Oh, I'm confident I can help you. And believe you me, the council would love to have our princess back in Athus instead of out there galivanting around, chasing old, forgotten legends. No, the real question is, what can *you* do to help *me?*"

Laval was suddenly energized. "I can pay you. Just name your price."

Apotri scoffed. "I don't need your coin. I have more than I know what to do with. However, there *is* something you could do for me."

"What?"

The room went silent for a while. Sihera had unknowingly leaned her ear closer to the door. She heard the screech of chair legs sliding along the wooden floor. Footsteps marched toward her. Sihera quickly sat upright and looked forward, placing her hands in her lap.

The door swung open. Standing tall above her, peering down over his round belly, was Apotri. He glared at her suspiciously as one arm held the door pressed open. Then he smiled.

"Sweetie, why don't you follow my men to the room down the hall, will you?"

Sihera's brow pressed down over her eyes. She didn't like that Apotri was trying to hide things from her.

Laval walked up behind Apotri and nodded at her. "Go wait in the room, like he said, Sihera."

She looked at Laval in shock. Why was he taking Apotri's side?

The guard beside her wrapped his large hand around her arm and pulled her up. As she was towed away down the hall, she glanced back angrily at Laval.

Laval's face looked strained. "It's just for a moment," he said, raising his hand to assure her.

The guard plunked her onto a bench in the next room, then she heard the small gears turn and click as the door was locked behind her.

Sihera was a well-behaved girl. She rarely, if ever, questioned what Laval asked her to do, but something stirred inside her about the way Apotri had grinned maniacally down at her. Something was wrong, and she wasn't about to sit there and do nothing.

A gentle breeze blew her hair to one side. Her spine straightened and her eyes lit up as she turned to look at the open window.

Sihera poked her head outside, glancing left and right. The room she was in was on the third floor of a tall stone building. There was no balcony, just windows spaced evenly along the wall made of limestone and mortar, and a perilous drop to the courtyard below. To her left she saw Apotri's office a few windows down.

The wall was made of stone slabs in a repeating pattern, two flush, then one jetting out slightly. The protruding stone looked like it was enough for a foothold, but if she fell from that height, she was pretty sure she would break a leg.

With a few quick breaths, Sihera bounced in place to muster up her courage. Then, reminding herself not to look down, she stepped up and pulled herself onto the window frame.

Perched on the windowsill, her eyes instinctively turned toward the ground. Her lungs tightened inside her chest and her eyes squeezed shut.

What am I doing?

She turned on her side, extending one leg and reaching her toes toward the narrow brick. The wind blew the end of her robe, obstructing her view of her feet. The farther her leg extended, feeling for the ledge, the more her lungs tightened.

The tip of her shoe touched the hard surface, and her weight rested comfortably on the stone. A small sigh of relief spread through her. All right. She could do this.

Placing her other foot and grasping the windowsill, she shimmied across the outside wall, taking careful steps. Soon, she reached Apotri's window. The window was shut, but she leaned her ear in and closed her eyes, making sure not to expose herself in front of the pane. Gradually, the muffled sounds of Apotri's voice filtered through the glass.

"…left two days ago."

Laval's voice was strained. "If the princess left two days ago, then how am I supposed to intercept her?"

"Hold that corner," said Apotri. Sihera heard a large paper being unfolded. "Based on when she departed, she must be sailing around the southern peninsula. That means she has at least another month before she arrives at her destination. We know the Origin is somewhere in this region. Wait three weeks then the Northern Pass will have thawed, and you can cut her off here. The pass is narrow, but the trip is only a two-day sail from Athus."

"All I have are transport ships. Once I catch up to her, how do I stop her?"

"Luckily for you, I control Athus' entire naval force, and a good portion of her soldiers. I'd be willing to grant you charge of a battle cruiser and thirty of my most trusted sailors. That will provide you with the force you need to stop the princess before she reaches the Origin."

"Why are you doing this? Why help the Archmagi?"

Apotri let out a deep sigh. "Because there is something I've been wanting for a long time now—something no amount of coin can buy, but *you* might be able to give me."

Laval was cautious. "What?"

There was a deep, resounding satisfaction in Apotri's voice. "Athus."

Sihera's brow pulled together. Apotri was even more vile than she had imagined. Why would Laval make a deal with someone like him?

"You want to overthrow the queen?" Laval sounded stunned. "But why?"

"She's had her time. And if the princess isn't willing to take her rightful place as queen, there will soon be a mad scramble for succession. Civil war is looming. I can't let that happen. I already command the majority of Athus' armed forces. However, one important group remains outside my control."

Laval's voice was low, stripped of emotion. "The queen's royal guards."

"Precisely," Apotri said in a pleased tone. "Now, it would be treasonous for the chairman of the royal council—or anyone associated with me—to even attempt to buy off the queen's guards. If I were discovered, I would be executed without question. *However*, if an overly ambitious leader of the Archmagi attempted to buy off the queen's guards and quietly handed control of them over to me, then my hands would be clean."

"What if *I'm* caught?"

"If you are discovered, then I will see to it personally that justice is done. You will be banished from Athus. I will then have thirty of my most trusted sailors escort you somewhere far away—oh, through the Northern Pass perhaps—and you will never be allowed to return. Of course, the rest of the Archmagi can stay in Athus, as they knew nothing of the crime."

Laval took a moment to think, but not nearly as long as Sihera thought he would. "I'll agree under one condition. We set sail tomorrow. I don't have the luxury of waiting around."

"If you uphold your end of the bargain first, I will have a ship ready to sail first thing tomorrow morning."

"Let's get started," Laval said with subtle eagerness in his voice.

Apotri laughed heartily. "You've surprised me Laval. You're more ambitious than you look. Just think of it. Soon, I'll have control of the queen's royal guards, and you'll be on your way to the Origin with that boy Dreamer you've wanted so badly."

Sihera gasped, rearing back, and her toe skirted off the edge of the brick. As her feet fell out from under her, all her body weight yanked on her arms—her head jerking back as her limbs were pulled taut.

Her feet dangled. Knots twisted in her stomach as her fingertips clung desperately to the bricks. Grunting, her arms strained to pull herself back up, her shoes digging away at the stone.

"What was that?!" called Apotri.

The edge of her toe caught hold of a brick and she hoisted herself back up, panting hard. She leaned her forehead against the cold stone, amazed at how close she had come to dying.

"Move! Out of my way!" Apotri demanded. She heard heavy footsteps pounding against the floor as the men ran. The sound of

Apotri's office door being flung open caused her eyes to go wide and her throat to tighten.

In a mad dash, Sihera shuffled her way back across the wall. She could hear muffled voices shouting inside as they ran by. Desperately, she tried to shimmy faster. With one final leap, she flung herself through the window. She fell short, grunting as her body landed half in, half out.

Across the room, the door handle rattled feverishly. Sihera stared at it with dread.

"Gah!" cried Apotri. "What idiot locked this door?! Who has the key?!"

Realizing she had been gifted a few extra seconds, Sihera wriggled and wormed her way through the window, tumbling to the floor. She rushed over and sat down on the bench.

The window! She forgot to close the window. There couldn't be any indication she had overheard Apotri and Laval's conversation.

The guard's keys rattled, and the lock began to turn. Sihera threw herself at the window and slammed it closed just as the sound of the lock clicked open.

The doorknob turned. Sihera took one long lunge across the room, sliding her butt along the bench as the door burst open. A pile of men—the guard, Apotri, and Laval—fell forward onto the wooden floor, groaning as they hit the ground. Sihera reared back, shocked and confused by the force the three men had used to throw themselves into the room.

The room was still for a moment as the men examined the room. Their eyes panned back and forth between her and the closed window. Sihera sat there, mouth agape, staring in surprise at them.

A look of embarrassment came over them; their brows pressed down, and their mouths stretched thin. They mumbled incoherent apologies as they rose and started to close the door behind them.

"What was that sound we'd heard?" Apotri asked.

Laval shrugged his shoulders. "I don't know, a large bird maybe?"

As the door clicked shut, Sihera's head slumped back against the wall. A long breath expelled out from her lungs. Her limbs felt loose and wobbly, like jelly. Somehow, she had gotten away with it, and Laval and Apotri were none the wiser.

* * *

The next morning, Sihera squinted her eyes in the early light as the crisp air frosted her breath. The sun was barely peeking over Athus' walls, but Apotri's sailors were busy loading a ship with fresh cargo. Laval had assembled a group of four mages to go with him and Sihera. The six of them stood on the docks, waiting.

"All aboard, sir," said the captain. "We are ready to make sail."

Sihera followed Laval and the other mages onto the ship. It was crowded on the deck; sailors scurried about like busy ants. They were a hardened-looking crew, not a smile on their faces, but the ship was clean and impressive in size. Three large masts stood tall as oak trees down the center.

Yesterday, after leaving Apotri's office, Laval had sent Sihera home by herself where she waited for several hours. When he finally returned, it was late in the night. Laval looked tired but pleased. "Pack your things," he had said. "We set sail in the morning."

Laval never told her what he had done. It bothered her that he seemed so content to withhold information from her. But more than that, she worried what might now happen to Queen Mehrabel because of them.

Sihera stood beside her mentor. "I don't like this. We shouldn't have gone to Apotri. He's not a good person."

"He's not so bad," Laval said, admiring the ship and crew.

"I don't care, we shouldn't have trusted him."

"You don't have to trust him, Sihera. You trust me, don't you?"

Her lips pressed together. It was surprising how difficult it was to answer that question anymore. Her eyes turned down as she forced the words from her mouth. "I trust you," she said in a quiet voice.

"Well, there you have it." He sounded pleased.

"Gentlemen," the captain signaled to the Archmagi. Then he

smiled down at Sihera. "Milady. If you please, I'll show you to your quarters and we can begin our voyage."

Laval placed a gentle hand on her back. "You see, the boy is as good as saved. With this ship and crew, we'll be able to catch up to the princess in a matter of days."

Sihera let out a small sigh and nodded. She supposed that was the silver lining. Soon, her Dreamer boy would be safe. Her spirits began to rise again. In less than a week, she could meet him in person. Perhaps that was worth it.

12

The Harsh Reality

It had only been two days since the *Nahktaio* left Athus, but they were already approaching the shoreline of a small island. As Jokahn looked over the ship's railing, he could smell the foulness radiating from the land.

He cupped a hand over his mouth. "Ugh, what is that?"

"*That* is Modalphia," Ticahrla glared at the shore.

Jokahn buckled over, holding back the retch in his throat. "I didn't know misery had a smell, but I think we found it."

As the ship laid anchor off the coast, he noticed Ticahrla, Drahig, and Bakta donning long, sandy-brown cloaks and masks.

"Here, put this on." Ticahrla tossed him a pile of rags, the same as she was now wearing.

The rags were easy enough to figure out. A large piece of cloth wrapped around the waist, a second piece draped over the shoulders and torso, and a third cloth wrapped around the face and head. The headpiece was his favorite; it helped block out that awful stench.

Ticahrla pulled a coin purse from her waist pocket and placed it in a lock-chest. "Hand me your valuables," she instructed. "Leave behind anything you don't want stolen." Bakta gave Ticahrla his tool belt while he chugged the remainder of his ale. Ticahrla's eyes glazed over, and she frowned at him impatiently.

Bakta held up a finger. "Almost done." He said with a quick breath and went back to drinking. Fed up, Ticahrla snatched the drink from Bakta's hand and glared at him. She set the mug down and was turning to Drahig when she stopped to do a double take. Bakta had—almost magically—materialized a small flask of hard liquor from a pocket somewhere and was inhaling it before she could steal it away. Jokahn chuckled at the way Bakta frantically suckled the last drops from the container. Ticahrla shook her head and turned to Drahig who handed her his gold buttons and cufflinks. Then she turned to Jokahn and waited.

He had nothing of value to leave behind.

Ticahrla stared down at him for a long while, waiting. And even though it was hidden behind her mask, he could see she was smiling at him—laughing at him.

Jokahn glared back at her. *Yeah, I know. I'm poor. I'm worthless. Thanks for rubbing it in.*

"Let's head out," Ticahrla finally said.

Jokahn followed them down a rope scaffolding into a small rowboat. With Drahig at the oars, Ticahrla mounted the bow, claiming leadership. Jokahn and Bakta were forced to sit in the rear.

As the land drew closer and more defined, so did the stench. It was the reek of death, Jokahn was sure of it. Rustic and bitter, like the decay of old blood. The smell was enough to bring a grown man to his knees.

The small boat ran ashore. As they trudged inland, the soil was remarkably dry despite its closeness to the ocean. It cracked and crunched under his feet. There wasn't a speck of green, just a steady brown as far as the eye could see.

"Where are we going?" he asked.

Ticahrla pointed at a small congregation of leather huts in the distance.

"That's Modalphia?" Jokahn asked in surprise.

Ticahrla nodded.

Soon enough, they arrived at the village's center. Modalphia was an astonishing sight of filth and poverty. The grisly huts were small and brittle, overcooked by the sun. Children ran about, their skin burnt and hardened like the leather huts they lived in. The few adults outside stared viciously at Ticahrla and her crew as they passed.

"Oh good," said Jokahn. "It looks like we managed to avoid the busy tourist season."

Ticahrla stopped in front of a larger hut. She turned to face her crew, taking time to examine each of them. "Now would be a good time to grow eyes in the back of your head," she said.

Jokahn frowned. He didn't know what her warning meant, but the intentional calm in her expression alarmed him.

With a final nod, Ticahrla threw open the tarp door and entered the large hut with Drahig, Bakta, and Jokahn following close behind.

He couldn't see anything, his eyes hadn't adjusted yet, but many chattering voices fell silent.

The low, coarse voice of a man dragged on as he spoke. "Princess Ticahrla, to what do I owe the privilege?"

Jokahn's vision came into focus. His attention was immediately drawn to an overweight, balding man seated at a small table in the back of the hut. His enormous belly pressed tightly against the confines of his tattered clothing, adorned with tarnished silver buttons and frayed threads. Scars littered his face and arms; his lower lip was permanently cocked to one side from the remnants of an old wound. A woman sat on each side as they fanned him.

Villagers were scattered about the floor and tables. Their clothes were nothing more than rags—worn pieces of fabric that hung loose over their bodies. Jokahn would have fit right in had he not been wearing the new clothes Queen Mehrabel had given him. He noticed Ticahrla, Bakta, and Drahig removing their tan rags and he followed suit.

"Hello, Miode," Ticahrla acknowledged the fat man.

"Please, sit, Princess," Miode welcomed her. His voice quickly turned harsh as shooed some locals, cursing at them in a foreign language that Jokahn didn't understand. The villagers reluctantly got up from their table. Miode cleared his throat and smiled at Ticahrla. "It has been too long. And look at how you've grown." He chuckled.

With a nod, Ticahrla gestured for her crew to sit at the open table while she remained standing. "You've grown too," Ticahrla mocked.

Miode smiled and rubbed his enormous belly. "I am not as young as I used to be." As Ticahrla took a step toward him, a sternness rose in his voice. "But don't think for a moment that this old man doesn't remember *you*." He dragged his finger across an old scar that ran down the side of his eye and neck.

Ticahrla strode toward Miode's table, glancing at a dusty but elegant sword propped up in the corner. "What a shame for such a fine weapon to waste away like that."

"Yes, well, I am no longer a fighter. I have other occupations these days," he squeezed his women and chuckled nervously.

Ticahrla smiled back half willingly, letting the falseness behind it show. She continued her approach.

Miode's voice started to become bitter. "What is it, Princess? What do you want from me?"

"You know what I want." The closer she got, the more Miode's gelatinous body jittered with fear.

"*That?* I—I don't have that."

"Yes, you do." Closer she walked.

"Well—uh… Nah—not on me I don't."

"Where is it?" Closer.

"It's—uh…"

It was too late. Ticahrla was at the foot of Miode's table, and the fear shook throughout his entire body. She rested her hands on the edge of the table and leaned forward to whisper, "I think I know where it is."

"Where?!" Miode seemed shocked, grabbing hold of a necklace that hung underneath his shirt.

Ticahrla's evil grin slowly etched across her face as her eyes glared up through her brow.

Miode squealed and shook his hands through the air as if to cleanse them. "Ticahrla, my princess," he pleaded. "Why do you do such things?"

"Give it to me!" she demanded, standing up tall and thrusting her hand out at him.

"But—I…"

"*Now!*"

As Ticahrla and Miode argued, Jokahn noticed movement in the corner of the room. Some of the locals were growing agitated and murmuring to each other. As their hands moved slowly toward their weapons, Jokahn's stomach tightened, and his limbs began to shake.

Bakta leaned over to Jokahn. "If this starts to go bad, you lay down and you stay down. You get me?"

Jokahn nodded, but Bakta's warning only made his body quiver even more. His heart was pounding in his chest.

Ticahrla slammed her fist onto the table and Jokahn jerked back with a gasp. "Stop wasting my time, Miode!" she snapped.

A few villagers drew their weapons, most of which seemed to be trade tools—pitchforks, knives, and hammers. Ticahrla glanced back at the men as they formed a half circle behind her, and Miode gave a wickedly victorious grin.

Ticahrla turned back to glare back at the fat man. "I will never forgive you for what you've done." She stabbed a finger at Miode. "And I *will* get that back."

Miode's smile widened as Ticahrla turned around. Jokahn let out a sigh of relief. This meeting had almost turned deadly.

As Ticahrla took her first step, Miode shouted, "Your father got what he deserved!"

Ticahrla's body came to a jerking halt, and her eyes erupted in flame.

Jokahn's heart lurched back into his throat.

Tearing her sword from its sheath, Ticahrla spun around, her blade slicing through the air and stopping right at the base of Miode's neck.

Miode cowered back in his seat as more locals surrounded Ticahrla, shouting and pointing their weapons at her. She focused solely on Miode, scowling down at him behind a cover of green flame.

Jokahn could tell these villagers were not fighters. They stutter stepped forward, screaming in a foreign dialect at her, but not one attacked.

"You're pathetic," she said, shaking her head. The fire in her eyes calmed to a simmer. "Look how low you've fallen."

Miode didn't answer. He sat there shaking beneath Ticahrla's blade, the rolls of his belly vibrating in fear.

"Quit your cowering!" Ticahrla shouted, twisting the edge of her sword into Miode's neck.

"D—don't kill me," Miode's voice shook. "I beg you."

This seemed to please Ticahrla. She cracked a wicked smile. "*Kill you?* Don't flatter yourself. You don't deserve a quick death. I'm going to watch you suffer."

One of the locals brandishing a small cleaver stepped forward. The man took a few deep breaths and cried out, *"Ahtept narue!"* as he thrust his weapon at Ticahrla's lower back.

Turning quickly, Ticahrla whipped her sword around to parry the man's attack, tearing a gash across Miode's throat. Blood splattered the face of the women at his side, and she shrieked. Jokahn's muscles went rigid as Miode gripped at his bloodied throat, gasping for air.

Ticahrla deflected a second attack and cut her blade back across the villager's abdomen. The man dropped his weapon and collapsed onto the dirt floor, screaming. The rest of the locals took a step back and gasped, their movement like water rippling outward from where Ticahrla had just gutted a man.

Ticahrla's eyes scanned the crowd. Her body was poised and ready, a sign of her training and skill. Also telling was the way the locals shied away just at the sight of blood. Jokahn knew which category he fell into. He began to retch as he stared down at the bloody man sprawled across the floor.

"This isn't your fight," commanded Ticahrla. "Don't die protecting a traitor. Niegh eit esth nat a gru."

The room was still for only a moment, but to Jokahn, the tension seemed to last forever. The emotions on the locals' faces shifted from fear, then to sadness, eventually settling on deep-seeded hatred. As their eyes slowly shifted back to Ticahrla, he realized the dreadful reality of what was about to happen.

A local raised his club into the air and chanted, "Ahtept narue!"

"Oh shit…" muttered Ticahrla.

The wave descended. As the locals rushed in on her, swinging their weapons wildly,

Drahig sprang from his seat, tossing the table into the air as he stood. Jokahn leaned back with a gasp as he felt the rush of air from the table soaring past him. A loud crash and the sound of splintering wood rang out, sending three locals tumbling to the floor. Drahig rushed to Ticahrla's side to fend off the attacking mob.

The sight of an enraged ergman was enough to halt the locals' advance. Ticahrla turned her attention back to the fat man, shoving the table aside. The two women next to him fled as Miode clawed at his throat, fighting for air.

Ticahrla grabbed the necklace from under his shirt and tore it off his neck. Jokahn struggled to get a glimpse of it. What was so important to these people that they would slaughter each other? As Ticahrla was about to turn and raise the necklace into view, Bakta cried out.

"Kid, get down!"

Two villagers wielding blades were charging toward him. Bakta jumped to his feet and pulled out a long knife he had tucked away in his baggy pants. Bakta deflected a blow and countered, slashing one of the men across the shoulder and piercing his weapon back into the man's chest. The first local fell to the floor, but the second was quickly pursuing his companion's killer.

Bakta deflected attack after attack as the villager hammered furious swings down at him. It wasn't long before Bakta was overpowered and struck across the stomach. Bakta gasped, falling to his knees. Jokahn sat there, frozen in horror as Bakta keeled forward onto the ground.

The villager's eyes turned and fixed on Jokahn. Slowly retreating down onto all fours, as Bakta had instructed, Jokahn became fear-stricken. He didn't know what else to do.

"Look out, boy!" Ticahrla cried.

Before Jokahn could turn, he caught a glimpse of a wooden club rushing into view. It struck him square in the face. His head whipped back, and the world became a blur of color as momentum arched his body backward onto the floor.

He hit the ground hard. Blood poured from his nose. His ears were ringing, and a black haze began closing in around the edges of his vision. *Oh no!* He was losing consciousness.

Desperate, he tried to sit up, but he had no strength left. A villager with a club in his hand stood over him, staring down at him with furious eyes as Jokahn's vision dissolved into darkness.

13

Suffering and Empathy

The world around him was dark and empty.

Why can't I open my eyes? Jokahn wondered, but as he thought of sight, he discovered he could see. Rippling outward from his feet, the world materialized around him, revealing a green, rolling hillside, and the rising sun at his back.

"Hello?" a girl's voice echoed through the void.

Jokahn lurched back as he turned around. His heart sped up and his lungs tensed, but he saw no one.

"Can you hear me?" said the voice, reverberating through the ether.

He searched every direction, yet he was all alone. "Wha—who—who's there?" he asked, eyes wide with panic as he stutter-stepped backward.

A girl with dark black curls and a long white robe appeared on the ground in front of him. Instantly, the fear drained from him, replaced only by a grand curiosity. She looked oddly familiar, but he couldn't place where he had seen her before.

"Hello?" he asked.

She didn't respond. Then he noticed she was toying with something, a small flame she held floating between her palms. She massaged it, growing it larger until she thrust her arms to the sky and hurled the fireball high above her.

Jokahn arched his head upward as the fire exploded into a thousand pieces. His mouth fell open as the embers trickled down and gradually burned out.

The girl laughed.

As Jokahn turned toward her, she smiled up at her creation, yet somehow her eyes seemed to peer straight through him. Jokahn waved his hand in front of her, but she didn't react. Then, with a rush of wind, the girl vanished.

Jokahn stepped back. He pressed his palm to his chest. His heart was pounding, like the rhythm of a hammer. Then he realized it wasn't his heartbeat. Something else was reverberating through his body. His brow pulled together.

Out on the horizon was a vast army, like a wave of darkness blanketing the grassy hills. As the army drew closer, their march became louder, until the small details of their faces could be seen.

Jokahn gasped as his chest tightened. An entire army of aiko loomed before him. He tried to call for help, but no sound came out of him. He tried to breathe, but there was no air. Jokahn screamed, only to see his muffled voice as air bubbles run upward from his lips. He was underwater.

* * *

Lurching up from Miode's dirt floor, Jokahn gasped for air. His face and shirt were dripping wet as he sat panting. Ticahrla stood before him holding an empty water jug, her face and armor splattered with someone else's blood.

"Get up!" she demanded.

"Wha—what's going on?" he asked, coughing up water.

"You were dreaming while the rest of us were fighting for our lives."

"I was…dreaming? But…there were aiko everywhere. A massive army of them."

"Stop exaggerating. It was just a dream. It isn't real."

None of that was real? Jokahn wiped away the water with his hand, smearing dirt across his face. A sharp pain ran down the bridge of his nose.

"Ah!" He flinched. Gingerly, he felt out the bump beginning to swell over his nose. "I think it's broken."

"It will be soon if you don't get up," she asserted.

Jokahn scowled at her, forcing himself to his feet. Behind Ticahrla, Drahig stood with Bakta's body flung lifelessly over his shoulder. A tan cloth was tied around his midsection as a makeshift bandage.

"Is Bakta going to be—"

"He'll be fine, now let's go!" she interrupted.

Jokahn could tell she was lying. He looked to Drahig for an honest answer, but all the ergman could do was shrug and shake his head.

A soft, agonizing groan came from behind him. He finally noticed the unexpected stillness that had fallen upon the previously chaotic room. He turned and stumbled backward, aghast at the horrific display.

Bodies were scattered haphazardly around the room, and broken pieces of furniture were strewn about. His gaze came upon Miode's oversized figure, still precariously perched in his seat. Blood was seeping from his neck and pooling on the ground beneath him. Another pained groan escaped Miode's throat.

He's still alive?! Jokahn spun around to Ticahrla. "What are you doing to him?"

Ticahrla looked down at him with an infuriated stare. "Don't you know who he is?!"

Jokahn glanced back at Miode's mangled body, but quickly had to turn away.

"Miode murdered my father!" she continued. "To this day, Athus suffers because of this man's greed. *I suffer!* Now I can watch as he suffers as well."

Ticahrla studied the damage she had caused and gave a satisfied nod. But as she turned back to Jokahn, a twinge of empathy stretched across her face. She frowned and knelt beside him.

"Listen," she said softly. "I know this might be hard for you to understand, but he deserves his slow death. Killing him quickly would have been too good for him."

Jokahn didn't reply; he sat there unable to make sense of anything.

Ticahrla sighed. Then she rose and nodded at Drahig. "Come on, let's get out of here."

Pushing open the hide flap, she stepped outside. Drahig was following close behind her.

Jokahn couldn't comprehend what was going on. He had to do something—anything—before he was left alone in that room of death.

"We can't leave him like that," he pleaded to the ergman.

Drahig stopped with the flap held open and looked down at Jokahn with empathetic eyes. "It had to be done," said Drahig. Then the ergman made his way out of the hut.

Jokahn felt hollow, or perhaps ill. He wasn't sure. The sensation was unlike anything he had ever experienced before. It was paralyzing, like a weight pinning him to the floor.

Alone in the room, Jokahn heard another whispered groan.

"—lease —" Miode's voice struggled to carry volume. The man was attempting to lift his head. "Pah—pah—please…"

Too petrified to move, Jokahn sat wide-eyed and in shock as Miode begged for him to end his suffering.

"Please…"

Jokahn couldn't take it any longer. He scrambled to his feet and rushed out of the hut.

As he hurried outside, back into the stinking heat, a small crowd was gathering. Near the middle, towering over them, was Drahig with Bakta still slung over his shoulder. Jokahn pushed and shoved his way to the ergman's side.

"Drahig, what's going on?"

Inside the ring of people stood Ticahrla. Across from her was a tall, burly teenage boy dressed in leather armor and chainmail. He paced back and forth with a large, curved sword in each hand.

"That's Miode's son, Terris," Drahig pointed out. "One of Miode's mistresses told him of his father's death, and now—"

Drahig didn't have to finish. Jokahn knew what he was going to say. "And now he wants revenge."

Terris, although hefty, was nowhere near overweight. Even from under the layers of armor, Terris' muscles bulged and flexed. His long, dark hair was pulled back into a warrior's knot behind his head. He had a strong jaw, and a thick brow that sat low over his eyes. Terris was a handsome young man, and much larger and stronger than Ticahrla.

"I always knew this day would come," said Terris. "I knew that ego of yours would never be satisfied until my father was dead."

"Don't do this, Terris," Ticahrla said in a firm tone. "It doesn't have to end this way."

"You know *exactly* how this has to end!" shouted Terris, jabbing a sword at her. "You just want to see me suffer like my father, don't you?!"

"*No*," Ticahrla said adamantly, her voice cracking. "I never wanted this for you. And…" Her voice softened into her angelic tone. "I never stopped caring for you."

Terris' repetitive march slowed to a stop. His fists clenched tightly at his sides. The anger in Terris' eyes was soothed, seeping slowly—almost unwillingly, reluctantly—from his body. Jokahn looked up at Drahig in confusion.

"They grew up together as children. They used to be very close," Drahig explained.

"No." Terris shook his head. He reared his shoulders and started pacing again. "No more mind games. I mean, what would you do if you were in my position? Would you show mercy?"

Ticahrla didn't respond.

A hint of sadness peered through the aggression in his eyes. "You know what has to happen, Tee."

Ticahrla gave a long sigh as her head drooped forward. Then, graceful as always, she lowered herself down onto one knee.

Jokahn's heart sank. What was she doing? Was she giving up? Wasn't she going to at least try to fight?

Resting her other knee on the ground, Ticahrla straightened her gown around her feet.

Terris belched out a laugh. "You always were a showoff." He twirled his swords in a vibrant display of prowess. "Well, I've been training for the day I got to fight you again." Dragging one sword against the other, Terris' blades ignited in flame. His voice became low and coarse. "*Waiting* for the day."

Ticahrla watched Terris' movements astutely. Apparently, there was nothing left to say.

Terris charged, screaming and raised a sword high in the air. Jokahn reeled back and peered through squinted eyes, not wanting to watch but unable to look away.

As the flaming blade came cascading downward over her, Ticahrla pivoted out the way on one knee and grappled Terris' wrist. Bracing behind his elbow, she sent him crashing down face first into the dirt. Terris grunted as he hit the ground, and Ticahrla thrust her knee against the back of his neck, pinning him where he lay.

A breath of amazement escaped Jokahn. *Holy shit, Ticahrla is good!* She made fighting Terris look easy.

Terris spewed dust as he panted, his face pressed into the dirt. He struggled to move, but his body was faceted to the ground beneath her. Ticahrla took her time as she gently pried a sword—the flames now extinguished—from his hand and rested the searing hot metal against the back of Terris' neck. Terris winced.

Her message was clear. She could have easily killed Terris if she wanted to.

Without saying a word, Ticahrla rose to her feet and thrust the smoldering blade into the ground. Terris sat upright, pressing his hand to the back of his neck and glaring up at her.

Tears swelled in Ticahrla's eyes. "Go home to your family, Terris," she said in a firm tone, but her voice quivered. Then she turned her back to him and started walking toward Jokahn.

Using his weapon like a cane, Terris pulled himself to his feet. His breathing was becoming erratic. His anger exploded as he shouted, "I'll die before I'm left to suffer in this rat hole any longer because of you!"

Terris charged again, thrusting his sword at her lower back.

"Ticahrla!" Jokahn cried out.

Ripping her swords from their sheaths, Ticahrla spun around and deflected Terris' attack. In a flash of speed, she sliced her sword across Terris' body. Jokahn didn't have time to realize what had happened when he saw Terris' decapitated head tumbling into the crowd. Terris' body collapsed, crumpling to the ground.

Jokahn's mouth gaped open. The locals began to disperse, running from the lifeless head.

Cleaning her blade, quiet and distraught, Ticahrla took long and heavy breaths. She sheathed her weapons, never looking at Terris' body, and stormed past Jokahn.

"To the ship," she said in a hard tone.

Jokahn couldn't take his eyes of the headless body, watching the blood pool around it, turning the dry dirt into a thick, umber mud. It all happened so fast. He barely knew what had transpired before it was over.

"*Move!*" she shouted from behind him.

Jokahn leapt at the sound of her voice and followed Ticahrla through the rabble of locals scurrying about.

He should have been glad Ticahrla was safe. She won the fight; she survived, but something stirred inside him. He glanced over his shoulder to get one last glimpse of Terris' body laying motionless in the dirt. It was sickening.

Ticahrla and her crew piled into the small boat and Drahig rowed them back to the *Nahktaio*.

"Unfurl those sails, boy," Ticahrla ordered. "Drahig, secure the rowboat and raise anchor. We're getting out of this shit hole."

Drahig gently laid Bakta's body on the deck and began hoisting the rowboat.

Jokahn was not as keen to take orders from Ticahrla at the moment. "But I—" he tried to dispute, but Ticahrla was even faster to interject.

Turning, she stared him down with fury in her eyes and growled at him through clenched teeth. "Boy, if you don't release those sails right now, I will throw you overboard and do it myself."

Jokahn grumbled, but begrudgingly made his way to the upper deck.

From behind him, Jokahn heard Ticahrla speaking quietly to Drahig. "Make sure the boy sets those sails correctly."

She didn't think he was capable of anything, did she? "I can set the sails myself," he called out.

Jokahn stomped up the stairs with a frown, but his march slowed as a saddening feeling filled his heart. He glanced over his shoulder at her. Ticahrla's eyes were still bearing down on him angrily. She looked monstrous. Tears began to fill his eyes. What happened to the glorious smile he cared for? *Who is this girl, really?* Maybe he had made a mistake choosing to come with Ticahrla.

He turned and continued upstairs.

14

Lurking Beneath

Ticahrla carefully watched Jokahn stomp up the stairs. Content to see the boy begin his duties, she nodded and walked to the side of the ship. She rested her palms against the railing, letting the weight of her upper body fall on her shoulders as her head slumped forward.

You pathetic weakling, she cursed herself. *How could you be so careless?* She had nearly lost everything. If the boy had been killed, she would have squandered her only chance of becoming an Arcane Bearer.

Her arms were trembling and her breathing was erratic. She had to compose herself; she couldn't let anyone see her this way.

How did Miode gather such a loyal following? Once she realized she was outnumbered, she should have come up with a better strategy. But when Miode spoke about her father, the rage took over.

Ticahrla grimaced. *That's no excuse.* She should have controlled her anger.

She didn't want anyone to die, well, except Miode. That fat traitor deserved to suffer a slow and painful death, but Terris and the people of Modalphia had done nothing to deserve her wrath. Even Bakta was on the brink of death because of her.

Ticahrla was no stranger to violence. War and death were the norm for any royal family, and she had grown accustomed to it at a young age. Still, she never sought to take someone's life who didn't deserve it.

She was a righteous person. No, she was *the most* righteous person. She was the princess of Athus, and if she was ever going to be worthy of sitting on that throne, she was going to have to do better than she had done in Modalphia. Much better.

Ticahrla's mind turned to the boy. Could she go through with it—killing the boy—when the time came? For her kingdom, for her people, for *herself*, she had to become an Arcane Bearer. But the weight on her heart after all the bloodshed that day made her question herself.

Disappointed and disgruntled, Ticahrla wiped the blood from her face and stared out at the water, helpless to subdue her downward spiral of thoughts. On repeat, her mind replayed every detail of her shortcomings and failures. Like an endless loop, the terrible memories ran through her head, judging her—punishing her.

Ticahrla reached into her leather breastplate and pulled out the necklace she had taken back from Miode. She stared at the large crystal attached to the end of the leather band, its sharp edges still speckled with blood. *Father's compass...* At last, she had gotten it back. She let out a comforted breath and tied the lace around her neck.

"Boat is secure, and anchor raised," reported Drahig.

Drahig's voice pulled Ticahrla from the deep, dark recesses of her mind, back into the present. "Thank you, Drahig."

The ship jolted forward as the wind filled its sails. She glanced up at the boy hanging from the rafters as he finished tying off the sail.

At least the boy isn't completely useless. "Help me carry Bakta downstairs," she said to Drahig. Ticahrla was walking toward Bakta when something strange caught her eye: water droplets scattered across the deck, forming a trail.

She turned, following the trail of water to the ship's railing. Stopping abruptly, her eyes locked onto three newly formed scratch marks carved into the wood. She leaned over the edge of the ship and peered down into the sea, waiting, watching the waves pass by.

Nothing... Just the steady pulse of the ocean breaking upon the bow of the ship. She glared down in discontent when a realization struck her. Ticahrla turned around and scanned the deck; her attention again drawn to the trail of water that wound to and fro about the ship.

Drahig had hoisted Bakta over his shoulder and was adjusting him as Ticahrla slapped a palm against his chest. "Hang on."

Drahig paused.

A terrible feeling began to stir in Ticahrla's mind. She followed the speckled dots around the deck, wondering what could have caused it.

The trail stopped at the shadow's edge, leading down the dark stairwell below deck. She gave a low grunt.

Ticahrla had traversed those stairs countless times without a care, but as she stared down into the abyss, the darkness was suddenly unnerving. She listened intently. A sound—*any sound*—would have been welcome. She could have come to some conclusion based on a sound, but the absolute silence that greeted her was unsettling.

Ticahrla's eyes shifted back and forth as her concern grew. From the corner of her eye, she glimpsed some small coils of rope hanging along the wall. She snatched up three of them and took one in her good hand.

Am I crazy? She lobbed a coil of rope down a side of the dark stairway. The coil tumbled down each step. *Thump, Thump, Thump,* and eventually came to a stop at the bottom, *Thu-dump.*

Ticahrla let out a small sigh of relief. She was content with that, but remained unnerved, so she tossed another coil down the center of the stairwell. *Thump, Thump, Thump, Thu-dump.*

Feeling a little surer of herself, she threw the last coil down the other side of the stairs.

. . .

No thump. Just silence.

"What are you doing?" Drahig asked, stopping by her side.

Ticahrla lurched back with a gasp.

"What's wrong?" Drahig sounded surprised.

"I—I don't know." Ticahrla tried to steady her nerves. "We might have a stowaway."

"What?" asked Drahig, gently resting Bakta on the deck again.

Ticahrla explained what she had found.

"Maybe it's a local from Modalphia," suggested Drahig.

That thought had crossed her mind, but something didn't feel right.

Ticahrla cupped her hands over her mouth and called out. "Whoever's down there, come on up and we'll take you back to shore." Then she remembered a person from Modalphia might not speak the common tongue. "Leh naf tru aytis?"

She waited, but no one replied. Ticahrla exhaled, growing tired of the unease.

"All right, well, I've had enough of this," she said, drawing her sword and extending a foot over the first step.

A rustle and a clash of wood rang out from the cluster of barrels across the deck. Ticahrla stopped, her foot suspended in the air. She heard feet shuffling as they scurried back behind the barrels.

She and Drahig exchanged glances. "Boy?" Ticahrla called out.

"Yeah, what do you want?" Jokahn replied, leaning his body out over the crow's nest, high above the deck. The boy looked down at her with a confused expression. "What's wrong?"

Ticahrla turned back to the dark stairwell. Her eyes narrowed and her face hardened into a glare. She contemplated what might be lurking below in the bowls of her ship. Her mind raced, eliminating the unlikely options until only a few dreadful outcomes were left. Despite a handful of possibilities that remained, she couldn't help but fixate on one horrifying word: *aiko.*

With her sword in hand, she took two large steps back and lowered herself into a fighting stance. "Drahig, get rid of those barrels."

Drahig dashed across the deck. With a forceful heave of his shoulder, he punted the barrels up and over the railing. A shrill cry echoed through the air, resonating from the barrels and the stairwell simultaneously.

The sound of desperate clawing and clamoring raced up the stairs. She focused and braced herself, steadying her breathing and holding her sword firmly in front of her.

Leaping from the shadows, its arms outstretched and claws bared, the aiko lunged at her. She thrust her sword forward with both hands, jolting the aiko to a stop as her steel pierced through the creature's chest and wedged into the ship's wall behind it.

Splashes were heard as the barrels Drahig had sent flying crashed down upon the waves. Ticahrla glanced out the corner of her eye and noticed two aiko faces floating amongst the barrels as the *Nahktaio* pulled away on a full sail of wind.

Ticahrla glared victoriously at the aiko she held skewered to the wall. Its arms had fallen loose, and its head slumped forward over her blade. The creature's chest convulsed as it wheezed and grunted.

This was her first aiko kill. She had never seen one this close before. She took a moment to examine its smooth, rubbery skin as it glistened in the sunlight. A thick, black goo oozed from the wound in its chest.

With a shriek, the aiko bust back to life. Ticahrla flinched back in surprise but managed to hold the creature pinned to the wall. Its talons reached out, desperately clawing at the air in front of her.

The aiko's aggression slowed, appearing confused as it looked down at the blade in its chest. Slowly, its eyes turned up angrily at her.

How is it still alive? Ticahrla's face grew concerned. She glanced at her sword to affirm she had hit her target, then came back to meet the creature's gaze.

The aiko wrapped its claws around her blade and pushed. To her amazement, the weapon slowly began to inch out of its chest. She leaned forward, expecting her sword to pierce deeper, but it didn't budge. Ticahrla frowned, confused. Again, she pressed all her weight against her weapon, but the aiko continued to edge the blade free from its body. Even with a sword through its chest, the aiko's strength was outmatching her own.

Ticahrla's face filled with dread. "Oh shit…"

Prying blade free, the creature batted the tip away, and charged. Shrieking furiously, it slashed a goo-covered claw at her. She stepped back, narrowly avoiding its razor-sharp talons.

The aiko stumbled weakly onto all fours but continued swinging its arms frantically through the air as it crept closer. Taking another step back, Ticahrla raised her sword. She struck the aiko at the base of its neck, but the steel barely penetrated its tough, leathery skin.

The creature appeared dazed. Quickly, before it could recover, Ticahrla began hacking away at the same spot with her sword. She cried out, screaming as her muscles grew tired, but she hammered on relentlessly. Slowly, a wound began to open around the base of the aiko's collar.

Exhausted, she hoisted her sword as high as she could and brought it crashing down. The blade crunched into the aiko's skull, becoming embedded across its left eye. Its head shook and its body collapsed, yanking her sword—still lodged in the creature's face—free from her hands.

Finally, all was still.

Breathing heavily, Ticahrla took a few steps back and slumped against the ship's railing. She looked down at her sore and trembling hands.

"What was that?!" she exclaimed, staring wide eyed at the lifeless creature. "I've never seen something take a beating like that and keep going."

Ticahrla looked over the railing. In the ocean, two aiko drifted in the distance. Ticahrla and Drahig laughed.

"Look at them out there," she chortled. "That's right! I'm still here! Come on, I thought aiko were supposed to be tough!"

A low hiss grew steadily from behind her.

Ticahrla's heart stopped, and dread overtook her face as she turned. The aiko was sitting on its knees, claws firmly grasping the hilt of the blade still wedged in its skull. It hissed as it wrenched the sword back and forth, finally prying it free. Its head lurched back, and a thick, black goo spouted from its eye. As the aiko feebly pulled itself back to its feet, it chucked her sword back across the deck.

"Drahig…" she said, too stunned to move. The aiko started to advance. "Drahig!"

Drahig threw himself between her and the aiko and thrust a palm down grasping at the aiko. It quickly scampered underneath and around him, circumventing Drahig all together and drove toward Ticahrla.

"Drahig, you good-for-nothing!" she scolded him, fear in her voice.

Ticahrla struggled to pull her remaining sword from its sheath, but her hands were trembling and weak, and her weapon bobbled to the floor. *You incompetent!* she thought, enraged. *This is how you die. Can't even hold your own sword!*

She stumbled and fell onto her back. The aiko clawed toward her as Ticahrla shuffled backward across the deck. With a single bound, the creature leapt forward. She clamped her eyes shut and turned her head away.

She heard a grunt and a slam, followed by desperate scratching against the wood. Ticahrla eased one eye open to see Drahig, feet planted on the floor, fists clenched around the aiko's ankle. As Drahig clung to the creature's limb, the aiko remained fixated on her.

"Ticahrla, what's going on?" Jokahn asked as he climbed down the center mast to the deck.

Everyone froze, the silence heavy in the air. Ticahrla's heart plummeted like a rock against her stomach. The boy stood there, wide-eyed and fear stricken, like a fool. It was suddenly all so clear to her; she could foresee the upcoming events unfolding in her mind. The boy would do what he did best, he would turn and run, and the aiko was sure to follow.

Jokahn's gaze was fixed on the creature sprawled out on the deck, one leg still in Drahig's grasp. Sure enough, the boy turned tail and sprinted for the stairwell.

"No! Damn it, boy!" Ticahrla cursed him as Jokahn ran like a coward below deck. The aiko wailed out a shrill cry and quickly scrambled after him.

Drahig, still clinging to its leg, pivoted in place with the creature. The aiko whipped around and sliced its claws across Drahig's forearm. He winced and groaned, releasing his grip. The aiko dropped to the floor with a thud and speedily clawed its way across the deck after Jokahn.

Time slowed as Ticahrla watched the aiko gaining on Jokahn. More terrifying than staring down an aiko was the thought of losing her one chance to become an Arcane Bearer. If Jokahn died now, then all the time she had spent searching, all the struggles she had endured, everything she had accomplished would have been for nothing. She glared furiously as all her efforts were being stolen from her, and all because of this stupid, cowardly boy!

"*No!*" Ticahrla cried as she rose to her feet. In her rage, her entire body erupted in flames. The aiko stopped and looked back at her. Her voice reverberated through her chest and echoed in a demonic tone. "That boy is *mine!*"

The aiko gazed up at her, petrified, and Jokahn continued obliviously below deck.

Ticahrla had never felt an explosion of anger like this before. Her body was heavy, and her clothing began to singe and darken from the flames engulfing her, but her eyes remained locked on the aiko. She stomped forward a heavy foot. Her body was surprisingly rigid and hard to move, but her thoughts were filled only with protecting what was hers—what was owed to her.

The aiko stared cautiously with its one good eye as Ticahrla struggled forward. The amount of energy she was expending was quickly depleting her. Her eyelids began to flutter and grow heavy as her consciousness waned, but she forced another foot forward. Her armored boot thumped forward with a thud, and the aiko finally gave in.

Never taking its eye off her, the aiko quickly wriggled its way between the ship's railing and fled back into the sea.

With her chance to become an Arcane Bearer safe once more, Ticahrla's body gave in to exhaustion and her eyes eased shut. Other than a few residual embers, the flames engulfing her quickly died out.

Unable to bear her own weight, Ticahrla keeled forward. Drahig's cool skin cradled her in his arms as she drifted unconscious.

15

Unveiling Darkness

Night fell over the open ocean as the *Nahktaio* sailed farther from Modalphia. A chilled breeze circled Jokahn as he sat on the deck, gazing up at the starlit sky.

He reached up to examine the swollen bump on the bridge of his nose. It was bigger than before, but the pain had dulled. He sighed, letting his arms fall limp beside him and leaning his head back against the ship's railing.

Ticahrla emerged from below deck. With her head down, she walked carefully up each step, bracing the wall with one hand. Her voice was coarse. "What happened?" she asked.

"You passed out after chasing the aiko off. Drahig carried you downstairs."

Ticahrla closed her eyes and grimaced, pressing her fingers to her forehead. "How long was I asleep?"

"A few hours."

Ticahrla groaned, shaking her head. "I shouldn't have slept so long. Bakta's bandages need to be changed."

"How is he doing?"

Ticahrla glared at him. Her body stiffened, her shoulders reared back, and her hands tightened into fists. But after a moment the bitterness in her face faded, and her arms fell loose. She sighed. "Not well."

"I'm sorry," he said softly.

That seemed to surprise Ticahrla. Her shoulders dropped, and her eyes turned heartfelt. She bit down on her lower lip, glancing around the ship—as if to ensure no one else was watching—and walked towards him.

Sitting down beside him, she leaned her shoulder against his. As the warmth of her skin pressed against his, Jokahn's heart fluttered briefly before calming itself.

Ticahrla closed her eyes and tucked her hands under her arms to shield herself from the cold. She was so calm, so beautiful. He couldn't help but admire her. But there was something unsettling, too. Beneath that beautiful façade was Ticahrla's darker side. Jokahn frowned, wondering which one was the real Ticahrla.

"What?" she asked firmly, not opening her eyes.

"Huh?" He jumped, startled.

"I can feel you staring at me. What is it?"

A flush of heat ran up through his cheeks. He didn't realize he was staring. "I—uh…" A glimmer of light silenced him.

A large jewel with a worn leather band was tied around Ticahrla's neck. As her chest gently rose and fell with each breath, the crystal swayed, creating an ebb and flow of color within it.

He already deduced where the necklace came from, but he was compelled to ask anyway. "What's that?"

Ticahrla's eyes creaked open as she raised an eyebrow at him. Sitting forward, she removed the jewel from its tattered strap and placed it on the floor in front of her. The crystal was perfectly balanced. Resting on the sharp edge of its side, it sat fixed in space, unmoving, even as the deck beneath rocked back and forth with the waves.

Her voice was soft. "It belonged to my father. It's his prized compass. This will lead me to the Origin."

The tail end of the compass pointed North by Northeast. With a gentle flick of her finger, Ticahrla spun the crystal. It circled in place and gradually slowed to a stop, its tail again pointing directly North by Northeast.

"Looks like I was right," Ticahrla grinned, looking down at the gem. "We're right on course. Only about three weeks before I reach the Origin."

"Your father's compass? How did it end up in Modalphia?"

"When I was young, Miode served as a general under my father. They were close friends once." Ticahrla picked up the gem up, twisting it back and forth in the moonlight, and smiled. "Father and Miode would always quarrel and laugh about politics. I still remember the times when Terris and I would…" her sentence slowed to a stop, and she pressed her lips together as the joy vanished from her face. Her eyes began to water.

Jokahn held his breath and shifted his eyes to the floor. He had never seen her cry before.

"Anyway," she continued, clearing her throat. "Miode apparently thought that, since there was no male heir to Athus' throne, if my father died then he would be the rightful king. So Miode had my father assassinated. I suppose he took Father's compass as a trophy before my mother banished him to that disease ridden island."

Jokahn eased his eyes up toward her as a tear ran down her cheek, yet she didn't try to hide it. She sat there, just as strong and confident as ever. It was the first time he had seen someone cry and not felt embarrassed for having witnessed it. Instead, the sadness in her eyes made him want to reach out and comfort her, and bring back that radiant smile of hers.

"What an asshole," he said.

Ticahrla chuckled. She turned and gave him an appreciative grin. Jokahn smiled back at her, happy he could make her laugh. She reattached her father's jewel to the leather band and tied the necklace around her neck.

"Yes, well, that's one way of putting it," she said, tucking the compass into her chest piece. Then she paused a moment and tilted her head at Jokahn, giving him a curious stare. "You know, you do have nice eyes."

Jokahn leaned back, an embarrassed grin coiling up on his face. His heartbeat rose. Was this another trick? Some game she was playing with him? "Uh—really?"

Ticahrla nodded. "I see the sincerity in them. Makes it hard to know what the right thing to do is sometimes."

Jokahn turned his head to the side. "What do you mean?"

"Never mind." She shook her head and smiled. "Learn to take a compliment."

Dammit! Ticahrla had given him a genuine compliment, and he still managed to screw it up. "Uh—thanks," he said, trying to recover. "I like your eyes, too." It was true. He had never seen anyone with eyes as green as hers. Eyes that were so strong and commanding of respect, and yet, somehow, also warm and welcoming.

Ticahrla shrugged. "If only you weren't such a coward. Maybe you wouldn't be such a pain in my ass then." She chuckled.

Jokahn's eyes blinked, and his head pulled back. *Wait. What?* "Such a what?"

"A coward," she reiterated astutely.

His brow pressed down over his eyes. How could she say that so calmly? It was like she wasn't even trying to be mean; she was just being honest. That's what hurt the most.

His voice came out quiet but firm. "I'm *not* a coward."

Ticahrla cringed, as if a bitter taste had soiled her mouth. "Denial is not appealing to anyone."

Denial? Coward?! Jokahn's eyes grew wide as his blood pressure rose. *Who does this bitch think she is?!* "At least I'm not some psycho who murdered my friend!"

Ticahrla's back stiffened as she glared at him. "I didn't *murder* Terris," she snapped. "I gave him the quick death he desired."

"A quick death? Is that supposed to be a good thing in that messed up head of yours?"

"It *is* a good thing. It's a warrior's death. When I die, it isn't going to be of old age in a bed somewhere. It will be at the hands of the opponent who has bested me."

"Like how Miode died, you mean?"

"*No.* Miode got what he deserved, a slow and agonizing end to his pathetic life."

"What's the difference?"

"I don't need to explain myself to someone like you."

Jokahn scoffed. "That's a convenient excuse."

Ticahrla snorted. "All right, listen carefully, you ignorant oaf. If your opponent kills you quickly, it means you led a good life and you were deserving of a peaceful death. If you are killed slowly, it means you were rotten and should be left to suffer at the end of your life. Got it?"

What stupid nonsense. "Sounds like you're trying to justify a guilty conscious."

Ticahrla's eyes filled with rage, and her jaw clenched as she stared him down. Jokahn quickly realized the dreadful mistake he had made.

Ticahrla's breathing steadily rose as anger filled her expression. With teeth bared, her hand lurched forward and struck him hard in the chest. Before he knew it, he was on his back with Ticahrla straddled over his belly, one fist reared back in the air as her other arm pinned his shoulder to the deck.

Jokahn winced and threw his arms up to shield himself. He peered up at her as Ticahrla's hair hung down over him. Through her bangs he could see her eyes baring down on him. She held him there, watching him—studying him. Gradually, her anger soothed. The tension in her grip relaxed, and a curious expression stretched across her face.

"Why are you cowering?" she asked in a stern but genuine voice. "Defend yourself." She shook his collar.

Defend myself? I am defending myself! "I—gah. Wha—what do you think I'm doing?"

Ticahrla's reared fist fell loose at her side. The anger in her eyes dispersed, and Jokahn carefully lowered his hands.

With an open palm, she slapped him across the face. He gasped and flailed his arms about. It didn't hurt. It startled him more than anything. "Agh! Stop it!"

"Make me," she said, smacking his other cheek.

That one stung a little. "Ow! Make you? What?"

"*Yes.* Stop acting like a cowardly child and fight me!"

He wasn't about to fight her. She was obviously much stronger and faster than him, even though he wasn't about to admit that. "I'm not going to fight a girl."

"But you'll get beaten up by one?" she asked, slapping him once more.

"I don't want to fight you, Ticahrla. Can you just get off me?"

Ticahrla paused. Her voice was calm with realization. "You don't know how, do you?"

Jokahn didn't respond. He wanted to lie. He wanted to tell her she was wrong, but it was obvious she already knew the truth. His hands slowly came to rest on his chest as he turned his eyes away. He didn't want to look at her as she saw the reality of how weak he was.

Great. Now she's going to hate me even more. The sadness filled his chest like a weight. She was so close to him, yet a great divide stretched between them. The tears began to swell in his eyes.

All he wanted was not to mess this up. Whatever it was he had with Ticahrla, he wanted—for once in his life—not to push everyone away. Yet here he was again, helpless to stop the inevitable fact that he was driving her away. It was debilitating to lie there on the deck and feel completely alone.

A hand grabbed his wrist. He gasped, startled to feel another's touch. Ticahrla's empathetic eyes stared down at him.

"Here," she said, gently taking Jokahn's arm and placing his palm around the back of her bicep. The tips of his fingers tingled as they brushed against her soft skin. "One hand like this. Your other braces my body." She hugged his other hand around the side of her ribs.

Jokahn's heart was beating against his chest. He looked down at the way his hand clutched her body and swallowed hard.

"Your leg needs to hook around mine, like this." Ticahrla laced her leg around his, all the while staring down at him. He looked up at her with a grateful longing. "Now," she said, lightly licking her lips, "raise your hips."

"Huh?"

"Just trust me. Raise your hips."

Jokahn struggled to decipher what she meant. He shimmied and adjusted beneath her before he could get enough leverage to press his hips upward. Arching his lower half into the air, Ticahrla rolled up and over the side of him, their bodies intertwined.

They tumbled together, and when they came to rest, Jokahn was on top of her. His head came to a jolting stop inches away from her face. He was so close to her he could see the pores of her skin and feel his hot breath bouncing back at him, mixing with the jasmine scents of her hair. Jokahn was breathing hard, but Ticahrla was calm. She lay on her back with her legs tied behind his waist, a subtle part to her mouth as her eyes looked back and forth into his.

"There," she said softly. "Easy, right?"

An odd feeling stirred in his stomach. A part of him was comforted by her, but there was something else that frightened him. He wasn't sure what it was, but he began to feel nervous, almost nauseous. When Ticahrla's eyes turned worried—probably reflecting his own expression—he couldn't control his urge to flee any longer.

Jokahn pushed himself up, turned, and started to hurry away.

"Where are you going?" she called out behind him.

His pace slowed to a stop. He had no idea where his feet were carrying him away to, or why his heart was aching so much.

"You can't keep running, boy."

Jokahn clamped his eyes shut at the pain those words caused him.

"You have to learn to stand up and fight."

His voice was faint, barely above a whisper. "How—" He stopped. *How do you see through me so easily?* How was it so simple for her to reach in and tug at his innermost core? Jokahn turned around. Ticahrla was lying on the deck, propped up on her elbows, with a concerned expression. "How am I supposed to do that?"

Ticahrla grinned a warm, heavenly smile. "I'll show you."

16

Memories

The sun rose on Sihera's third day at sea. As she made her way up to the helm, Laval was already awake and speaking with the captain. A warm gust of wind wafted in from behind her, carrying with it a pungent odor. She gagged and covered her mouth.

Laval choked and coughed. "What's that horrid smell?" he cried.

The captain pointed to a small island behind them. "Modalphia. It's a tiny, disease-ridden place where Athus and other nations send their unwanted. Don't worry, the smell will pass. We're on track to catch up with the princess soon."

It was hard to believe at first, but she was actually enjoying her time on a warship. Sure, the same terrible vision continued to haunt her nights, but her days were pleasantly optimistic. She was on her way to rescue her Dreamer boy and Laval had allowed her to practice her magic again.

"Ready to begin your morning practice?" asked Laval. Sihera beamed a wide smile at him.

With a deep breath, she closed her eyes and placed her hands together out in front of her. The sounds of the crew clamoring around her faded, and the heat in her chest began to churn. Yes, that familiar warmth was growing inside her. Feeling the heat running through her body again was such a relief—like stretching a muscle that had sat stiff and unmoving for too long—and she let out a soft, pleasurable groan.

The energy, hot like flowing magma, poured down her arms and crawled up into her throat and skull. As her eyes eased open and the flames spilled out, her vision turned into vibrant hues of orange and red.

Electricity leapt between her hands. Her fingers curled inward, forming a claw-like grip. With a light tug, she snapped the current in two and ignited a small flame. Her arms flexed as she caught it, straining to hold the flames suspended in the air, fueling the fire by continuing to feed her energy into it.

"Good," Laval said encouragingly. "But how long can you sustain it?"

She gave him a sly grin. She would do one better. She wouldn't just sustain the flame, she would grow it.

Sihera enjoyed it when Laval pushed the limits of her magic. She had always been a gifted mage, and she relished that look of pride in his eyes.

She focused and poured her energy into the flames. Steadily, the fireball grew to the size of a coconut.

The pop of a small explosion shoved Sihera to the side. She gasped, barely managing to hold onto the fireball, and shot a fierce glare at Laval. He stood there, his hand still shaped like a claw, and a conniving grin across his face.

He did that on purpose! She might have blown a hole in the ship if she had lost her focus. *He wants to play games, huh?*

Sihera grinned a wicked smile and reared back her arms. With a grunt, she heaved the fireball at him. Laval reached out and caught it from the air. He staggered backward a step as he pulled it toward his center, then he gave her a wide smile.

"Come on, Sihera. You can do better than that." Laval hurled her fireball back at her.

She yelped as the flames came hurtling toward her. Out of reflex, she focused her energy, bringing her forearms together in front of her like a shield, and created a small blast as a protective barrier. The heat from the fireball hit and then quickly dispersed as it was deflected away.

A crowd of sailors had started to gather around them. Laval stood tall and confident, looking smug in front of her. Sihera was breathing heavily.

"Have at me, Sihera," Laval cheered. "Show them what you can do."

Sihera let out a sharp breath as she glared at him through her brow. Then she smiled.

She planted her feet and clasped her palms together. With bared teeth, she pulled lightning wide across her chest. She held it there for as long as she could, her arms straining. When the current finally snapped, the explosion sent a shockwave racing across the deck.

Laval held up an arm and deflected the blast. The gust of wind filled the sails and lurched the ship forward. The sailors shouted as they struggled to keep their footing. Then the wind died down, and everything was quiet.

Sihera panted as she scanned the sailors' faces. The men were startled, almost frightened, as they exchanged glances. She may have been a little overzealous, and a sickening tension twisted in her belly. She huddled her head between her shoulders and tried to swallow, but her throat was surprisingly dry.

The sailors shouted as they ran toward her. Startled, she shook and hugged her arms close to her body. They circled around her, shaking her by the shoulders and patting her hard on the back. Her worry eased a bit as they started cheering, wide smiles across their faces.

"This one's got some fire in her!" shouted one man.

As they shook her from side to side, hailing her praise, Laval was staring proudly at her. She cracked a half smile at him.

Slowly the crowd dispersed, and Laval stood beside her. "You are an impressive mage," Laval said as he placed a hand on her shoulder. "You will make an amazing Arcane Bearer one day."

Her smile faded. "I'm not going to become an Arcane Bearer, remember?"

Laval's prideful expression faltered, but only for a moment. "Of course… My mistake. Old habits, that's all."

Was it? She hated not being able to tell if Laval was lying to her; she hated not knowing if she could trust him anymore.

It wasn't always like that. For the longest time, she never

questioned him. After all, Laval rescued her when she was only eight years old. Back then, she and her family were nothing more than simple farmers in a small village.

Sihera was the oldest of three girls. Her parents were hard working. Her father spent most of his time in the field, and her mother tended to the sheep in between caring for her and her sisters.

It was strange thinking about her old family again. She barely remembered their faces anymore. It was so long ago; it almost felt like a different life. Although, she still remembered the first time she had met Laval.

* * *

It was a particularly warm summer back then. Sihera and her two sisters, Deania and Lysahndra, were playing outside when a beautiful horse-drawn carriage rode down the dirt road toward her family's farm. Men and women in long, elegant robes walked alongside. Coming from a village of clay and straw houses, Sihera had never seen anything like it.

The carriage stopped, and a servant opened the door. A man—Laval—stepped out. He was tall and square-jawed, wearing his Archmagi robes. He looked like royalty. Back then, Sihera had never heard of the Archmagi and knew nothing of magic or mages.

It was surprising to see one of the neighbor boys, still covered in dirt just as she was, step out of the carriage behind Laval. Laval bent down and whispered something in his ear. The boy nodded and pointed at Sihera. Laval's head turned and their eyes met for the first time.

Laval didn't speak to her that day, but soon after, her parents invited him to dinner. Her mother made sure everyone was washed and dressed in their best attire. At the dinner table, Laval spoke enthusiastically about the Archmagi Refuge and the great things they were doing. He even offered to let Sihera and her sisters attend a school at the refuge, free of charge.

Education for young kids was expensive and a privilege. Deania and Lysahndra bounced with excitement, but her father ground his teeth and glared.

"What do you think, Sihera?" her mother asked in her usual, gentle tone. "Would you like to go to school?"

Everyone turned to look at her. She didn't know what to think, so she kept quiet and looked at the floor. The weight of everyone's eyes made her nervous.

"We'll take some time to consider it," her father interjected.

Her parents never had the chance to decide. A few days later, as Sihera and her sisters slept in their room, a loud crash woke them with a jolt. Deania and Lysahndra clung to her as their mother let out a shrill cry.

A man dressed in black, his face covered and a torch in one hand, pushed open the cloth door to her room. Sihera's lungs tightened, holding her breath, as her sisters shrieked. She knew what this man was. The neighboring kids had told her stories of men in black shrouds that snatched children from their families in the night. They were slave traders.

More men with torches entered, grabbing her and her sisters by their arms and dragging them out of the room. Her siblings kicked and screamed, but Sihera was quiet. She stared in wide-eyed disbelief at her mother and father lying in a pool of blood.

Outside, the men's torches illuminated a steel cage with wheels, towed behind a lone donkey. The men pushed and shoved Sihera and her sisters inside and locked the cage shut.

Sihera's family was not wealthy, but she had never known hunger. During the week that followed inside that cage, she and her sisters learned what it truly meant to be frightened and starving.

Being the oldest, Sihera felt a certain sense of responsibility for her sisters but had no idea how to help them. The men escorting them paid no attention to her pleas or her sister's cries.

One day, the cart stopped, and the cage opened. She and her sisters huddled together. The men grabbed Lysahndra first, then Deania, and pried them from her arms. Tears streamed down her sisters' faces as they wailed uncontrollably. She wanted to call out to them, tell them everything was going to be all right, but she knew that was a lie. Sihera sat there as those men took her sisters away, powerless to stop them.

It rained nonstop for the next several days. She was cold and wet as she sat alone in the cage, her hair and clothes soaked through. Sihera rocked back and forth as her steel prison rattled along relentlessly through the night.

The cage stopped. Sihera's head rose, and she turned to look behind her.

In the middle of the muddy road, standing tall and defiant in front of the slave traders and their donkey, was a lone man wearing a long robe. It was hard to make anything out through the pouring rain, but what appeared to be fire ignited in the man's hand.

The slave traders took a step back and looked at each other in confusion. Before any of them could react, a fireball was hurtling toward one of them. It hit with an explosion that sent the man flying backward, rocking Sihera's cage. A bolt of lightning streaked through the air with a loud crack, dropping another two men and leaving a ringing sound in her ears.

She panted and clasped her hands over her ears.

The one remaining slave trader was screaming as he sprinted in the opposite direction. The robed man stopped beside the cage. She recognized Laval from his square jaw.

Laval didn't look at her. He glared and gritted his teeth at the fleeing man as a ball of fire swelled between his palms. Laval lobbed the fireball through the air. It hit the slave trader square in the back, bursting into a shower of embers, and the man dropped.

Sihera looked cautiously at Laval. His face was hard at first, but as he turned toward her, his eyes softened.

"You're all right, little one," he said, holding his hands up.

Laval pried the keys from a man's belt and opened the cage door. He held out his hand to her. Her eyes blinked as they strained to see through the pouring rain.

"Come now, my child."

Sihera sat quivering at the back of the cage. Her voice was weaker than she expected. "Where are my sisters?"

Laval searched behind him, then turned to Sihera again. "I will find them, but right now I need to get you somewhere safe."

Sihera hesitated, pressing herself further back against the metal frame.

Laval frowned. "I promise, I will find your sisters."

Sihera pursed her lips, but she placed her hand in his and stepped out of the cage.

Laval brought her back to the Archmagi Refuge and sent his men to search for Deania and Lysahndra. A week later, they brought back the terrible news. Lysahndra had died from heat exhaustion working the field, and Deania was killed trying to escape. Laval was devastated, even more apparently so than Sihera was. She didn't even cry. She sat and stared at the floor, a hollow ache resting against her chest.

That same day, Laval sent mages to eliminate what remained of the slave traders and seize the assets of whoever had bought Sihera's sisters. A public hanging was quickly organized.

Sihera learned that with Laval, justice was swift. He avenged the death of her family, but it did little to relieve the constant strain on her heart. The only real solace she found was in practicing magic.

At the time, Sihera wanted more than anything to become an Arcane Bearer; she wanted to be the most powerful mage in the world. If she could become strong like Laval, then she could protect the people she cared about from ever being harmed again. Of course, her ambitions changed slightly after learning she could only become an Arcane Bearer by sacrificing her Dreamer boy.

"Sihera?" Laval's voice echoed through her mind.

* * *

Her eyes blinked as she took a deep breath. Glancing around the warship, she realized she had fallen behind as Laval walked ahead of her.

Sihera's brow pressed firmly down over her eyes. It was strange reliving that memory. She had never noticed the coincidence between Laval's arrival and the murder of her family. She was so young when it happened. Her eyes looked up through her brow at the square-jawed man, and she began to question, did Laval have something to do with the death of her family?

"Is everything all right?" Laval asked.

She wasn't sure. Laval stared back at her with those same caring eyes. The joy she had shared with him was suddenly confusing. It was becoming harder to tell if Laval was a friend or foe, and it frightened her to realize he was the only family she had left.

17

Ergman Island

"*Wrong*, do it again," Ticahrla said in a disgruntled tone, clamping her eyes shut and massaging her forehead.

Jokahn was breathing heavily, his muscles sore from two days of training, but he still struggled to learn the most basic self-defense techniques. Ticahrla assured him they would reach the Origin in just three more weeks, but he wasn't sure if he'd survive her training that long.

Ticahrla paced around him as she barked orders. "Listen carefully this time. Legs shoulder-width apart. Hips low."

Jokahn exhaled sharply and focused, shifting his feet wider and bobbing up and down.

"Good. Keep your hands up. Your arms are not only your first line of defense, but they also assess the distance to your opponent."

Holding his hands out in front of his eyeline, Jokahn tried to imagine an opponent standing before him.

"Now, move forward."

Jokahn stepped forward.

"Wrong! Wrong! *Wrong!*"

He groaned as his arms fell limp in front of him. "What is it this time?"

"You aren't even trying."

"I did exactly what you told me to do."

"No, you didn't. Look at your footing."

Jokahn glanced down at his feet. They looked all right to him. He was trying to do what she said, but learning to fight was harder than he thought. Everything had to be perfect with Ticahrla, or it wasn't good enough.

"I don't understand. Why am I learning how to fight again?" he asked, staring down, adjusting his feet.

"So you can defend yourself," she said bluntly.

"But I don't want to fight."

Ticahrla frowned, her voice flat, "Yes, I realize that."

"What's the point then?"

She gave him a forceful shove.

"Hey!" he cried.

"What are you going to do when someone pushes you?"

"I—I don't know."

She gestured to him. "Here, try to push me."

"What?"

"Push me!"

Push Ticahrla? The thought was enticing. A smug grin stretched across his face. "Fine," he said, extended his hand. Before he could reach her, Ticahrla snatched up two of his fingers and twisted. Pain shot through his arm up into his spine. "AH!" He cried as his legs gave out and he crumpled to the floor, his fingers still imprisoned in her grip.

"Ticahrla!" Drahig called as he rushed upstairs onto the deck. She released him, and Jokahn sat there quivering, trying to rub the feeling back into his fingers. "You need to check on Bakta," continued Drahig. "He's not looking well."

* * *

Jokahn and Drahig stood outside the sleeping quarters below deck as Ticahrla pulled up a stool and sat at Bakta's bedside. As she began removing the bandages from his abdomen, she flinched back and held her forearm across her mouth.

A moment later, Jokahn was hit with a sour-tasting waft of air and cupped his hand over his mouth, trying to force back the retch rising in his throat.

"Ugh, great…" Ticahrla groaned. "Bakta needs medicine. We'll have to make a stop."

Drahig frowned, glancing from side to side. "But there isn't another port for three days."

"You're right," she said, turning to give Drahig an empathetic glance. "We have to go to Ergman Island to find some herbs."

* * *

Ergman Island was a small speck of land in the middle of the ocean, filled with tall, dense trees that reached the sandy coastline.

At first, Jokahn was excited to meet more ergmen, but when Ticahrla explained that most ergmen were not like Drahig and wouldn't hesitate to kill a human, he became cautious of the unexpected detour. To make matters worse, Ticahrla decided to go during the dead of night.

Ticahrla led Jokahn and Drahig into the dark forest as Drahig carried Bakta over his shoulder. It was unnervingly quiet. Jokahn heard nothing but his and Ticahrla's own footsteps rustling through the thick brush. Despite Drahig's size, the giant ergman moved silently behind him, as if his body molded to the environment.

A glimmer of moonlight caught Jokahn's eye, reflecting a yellow hue from the shadows. There was something odd; the glint of light seemed to follow him as he walked. Then it blinked.

Jokahn's eyes swelled with fear as he gasped loudly and pressed his back against a tree. Ticahrla whipped around and pressed her hand over his mouth.

She whispered harshly at him. "*Be quiet!* You want to get us killed?"

He clawed at Ticahrla's arm in a panic, mumbling indistinguishable sounds of worry into her palm.

"Ticahrla…" Drahig's voice was low and cautious. "We're not alone."

Ticahrla stepped back and scanned the forest, her hand on her weapon.

A huge mass plummeted down from the treetops, landing on all fours with a loud thud. The ergman spoke in a deep, throaty tone. "You have got some nerve coming here, *humans*."

Drahig placed Bakta on the ground and threw himself between Ticahrla and the ergman, snarling as his upper body rose and fell with deep breaths.

As the ergman rose, Jokahn's head craned back and his jaw fell open. It was huge, easily dwarfing over Drahig.

The giant trudged forward from the shadows and into the moonlight. His wide shoulders swayed as he walked, wearing nothing but some beads and organic jewelry. His scales were weathered and coarse—aged.

Drahig snarled again as the giant ergman strode closer to Ticahrla.

"Down, puppers," said the giant. "If dead is how we wanted you, then dead you would be."

Slowly emerging from the forest, over a dozen ergmen came forward, all of them larger than Drahig. Some climbed down from treetops, others crept forward from the darkness, circling around them.

The range of sizes, shapes, and colors in the ergmen was shocking. Still, Drahig stood out being the only ergman wearing clothes. It was the defining feature that sided him with the humans against the ergmen. The ergmen raised their spears and held them high, ready to strike. Jokahn's body tensed, and his heart raced. His feet wanted to run, but the giant beasts had encircled him.

A young, female ergman, barely taller than Ticahrla, gently pushed her way through the ring of ergmen. Her shoulders were narrow compared to the others, and her face had a gentle appearance. Her skin was shiny and new, like Drahig's.

"Nalia, what are you doing?" warned the giant. But she continued forward, her focus centered on Drahig.

"It's all right, Dargo," she replied. "I just want to see." Drahig stood up tall, appearing more intimidated by this little ergman than any of the others.

As Drahig's muzzle opened to speak, Nalia smiled bright up at him, and Drahig quickly locked his mouth shut again.

"*Ahem.*" Ticahrla jabbed Drahig in the side with her elbow.

Drahig cleared his throat as he looked nervously down at the tiny ergman. He extended his hand toward her. "My name is Drahig. How do you do?"

Ticahrla slumped her shoulders and sighed in disappointment.

Nalia looked at Drahig's open hand and cringed. "It has been a long time since someone tried to shake my hand. My previous owners taught me all about human customs, but it still saddens me to see it come from an ergman." She glared at Ticahrla for a moment, but as she turned back to Drahig, she smiled, giving him a playful jab against his chest. "Come on, I want to introduce you to the rest of my clan."

"No," Dargo said firmly. "He's one of them."

"They are no threat to us," she assured.

"*Nalia!*" Dargo shouted, stomping his foot. Then he began ranting in a language Jokahn didn't understand.

Nalia stormed over to the giant and reached up high to jab a finger at his chest. Dargo's head and shoulders began to slouch as Nalia berated him.

"Wait," Drahig interjected. Nalia turned to look at him. "Please, my friend needs help." Drahig stepped aside, pointing to Bakta as he lay motionless on the ground.

Nalia approached Bakta cautiously. With a gentle hand, she pulled back the old bandages. The stench hit her nostrils, and, with a short gasp, she lurched back in surprise. Her snout crinkled and she cupped a hand over her muzzle. "This wound is rotten."

"He was injured in a fight," Ticahrla replied. "Can you help him?"

Nalia nodded. "I have some herbs that might help. Follow me."

"Thank you." Ticahrla smiled.

"Drahig," Nalia called, waving him over. "Take your wounded human and follow me. Dargo will carry your female." She said, pointing at Ticahrla. Then Nalia walked over to Jokahn and smiled. He leaned back at Nalia's sudden closeness. "And you can come with me."

The way her muzzle pulled back into a grin, exposing her large white teeth, was off-putting at first, but the odd sensation quickly faded as he saw the look in her eyes. They seemed genuine and comforting—kind. He smiled back at her, and Nalia picked him up and slung him onto her back.

Jokahn looked back at Ticahrla as Dargo reluctantly offered her his back.

"I think I'd rather walk," said Ticahrla, looking cautiously at the hulking beast who was obviously repulsed by her presence.

"Are you sure you can keep up?" asked Nalia as she adjusted Jokahn on her back.

Ticahrla glared at her. "I'll manage."

"Fine by me. Do you have a good grip, little boy?"

Jokahn didn't like being called *little*, but compared to an ergman, he assumed any human would seem small. He nodded.

"Let's go," announced Nalia, and the group of ergmen sprinted forward. Jokahn's head whipped back at the sudden jolt of speed through the dense forest.

Nalia and the others were moving so fast, he couldn't imagine how Ticahrla would ever keep up. He glanced back over his shoulder and—never one to be outdone—at the tail end of the pack was Ticahrla. She sprinted through the brush, agile and quick with the rest of the ergmen.

Nalia called back to Jokahn. "We are going up now, so whatever you do, don't let go."

"Up?" he asked.

Without a pause in her stride, Nalia leapt from the ground and soared through the air. He screamed as his feet dangled behind him, clinging around her neck.

Nalia came to a hard stop, gripping to the trunk of a tree, and Jokahn crashed into the back of her.

"How are you doing?" asked Nalia.

He shrieked, "I'm slipping!"

"I've got you," Nalia assured him in a calm voice. She lifted him up, one hand supporting his butt, and allowed him to readjust his grip. "Better?"

"I think so, but I don't like going so fast."

"You are doing fine. Just hold on. We're almost there."

Once again, Nalia lunged forward in a burst of speed, climbing her way easily up the tree. Jokahn could see the shadowy figures of other ergmen scaling the surrounding trees as he glanced around him. It was incredible to watch. He could feel Nalia's muscles grinding beneath her sleek and shimmery skin as she clawed upward.

She stopped and set Jokahn down on one of the high, outstretched branches of the tree. His head was spinning. He looked around and saw dried fruit across vines, and hand painted symbols on the trunk. "Where am I?" he asked.

"This is my stay," said Nalia as she rummaged through some woven baskets.

"You live here?"

"Of course," she chuckled. "Now where are those herbs?"

Jokahn glanced out at the nearby trees. Drahig was climbing up the trunk of a nearby tree with Bakta in his arms. An entire village of ergmen lived in these treetops, each ergman with their own stay. They shied away, looking surprised to find humans amongst them in the middle of the night.

"I found them," cheered Nalia. She picked up the basket of herbs and leapt to the nearby tree with Drahig. "You'll have to change these out every day," she instructed Drahig as she began replacing Bakta's old bandages with long, green leaves.

Drahig gave a grateful sigh. "I don't know how else to say it, but…" Drahig and Nalia looked warmly at each other. "Thank you."

Nalia smiled. "This is how we say thank you," she held her open palm against her chest, "and you're welcome," and then took the same hand and pressed it over Drahig's heart.

It was strange for Jokahn to realize how foreign ergman customs were to Drahig, but Nalia didn't seem to mind. She smiled affectionately at him, and Drahig nodded his head.

"I can teach you more," continued Nalia. "If you would like, you can stay with me and my clan."

Drahig looked surprised. His muzzle pursed together as he

thought about it, but eventually he shook his head. "I can't," he said somberly.

"I understand. I had trouble leaving my owners too, no matter how negligent and abusive they were."

"Ticahrla isn't—"

Nalia held up a hand. "You don't have to explain. Although, if you ever change your mind, you will always be welcome here."

Drahig nodded a grateful head.

Nalia and Drahig went back to silently mending Bakta's wound as Jokahn's attention was drawn to an unsettling rustle coming from beneath the branches. The leaves shook; something was coming. Jokahn's heart started to beat heavy in his chest as the sound grew nearer. A limb shot up through the branches and grabbed him by his leg.

"Ahhh!" he shrieked.

Ticahrla's head emerged from the brush. "Stop shouting," she panted.

"You're crushing my leg!"

"What a crybaby." With a grunt, she heaved herself up onto a large branch. Relinquishing Jokahn's leg, she sprawled out onto her back and released a long, drawn-out breath. She lay there, her arms hanging limp over each side of the tree branch as she breathed heavily.

Nalia's voice was soft in the distance. "Drahig, hold here."

Ticahrla sat upright and looked over at Nalia and Drahig working over Bakta's body. "Hang in there, Bakta."

As Nalia tossed a bloody and puss-covered bandage to the side, Jokahn felt a retch rising up from his stomach. He still wasn't used to the sight of blood.

Ticahrla gestured to him. "Come on, let's let them work." She started climbing back down, and Jokahn followed behind her. One branch at a time, they made their way down the trunk of the tree.

"So, what do you think about the wild ergmen?" she asked.

Jokahn grunted as he lowered himself down another branch, "They—ugh—aren't as scary as you made them out to be."

"Yeah, we got pretty lucky finding Nalia's clan. She's a good leader."

"I've never seen an ergman's stay before. Why—ugh—why do they all live in trees?"

"Ergmen are different from us; they like it up there. I think that's why Drahig is always sitting atop the center mast of the *Nahktaio*."

Ticahrla and Jokahn reached the forest floor.

"Is it safe to be walking around?" asked Jokahn.

"We'll be fine. This is Nalia's territory. Ergmen don't cross into each other's land unless it's to fight." Ticahrla gave him an unexpected slap on the shoulder. "Hey, speaking of which, let's get some training in."

Jokahn groaned. "I don't want to train right now."

"Not even to learn some magic?"

Jokahn stopped. His brow perked up slightly as he looked back at her with a spark of curiosity.

She gave him a sly yet victorious grin, beckoning him closer with the slow gesture of her finger. Jokahn walked toward her. Ticahrla grabbed him by the hand and pulled him in close. He held his breath. She looked down at her open palm as she held it out in front of her.

As her skin became warm to the touch, sparks leapt between her fingertips. He was transfixed, marveling at the spectacle.

Slowly, the electricity died out. Ticahrla gave Jokahn a cocky smile as she returned his hand and said, "Now you try."

Jokahn belched out a laugh. "Yeah, right. No problem." How was he ever supposed to replicate that? He shook out his arms and legs and held a hand in front of his face. He groaned, staring intensely at it.

"No, no, no," Ticahrla laughed, quickly stopping him. "You'll give birth to your colon if you keep that up. It starts inside you. Feel your energy building up, then let it flow. Don't try to squeeze it out."

He toiled alongside Ticahrla for several hours, but made no signs of progress. After a long and arduous struggle, they were both visibly tired.

Ticahrla placed her hand on Jokahn's chest. "Remember to relax.

Let your energy flow."

He was trying, but it was harder to relax with her touching him.

This is ridiculous. He knew it was never going to work. Ticahrla had stood beside him encouragingly this long and still nothing had happened. Maybe he didn't have what it took to learn magic. Maybe he wasn't cut out for it.

A pulse of heat rushed through his body. He stepped back with a gasp and stared up at Ticahrla.

Her eyes were big as she nodded quickly, the hint of a smile appearing on her face. "Come on," she said, quiet but eager.

He licked his lips and concentrated. *Come on, Jokahn, you got this.* He tried to visualize the energy inside him, picturing it as a hot, dense sphere, like the core of a planet, slowly churning and bubbling.

Ticahrla's velvety voice urged him on. "That's it."

As his heart beat faster, filling his chest with a coursing hot magma, his arms and legs began to shake, and the heat crawled up into his throat. Jokahn turned his head to the sky. A hot, coarse breath exhaled from him, and his vision shifted to a vague tint of blue from the hot vapor seeping out of his eyes.

Ticahrla cried out. "You're doing it! I can't believe you're doing it!"

He was. He was *actually* doing it. A sudden sense of dread rose up into his chest, and the fire inside him quickly died out.

Jokahn keeled forward, resting his hands on his knees as he breathed heavily.

Ticahrla held her arms out as she glared at him in astonishment. "Why did you stop?! You had it!"

"I—I don't know," he panted. "Something didn't feel right."

"You're insane! Do you have any idea how long it took me to do that?! And you did it on your first day!"

Jokahn shook his head. "No, something was wrong. I think I might be too tired."

"Too *tired?*" Ticahrla pressed her palm to her forehead and ran her fingers back through her hair in frustration. "Seriously. How did I get saddled with *the* most timid and whiney Dreamer of all time?"

Jokahn grimaced and his blood pressure rose. "Yeah, well, why did I get stuck with someone who's always pissed off? Seriously, it's like you've turned anger into an artform."

"I'm not pissed off all the time. You are just a coward. It's frustrating."

Jokahn let out an irritated snort. He was fed up with being insulted. "Stop saying that! I'm not a coward!"

"Then quit acting like one! Show some confidence already!"

"I said I'm tired! Being tired doesn't make me a coward!"

Ticahrla inhaled sharply and her claw-like hands jutted out toward Jokahn's throat. With rage engulfing her face and her arms shaking, she looked as though she wanted to strangle him, but he knew she couldn't; she needed him to become an Arcane Bearer. Jokahn chuckled. He could almost see the logical impasse running through her mind.

Ticahrla let out a groan, turned around, and punch the bark of a tree. Jokahn reared his head back and glared.

She rested her forehead against the trunk and tried to slow her breathing. "You can't keep running from your problems, boy," Ticahrla said in a calmer tone. "Eventually, you've got to learn to face them."

He didn't understand why she continued to harp on this topic. He wasn't a coward. He could argue with Ticahrla, after all, and she could be scarier than any beast or creature.

Drahig walked up with Bakta in his arms and a puzzled look on his face. Around Drahig's shoulder was a leather satchel with green herbs hanging out of one end. "Ready to go?" asked Drahig.

Ticahrla nodded a heavy head. "Let's get out of here."

18

Something in Her Smile

The next morning, the *Nahktaio* was back at sea. It would take just twenty more days before they reached the Origin. Jokahn woke to find Ticahrla waiting for him on the deck. She stood tall and assertive, holding a long wooden stick.

"Today, I teach you how to face your fears," Ticahrla said with a smile that was a little *too* happy.

Jokahn groaned. "Training already?"

Ticahrla cracked the wooden stick against Jokahn's thigh.

"Ah!" He winced, clutching his leg and hobbling back. "What was that for?!"

"That was the start of your lesson today." She placed the stick down and gestured to him. "Now, come here. I'm going to show you how to defend yourself from an attack like that."

Jokahn was reluctant at first, but seeing the stick was safely on the ground, he limped over to Ticahrla's side. "What do I need to do?" he asked, massaging his leg.

Ticahrla walked behind him and whispered in his ear, her lips brushing lightly against his skin, "I'll show you."

Jokahn's heart beat faster as Ticahrla's body slowly molded up against his. Her hands glided down his forearms. "Keep your hands in front of you." Ticahrla spoke softly as she extended his arms. Jokahn's body was helpless to do anything but comply. "Good. Now, stand your legs a little wider." Ticahrla's palms pressed against the inside of his thighs, pushing his legs outward. "There you go. Now, lower your hips a little. Shoulders back, head up." Ticahrla pointed out in front of him toward the horizon. "And eyes on your enemy at all times."

Jokahn was frozen in a daze; he couldn't move, but his skin was tingling and his head was spinning in an dizzying blur of senses.

"Perfect," Ticahrla whispered. Then she pulled away.

As soon as her body left his, a chill of ocean air circled around him. He shivered, yearning for her touch. Footsteps: he heard someone walking around him, but the world was a haze.

"And remember," Ticahrla's voice echoed as she moved around him, "as the attack comes, move *toward* your opponent." Ticahrla appeared, lowering herself into an odd stance. "Now, let's try this again."

A loud crack rang out as a searing pain ripped through his thigh. He grimaced, hissing as he pulled air through his clenched teeth. The haze cleared from his mind and Ticahrla stood in front of him with wicked grin and a stick in her hand.

"What are you doing?" he cried. Ticahrla reared back and struck him again in the same spot. "Ow!" he wailed. She raised the stick, and Jokahn turned away.

Her voice became heated. "Why are you running away? You know how to defend yourself." She hit him again.

"Stop it!" he said, hobbling away. His leg was going numb.

Again, she hit him and roared back, "Why? What are you going to do about it?!"

Jokahn's face became enraged. As she swung, Jokahn turned and stepped toward her. He caught the stick against his side and pressed his shoulder into her stomach, letting out a furious cry as he pulled Ticahrla's knee out from under her. She fell onto her back and Jokahn landed mounted on top of her.

He was breathing heavily as he glared down at her, but she looked up at him with a warm smile. Her voice was soft, yet proud. "Now you're getting it."

Jokahn glowered at her in rage. *Why is she always smiling whenever I'm in pain?* With an anguished groan, he struggled to his feet. "See, this is why I didn't want to do this. I knew I was going to get hurt."

With a crumpled look of disgust, Ticahrla rested her weight on her elbows. "Why are you always so afraid of getting hurt?"

What kind of a stupid question is that?! Jokahn looked back at Ticahrla with an aggravated expression. "Because it *hurts*, of course!"

"*So?* Growing isn't easy. Growing hurts!"

"Oh, forget it," he grumbled and stomped away.

"All right, fine!" shouted Ticahrla as she rose to her feet and angrily beat the dust from her gown. "Spend the rest of your life too terrified to even get a scratch. See if I care. Just go about living your life frightened and alone all the time."

That one hurt. Ticahrla's words shot a solemn pressure through his body, and his march slowed to a stop. Jokahn didn't want to be afraid anymore, he hated it. He had always been afraid; it kept him safe as a child, but it also kept him sad and alone. Now that he had finally found someone he cared about, someone he wanted to trust, he was driving her away too.

Ticahrla turned, clenched her fists, and started to walk away.

"Wait…" Jokahn said quietly, too quietly for Ticahrla to hear.

He reached out and grabbed her wrist. Ticahrla was yanked to a stop. She stood there and released a long, frustrated sigh, but she didn't look back at him.

"Please wait…" Jokahn said again, struggling to add volume to his voice.

Ticahrla glanced back at how he had anchored himself to her wrist. She looked furious at first, but as their eyes met her brow rose and her expression shifted toward surprise. A single tear ran down Jokahn's cheek.

"What, are you crying now?!" exclaimed Ticahrla.

"I'm not crying." He quickly brushed the tear away with the back of his hand. "It's just that…I don't want you to go."

"Hmph." Ticahrla snorted. "Are boys always this emotional?"

Jokahn frowned, slightly embarrassed. He didn't know how to respond, so he moved on. "Will you teach me?"

"Huh?"

"You said you would teach me to fight—to face my fears. Will you still teach me?"

"Why should I? You obviously don't want to learn."

Jokahn looked down at the floor. She was right, as usual, but that was only the half-truth. Sure, he didn't care about learning to fight, but he wanted to be with Ticahrla. "But…I still want you to stay," he said softly, trying to explain as best he could.

The deck of the *Nahktaio* was quiet for a moment. Ticahrla didn't respond, and Jokahn couldn't summon up the courage to look at her. He didn't have to look; he already knew he had driven her away, just like everyone else. As Jokahn clung to her wrist, the small space between them suddenly seemed to stretch on forever, like a chasm he would never be able to close. Once again, he felt alone. The realization of it was difficult, and it settled hard against his stomach.

A hand gently cupped the back of his head. The subtle touch startled him, and he let out a small gasp. Ticahrla pulled him in close to her. He stood there, frozen, pressed against her body as she hugged him warmly.

"I'm not going anywhere," she said softly. "I'll always be here for you."

Jokahn was numb from head to toe. He couldn't move, he couldn't speak, but tears began streaming down his face. These tears were different, though. Not sad. Even though he was helpless to stop crying, he actually felt…*happy!*

He wrapped his arms around her. For the first time, the pain that had been weighing on him for so long began to dissipate. He let out a long, glorious sigh of relief. He was right; Ticahrla was the best thing that had ever happened to him.

* * *

Ticahrla held Jokahn lovingly in her arms as he pressed his face against her. She looked down at him and grinned a wicked smile, for she knew—at that very moment—she had the boy right where she wanted him, and he would be helpless to defy her.

19

A Looming Threat

Two days had passed on the *Nahktaio*, and life for Jokahn had become increasingly grueling with each day. Ticahrla kept him occupied with nonstop training and chores, and there were still seventeen days to go before they reached the Origin.

He sat hunched over on all fours, drenched in sweat, and panting as he pushed a large brush back and forth across the deck. Ticahrla stood above him at the helm, studying her father's compass. Her eyes shifted toward him, and a coy smile stretched across her face.

"Boy," she called. He paused, resting his elbows on his thighs. "Don't forget to scrub the stern. That's where things get really mucky." She beamed a wide smile.

Jokahn gave a tired glance toward the rear of the ship and let out a long breath. Of course, he knew what she was up to—he wasn't an idiot. She was manipulating him, but Jokahn couldn't care less. As long as she continued to shine that glorious smile down upon him, he was happy. Wiping the sweat from his brow, he smiled up at her. He adored the attention she gave him; he loved every minute of it.

After he finished scrubbing the entire ship, Ticahrla had him reorganize the freight and adjust the rigging. It was just past noon—although it felt much later than that—when he noticed Ticahrla standing on the deck with two wooden swords, one in each hand.

"Today, you learn to use the sword," she declared. With the utmost respect, she presented the hilt of one sword to him.

He smiled brightly and snatched the training weapon from her hand, swinging it wildly as he fought off dozens of imaginary foes.

"Come on, Ticahrla," he cheered, playfully jabbing his sword at her. "Duel me, if you think you can."

Ticahrla stood there looking unimpressed, her eyes glazed over with disappointment. She slapped her wooden sword down on top of his, nearly toppled him forward onto his face.

He caught his balance and shook the sting from his hands. "Ah, that hurt."

"Good," she said sternly. "Maybe you won't do it again. Now focus. This is serious business."

He grumbled but did as he was told.

They spent the entire day, practicing the basics of sword fighting. He had no idea there was so much to learn: the subtle nuances of how to grip the hilt, the importance of balance and how he positioned his feet. Each movement had to be executed with precision.

As they wrapped up their training, Ticahrla collected the wooden swords and placed them back in her quarters. Jokahn noticed the two swords sheathed on her left hip.

"When do I get to have a real sword?" he asked.

Ticahrla chuckled. "You haven't earned it yet."

"Yeah, but when will I earn it?"

She shot a snide glare at him, "When you learn to grow up."

Jokahn frowned and grumbled. That wasn't a real answer. That was a copout answer.

* * *

Early the next morning, Ticahrla was woken with a jolt. She lurched back in her hammock and peered up through sleepy eyes. Drahig's large frame was hovering over her with his hand on her shoulder.

There was caution in his eyes. "You need to see this," he said.

She leapt from her hammock and Drahig led her up to the helm.

Drahig handed her a retractable telescope and pointed off the stern. "Someone is following us."

Ticahrla extended the telescope and peered through the lens. In the distance was a large, three-sailed vessel. A long sigh escaped her lips. "That's an Athus warship."

"Coincidence?"

"Not with my luck."

She frowned, tapping the telescope repeatedly against her thigh. *Who is on that warship? What do they want?*

"Turn hard to port," she ordered, marching over to the helm's railing. Drahig hurried to the wheel and cranked it left. "Head toward that shoreline. We'll see what their intentions are."

The *Nahktaio* groaned as the bow dipped and turned into the waves.

Not long after, the boy rushed up to the helm with a confused look, still groggy and half asleep. "What's going on? Why are we turning?"

Ticahrla's eyes were hard and focused. "We're being followed. Or we're about to find out if we are."

She returned to the stern and glared at the warship. If it continued its path, she knew the ship wasn't interested in her, but if it changed course, there was going to be trouble ahead.

The warship carried on, unchanging, and a sense of relief began to ease through her shoulders. She was already behind schedule reaching the Origin; the last thing she needed was another delay.

A shift in the warship's sails caught Ticahrla's attention. Her eyes narrowed as the sails turned and the hull pivoted toward her.

"Dammit…"

"What's wrong?" asked Jokahn.

"They're steering toward us."

The boy's head turned to look nervously out toward the water. "Can we outrun them?"

"Not a chance. That's a battlecruiser, much larger and faster than us. They'll close the distance and then either ram or wrangle us."

"Wrangle?"

"Get in close, then hook and tether their ship to ours so they can board us. With a ship that size, there are at least two dozen armed sailors on board, and they're all well trained swordsmen."

His voice cracked, "What do we do?"

Poor boy. He was shaking. She smiled at him. "Simple. We take away their advantage." She pointed at a harbor city along the coastline. "We make a stop in Broich territory, pull into a shallow port where a large ship's size and speed won't help them."

"What's Broich territory?"

"One of the seven sovereign kingdoms. They're brutish people, but Athus buys a lot of steel from them, so we'll be welcome."

As the *Nahktaio* sailed through the narrow mouth of the harbor, she realized this port was even more perfect than she had hoped. If the Athus battlecruiser was stupid enough to follow her into the harbor, it would run aground on the rocks, and her smaller ship could escape.

"That's far enough, Drahig. Turn us about and secure the sails."

The *Nahktaio* turned and gradually slowed to a stop as it drifted in the center of the harbor.

The warship moved steadily closer, but it raised its sails and eased to a stop just outside the mouth of the harbor, blocking her only escape route.

She grunted and glared at the battlecruiser. They didn't take the bait. The ship's captain was smarter than she expected.

Ticahrla raised the telescope. She could make out small figures moving across the deck and spotted a group of men wearing red and white robes.

"Son of a bitch," Ticahrla muttered, lowering the telescope and shaking her head.

"What is it?" asked Drahig.

"Why are there Archmagi on an Athus warship?"

"They've blocked us in. What now?"

"Easy, we sit and wait. The real question is, what do *they* do?"

* * *

Sihera stood on the deck of the warship looking out into harbor. Amongst the small cluster of ships that sat in front of them was the princess's vessel, and on it was her Dreamer boy. Sihera let out a long sigh. She was so close to him it almost felt surreal.

A low grunt drew her attention. Laval was stewing angrily beside her as he glared across the water at Ticahrla's tiny ship. His hands gripped tightly around the railing and twisted, as if he was trying to ring the wood dry.

"She's mocking us," Laval growled.

"This is as far as we can go, sir," the captain said. "We'll run aground if we follow her in there."

"Should we wait her out?" asked one of Laval's men. "She can't stay there forever."

Laval stroked his square jaw. "No, I have a better idea. We'll wait until nightfall and use the rowboats to move in when she least expects it."

20

Courage and Cowardice

The sun was disappearing over the horizon and the sky was growing dark, yet there was still no movement from the Athus warship. Ticahrla had eventually decided to dock the *Nahktaio* where it now sat.

Broich was a strange place. Instead of the pleasant seaside breeze Jokahn was familiar with, the acidic tang of dirt and coal hung constant in the air, so thick he could taste it. Clearly a mining town, the harbor was lined with gemstone and metal worker shops. A thick layer of grime clung to the stone and dark timber buildings, painting everything the same drab color.

Jokahn stood at the ship's railing, watching the shadowy vessel looming in the distance. Sitting there and waiting was difficult for him. Ticahrla, however, seemed unfazed. She went about her day pretty much as usual, moving cargo around and practicing her sword techniques, as if a giant warship wasn't holding her trapped in this harbor. How was she so calm? Did Ticahrla even have a plan if the warship attacked?

A crash of wood and the sound of angered voices nearby caught his attention. It seemed Ticahrla and Drahig had noticed as well. They all hurried over to the other side of the *Nahktaio* to see the commotion.

Near the docks, a scuffle was about to break out between the Broich locals. A husband and wife were backed into a corner by a group of five men. Ticahrla was right, the people here were aggressive, all with short, stocky builds and thick, strong hands. Their clothes and skin were laced with dirt, just like everything else.

The man in the front shoved the husband hard against his chest, slamming the husband's back against the wall.

The wife pushed the man off her husband and the mob swarmed, punching and kicking her. She screamed and fell to the floor, but they continued pummeling her mercilessly.

Jokahn's chest tightened with anxiety. His heart ached as he watched the woman being beaten. Ticahrla's body instinctively lurched forward a step, but she stopped as the husband stepped in, trying to shove the men away. The group tackled the husband to the floor, and the couple covered up, desperately trying to protect themselves.

Jokahn's face strained as he massaged the back of his neck. He imagined what it would have been like if the same thing had happened to him and Ticahrla—him being viciously assaulted, and Ticahrla either forced to watch or suffer the same fate.

"If I'm ever being beaten like that, just let them beat me," he said. "It isn't worth getting you beaten up as well."

He cared for Ticahrla and would never want her to suffer like that. There was no point in her needlessly being injured as well, or even worse, killed.

"*Fuck that!*" exclaimed Ticahrla. Her response was so firm that it caught him off guard, and he looked up at her with surprise. "If that was you," she continued, jabbing a finger at the couple, "I would be right there next to you, kicking ass or getting our asses kicked. I don't give a shit how many people I have to fight off."

Hearing her say that with such conviction threw Jokahn for a loop. On one hand, it filled him with pride; it made him realize how lucky he was to have Ticahrla, to have someone who was willing to stand up for him, no matter the opposition. But on the other hand, it caused a sickening feeling to twist in his stomach; it was the feeling of guilt and embarrassment upon realizing he didn't have the same courage she did, and it sat heavy on his belly. *Maybe Ticahrla was right. Maybe I am a coward.*

"Come on, let's go help them," Ticahrla said, lowering the ramp onto the dock.

His body went rigid, and his feet planted. "Wha—what do you mean, 'go help them'?"

Ticahrla either ignored him or chose not to answer his question. "Drahig, keep an eye on that warship. If you see anything change, ring the helm's bell."

"Understood," Drahig said astutely.

"You," Ticahrla said, tapping Jokahn's arm with the back of her hand. "Follow me."

His voice was shaking. "What are we going to do?"

"I'll take out the guy in front, you take out the smaller one on the right. After two or three of them are dealt with, the others will likely scatter." Then she marched confidently down the ramp.

Jokahn's mind was racing. They didn't know this couple, but that didn't seem to matter to Ticahrla. She always did what she felt was right in the moment. That was just the way she was. But he wasn't built that way. He couldn't leap heroically into action.

He looked over at the so-called "smaller one" on the right. The man was the smallest of the group, but he was still much larger than Jokahn. As he watched the man beating relentlessly on the husband, Jokahn was not instilled with confidence. "This is stupid. We can't jump into some random street fight."

Ticahrla stopped to look back at him, and exclaimed, "Don't you want to help them?"

He scoffed nervously. "Of course, I *want* to help. But there's a difference between wanting to help and jumping headfirst into a brawl for some people we don't even know."

"Yes. One is *wrong*, and one is *right*," Ticahrla said bluntly. "How do you want to be remembered when people tell stories about you one day? Do you want to be remembered as a coward who waited on the sidelines, or as someone who stood up for what was right?"

Jokahn groaned, still hesitant. "I'd like to be remembered as the person who strategically did not die."

Frustrated, Ticahrla stormed back up the ramp. She grabbed him by the arm. "Listen, if I don't see you in that fight with me, when

I'm done with them, I'm coming back to pound your face next. You got that?" She didn't wait for him to respond. Without another word, she turned and charged into the fray.

Jokahn didn't follow. He had never been in a real fight before. He cautiously thought about joining her, but quickly reasoned against it. For a moment he considered running away. He could do that. He could hide in the sleeping quarters and wait for Ticahrla to return. But what would she think of him then? Or, even worse, what if Ticahrla didn't return? What if she got hurt?

He stood there and pressed his palms to his temples, unsure of what to do. Why was she always causing more trouble for him than there needed to be? She couldn't just make things easy for once, could she?

Ticahrla rushed up behind one man and cracked her armored boot against the side of his knee. The man wailed as one leg gave out beneath him. With a swift elbow, the sharp edge of Ticahrla's bone crunched against the man's nose, sending blood arcing through the air. Jokahn grimaced as the man fell onto his back and went silent.

With both hands, Ticahrla grabbed the next closest person by the scruff of his collar and hefted him up and over her hip. The man's legs flung through the air, and he landed with a loud thud against the ground. The man groaned and wheezed as he curled up on the floor.

The group finally noticed Ticahrla. The largest man came up from behind and bearhugged her, lifting her off the ground. Jokahn's lungs tensed, and his face turned angry as she struggled to break free.

"Hold her still," said the smaller man. He reared back his fist and struck Ticahrla across her left eye.

A furious heat surged up into Jokahn's face. He let out a groan and charged at the smaller man. With a loud cry, he rammed his shoulder into the smaller man's gut and tied his arms around the man's waist. Jokahn drove his feet forward, and the man started to topple over. Landing with a shocking amount of force, the two hit the ground as Jokahn's weight fell hard on top of him.

Jokahn was dazed for a moment. As his senses realigned, he realized he had landed with his legs straddling the man's chest. It was the perfect position to rain blows down on his opponent.

Left, right, left, right. Jokahn hammered his fists down. The man shielded his head with his arms.

Jokahn sat up tall and grinned, amazed at how well he was doing. Confidence surged through him. The fear that had once handicapped him began to dissipate. *Damn this feels good!*

Suddenly, the man beneath him began to buck. A look of dread overtook Jokahn's once confident expression as he fell forward. He caught himself, bracing his upper body with his hands on the ground around the man's head. The man squirmed, trying to wrestle him off. Jokahn felt his hips rise, and his weight began to fall to one side.

No! No! No! The man rolled Jokahn over onto his back and postured up, throwing vengeful punches down at him. Jokahn deflected one blow, and then another, but the third struck him across the cheekbone, whipping his head back against the ground.

Jokahn's vision blurred, his ears began to ring, and the side of his face was numb. Time seemed to move much slower after that. He couldn't see the man standing above him anymore.

Oh, no... Jokahn's outstretched arms desperately tried to protect his head, but there was nothing he could do. Another fist brushed past him, grazing his ear before hitting the ground. The man had missed. The fist retracted, and Jokahn knew another blow would soon be coming.

Jokahn's vision began to focus. The man above him was cocking his arm back when a metal boot came into Jokahn's peripheral, hitting the man square in the ribcage. Like a whip, the man's body launched backward, first his chest, then his head, and lastly his limbs as he jettisoned out of view. Ticahrla planted her foot and stood above Jokahn in an aggressive posture. Time steadily returned to normal as Jokahn groaned and sat upright.

Ticahrla knelt and braced an arm around his back. "Are you all right?" she asked in a panicked voice, running a hand over his body.

"I'm all right, I'm all right," he groaned, waving away her concern. As she helped him to his feet, he noticed her left cheek was bruised and swollen, and her right lip was bleeding. "Ticahrla, you're hurt," he exclaimed.

She smiled and raised an eyebrow. "You've got quite the shiner yourself."

Jokahn's hand touched his cheek. It was sore, but in a strange way, it felt good.

He turned to view what was left of the brawl. In the distance, two men from the group were hobbling away through the crowded street. On the floor lied one man writhing in pain and two more completely unconscious. The husband and wife stood in the corner as they held each other and cried. They were both beaten and bruised, but they would be all right.

Jokahn and Ticahrla looked at each other and smiled. His heart was still racing, but in a good way. He had never felt more alive. It was strange. He had gained nothing he could show to someone. There was no coin as a reward. He would not be hailed as a hero in the city. The couple they helped never even thanked them. And yet, nothing he had ever accomplished before that day had felt nearly as rewarding.

Ticahrla looked at him with a proud grin.

As they made their way back onboard the *Nahktaio*, Ticahrla stopped beside Drahig who was still diligently watching the warship in the distance.

"Any change?" asked Ticahrla.

"Nothing," replied Drahig. For the first time, the ergman took his eyes off the sea and turned to look at Ticahrla. His head reared back in surprise. "Umm…you—you have some blood…" Drahig indicated by pointing at his own lip.

Ticahrla's face puckered and squinched as she sucked on her bottom lip to clean the blood off. Then she pouted her lips at the ergman. "Better?"

Of course, it wasn't better. Drahig chuckled and shook his head. Jokahn and Ticahrla looked at each other and laughed.

For the first time, Jokahn felt like he finally understood what Ticahrla was thinking. He was proud of his battle wounds, and he was sure she felt the same.

21

Strike from the Shadows

Sihera looked up at the night sky, now shrouded in clouds with scarcely any moonlight. The air was still, but the bitter cold stung at her face. The water was flat, like a mat blanket stretched across the harbor, and the ships had become an indistinguishable cluster of silhouettes. She peered over the warship's railing at three rowboats, all filled with men, drifting in the water below. A rope scaffolding hung off the side of the ship.

"Come. Easy now," Laval called up to her. "Watch your step."

Climbing over the railing, she scaled down the side of the ship as the rope wobbled beneath her, eventually making it onto a small rowboat with the Archmagi and some sailors. Eight men were crowded into each of the tiny boats. Laval helped her to her seat, and the sailors began rowing quietly toward land.

Sihera clasped her hands between her knees. It wasn't just the cold that bothered her; she had a terrible, unnerving feeling about what was to come. There was so much at stake. Her Dreamer boy's life rested in the hands of these men, most of whom she hardly knew. Would Laval's plan to rescue the boy work? She couldn't be sure.

It didn't take long to reach Ticahrla's ship. It sat docked peacefully in the night. No one even seemed to be standing guard.

The three rowboats pulled up alongside the princess's vessel. The sailors raised tall ladders with hooks and climbed up the side, swords in hand. They moved quickly and stealthily. In no time, the rowboats were nearly empty, and only her and the five other Archmagi remained.

From atop Ticahrla's ship, a sailor leaned over and waved them up. Laval went first, clumsily making his way up the ladder, then the rest of the Archmagi mages followed. Sihera was the last to exit the rowboat.

As she reached the top, a sailor offered her a hand and helped her over the railing. Men were quietly scurrying about the ship.

"Well?" Laval whispered to one of the sailors.

The man shrugged. "The vessel is empty. There's no one here."

A loud crack rang out from above, then the whir of rope being pulled through bearings filled the air.

"Look out!" cried one man.

Sihera looked up with a gasp just in time to see a net filled with large crates crashing down over her. She shrieked and covered her head.

Laval shot his hand up, creating a fiery explosion that lit up the darkness with vibrant oranges, sending a few boxes flying overboard. The crates he missed came crashing down on top of two mages. Sihera reared back and pressed up against Laval. One man lying beside her was unconscious, the other groaned in misery under the heavy boxes.

A shadowy figure repelled down from the sails and landed on the docks. Everyone hurried to the ship's railing to see.

Ticahrla stood alone on the dock with her hands on her hips as she looked up them.

"Traitors!" her voice roared through the night air. "How could my own sailors turn against me to side with the Archmagi?!"

"You misunderstand, Princess," Laval called down to her. "We're here on orders from your royal council. We simply want to see you, the boy, and the compass all returned safely home to Athus."

"If you're so concerned about our safety, then why are you all so well armed?"

Laval chuckled. "You'll come quietly, Princess, if you know what's best for you."

Ticahrla belched out a laugh. "Yeah, right. As if I'm intimidated by some old man in a dress."

Laval stood tall, glaring down at her. "It's a robe," he

proclaimed.

"Whatever makes you feel better."

Sihera turned a cautious eye toward Laval. He looked furious. His mouth was puckered into a tight knot, and his eyes bulged as he inhaled sharply through his nose. "Stupid girl. I have twenty-two men."

"You're down by two if my count is correct." Ticahrla thrust a hand into her chest piece and pulled out a leather necklace. "Did you say *this* is what you're looking for?"

Sihera held her breath as the king's compass shimmered in the dim moonlight, dangling at the end of the band. Laval's body lurched forward, leaning over the ship's railing. His eyes looked hungry, and a narrow grin exposed his bared teeth.

Ticahrla grinned wickedly up at them as she tucked the compass away again. "If you want it, then come and get it, *Man-dress*." She turned and ran into the city.

"Quickly, after her!" Laval cried.

As Ticahrla sprinted around a corner, the men charged onto the docks and Sihera hurried behind them. Laval and the Archmagi led the pack, hurling fireballs out in front of them as they ran.

The group slowed to a stop. Sihera pushed her way between the sailors to Laval where she found Ticahrla laying on the ground, panting as she pressed her hand over a scorched mark on her armor. The princess sat there with an aggravated stare, looking up at them like a rabid dog.

Laval stood tall over her. There was a glee in Laval's voice as he spoke. "Don't make this harder on yourself, Princess."

Sihera cringed. *Why is he acting this way?*

Ticahrla winced, scooting herself back against a wall. "*This?*" she gestured at her side. "This is nothing. I just felt like resting, that's all."

"Play coy all you want; it doesn't change anything."

Ticahrla laughed. "Don't you get it? I wasn't running away. I was distracting you, you morons. See?" Ticahrla jabbed an arm out, pointing behind them.

Sihera held her breath as everyone whipped around, the sailors brandishing their weapons. Sihera hugged her arms to her chest as she searched the dark city streets behind them, frightened by what might jump out at her from the shadows…but there was nothing.

The sound of a dull thud pulled Sihera's attention back. Laval gave a low wheeze as he grimaced, hunching over, and clasping his ribs. Ticahrla was already up and racing down an alleyway.

"Get after her…" Laval groaned as he pushed himself into a sprint behind Ticahrla, still clutching his side. The Archmagi ran after Laval with Sihera and the sailors following behind.

They chased Ticahrla through the empty city streets until Sihera grew winded. Gratefully, the group came to a stop again. She rested her hands on her knees to catch her breath.

"Where'd she go?" a man asked.

"She was right here."

"You lost her?!"

Laval ordered, "You search that way. You check the alley. She can't be far."

Sihera lost track of Laval. As the men spread out in different directions, she rang her hands together, unsure who to follow.

A crash caught her attention. One of the sailors stumbled past her. Ticahrla lunged forward, swords drawn, and rammed her shoulder into the back of a sailor. He tumbled forward and a second sailor slashed his sword at her. She parried and kicked the man in the chest.

"Here! Over here!" someone cried.

Ticahrla vanished back into the darkness of a backstreet as the men chased after her. Sihera jogged as fast as she could down the dark alleyway after them, but her chest was aching and her legs were weak.

"Wait for me!" she called.

The world was growing quiet again as the men's voices grew distance. Only the panting of her labored breathing remained as she watched them sprinting away.

A hand clasped over her mouth and jerked her head back. She let out a muffled cry as she was pulled down to her knees.

"Quiet," Ticahrla whispered, pressing a dagger to her throat.

Sihera knelt on the ground, breathing heavily through her nose as she watched the group of men disappear into the darkness. She tried to call out to them but couldn't manage anything more than a quiet moan through Ticahrla's palm.

Laval, come back! Don't leave me! A somber breath escaped her. They were gone. It was just her and the princess.

Ticahrla let out satisfied grunt and turned to look at her. Sihera glared back from the corner of her eye.

"So, this is the Archmagi's Dreamer," Ticahrla said, giving Sihera a glance up and down. "I have to admit, I was expecting something more."

Sihera's eyes narrowed. She wanted to rebuttal, trying to wrestle her mouth free, but couldn't. Finally, Ticahrla released her grip over her jaw, but continued to hold the blade firm against Sihera's throat.

With a deep breath, Sihera demanded, "What have you done with the boy?"

Ticahrla leaned her head back. "The boy?"

"The boy Dreamer. You haven't hurt him yet, have you?"

Ticahrla was quiet for a moment. "How do you know the boy?"

"So, you haven't yet. No, of course not. You have to find the Origin first."

Ticahrla's mouth flattened into a hard line. "Girl, I don't know what you think you know, but you are wearing on my cheerful demeanor."

Ticahrla pressed the blade harder against Sihera's skin. The sting of the knife's edge gave her voice a slight rasp. "You're not going to kill me," she said confidently.

"What makes you say that?"

"I saw you fighting those men. You could have killed any one of them, but you let them all live."

"Those are my people, no matter how misguided. Don't make the mistake of thinking I hold an Archmagi pawn with the same regard."

"Then why haven't you killed me?"

"I'm still trying to figure you out. So, tell me, why are the

Archmagi pursuing me?"

Sihera grimaced and turned her head to relieve some of the pressure on her neck. "We—we're here to rescue the boy."

"I see, trying to stop me from reaching the Origin."

"No, we don't care about the Origin anymore."

Ticahrla belched out a laugh. "Yeah right. I saw the look on all your faces when you saw the compass. Your mouths were practically salivating."

Sihera turned her eyes to the ground and frowned. Ticahrla was right. Sihera had noticed that as well.

Ticahrla continued. "Why are my sailors working with the Archmagi?"

"It's like I said, they are helping us rescue the boy."

"Stop bullshitting me." Ticahrla pressed the knife tighter against her throat. Sihera clamped her eyes shut and winced. "Who commissioned the warship?"

"The chairman. Ah—Apotri." Sihera let out a groan. "He made a deal with Laval."

"What deal?"

Again, Ticahrla pressed her dagger harder against Sihera's jawline. A line of blood ran down her neck.

"You don't scare me, Princess. The Archmagi and I will destroy you before you ever hurt that boy."

"What is your obsession with this boy? You want to use him as a sacrifice?"

"No!" cried Sihera.

"What then? Do you know him?"

Her voice became quiet. "No, not really. I—I mean, I don't even know his name, but I see him in my dreams. And I know what you are going to do to him is wrong."

Ticahrla's grip loosened, and the blade eased away from her neck. Sihera peered back at Ticahrla. The princess had a stern scowl as she stared at the ground.

Sihera's heart began to race. This might be her only chance to escape. She focused her energy and sparks began to arc from her hand. She turned slightly, pressing her palm to Ticahrla's chest as she let out a sharp cry.

A small blast knocked Ticahrla back. Sihera cringed as the blade nicked her jawline. She staggered to her feet, pressing her fingers to her throat and examining the blood. It wasn't too bad, just a small cut.

Along the pier, Ticahrla gave a soft but maniacal laugh as she rose gingerly to her feet. "You had me going there. Did you actually mean any of the shit you just said?" she said, holstering her dagger behind her back.

Sihera lowered her stance and let out a long breath. She glared at Ticahrla across the pier. The heat began to churn in her chest, flowing down into her fingertips. Steam began rising from her shoulders in the cold, night air, and flames poured from her eyes. She ignited a fireball between her hands. "I meant it when I said I would destroy you."

Ticahrla grinned a wicked smile and slowly unsheathed her swords. "Better mages than you have tried."

Ticahrla charged. Sihera let out a loud cry as she hurled the fireball forward, illuminating the pier with vibrant oranges. Ticahrla ducked as she sprinted forward. The flaming inferno shot by her and disappeared into the ocean.

Sihera took a deep breath in, shocked by how quickly Ticahrla had closed the distance. With rage-filled eyes and teeth bared, the princess reared her sword back. Sihera's eyes grew wide, and her lungs tightened. She quickly pressed her forearms together to form a deflection. Ticahrla's blade struck the shockwave protecting her, but the force of the blow knocked Sihera onto her back.

She struck the wooden planks harder than she had expected, nearly knocking the wind out of her. Ticahrla thrust another sword at her. Sihera jutted her hands out, creating a small explosion that pushed Ticahrla's hips out from under her.

Ticahrla came crashing down on top of Sihera, and the two tumbled across the pier. As they rolled, the two were flung apart from each other. Sihera's head was spinning as she came to rest, but the fight wasn't over. She had to get back up. Her vision focused on two swords that laid on the dock in front of her, but where was Ticahrla?

A shuffling sound came from beside her. Before she could turn, a heavy weight pushed her over, pinning her back to the floor. Ticahrla climbed on top of her, trapping her left arm against her body as Ticahrla shoved her forearm against the side of Sihera's jaw. She winced at the twisting pressure in her neck, her cheek pressed down against the wood.

It was becoming difficult to breathe. She had to get Ticahrla off her. She sent the heat of her energy down into her right arm. Sparks began to arc from her hand, but Ticahrla grappled her by the wrist.

"Nuh-uh, not this time," Ticahrla said.

Sihera let out a pained groan, almost a whimper. She couldn't move. She couldn't breathe. She tried to pull air into her lungs, but all she managed were small wheezes from underneath Ticahrla's weight. It wasn't enough. She could see the darkness closing in around the edges of her vision. Her eyelids began to flutter.

"That's right, go to sleep," Ticahrla whispered to her in a soothing voice.

Sihera's legs kicked and wriggled desperately, but Ticahrla didn't budge. Sihera's vision had gone black. Her eyes clenched shut. She had to do something, but she couldn't even move.

"Don't worry. I'll take good care of the boy."

No! You can't! There was only one thing she could do, but it might hurt her just as much as it would Ticahrla. Her consciousness fading, she realized she didn't have any other choice.

Sihera's eyes shot open; she couldn't see, but she felt the heat from the flames. Electricity leapt in all directions off her body. Ticahrla's spine arched backward, relieving some of the pressure off Sihera. Her vision started to return just as the electricity running through Ticahrla came surging back into Sihera's shoulder and down into her vertebrae.

It burned, like fire scorching her from the inside. Her body convulsed, writhing in pain, but she concentrated all of her will on maintaining the flow of energy for as long as she could. Her muscles spasmed, and her jaw clenched together as she let out an anguished cry through her bared teeth. She had never heard such a ghostly tone escape from her own lungs before.

She couldn't take it anymore. Sihera's muscles went loose, the crackle of electricity died out, and Ticahrla's weight collapsed beside her with a thud.

Gasping and wheezing for air, Sihera slowly rolled over and flopped onto her stomach. Every part of her was trembling. She tried to pull herself up, but she was too exhausted. Her forehead slumped forward against the wooden planks as she breathed heavily.

If only she could have stayed there, taken a moment to rest, but she knew she couldn't let herself relax. Not yet. With a grunt, she pressed herself up on all fours and turned her head slightly to see Ticahrla. Amazingly, the princess wasn't dead.

Ticahrla looked dazed, but she was moving. She knelt on the floor, feeling out the terrain with her hands as a blind person might do, somehow managing to grab her swords.

Sihera couldn't let Ticahrla recover. She had to finish this while she still could. With all her strength, she groaned and thrust herself to her feet. Her muscles quivering, she turned her feet inward and locked her knees to hold herself upright.

Ticahrla grunted, using one sword as a cane to press herself to her feet, and glared down the pier at her.

"Sihera!" Laval's voice called out from the distance. She looked back into the dark city and could hear the men racing toward her. She just had to keep Ticahrla in place long enough for help to arrive and her Dreamer boy would be safe.

"Looks like the cavalry has come to the rescue," Ticahrla said, gingerly sheathing her swords.

Sihera turned back to glare at Ticahrla. "I don't need to be rescued. I can take you myself."

Ticahrla chuckled. "In your dreams, maybe."

Sihera's eyes ignited as sparks leapt from her palms. Ticahrla remained calm and cocky as ever, not even attempting to defend herself.

"Ticahrla! Grab hold!" a boy's voice called out.

The fire in Sihera's eyes vanished, and her jaw fell open as a ship sailed by the end of the pier. On it was her Dreamer boy, in real life, just a few feet away from her. Sihera's heart stopped, and her arms fell loose by her sides. She couldn't think. She couldn't move.

The boy tossed a long rope over the railing. Ticahrla gripped it with both hands and was carried away as the ship sailed by.

The sound of footsteps came rushing in from behind her.

"Sihera, are you all right?!" Laval cried.

Sihera stood there, unable to speak, and stared in disbelief as Ticahrla and the boy sailed away.

"Quickly, to the rowboats," ordered Laval.

A stampede of running feet took off down the docks.

"Sihera, hurry, my child." Laval grabbed her by the shoulders and led her down the docks behind the other men.

"Where are they?!" asked one sailor. "What happened to the boats?"

In a daze, Sihera's eyes turned down to the water in front of her. There sat three small boats, right where they had left them. Only now they were sunk several feet beneath the surface of the ocean.

"Dammit!" cried Laval. "She's getting away!"

* * *

Ticahrla grunted and gritted her teeth, pulling herself up the rope. Jokahn extended his arm over the railing, and she grasped his forearm. The boy arched his back, pulling her up and over the side of the *Nahktaio*, and they fell to the deck with a thud.

They both panted heavy breaths as they sprawled out across the floor, her muscles sore with fatigue. The boy chuckled like a child, but she knew they weren't out of danger yet.

"Drahig!" she called up to the helm as she rolled over and forced herself to her feet. Drahig was at the wheel and dripping wet, steering the ship toward the mouth of the harbor. "Tell me you disabled that warship."

Drahig looked down at her with a proud grin and nodded. "I took out their rudder and sank their rowboats, just as you asked."

"Boy, you got Bakta back on the ship, right?"

Jokahn nodded.

She let out an exhausted breath. "Good."

Making her way to the bow, she could just make out the silhouette of the Athus battlecruiser against the night sky, sitting anchored at the mouth of the harbor.

Ticahrla grinned. "Take us right behind the stern of their ship, Drahig. I want to see the look in their eyes as we sail past them."

As the *Nahktaio* drifted closer, a whistle blew, and the sound of men's voices filled the night air. The warship began raising anchor and lowering its sails.

The helmsman wrestled frantically with the wheel. "Captain, the rudder! It's not responding!"

A wide grin stretched across Ticahrla's face as she grabbed a rope and leaned over the side of her ship. She cupped a hand to her mouth and called out in a cheerful tone, "At ease, boys! I'll take it from here!"

As the *Nahktaio* glided out of the harbor and back into the open sea, no one followed her.

22

Twisted Dreams

As Sihera dreamt, she walked down that same cavernous hallway, her chest aching, her head heavy, and her senses dulled. Her Dreamer boy walked in front of her. She had come so close to saving him, but she had failed.

The boy came to a stop at the water's edge, his back towards her, the same as always. On cue, her left arm reached for him, but something was different. Her arm was shimmery, almost ink-like in color. Her fingers were long and sharp. She stared curiously at the unusual limb until it dawned upon her. It was the claw of an aiko.

The boy spun around to face her—he had never done that before—and his expression turned pale. His blue eyes widened with fear as the aiko's claw thrust forward and sank its talons into his chest.

Sihera lurched upright from her dream. She sat in her hammock with a strained expression, panting heavily with sweat dripping from her brow.

What was that about?

* * *

Two days later, the warship was limping back toward Athus for repairs. Sihera continued to have the same dream, but it was always changing now. A vision that had once been so predictable was suddenly filled with uncertainty. What was going on? Was Sihera losing her focus, or was there something else she couldn't see, creating waves of uncertainty in the boy's future?

She clamped her head between her hands, trying to make sense of it. There was a terrible sense of guilt that sat with her for failing to rescue her Dreamer boy.

She approached Laval one evening. "So…what do we do now?" she asked solemnly.

Laval slumped his head between his shoulders. For the entire trip back to Athus, he never spoke a word. He just stayed in their quarters, looking hollow and defeated.

When the ship finally pulled into port five days later, Laval and Sihera returned to their home in Athus. They walked through the front door and quietly sat their luggage down.

"I'll get us something to eat," Laval said as he shuffled into the kitchen.

She sat down at the table as Laval set a plate of bread and dried meat in front of her and then sat himself across the table. She waited for him to say something, but he just quietly picked at his food, never looking up.

Sihera frowned. Laval used to be like a father to her. Now he just felt like a ghost—some lost spirit that lingered around. She wanted to tell him about the vision she'd been having, but she wasn't sure if he would even listen to her.

"I—I've been having a dream lately," she said in a quiet voice. Laval's head rose, and his eyes blinked as if pulled from a deep sleep. "My vision… It's changing."

Laval swallowed his food and cleared his throat. "Changing, you say?"

Now that she had started, it was rather embarrassing to talk about, but it was too late to turn back. "Every night I would watch him die. It used to be so clear, so consistent. But lately, it's different every time."

"What's different?"

"The way he dies. Sometimes it's a dagger, or a sword, or an aiko's claw. But no matter what, he always dies. What do you think it means?"

Laval shrugged. "The future is hard to predict."

"He still needs our help, you know?"

Laval shook his head. "We've done everything we can."

"We can't just give up," Sihera said, adding some sternness to her voice. "I have to help him."

Laval's voice became hard. "Yes? And how do you intend to do that? Do you know where to find him? Have you commissioned a ship to take you there? Be realistic, Sihera. We lost our chance."

"Well, we have to do something!"

"*We* have to focus on ensuring our own survival now! Look at you. You take for granted the sheltered lifestyle I fight so diligently for us to have. Do you think everyone in Athus has the luxury of a home like this? Are the rest of the Archmagi living so comfortably?"

She couldn't believe what she was hearing. *How can he sit there and talk about creature comforts? The boy might be dying out there!* "But—"

"But nothing!" Laval shouted, slamming the utensil against his plate. The table shook, and Sihera lurched back with a gasp. Laval glared at her with intense fury from across the table. Her eyes turned down to her lap. Her arms were shaking. She clasped one hand over the other to steady them.

Why is Laval acting this way? He had never yelled at her like that before.

He exhaled. When Laval spoke, his voice was stern, but calmer. "Sihera, I'm doing the best I can. Don't you see that?"

Sihera nodded her trembling head.

"I know it's hard to accept, but we have to learn to move on, no matter how badly we wanted that boy's sacrifice."

Sihera's heart stopped, and her body froze. Her vision blurred around the edges as she stared off into nothingness. *What did he say?*

Laval coughed, choking on his food. "No matter how badly we wanted to help that boy, Sihera," he repeated, clearing his throat. "You understand, don't you?"

Her eyes were still locked out in the distance, and her throat was dry, but she managed to push the word past her lips. "Yes." Her voice came out quieter than she expected.

How could she have been so stupid? Had Laval been planning this the whole time? If even Laval—the man who had raised her; her closest friend—was plotting against her Dreamer boy, who did she have left she could trust? A sickening feeling began to twist in her stomach, almost to the point that she thought she might throw up. Her eyes were beginning to water.

She took a breath, blinking as her vision came back into focus. "I'm done with my food. May I be excused?"

"Done?" Laval sounded surprised. "You hardly ate."

"I guess I'm not hungry. I think I might go lie down for a bit."

Laval's voice was slow, almost cautious. "Yes… All right then."

Sihera walked to her bedroom and closed the door behind her. Her head was spinning. She laid down on her bed and cupped her hands over her mouth, feeling the quiver of each warm, trembling breath.

What am I supposed to do now?

The doorknob rattled. With a gasp, she quickly brushed her tears away and faced the door. Laval's shadow stood at the base of her door, unmoving. She listened and waited, expecting him to say something, but after a moment, the shadow simply walked away.

Her brow came together, confused. Laval was acting so strangely; it was almost as if she didn't know him anymore. What was he doing?

Sihera's eyes widened as a chilling thought began to stir in her mind. Slowly, she pulled herself out of bed and glared at the door handle. Her tongue licked unnervingly across her bottom lip as she contemplated. She hated the question racing through her mind but, somehow, she already knew the answer. Sihera reached out and quietly turned the nob. It stopped with a rattle after only half a turn. It was locked.

She knew it. Laval didn't trust her anymore, and it suddenly terrified her to realize how little control she had over her own life.

* * *

Later that night, Sihera lay in her bed, unable to sleep, her mind racing with a mix of emotions. Laval, of course, was sound asleep and snoring in the other room.

As she lay there, Sihera realized she could never protect the boy while she was with Laval. Her eyes widened at the wave of enlightenment that washed over her; like a warm blanket comforting her. Laval wanted to sacrifice the boy to make her an Arcane Bearer, but without her, there would be no reason for him to kill the boy.

She sat upright in her bed. It all came to her in an instant. Her plan was so simple, it was amazing she hadn't thought of it sooner. She would run away, acquire a ship of her own, sail through the Northern Pass, and meet up with her Dreamer boy and the princess before they reached the Origin. It was perfect!

Leaping out of bed, she threw on her Archmagi robe and shoved some extra clothes, coin, and food into a satchel. She paused as she opened her closet, spotting an unfamiliar jacket.

It was long and purple, with a fur trim around the neckline. It was beautiful; nothing like what she was used to wearing. It must have been left there by the previous homeowners. Her hand reached out for it. She knew she shouldn't; Laval would never approve of her wearing something like this.

Her lips pressed together. She snatched the jacket from the closet and pulled it over her shoulders. It fit perfectly, as if it was meant for her. Smiling, she exhaled a pleasant breath. She slung the satchel over her back and headed for the door.

She stopped. That's right, she was locked in her room. She turned to the window and gave it a tug, but it wouldn't open.

Pressing her hand to the chilled glass, she took a moment to glance out the window. The wind blew shrubs back and forth. It looked cold outside. Still, what she wouldn't have given to be out there. It was ironic that someone as skilled in magic as her could be held prisoner by such a thin pane of glass. If she really wanted to, she could tear down this entire wall.

Slowly, Sihera turned her hand and stared down at her palm. Her arm began to tremble as her fingers curled inward. *But what will*

Laval think? Could she do it without him?

Her breathing quickened, and her heart pounded. She peered up at the window again through an angered brow. She could do it. She didn't need him. She didn't need anyone.

The warmth rose in her chest. She let the wave of heat fill and pour over her body. Her muscles flexed. As she sent the heat coursing down into her arm, lightning crackled loudly from her fingertips. A red hue engulfed her sight.

"Sihera?" Laval's voice called from outside her room as the doorknob rattled aggressively. Her eyes shot a vicious stare back at the door, but she focused on maintaining her energy. "Sihera! Stop this! Stop this at once!" he cried as he fumbled with the keys.

The sound of his voice alone made her lips pull back over her teeth. She turned her eyes back toward the feeble pane of glass standing between her and her freedom and, with a loud cry, thrust her hand at the window. An explosion rang out, whipping her hair back and shattering the glass as the window frame was blown out from the wall. The shockwave pushed her back a step.

She panted as the heat subsided, staring through the gaping hole. A rush of cold air circled around her. She closed her eyes and breathed it in, relishing the chilled crispness being pulled into her lungs.

As the air settled, and her eyes opened, a line of streetlamps illuminated the road in front of her. She chuckled, unable restrain her smile. There it was: her path to freedom; her path to her Dreamer boy.

Without a second thought, she leapt through the opening and sprinted down the dark, city street.

23

Old Wounds

Ticahrla sat at her desk in the captain's loge of the *Nahktaio* and rolled out a large map. Using a metal prong, she walked the tool along the marked path. She was rounding the southern tip of the peninsula; only ten days until she reached the Origin.

She removed her father's compass from around her neck and placed it on the tabletop. With a gentle spin, she set the crystal in motion, watching as it slowly came to a halt, the tail end pointing North by Northeast. Good, she was still on course.

At this rate, she would have just enough time to get to the Origin, become an Arcane Bearer, and make it back to Athus before her seventeenth birthday. As long as she didn't run into any more delays, things were looking pretty good. The boy finally seemed to be taking a liking to his training, and he was showing excellent progress. And with the Archmagi left stranded behind her, there was little left that needed to be done. Ticahrla let out a gentle sigh. She was nearly there, and she could finally relax a little.

She sat back in her chair, unsure what to do with herself. The ease was unfamiliar to her. She rolled up the map and refastened the compass around her neck.

Making her way down into the sleeping quarters, she pulled up a stool, sat beside Bakta's hammock and pressed a cool, damp rag to his forehead. Bakta's wound was finally on the mend. However, there was one unexpected side effect.

Bakta's body jerked violently—as it had started to do recently— and Ticahrla retracted her hands. His body shook briefly and then came to rest. Ticahrla grimaced. It pained her to see him suffering, and she knew him well enough to understand what he was struggling with.

Due to his injury, Bakta had spent much of his time unconscious, and—as Bakta was not a Dreamer—his unconscious mind was spared of any dark and depressing thoughts he might have had. But now that he was starting to heal, his awake and sober mind would be free to dwell on the dreadful memories of his past.

Again, Bakta's muscles tightened, and his limbs shook as he wriggled in his partial state of consciousness. Ticahrla looked down at him with empathetic eyes and pressed the rag to his brow, knowing exactly where his mind would take him.

She thought back to the day when she'd first met Bakta.

* * *

Over a year ago, Ticahrla strode through the crowded streets of Teska, a trading hub in the Celara kingdom famous for its underground network of informants. With enough persuasion or coin, one could find information on just about anything in Teska, even where to find dreamers. Drahig—who was a bit smaller back then—was waiting alone on the ship.

It was actually quite nice for her. In Celara, the princess of Athus could roam freely and not be recognized. There were no hard stares, or judgmental glances as she walked amongst the local vendors. She casually perused the merchants when a loud crash rang out in the street.

The door of a nearby building had been kicked open and slammed against the outer wall. As a group of men dragged a beaten and bloodied family out onto the street, very few people seemed to take notice, but Ticahrla's eyes narrowed. The men all wore matching colored leather vests—a local gang. Celara was never known for their military might, which meant gangs were rampant in these parts.

The men chucked the dead bodies of a woman and a young boy to the floor and dragged a skinny man across the ground by his ankle. He was barely conscious, his face bloody and beaten to a pulp, as the gang laid him next to the woman and child. Ticahrla's blood pressure began to rise as she found herself unconsciously moving closer.

The leader of the gang, the man adorned with the most trinkets and piercings to show off his status, jabbed his finger at the beaten man. "Ya got one week, Bakta. And ya better get us that coin."

Bakta didn't respond. He lay there using what little strength he still had to reach out for his wife and child.

The leader signaled to his men. "Get this trash outta my sight."

They picked Bakta up and threw him into a nearby gutter. As they turned to walk away, the group stopped, apparently taken back to find a teenage girl standing defiantly in their path.

Ticahrla's arms were shaking as her hands tightened into white-knuckled fists at her sides. The sight of Bakta reaching for his dead family caused her teeth to clench so tightly that her jaw ached. Her breathing was heavy. She couldn't help it. Her heart pounded, pumping rage through her veins.

"Yeah, whatcha ya lookin' at, girly?" the gang leader called out to her in that stereotypical southern peninsula accent; it was like a mishmash of all dialects combined, yet somehow distinctly its own.

Her eyes turned up to glare at the man in front of her. She took several calming breaths before she spoke. "Tell me," she growled. "Tell me why I shouldn't kill you all."

The man scoffed. There were eight of them and only one of her. "Get outta the way, kid. Ya don't know what ya're talkin' about."

But Ticahrla wasn't about to budge. She dug her metal boot into the mud and slowly unsheathed both of her swords.

The leader watched carefully as she held her blades at her sides. Then he snapped his fingers to signal to one of his men. "Get rid o' this thing."

One man drew a long sword from his waistband as he approached her. "I'ma have fun with this one," said the man with a wicked grin, half-heartedly drawing back his weapon.

With ease, Ticahrla kicked his leg out from underneath the man. As he fell back onto the floor, she drove both blades into his gut.

The man seemed surprised to find himself on the floor. As he looked down at the two swords protruding from his belly, he began to wail uncontrollably. Hearing his cries, Ticahrla took in her first breath of relief, but the satisfaction was short lived. She knew what she really wanted. Glaring furiously at the gang leader in front of her, she pried her weapons from the fallen body and stood ready once more.

The leader stepped back, startled and wide-eyed at first, but he managed to recompose himself rather quickly. "What's wrong with ya, girly? Ya got a death wish o' something?"

"I'm here to make you suffer for what you did to that family."

"I see…" The leader clicked his tongue and stroked his chin, looking her up and down. He pointed his thumb behind him toward Bakta. "Family o' yours?"

Ticahrla shook her head.

"Friend, then?"

She just glared.

"Hold up! Ya don't even know this guy?! Ya *do* know he's a worthless drunk and a gambler who ain't give two shits about his wife and kid 'cause he gambled away everything he had and then some, don't chya?"

Ticahrla glanced at Bakta who still lay in the street. He was apparently becoming conscious enough to realize something was going on around him. Her heart was swaying between the ache she felt for Bakta's family and the hatred she held for this gang of thugs. "Whatever he did, his wife and child didn't deserve that."

"This punk owes us a lot o' coin!"

She turned back to the man shouting in front of her and looked him straight in the eyes. "Not anymore."

The leader narrowed his eyes and cocked his head to the side. "What's your name, girly?"

"Ticahrla."

"Ticahrla, huh?" The leader nodded as he looked her over once more. He learned forward and said in a gentle voice, "Ya sure you wanna do this? I mean, why risk your neck for some loser like him? Huh? Why gut my man like that?"

She glared back and said with a stern voice, "Because I can."

The leader snorted a laugh and shook his head. "You got guts, girly. I hate to do this to ya, but it looks like you're leaving me no choice." He drew his sword, and each of the men behind him followed suit. Lowing himself into a fighting stance, he shrugged his shoulders. "All right, let's do this."

Two men charged full speed at her. Ticahrla ducked under the first swing, cutting out the back of the man's knee, and sliced through the collarbone the second attacker. Having dispensed the first two, she marched forward toward the gang leader.

The leader stabbed his sword straight at her, forcing her to parry and sidestep. The rest of the men were circling around her. There were too many to fight all at once; she had to finish this quickly.

Ticahrla tried to force an offhanded joust at the leader, but he cut his blade down on top of hers, knocking the sword out of her left hand. She winced at the sting that ran through her fingers.

As the leader swung wildly in the front of him, she had to take a few steps back stepped back toward his men. On the next swing, Ticahrla parried the tip of his blade into the dirt and punched the hilt of his sword out of his hand. Now disarmed, the man backpedaled frantically.

Lunging forward, Ticahrla drove the tip of her blade up and under the man's ribcage. As he began to fall back, the whites of his eyes bulging with fear, Ticahrla grabbed him by the collar. With a strained expression, she pulled the man in close to her, driving her blade deeper into his gut.

The man collapsed onto his back with Ticahrla straddled over him, her face so close to his she could feel each of his warm, panicked breaths. A wicked smile carved across her face, relishing the look of agony in his eyes, feeding off the nourishment of his terror.

She didn't have long to revel in her victory. The sound of footsteps came rushing in from behind her. With a subtle glance, she saw the remaining four men charging in.

With her sword buried in the chest of their leader, Ticahrla reached behind her back and pulled out her dagger. She plunged the blade repeatedly into the leader's chest with quick, vicious blows. The man was already defeated, but she had to make him suffer; she needed the rest of his men to see what happened to anyone who was foolish enough to fight her.

The men charging slowed to a stop well outside of striking range, and Ticahrla whipped around to face them. Still crouching on the bloodied body of their leader, she snarled up at them like a rabid dog, her teeth bared, and the man's hot blood dripping down the scowl of her face.

They looked down at the flayed and tortured body of their leader, and then back at the ravenous eyes of his murderer. It wasn't a surprise when the remaining men turned tail and ran.

Ticahrla let out a long, exhausted breath as her arms fell weak at her side. Her limbs were shaking, and her fingers were locked in a tight grip around her dagger, but she could finally breathe a sigh of relief. Wiping the blood from her face, she gingerly pulled herself back up to her feet.

After sheathing her dagger, Ticahrla wrestled to pry her sword from the leader's corpse. The blade came loose, and she stumbled backward a step to retain her footing. Searching the ground around her, she bent over to pick up the sword she had dropped and wiped both blades clean of blood against the length of her gown.

As she holstered her weapons, Ticahrla spotted Bakta still lying in the same spot, his mouth agape as he gawked at her. She walked over and knelt in front of him. From behind his bruised and swollen eyes, Bakta stared up at her in disbelief. His mouth moved as if he was trying to say something.

"Is—is this real?"

Ticahrla looked over at the bodies of his wife and son. If only she had gotten there a little sooner, maybe she could have saved them. She turned back to Bakta and placed a tender hand upon his shoulder.

"Come on," she said in a soft and caring voice. "I'll help you bury your family."

* * *

Ticahrla and Bakta sat in silence at the table of a local tavern, both covered in mud from the burial. Bakta clasped a large mug of ale and stared blankly down at the drink. He hadn't even touched the meal she had bought for him.

"Eat," she said. "You need to regain your strength."

Bakta's voice was barely above a whisper. "What for?"

Ticahrla gave a disgruntled sigh, frustrated to see Bakta so eager to give up on his life. She recalled a quote that had helped her through times of loss and recited it with ease. "Grief is a burden that only someone who has truly loved will ever have to endure. Love is your gift that you shared with this world, a gift that is sorely needed now more than ever. And as much as it may pain you, understand that you must continue spreading it. You owe it to yourself and to others, just as you owe it to those you have lost."

Bakta's head slowly rose from his drink as he stared at her with a baffled, almost aggravated, expression. His voice came out as a high-pitched cry. "What are you?!"

Ticahrla tilted her head, unsure what he meant.

Bakta looked around for a moment with a strained expression, trying to compose his thoughts. As he spoke, the words came spilling out of him. "I mean, you—you're just a *girl!* Yet you are *loaded* with coin. You sit there spouting off, no, *reciting* life lessons like some ancient wise man, all calm and collected. And all of this after doing—doing *that!*" Bakta jabbed his hand out at the dead bodies of the gang members that still lay in the street. "I mean you—you killed those guys li–like–like it was nothing! And why?! You don't know me! You don't owe me anything! What—what was it? What did you say to them? 'Because I can'? *Because I can?!* Are you shitting me?! What does that even mean? Or were you just trying to look like a badass back there?"

Bakta was panting. Ticahrla's eyes remained fixated on him, but a bright smile began to slowly stretch across her face. She was happy to see some life return to Bakta, and his manic personality nearly made her laugh.

She glanced down at the table, still smiling, as she thought to herself. Then she turned back up to look at him. "I felt…obligated," she tried to explain, but Bakta clearly didn't understand. So, she went on. "I said, 'Because I can' because I knew there was something I could do to help you. And if I *could* do something to help, then it would have been wrong for me not to."

Bakta glared at her. "You know…I really hate how, in a crazy kind of way, that almost makes sense."

Ticahrla and Bakta chuckled together. She enjoyed his sense of humor.

His jaw opened and closed a few times, as if struggling to find the right words. "How old are you?" he eventually asked.

Ticahrla's smile faded slightly, and she pulled back her shoulders. "I'm fifteen."

"Well, I'm thirty-four, and when I saw you gut those men back there, I thought you were about as psychotic as they were."

Ticahrla's brow pulled together slightly. Bakta must have noticed because he held up a finger to stop her before he finished speaking.

"And even though you may be the single most insane person I have ever met…" Then his voice turned soft and comforting. "Somehow, you are also the most genuine." Bakta grabbed a utensil and stabbed a piece of food. Then he turned to her and smiled. "You're a good person, Ticahrla. Thank you."

Ticahrla nodded and smiled back.

* * *

Back on the *Nahktaio*, Ticahrla flipped the cool rag over and pressed it to Bakta's forehead again. A somber smile stretched thin across her face.

She remembered how hard it had been for Bakta to go on after losing his family. A short time later, Bakta had joined Ticahrla and Drahig on her search for the Origin. She still wasn't sure why he had accepted her offer to become part of her crew. Maybe, on some level, he believed in what she was fighting for, too.

Of course, following her and Drahig across the world could never get rid of the constant pain he felt, but perhaps it was enough of a distraction. Maybe it gave him a purpose—a reason to get out of bed each day.

If Bakta had been a drunk before his wife and son died, then he had become doubly so after. He managed to stumble his way through life as a high-functioning alcoholic. There wasn't a waking moment when he didn't have some form of drink in his hand, but Ticahrla allowed it because she knew it was the only thing that got him through the day—the only thing that gave him some resemblance of peace.

Sure, life with her was more violent than Bakta was used to. She never hesitated to stand up for what was righteous and moral, and she was unapologetic about the brutality of her ways. She understood why it was a little hard for Bakta to get used to it at first, but after a while, he stopped questioning all-together if what she was doing was right or wrong.

Again, Bakta's body lurched and squirmed in his semi-conscious state. She leaned over him and pressed her palms to his chest, trying her best to hold him down. He hadn't had a drop of alcohol for weeks now. She knew his mind and body were begging for release—begging for the emptiness of sleep or the deadened nerves of alcohol so he could escape his tormented memories—but a body can only remain asleep or numb for so long. Eventually, the agony always returns.

Bakta gasped as his eyes shot open, and his fingers latched tightly around her arm.

"Ale," Bakta said in a coarse voice. His bulging eyes searched frantically around the room.

Ticahrla shook her head. "You need to rest."

"*Ale!*" he repeated desperately.

"You haven't fully recovered. You shouldn't be drinking—"

Bakta reached up, grabbed her by the collar, and pulled her face in close to his. She saw the look in his tear-filled eyes. It wasn't anger. It was desperation; it was pain. "Get me some damn drink, you wicked girl," he said through gritted teeth.

Ticahrla stubbornly pursed her lips, but her eyes were sympathetic. She stared back at him for a long while, neither one of them saying a word. She knew she shouldn't. His health was close to failing him. Eventually, though, she gave in and nodded.

Bakta released his grip and let out an agonizing groan as he collapsed back onto his hammock. Ticahrla hurried out of the room to gather some ale.

* * *

The next morning, Bakta had finally regained enough strength to pull himself out of bed. Ticahrla watched him hobble across the deck and slowly make his way up to the helm where she was waiting.

Bakta carefully pulled himself up the stairs, his head down, focusing intently on each step. He glanced up at her and smiled, almost a chuckle, as he struggled with such a simple task. It made her smile to see him acting himself again.

Bakta stopped by her side as they stood together, looking out at the vast, empty ocean in front of them. He rested his hand lightly on her forearm. "I'm sorry for—for grabbing you. And for speaking to you like that."

She patted the back of his hand and nodded, letting him know she understood.

Later that day, over supper, everyone was excited to see Bakta back on his feet. As they ate together in the dining quarter, Jokahn told Bakta all about the adventures he had missed out on—about the aiko, the ergmen, and the warship. He even told him about the couple they had protected.

"I believe it," Bakta smiled and nodded at her. "Ticahrla always has been the right hand of justice."

She grinned warmly, appreciating the flattery they were unnecessarily doting upon her, but the truth was Jokahn had done his fair share as well. "Don't be so modest," she said, reaching across the table and shaking the boy by his shoulder. "Tell him what you did."

Jokahn blushed and beamed a bright smile. "Well, Ticahrla did most of it, but I came in and I tackled this guy, just like she taught me…"

As Jokahn recounted the tale with enthusiasm, Ticahrla caught the glimpse of Bakta's once pleasant smile slowly fading. Jokahn's voice gradually became muffled and faded into the background as she watched the subtle shift in Bakta's expressions. His gaze turned to meet hers.

Her head tilted to the side. The dead stare in Bakta's eyes was unsettling, and it caused a nauseating churn in her stomach. Bakta turned his attention back to the boy and feigned a smile.

Ticahrla grimaced. *What was that about?* She pushed the thought from her mind and turned her focus back to the boy.

"Well, that was the gist of it anyway," Jokahn said in a pleasant tone as he concluded his story. "Like I said, Ticahrla did most of it."

"Hmm…" She gave an exaggerated expression as she playfully mused with herself. "I guess you were right after all."

"What?" asked Jokahn.

She pointed a finger back at herself and gave the boy a cocky grin. "Best thing that ever happened to you, am I right?"

Jokahn shook his head and chuckled, rolling his eyes at her. Everyone except Bakta laughed.

After their meal, they all headed outside for some fresh air. As Drahig and Jokahn made their way upstairs to the deck, Bakta called out from behind her. "Ticahrla, can I speak to you for a moment?"

As she turned, she could see something was still troubling him. "Sure. What is it?" she asked.

Bakta pondered for a moment. Then he looked up at her, his mouth agape, and shrugged his shoulders. "How do you do it?" he asked.

She squinted her eyes and tilted her head. "What do you mean?"

"How can you laugh and joke with a boy you are going to murder in a few days?"

A twinge ran through her. It suddenly felt as if something was lodged in her throat. She quickly swallowed down the unsettling emotion, but as a horrified expression spread across Bakta's face, she knew he had caught the faint sign of conflict within her.

Bakta's eyes grew wide, but his voice was calm. "You can't do it, can you?"

She scoffed, almost a laugh, as she waved away Bakta's concern. "Oh, please. He's just some worthless boy." But despite her facade, a panic of insecurity was building up inside her.

Bakta apparently wasn't fooled either. "Are you sure about that?"

In an instant, the rage boiled up inside her—insulted for reasons even she didn't fully understand—and she doubled down with fervor. "How *dare* you question if I have the muster to do what needs to be done!" She spoke in an aggressive tone but made sure her voice wasn't loud enough to carry far. "I would do anything for Athus! And I will destroy that boy in an instant if it gives me even the most miniscule chance of becoming an Arcane Bearer!" With that, she shoved her way past Bakta and stormed off down the hall.

Ticahrla paced in tight circles within the confines of the sleeping quarters, grumbling to herself. "Idiotic drunk. What does he know?" But a lingering fear lurked in the back of her mind. What if Bakta was right? Had she grown too attached to Jokahn? What if she couldn't bring herself to kill him?

No. This is too important. She had to become an Arcane Bearer. She couldn't return to Athus empty-handed again. Everyone was counting on her. She needed that power to rid Athus of the council's tyranny and injustice. She needed it to prove to herself she was worthy of ruling.

Ticahrla planted her feet and exhaled, reaffirming her decision. "I *will* kill him."

* * *

The next day, Ticahrla stood at the helm, watching Jokahn practicing his techniques in the middle of the deck, when she heard

Baka slowly clomping his way up the stairs. She frowned, not wanting to deal with his meddling worries.

"You have to tell me how you do it," he insisted as he stood beside her.

She groaned. "Not this again."

"You have to tell me. It's killing me."

Baka's face looked in pain. She sighed, empathizing with him. "I know how you feel, Bakta."

He raised an eyebrow at her. "You do?"

"Of course, I do. Trust me, this decision has been brutal on me as well."

Bakta let out an enormous sigh of relief and smiled. "I can't tell you how good that makes me feel. I thought I was going crazy. I thought—"

She stopped him before he could ramble on. "*But*…the simple truth is that there is no other way." Bakta's smile slowly faded as she continued. "I don't want to kill Jokahn. I love the little bastard, I really do. But I didn't make the rules, Bakta. And I *need* to become an Arcane Bearer. *Athus* needs me to." Ticahrla shrugged her shoulders and looked deep into Bakta's eyes with care and compassion. "Sometimes…sacrifices have to be made."

"Ticahrla…" Bakta frowned, shaking his head. Seeing the hesitation in Bakta caused her caring expression to fade. "Ticahrla, you know I've always backed you. I've never questioned your methods, no matter how brutal or bloody, because I knew deep down inside me that you wouldn't do something if even for a second you thought it wasn't right." As Bakta continued, the rage began to simmer inside her. "And *I know* with you as an Arcane Bearer, you could change the world for the better. But…I don't know…" Bakta let out a sigh. "The thought of killing Jokahn just doesn't feel…all that righteous anymore."

"That's enough, Bakta!" Ticahrla roared, her voice turning dark. Bakta leapt back at her sudden outburst. "It has to be done! We've come too far. I can't turn back now. I've sacrificed too, you know!"

Bakta leaned far back with fear in his eyes. His words came out as a whisper. "You're obsessed."

Her head was throbbing from this annoying little man. She didn't want to listen to his ramblings anymore. "And you're an idiot," she said, massaging her forehead.

Bakta's voice was cautious as he spoke. "What happens, Ticahrla? What happens when someone as powerful as you becomes driven by greed instead of righteous duty?"

"Just shut up," she groaned, shoving Bakta with her shoulder and storming past him.

24

A Glimpse Inside

Jokahn sat in the dining quarter quietly eating his dinner as he watched Bakta groan and grumble to himself. Ticahrla and Bakta must have had an argument because the two refused to eat in the same room or talk to each other. Whatever had happened, it appeared Bakta was having a harder time dealing with it, so Jokahn thought he would keep him company.

As Bakta took another swig of ale, Jokahn looked curiously at the wooden cup. "Why do you always carry that same old mug around?"

Bakta paused. He chuckled, and his cheeks turned red as he lowered his eyes. "I hadn't realized a mug of ale had become my trademark." He sighed, setting the drink on the table and gazing at it. "I suppose when you get to be my age, and you've been through some nasty things you'd rather forget about, sometimes it's easier to wash those memories away with a bit of ale." Bakta's mouth twisted. "Actually, it's always easier that way." Bakta strained to press his lips together into a thin smile, but the tears were swelling in his eyes.

"I'm sorry," Jokahn said in a heartfelt tone. "I didn't mean to pry."

Bakta shrugged. "Meh, that's life, you know?"

"Yeah," Jokahn said, turning his eyes down. He knew. He knew all too well. "I remember, back in Anchorsfell, I didn't have anyone. I mean, there was a town full of people there, and not one of them cared if I lived or died. But you know what?" He looked up at Bakta and smiled. "Everything turns out all right in the end."

Bakta's eyebrows raised as he stared at him. "How do you do it, Jokahn? What makes *you* happy?"

Jokahn frowned. "I don't know. I never thought about it." He didn't have to think for long. He knew what made him happy. Just the thought of her glorious smile was enough to light up his face. "Being here, training with Ticahrla, helping Drahig with chores, and playing chips with you. I think that's what makes me happy."

Jokahn thought his encouraging words would make Bakta feel better, but the man appeared more dead inside than ever.

Bakta looked down at his ale with sullen eyes. "I'm afraid, Jokahn," he said in a low voice.

"Afraid of what?"

"I'm afraid that, someday, no amount of alcohol is going to be enough to save me."

The unexpected sound of trickling water caused Jokahn and Bakta to pause and exchange puzzled glances.

"Ah, shit…" Bakta said looking down under the table. "I think I've pissed myself."

Jokahn leaned his head under the table, but what he saw wasn't at all what Bakta thought it was. A leak had sprung in the ship's hull and a jet of sea water was streaming in.

"Welp, that's not good," said Bakta.

Jokahn and Bakta raced upstairs to get Ticahrla and Drahig. They all hurried back down into the hallway to peer into the dining quarter.

"Shit!" Ticahrla reared back, squeezing her fists tightly against her temples. "Damn it! This is the last thing I need right now."

Jokahn looked up at her as she started pacing angrily back and forth.

She turned to Bakta. "All right, what do you need to do to patch it up?"

Bakta gave an intoxicated snort. "Patch it up? That's a hull leak. You have to dock this girl and pull the whole thing out of the water."

"You're joking, right?"

"Afraid not."

Ticahrla put her hands on her hips and let out a long and frustrated sigh. "Fine. We'll stop at the nearest port. Until then, do what you can to plug that hole."

"Yes, ma'am," Bakta saluted mockingly.

* * *

A few hours later, the *Nahktaio* was sitting in a drydock in a place called Prixia, a vibrant city in the Olthar kingdom. Even well into the night, buildings and streets were illuminated with colorful lanterns, and people bustled about. The piers were packed tightly with fine oak buildings, providing all matters of recreation: lavish taverns, gambling dens, fight clubs, and performers. The trill of music and cheers filled the air from all directions. The entire city was like one large party. A grin stretched across Jokahn's face. Finally, a place he might enjoy.

Jokahn watched as Ticahrla paid the mechanic to begin his repairs, then they started off into the city.

"Ah, miss," the mechanic called out to Ticahrla. They all stopped and turned toward the man. "I'll repair your ship for you, but that one's going to have to stay on board." He pointed at Drahig. "People here are not as welcoming to certain creatures as I am." Everyone turned to look at Drahig.

"Why don't you stay on the ship, Drahig," instructed Ticahrla. "We won't be long."

Drahig's head pulled back slightly in his confusion.

"Don't worry, big guy," Bakta said encouragingly. "I'll bring you back something good to eat."

Drahig seemed reluctant at first, but he did as he was told and went back to the ship.

Jokahn didn't understand. "Why can't Drahig come with us?" he asked Ticahrla.

As they approached the nearest tavern, Ticahrla pointed to a sign hung next to the entrance that read, *Humans Only*. "Not all cultures are as accepting as others."

Jokahn stared curiously up at the placard. *Why would anyone not want Drahig?* He was the gentlest creature Jokahn had ever met.

As Ticahrla, Jokahn, and Bakta entered the tavern, it reminded

Jokahn of the taverns back in Anchorsfell, although this one was much cleaner and more refined. Everything from the tables to the decor had a polished finish.

"Grab me a warm meal, Bakta," instructed Ticahrla. Then she let out an exhausted sigh and slumped her shoulders forward. "I'm going to find us a table."

Bakta nodded as Ticahrla headed toward the back of the tavern. "Come on, Jokahn." Bakta gave him a solid pat on his back. "Let me show you how to order a proper ale."

Jokahn smiled up at him as they made their way to the bar, happy to see that Bakta was beginning to act like his pleasant self again.

It was a welcome change for Jokahn not to feel as though he had to hide himself when walking through a tavern. He had spent so many years of his life stealing from people. It was exciting to be a customer for once.

Bakta approached the bar and surveyed the alcohol that was displayed aesthetically on the back wall.

"Fancy gig you got here," Bakta said to the man behind the counter.

"I appreciate that," said the barman. "What can I get you?"

As Bakta placed his order, Jokahn was looking around the lavish room when a girl with long, golden hair caught his gaze. There was something different about her, something strange. She was smiling at him. He tilted his head to one side, perplexed.

The girl sat at her table, fidgeting, running her fingers through her hair.

What is she doing? He didn't understand any of it. Jokahn chuckled and smiled back at her.

The girl's cheeks flushed bright red, and she dropped her gaze to the floor.

"Careful, kid," Bakta said as he placed a hand on Jokahn's shoulder. "Lust can be a dangerous—" His words trailed off as his gaze fell on the blonde girl. "Wow, what are they putting in the water over here?"

Jokahn looked up at him in confusion.

Bakta shook his head, "I gotta get out of here," he said, searching for the exit. "Good luck, Jokahn. You are on your own now." Bakta hurried toward the door.

Jokahn sat up straight. "What? What about the food?"

"Just wait for the barman to get it for you. I've got everything *I* need right here," he said holding up an ale. "I'll see you around, kid." Then he exited the tavern.

Jokahn laughed at the way Bakta had scuttled away in a hurry. He never quite understood Bakta's quirky nature, but the man always managed to make him laugh.

Jokahn continued to glance around the tavern. At a table in the back of the room, sitting poised and beautiful as ever, was Ticahrla. Jokahn smiled warmly as he looked at her. Her eyes were carefully panning across the faces of each person in the room until her gaze met Jokahn's.

She paused, sitting up slightly, apparently surprised to find him staring back at her. Jokahn smiled and waved. Ticahrla chuckled, shaking her head, and smiled back at him with a coy grin. With a cool calmness only she seemed to possess, Ticahrla leaned back and rested her arms across the top of the bench. Then, with a subtle raise of her hand, she lifted two fingers to wave back at him.

Jokahn's heart melted as he nearly fell back off the bar stool.

Again, Ticahrla let out a chuckle. She mouthed to him, "You are so odd."

Suddenly, Ticahrla's face turned hard as her eyes shifted to Jokahn's left.

"Hey, boy," a man said beside him.

Jokahn looked up to see four angry men dressed in finely tailored coats approaching him. Uncertain what they wanted, Jokahn looked to Ticahrla for help. She had started to rise from her seat but paused. She stood there—half sitting, half standing—and then gave Jokahn a stern glare as she sat herself back down.

"Hey, I'm talking to you!" the man said as he gave Jokahn a shove. It took him by surprise, and Jokahn struggled to keep his footing as he stumbled off the stool.

Jokahn turned to face the man who had pushed him. He was well dressed and obviously wealthy, but rather thinly framed for an adult. The man stood and jutted his chin out at Jokahn with a snide and disapproving attitude.

"That's a nice shirt," the man said as his group of friends circled in around Jokahn.

Jokahn glanced down at the clothes the queen had made for him. "Thanks…" Jokahn said cautiously.

"Where did you get it?" asked the man.

"It was a gift," Jokahn replied honestly.

The man's voice was low as he clicked his tongue and glanced disgustingly up and down at Jokahn. "Yeah, I bet it was." Then the man took a small but assertive step toward Jokahn. "I think it's about time you left," said the man in a firm tone.

Jokahn looked up at the man in confusion. "What?" He couldn't understand what the man was talking about, but it wasn't pleasant. "Listen, I'm just waiting for my food. Even an idiot can see that, right?"

The man's head reared back in shock, his voice quiet. "What did you say to me?"

Jokahn shook his head. "That came out wrong. What I meant was—"

The man's eyes turned livid. Taking one step closer and forcing Jokahn backward, the man shouted, "Take your shit and get out of here!"

Jokahn's face sank, and he leaned away from the aggressive closeness of the man's posture. He'd done it again. Jokahn looked over at Ticahrla who still sat at her table with a stern expression on her face. She gave a quick nod toward the man and then stared fiercely at Jokahn, as if to say, "Don't look at me, look at him!"

"Now you listen to me, boy. You aren't fooling anyone. We all know you stole those clothes. So just get out of here before I stop feeling so nice and have you arrested."

Stole?! I didn't steal anything! "I didn't—"

"I said move it, thief!" The man shoved Jokahn hard.

Jokahn's back slammed against the countertop. It hurt. He fell to his hands and knees on the floor and winced in pain. He couldn't understand why any of this was happening. Even wearing nice clothing apparently couldn't hide the fact that he was nothing more than a petty thief. Was it that obvious? What was it that gave him away? The way he carried himself? The way he spoke? How was he so easily singled out from the crowd like that?

Jokahn's eyes began to water. His breathing grew heavy as he started to weep on the floor.

The man scoffed. "See, they're all the same. Pathetic, low-class pieces of shit." A rage stirred inside Jokahn, and his hands tightened into fists. The man continued in a low, disgusted tone. "Nothing ever changes."

As the man reached down and grabbed him by the collar, Jokahn clasped the man by his fingers and twisted them backward. The man reared up and cried out in the agony.

One of the men drew back his fist and punched Jokahn across the jaw. Jokahn's grip gave out as he fell to the floor. Another man reached down and rolled Jokahn onto his back, pinning him to the ground.

The side of his face was throbbing, and he struggled to wrench his way out from under the man's weight, but he was stuck.

The man Jokahn had grabbed was massaging his hand as he stood angrily over him. "Oh, now you're going to get it, you pathetic little pipsqueak." Then he bent over, grabbed Jokahn by the shirt, and cocked his fist back into the air.

"*Hey!*" Ticahrla's booming voice rang out from across the room. The entire tavern came to a halt, and the man paused with his fist held high. Everyone's gaze turned toward Ticahrla. "You want to talk about pathetic?!" Ticahrla shouted as she marched aggressively across the room. "Why don't you try looking in the mirror for once!"

As Ticahrla approached the group of men, they released Jokahn. He slumped back onto his elbows as he watched the men stand up tall to face the enraged girl.

"Who's this bitch?!" The man pointed a finger at Ticahrla as she stormed angrily towards him, stopping right in his face.

"I'm the bitch who's about to break your nose in if you lay another hand on that boy."

The man was suddenly at a loss for words. He leaned back, pressing himself up against the bar.

"You disgust me," Ticahrla growled. "Never before in my life have I seen such a cluster fuck of privileged, overgrown children more devoid of a spine. Look at you!" The men glanced cautiously back and forth at each other. "Is this what you do to feel good about yourself? Take your frustrations out on those smaller and weaker than you?"

"What, you're sticking up for this piece of scum?" the man finally said, shocked as he pointed down at Jokahn.

"He's not scum! And he's no thief either! I gave him the clothes, you half-witted moron!"

The man leaned back far away from Ticahrla's aggressive posture, and his anger quickly diminished. His body—now pinned between Ticahrla and the counter—surrendered, raising his hands in the air. "Hey, how was I supposed to know? I thought he stole it. I was just trying to do the right thing—"

"You were just trying to do the only thing that gives you the complete misconception of being a man. I swear, I would bash my heel into your jaw right now, but a piece of shit like you isn't worthy enough to lick the stink from my boot."

"I—I'm sorry!" exclaimed the man.

Jokahn looked up as he watched the once confident man shrink and cower beneath Ticahrla.

"Don't apologize to me, you imbecile! Apologize to him!" Ticahrla said, grabbing the man by the collar and jabbing a finger down at Jokahn.

The man looked down at him. "I'm sorry."

Ticahrla pulled the man's face in close to hers, and he tried desperately to turn away his gaze.

She stood there, watching the man cower until—apparently content with the way he now submitted before her—the anger in her face subsided. Her grip loosened around his collar. With a warm yet somber expression, she extended her hand to Jokahn.

Jokahn looked around the tavern. All eyes were fixed on him, their wide and judgmental stares piercing through him. He cringed and his head sank between his shoulders. He was so embarrassed. *Why are they all staring at me?* Tears were swelling in his eyes, and his breathing was growing manic. He couldn't take it anymore.

Jokahn batted Ticahrla's hand away and scurried to his feet, hiding his face in shame as he sprinted toward the back exit. He plowed through the door with his shoulder and stumbled out into the cold, dark alleyway behind the tavern.

He wanted to run and keep on running, but his heart had given out. His legs slowed to a stop and his shoulder leaned up against the outside wall of the tavern. He couldn't stand it. Why did he have to be such a worthless lowlife? Why was she so perfect?!

"Are you all right?" her gentle tone asked from behind him.

Jokahn clamped his eyes shut. Just hearing her voice made his chest ache. He was breathing hard. His sobs made it hard for him to speak. He didn't want to face her. "Why am I such a coward?" he whimpered. "Why can't I be like you?"

"Don't be ridiculous," Ticahrla said in a confident, upbeat tone. "You did great in there. You stood up to that bully, and you should be proud of yourself. That idiot is just lucky he had his friends, otherwise you would have mopped the floor with that scrawny punk." Ticahrla laughed encouragingly, but he didn't feel like laughing. He felt awful. He stood there with his head hung low, trying to breathe between sobs. Ticahrla's laughter subsided.

Jokahn couldn't stand to have her see him like this. The night had been embarrassing enough already. He didn't want her to see him cry. "I have to go," he said as he pushed himself off the wall and started walking around the corner of the back alley.

"Wait," she cried.

Jokahn stopped, and he turned to look over his shoulder at her. Her face was strained, and her arm was outstretched toward him, as if trying to command him to stop. Ticahrla lowered her hand and rubbed her forearm anxiously.

"Listen to me, Jokahn," she said, her voice calm, almost intentionally steady. "I know it hurts right now, but I need you to understand that there's something special about you—something great that I…that I can't even begin to explain."

Jokahn's brow raised. He could see water beginning to swell in her eyes, but her voice remained strong.

"You are so much more than you think you are. You might not see it yet, but believe me when I say, one of these days everyone is going to realize just how amazing you truly are. And when that day comes, I hope with all my heart that I'm there with you, giving you a wink and a smile, just so I can say I told you so."

Jokahn was surprised to find himself gasping for breath as tears ran down his face. Wiping the blurriness from his eyes and the snot from his nose, he was amazed to feel his spirits rise again.

How does she do that? How did she know just what to say to make him feel better? Ticahrla was the only person he knew who could pick someone up or tear them down with nothing but her words.

Still breathing hard, Jokahn felt a joyful relief spreading over him, and he smiled at her. Apparently, that was the expression she was striving for, and she gave a weary smile back.

Thank you, Ticahrla. He nodded gratefully at her, then quietly made his way around the corner, and left.

* * *

As Jokahn walked out of view, Ticahrla thought she should have felt better about herself, but instead she found herself left with an uneasy twinge in her stomach. Why had she said that to him? Was it a lie? She didn't think it was. And yet, at the same time, why would she care? The conflict inside of her was growing. She realized she was starting to do more than just like Jokahn for his company. She genuinely cared for him.

Her heart had ached at just the sight of him crying. How was she supposed to sacrifice him now? And yet, she knew she had no other choice. In a few days, she knew she would have to kill him. Ticahrla sighed and dragged her hand across her mouth.

I can do this, she assured herself. But even as she thought the words, she could not deny the doubt she felt.

Slowly, she stumbled her way back into the tavern—almost in a daze—confused by her actions to stand up for the boy. As she entered, a crowd of people circled around her and cheered. Ticahrla was taken aback and glared harshly at the unexpected attention. She took a quick glance around the room. The group of men who had bullied Jokahn were gone.

People came up from every angle to shake her hand and pat her on the back.

"Well done," said one man.

"You're a good person, you are," said a woman.

A young man approached Ticahrla with a wide grin. "A fine show, miss. That boy is lucky to have someone like you."

Ticahrla stopped abruptly and turned to the young man. "What?" she said in a low voice, almost a growl. "What did you say?"

The young man appeared shocked by the sternness in her voice and took a small step backward. "Wha—well I—I've never seen someone dish out a lashing like that in my life," he said with a nervous chuckle. "You must really care for that boy. Who is he to you? A close friend? Family?"

Ticahrla's breathing grew faster, and her eyes shifted back and forth as she stared at the floor. The people surrounding her suddenly made her feel constrained and claustrophobic. "I have to go," she said as she pushed her way through the cheering crowd and hurried out of the tavern.

* * *

Jokahn meandered through the streets, walking slowly and in no particular direction. *I am a coward,* he realized. He hated being a coward, but no matter how hard he tried, he felt helpless to change

195

it. Why was it so hard to stand up for himself? Why was he still running away all the time? Why couldn't he be strong and confident like Ticahrla?

"Jokahn?" a man's voice called out over the crowd. Jokahn's head rose. "Over here," Bakta called again, waving at him. Jokahn's heart sank. He didn't want Bakta to see him like this.

As Bakta walked over, Jokahn tried to brush the tears away in a hurry, but his eyes were still red and swollen.

"Jokahn, what's the matter?" asked Bakta.

Jokahn wondered if Bakta would understand his plight. He wasn't sure, but he had no one else to turn to. Right there, in middle of the street, Jokahn recanted the terrible events that had occurred after Bakta left. Bakta's face crumpled.

"Why, Bakta? Why can't I be more like Ticahrla? She always knows what to say and what to do. She never makes a mistake. She's perfect."

Bakta chuckled. "Cheer up, kid. She's far from perfect."

Jokahn rolled his eyes, knowing Bakta was only lying to try to make him feel better.

"Trust me, she's human just like the rest of us," assured Bakta. "I understand, you went through a rough spot today. And where you failed, she succeeded. But don't feel bad about it. Nobody gets things right on the first try. Why, look at me," he said with a chuckle. "I've been wanting to quit drinking, and here I am with another ale in my hand."

Jokahn's frown flattened his lips into a line, unimpressed with Bakta's attempt at a motivational speech.

Bakta continued, "What I'm trying to say is everyone deals with failures in life, and that's a good thing. Ticahrla's success tonight was only because she had failed at that same thing many times before until, finally, she started getting it right. But you weren't around to experience all those failures with her. You only got to see the end result. You know, my pap used to tell me, 'Learn from your failures, because—" Bakta's speech slowed as he glanced down at his mug. "—because you have only truly failed when you stop trying.'"

Jokahn's brow raised a little. He hadn't expected anything profound to actually come from Bakta of all people, but what he said started to make sense. A gentle smile grew across Jokahn's face. "Thanks, Bakta. That helps."

"No…thank you, kid." Bakta said, slowly pouring the remainder of his ale out onto the ground.

* * *

As Bakta and Jokahn made their way back to the *Nahktaio*, Ticahrla continued to lumber through the city streets. Her head was spinning. What was she supposed to do now? It was becoming clear to her she was never going to be able to kill Jokahn. She had grown too attached to the boy. She should never have gotten so involved. She should have found the Origin, killed Jokahn, and gotten it over with.

What was I thinking?! she scolded herself. Ticahrla's face crumpled in frustration as she dug her fingers into her skull. *Ugh! I'm such a weakling!*

Her arms fell loose at her sides. Bakta was right. Killing Jokahn was the wrong thing to do. She couldn't lie to herself anymore.

She let out a long breath. *What am I going to do now?* There wasn't any other choice really. Her birthday was just a few weeks away. For her mother, for her people, she had to go back to Athus.

Ticahrla pulled the necklace out from around her neck and looked down at the compass. "I'm sorry, Father," her voice quivered. "I almost had it."

* * *

Ticahrla meandered back to her ship, feeling more depressed and disheartened than ever. As she returned, Jokahn came running down to the docks to greet her.

"Hey, Ticahrla," he welcomed her with an uplifting tone.

Ticahrla frowned at his cheerful expression, annoyed to see him in a better mood than she was. She didn't want to be bothered by anyone at the moment. She just wanted to check the repairs and be on her way—back out on the open ocean, headed for Athus.

She turned away from him and began examining her ship. It looked like the repairs were complete. The dry dock had been filled and the ship appeared ready to sail.

Jokahn seemed to pick up on her mood. This time when he spoke, his voice was a bit more reserved. "I—I didn't get a chance to say thanks for…well, for what you said earlier."

She didn't look at him. She just rolled her eyes.

He continued. "I just wanted you to know, it meant a lot to me, and I appreciate it."

"Listen, Jokahn, there's something I need to talk to you about." She turned around to face him, but as she did, she noticed movement behind him. Ticahrla paused, and her eyes narrowed as a pair of deep-set black eyes stared intently back at her from beneath the ocean's surface. A deep breath pulled into her lungs as the dread overtook her.

Apparently seeing the shift of emotions on her face, the aiko's claw extended upward out of the water.

"Get back!" Ticahrla cried, pulling Jokahn behind her as she drew her sword and shuffled backward across the dock.

The aiko pulled itself up onto the dock and sat there, hunched over with one leg still in the water, just staring at her. And there it stayed.

Her muscles were tense, and her weapon ready. She glared at the aiko. *What is it doing? Why is it just sitting there?*

Finally, the aiko rose. Pulling the last of its body from the water, it stood up tall, water dripping off its body and pooling on the wooden planks beneath it. She had forgotten how tall an aiko was when standing upright.

The creature didn't appear to be aggressive. Was this some sort of trap? A ploy to lure her in? That was when she noticed a large scar running across the aiko's left eye.

She gasped, and her words came out almost as a whisper. "That's impossible…" Ticahrla looked closer at the aiko's chest and saw the wound she had made weeks ago. Two more aiko pulled themselves out of the water and stood beside the first.

How did they follow me all this way? Not only that, *why* had they followed her? And why show themselves now? If the creatures wanted to attack, they would have had the perfect opportunity to ambush her and Jokahn earlier, but they didn't.

"Oh shit!" Bakta's voice called out from aboard the *Nahktaio*. Everyone's eyes turned toward him. "Drahig, get down here now!"

"*No!*" Ticahrla commanded. "No, everyone stay where you are." She leaned her head over her shoulder, and whispered to Jokahn, "Stay close to me."

Jokahn nodded nervously.

Ticahrla moved in a large arc around the aiko. The creatures didn't budge except to turn where they stood as she and Jokahn made their way up the ramp, and onto the *Nahktaio*.

"Get us out of here, Drahig," Ticahrla ordered as she sheathed her weapon and stood at the railing. The creatures remained on the dock as the *Nahktaio* drifted slowly away from the pier.

"What was that about?" asked Bakta.

Ticahrla stared back at the creatures with stern gaze as they gradually shrank into the distance. "I have no idea."

The jolt of a boy's laughter startled her. She turned angrily to see Jokahn chuckling beside her, a brilliant smile on his face. "How are so you happy at a time like this?"

Jokahn shrugged. "We're together and we're alive. What's there not to be happy about?"

Ticahrla frowned, and her brow pulled together in frustration. "You're an idiot," she said, shaking her head as she stormed away.

25

Streets of Athus

Sihera had spent three days living on the street and was no closer to finding a ship to take her through the Northern Pass. She had tried to convince captains and crewmen to let her sail with them—or even to stow her on board—but lacked enough coin to convince anyone. Things were not going at all like she had planned.

She grimaced as she made her way through the market district, where the normally civil people of Athus turned short-tempered and irritable. Leaning her back against a wall and sliding down to the floor, exhausted, she rested for a moment.

Sihera hadn't bathed since she ran away. Her hair was twisted into knots, her clothes were filthy, and her stomach was tight and protesting in hunger. She pulled open her satchel and grabbed one of the few remaining snacks she had packed away.

As she nibbled on the tiny morsel, merchants dished out plates of fried fish. Her dry lips parted as the tantalizing aromas circled around her. The thought of purchasing some fish had crossed her mind, but she needed all the coin she could get for more important things like travel.

Swallowing the last scrap of food, Sihera leaned her head against the wall and let out a disheartened sigh. This was so much harder than she had anticipated. A part of her wanted to give up and turn back. Perhaps Laval wouldn't be too upset, although she did put a hole in her bedroom wall.

No, she couldn't give up. She had to find her Dreamer boy. With a grunt, she forced herself back onto her feet and marched forward through the crowded streets.

* * *

It was now nearly noon, and Sihera had managed to escape the market district onto the more peaceful streets of the residential area.

Sihera waved down a woman passing by. "Excuse me, can you tell me where the dockyard is?"

The woman snickered lightly. "You're a ways away if you're trying to get to the docks."

Sihera's shoulders drooped forward, cringing as she surveyed her surroundings. How was it possible to get so lost in one city?

The woman looked down at her with a heartfelt expression. "To get to the docks, you will want to go back the way you came. Keep going until you reach the courtyard. You'll see the palace on your left. Take a right and follow the main trade road to the harbor. If you get lost, just keep going southeast and you'll reach the docks."

Sihera squinted, signing with her hands as she tried to memorize the directions. "Courtyard… Palace on my left… Follow the trade road southeast…" *What's a trade road?*

"Would you like someone to go with you?"

Sihera was trying to keep a low profile; Laval's men were undoubtably looking for her. "No, I think I got it. Thank you." She headed back the way she had come.

"Good luck," the woman called.

Find the courtyard. Find the courtyard, she repeated to herself.

She walked for a long while feeling more lost with every passing minute, until she spotted a familiar sight.

"The palace!" she cheered. But it was on her right. Wasn't the palace supposed to be on the left? Maybe the palace was supposed to be on the right and the courtyard on the left. Wait, where was the courtyard?

Sihera grunted but, undeterred, she pressed forward. Eventually, she came to another crowded street. Perhaps this was the trade road the woman had spoken of. With renewed life, she navigated through the bustling street. It had been a long day with hardly anything to eat, but she was feeling confident she would find her Dreamer boy.

Sihera stopped dead in her tracks to do a double take, not believing what her eyes had seen. She gawked at the familiar looking merchant; it was the exact same man selling fried fish.

No… The hope was sucked dry from her body, leaving a defeated expression on her face. She was back in the market district.

Someone rammed into her shoulder. Sihera stumbled, wincing as she grasped her shoulder.

Hey! That really hurt!

"Keep moving, girl. You're slowing people down," a man said in a rough voice as he hurried by.

Sihera pressed her lips together in frustration. She was tired of being pushed around. Gritting her teeth, she started elbowing her way through the herd, leaning her full weight into them. She wanted them to feel the pain and frustration she felt. As another person corralled through her, she tumbled to the ground.

That was it. She couldn't take it anymore. Her eyes erupted into a rich, red flame. An enraged heat went surging through her. Lightning crackled, arching across her body.

"Get off me!" she shouted. A deafening blast reverberated through the air, and a shockwave rushed outward from where she stood, sending people falling to the ground in a circle around her.

The bustling crowd fell silent. Everyone's gaze fixed on her as she stood centered in a ring of terrified faces, flames still pouring from her rage-filled eyes.

She glared angrily at the people around her as her shoulders rose and fell with each heavy breath. However, it soon dawned on her the grave mistake she had made.

"A mage…" murmured one woman in the crowd.

The fire in Sihera's eyes dissipated, and the scowl on her face eased.

"Is it really?" said one man.

"It is!" cried another woman. "I told you they should have never let the Archmagi stay here."

Sihera's anger was quickly replaced by fear as the ring of people began closing in around her. She hugged her arms around her chest. She couldn't let them catch her. They would send her back to Laval for sure, or worse.

She burst into a sprint, shoving her way through the crowd as she hurried down a back alley. Huddling between some piles of garbage, panting and out of breath, she buried her face in her hands and sobbed uncontrollably. She couldn't help it. Her lungs quivered with each aching breath. There, amongst the trash, she hid herself for the rest of the day.

As the sky darkened and the air grew cold, the noise of the city died down. She hugged her jacket around her. The floor was hard and uncomfortable, but it wasn't long before her eyes became heavy, and Sihera began to dream.

* * *

The boy walked in front of her again, leading her down the long and winding cave. His attire had changed—he now wore a robe with the hood raised, covering the back of his head—but that was hardly surprising. Sihera's vision of her Dreamer boy was always changing now.

How will he die this time? she wondered. At the hands of an aiko? A dagger? Poison? Anything was possible at this point. Sihera looked down at her hand. It was a human hand, and inside its grasp was a dagger. Back to the blade, it seemed.

As the boy reached the edge of the pool, a group of men in robes circled around him. Sihera glanced curiously at them; they were Archmagi. Sihera's free hand reached out and turned the boy around to face her. As the boy turned, her heart seized up. The hood still covered his face, but there were black curls of hair that hung out the opening of the hood. Sihera's hands—one hand still grasping the dagger—gently pushed the hood back. A face looked up at her, but it was not her Dreamer boy. It was her own face looking back at her.

Sihera stared at herself in shock and awe, terrified to see the trembling look in her own eyes. The girl's brow pressed together into a high point upon her forehead, her eyes were somber and red, as if she'd been crying.

The dagger in Sihera's hand raised up high. She watched on, stunned, as the girl—herself—clenched her eyes shut and braced for the pain. The dagger thrust downward. As the blade pierced through the girl's chest, Sihera felt a searing pain shoot through her heart.

Sihera's eyes burst open, and her lungs pulled in the cold, crisp Athus air. Sitting up on the alley floor, her fingers frantically pulled away at her jacket and clothes as she examined her skin. She could still feel the slight sting in her chest from the blade, but there was no wound. With a long, relieving sigh, her head slumped back against the stone wall and her arms fell beside her.

What a nightmare. She had never dreamt of herself dying before. Actually, was that a dream or a vision? She wasn't sure anymore.

It was terrifying to look into her own fear-stricken eyes as she died. She tried to push the thought from her mind, but once implanted, it became frustratingly hard for her to shake.

"Sihera?" asked a man's voice.

She lurched back. The silhouette of a man was standing in front of her. As he knelt to get a closer look at her, she recognized the Archmagi robes he wore; he was one of Laval's men. Her heart sank low and heavy in her chest. *Oh no...*

"Sihera, look at you," the man scoffed, pushing away the trash she had unknowingly huddled beneath for warmth.

"How—how did you find me?" she asked.

He chuckled, but quickly stifled his laughter. "You made quite the spectacle earlier today."

Sihera frowned and lowered her eyes.

The man's voice turned soft. "Come. Let's get you home. Laval is waiting for you."

* * *

The Archmagi man pushed open the front door to Sihera's house. It must have been around midnight, but Laval was dressed and waiting in the entryway, arms crossed tight against his chest. She stood there, not wanting to go in. How long had Laval been waiting there?

Laval jutted his chin out angrily. No one said a word. The Archmagi man gave her a nudge and she staggered forward, stopping just in front of Laval, but she could not bring herself to look at him.

"Sorry…" she grumbled under her breath.

Laval tapped his foot frantically on the hardwood floor, but after a moment, his tapping stopped. He bent down and hugged her, whispering in a stern yet loving voice, "Don't ever frighten me like that again."

She didn't say anything, but she began to feel a strong empathy for Laval. She hadn't thought about what he must have been going through in her absence. As she felt the cool line of a tear running down the side of his face, she realized the hurt she had caused him.

She hadn't meant to hurt Laval; she was grateful to him. Ever since she was a little girl, Laval had raised her as if she were his own child. She still hated him for what he wanted to do to her Dreamer boy, but at least she realized now that he did care for her. Slowly— albeit reluctantly—she tied her arms around his back, and the Archmagi man closed the door behind her.

Laval sat her down at the table and served her some food. That night, in the dim, candlelit room, she ate as though she had never eaten before. Her stomach was so appreciative to be swollen and stuffed with food again.

"I'm sorry for the way I acted," Laval said. "I realize now that it was wrong. From now on, I promise you, I will be a better parent for you."

She looked up at him and smiled. It was comforting to hear Laval say that.

"But you must tell me," he continued, "why did you feel like you had to run away?"

Her smile slowly faded. She looked down at the table and began to feel shy. "You—you said you were going to hurt him. My—the boy."

Laval's brow crinkled in confusion. He shook his head and exhaled, almost a chuckle. "Sihera, believe me, I want nothing but what is best for you and this boy."

A frown pressed onto her face. She was frustrated by his blatant lie, but her voice came out softer and more disheartened than she expected. "You said you were going to *sacrifice* him."

The pang of frustration tweaked Laval's head to the side. His eyes narrowed, but he didn't answer.

Her throat tightened, and her eyes began to water as she continued in a strained voice. "You hid things from me, Laval. You *lied* to me."

Laval's brow turned upward, and his eyes grew empathetic. "Sihera, I'm sorry I lied to you. I never meant to hurt you. If I have ever withheld anything from you, please know I did it only to protect you. I did it because I *care* for you."

"How can I trust anything you say?"

Laval reached out and held her hand. "Let me prove it to you. Come with me. It might not be too late. We'll set sail first thing in the morning through the Northern Pass to rescue him. Then you'll see, we will all be together—you, me, and the boy."

The weight of her emotions lifted briefly; the thought of being together with her Dreamer boy made her feel unexpectedly light. Her brow raised slightly, and Laval gave her a weak smile.

"I am a flawed person, Sihera. I have made many mistakes trying to be the parent you deserve. But if you ever thought of me as a father in the same way that I look at you as my daughter, then *please* give me a chance to make this right again."

Sihera's heart ached. More than anything, she wanted to believe him; she wanted what he said to be true. But somewhere in the dark recesses of her mind she knew he might still be lying to her. *What should I do?*

"All right," she said, giving in. She was tired of fighting. She didn't want to struggle on her own anymore. She wanted to go back to the days when she and Laval were happy together. Her shoulders slumped forward as she let out a long breath. "In the morning, I'll go with you."

26

Shattered Dreams

Jokahn stood alone on an open, grassy plain beneath the moonlit sky, admiring the stars. He enjoyed the peace and quiet of this place.

"Hello?" echoed a gentle voice.

The face of a girl appeared in front of him. She smiled, and her big brown eyes pinched at the corners with joy from behind the dark curls of her hair.

"Oh, it's you again." Jokahn smiled back.

The girl's joyous expression turned grievous as she gasped and vanished from sight.

"Wait! Where are you going?" he called.

The girl's voice reverberated through the void. "Are you talking to me?"

"Yes. Where did you go?"

"You—you can hear me?" she said. Jokahn searched all around him as her words bounced from one place to another. "And you can see…" The girl's voice stopped as he turned and found himself standing in front of her. "…*me?*"

He stood there, mesmerized, as her eyes began to flicker. Like a ripple of water, the color of her irises changed from brown to blue.

"Your eyes…" he wondered aloud.

"Huh?"

"Your eyes. They just turned blue."

"Oh." The girl's cheeks flushed red as she shied away. "Yeah, I've kind of always liked the color of your eyes."

"My eyes? But how did you do that?"

She faced him—her eyes back to their original brown—and

laughed. "It's a dream. You can do anything you want."

The girl twirled and burst into a thousand bright lights that shot out in every direction. Jokahn ducked and shielded himself with his arms.

"What's the matter?" she asked, standing whole in front of him again, a pleasant but confused look upon her face. She rested her palms on her knees and bent down, cocking her head curiously to one side.

He crept carefully out from behind his arms, unsure of what was going on.

"Don't be afraid." The girl smiled. "What's your name?"

"Jokahn," he said cautiously.

"Jokahn," the girl repeated with a long sigh of relief, as if finally releasing some long-held tension. "My name's Sihera."

"Get away from him!" a familiar voice rang out from behind him. "The boy is *mine!*"

Ticahrla stood firm and tall in the distance. She looked furious; her eyes were spewing green flames, and her hands were molding a small fire.

"*You…*" Sihera glared at Ticahrla. "Jokahn, get back."

"No, it's all right. It's just Ticahrla."

Sihera looked up at him in astonishment. "Don't you know who she is?! She is trying to… *Eeek!*" Sihera shrieked.

Jokahn looked up just in time to see a pillar of fire crash down in front of him. The blast of heat lifted him off his feet and flung him back through the air. He hit the ground with a hard thud as the air was ripped from his lungs.

As he lay sprawled out on his stomach, his head was spinning, and his ears rang. He groaned, struggling to breathe, as he pushed himself up onto his knees. *What was that?!*

Ticahrla planted her steel boot and stood next to him. With a twirl of her arms and a loud cry, she sent a second pillar of flame shooting through the air.

Jokahn's brow pulled together. Something was wrong. Ticahrla didn't know how to use such powerful magic. Then he remembered that this was all just a dream; none of it was real.

The pillar of flame cascaded down over Sihera's already motionless body, but as the flames cleared, Sihera was gone.

"Ticahrla, what's going on?"

"Shut up, boy!" Ticahrla's eyes frantically scanned the area.

Jokahn sat up, massaging the ache in his forehead, trying to make sense of his dream, when an odd sensation wrapped around his back and chest. He gasped, lifting his arms and examining his torso but saw nothing. "Do you feel that?" he asked.

"Feel what?" Ticahrla said harshly.

"Shhh," a voice whispered into his ear.

The world around him started to dissolve—vanishing before his eyes—and he found himself transported into the midst of a lush rain forest. Sitting behind him was Sihera, her arms still hugging his body.

"Sihera!" Jokahn exclaimed as he turned to face her. "Are you all right?"

"I'm fine," she said dismissively, holding up her hands to silence him. "Now, listen to me. You can't trust Ticahrla. No matter what she says or does."

A chuckle escaped him. "What are you talking about?"

"Just listen," Sihera demanded, clenching her eyes shut and shaking her fists at him.

A hand shot out from the ground like a claw and clenched tightly around Sihera's throat. Jokahn lurched back in fear as Sihera struggled to pry herself free.

The ground beneath him began to quake. As the earth shook and parted, Ticahrla emerged from the soil, rising high into the air with her fingers still clasped around Sihera's throat.

Sihera kicked and wriggled, trying to break free. Ticahrla glared viciously up at her with teeth bared and emerald flames lapping from her eyes. "Can't trust *me?*" Her voice was low and demonic. "That's rich coming from an Archmagi pawn."

Sihera turned a furious gaze down at Ticahrla and gritted her teeth as her eyes erupted into a bright red flame. Electricity began to spark between her hands. With a loud crack and a flash of light, Ticahrla was launched backward, her body careening through the air, ricocheting like a rag doll against the trees. Jokahn stared off into the distance, his eyes wide and jaw slung open.

Sihera was hovering in the air. Her eyes expelled a tremendous red flame. Her face was tight and angry as electricity crackled across her entire body.

Never one to be outdone, Ticahrla came racing back to the fight. At first, she appeared small and distant, but as she marched closer, she grew exponentially in size. Ticahrla continued to grow until she stood as tall as a tree.

Jokahn's mind was a blur. He sat there helpless to do anything but watch in awe at the spectacle his dream had become.

Ticahrla and Sihera charged at each other, Ticahrla rearing back a colossal fist, while Sihera soared through the air, ready to unleash a blazing ball of fire. Just before they could reach each other, Sihera stopped midair with a gasp.

"Oh, no…" Sihera said with dread in her voice. The flames in her eyes went out and she gently floated down to the ground. Falling to her knees, her fear-filled eyes stared blankly out into the horizon. Ticahrla—having shrunk back down to normal size again—stood beside Jokahn and stared curiously at Sihera.

Fear enveloped Sihera's expression. Her voice was quivering. "The aiko… They're here." Then, in an instant, she vanished.

"Sihera?" Jokahn called out. He searched the forest around him, but she was gone.

The landscape beneath him began to change, and the trees disappeared. Distant cries and screams, mixed with a steady hiss, filled the air. He turned to see a kingdom on fire. The grand, white stone walls of the city were easily recognized. It was Athus, and the city was burning. Bright red flames illuminated the night sky as large clouds of black smoke bellowed out from within the walls.

Jokahn turned to Ticahrla. "What's going on?" he asked.

Ticahrla didn't respond. She just stared in horror.

Then, just as Sihera had done, Ticahrla vanished from sight, and

Jokahn was left all alone on the hillside.

One of Athus' walls crumbled and fell. More screams and cries of terror filled the air. The fires roared.

A familiar voice called out to him in his mind. "Jokahn!" Her voice was panicked.

"Ticahrla?" Jokahn looked around him, but she was nowhere to be found.

"Jokahn!" Her voice rang out again.

A heavy sensation pressed against his chest. It was suddenly difficult to breathe. Again, the pressure hit him.

"Jokahn! Wake up!" Ticahrla cried.

Gasping for air, Jokahn's eyes shot open as he lurched up in his hammock.

"What did you see?!" Ticahrla shouted as her fists clung to his shirt, panic enveloping her face. "Tell me what you saw!"

He was in a daze. "Ah—Athus," he managed to say. "I saw Athus. It was burning."

Ticahrla stared at him with an anguished—almost lifeless— expression. Her grip loosened, and she slumped back against the wall. Slowly, her body sank down onto the floor. She appeared dead inside.

Jokahn looked over at her with worry. "Why? Ticahrla, what's wrong?"

"Because..." Ticahrla said in a weak voice as she stared blankly off into the distance. "I dreamt it, too."

27

Echoes of Her Remorse

From the deck of the *Nahktaio*, Jokahn looked up at Ticahrla with a concerned expression. She stood at the helm, steering the ship, focusing all her attention on the horizon in front of her. Ticahrla had decided to change course and told him they were sailing back to Athus. She had given up on finding the Origin, although she refused to explain why.

He stood there watching her, troubled by what she had said before: "I dreamt it, too." These few simple words threw everything he thought he knew into question. She *dreamt* it? Was she a Dreamer too? If so, then why did she need him? What was the point of this whole endeavor? Had she been lying to him?

So many questions were swirling through Jokahn's mind, but despite several attempts to speak with her, Ticahrla was never in the mood. If he tried to strike up a conversation, she would say, "I'm busy," or, "Not now, I need to focus."

It took sixteen days to reach Athus. Sixteen days of being ignored and alone as he watched Ticahrla sulking in solitude. He did his best to keep up with his chores and training, but it was difficult for him on his own.

The day came when the fallen gates of Athus appeared in the distance, and Jokahn knew that if he ever wanted to get any answers from her, he had to talk to Ticahrla before they docked.

He stood beside her and stared at the floor. "Ticahrla," he said quietly. She pretended not to notice him, as usual. He massaged his hands together. Why was he so nervous? He looked at her with a drained expression. "Ticahrla, you wouldn't lie to me, would you? I mean, if I asked you something important."

That seemed to catch her attention. With a pained expression, she turned to look at him from the corner of her eye.

"It's been bothering me," he continued. "I have to know. Are— are you a *Dreamer?*"

With a long, drawn-out sigh, her shoulders drooped, and her eyes turned sorrowful. She nodded a heavy head at him.

Jokahn released a long breath—a breath he felt he had been holding in for weeks now. He was relieved for a moment, but then his face slowly shifted toward concern. "But then why did you need me? I was nothing; a worthless pickpocket from Anchorsfell."

"Jokahn, I already told you; we're not going to the Origin anymore. I can't talk about this right now. I have more important things I need to focus on."

Jokahn's face scrunched together. That wasn't the answer he had been hoping for, and it showed through his expression.

Ticahrla sighed. "Let's just say this," she said, turning away to look out at the ocean as she spoke. "To become an Arcane Bearer is a…difficult process. It would have helped to have had you with me. Other than that, you'll just have to trust that I needed you. Trust that I need you still, Jokahn. I need you now more than ever."

That response was better. He was content with that. Ticahrla needed him; for what reason, he wasn't sure. But, nonetheless, she needed him. After all she had done for him, he would give her that; he would be there for her in her time of need.

As the ship drew closer to Athus, Jokahn could see the city was completely destroyed. He looked out in awe and horror at the smoldering rubble of the once grand kingdom. The *Nahktaio* pulled into the harbor through an opening where one of the large sea doors hung crooked and collapsed in the water. Everything was quiet. The city was empty. Only the dead remained.

As Drahig tied the ship to the dock, Ticahrla ordered everyone to stay on board and hurried onto dry land.

"Wait, where are you going?" Bakta leaned over the railing.

"I have to check something," she called back and marched off alone.

* * *

As Ticahrla walked through the destruction that was once the palace, she had one destination on her mind. Her movement slowed and then stopped as she approached the hallway leading to the queen's chambers. She stared at the door to her mother's room.

The hallway was dark, but she could see moonlight peeking through the door as it sat slightly ajar. Claw marks were etched into the wood from where the aiko had pried it open. Ticahrla looked around the hallway, but there were no other signs of struggle; no trace of the queen's royal guards, no last stand to defend their queen. Ticahrla's brow tightened as her eyes focused back on the door. She walked forward.

There are no guards because Mother escaped, and her chamber is empty, she tried to assure herself, but she couldn't shake the unnerving feeling that twisted around her heart.

She stood in front of the door and glared at the handle, her hands in tight fists at her side. Pressing her lips together, she closed her eyes and, with a deep breath, pushed open the door.

As she willed her eyes open, moonlight shined in from the window, illuminating the bedroom. Her eyes panned across the destruction. In the shadowy corner of the room rested a crumpled mess of white silken blankets that had torn from the bed. They were stained red with blood. Extended out from beneath the sheets lay her mother's hand, lacerations running up and down her arm.

Ticahrla's heart collapsed and her legs gave out from beneath her. Falling to her knees, the tears began pouring down her face. Her jaw fell open, struggling for breath, her sobs coming out as small, stuttered gasps.

Weak and trembling, her body keeled forward as she held her face in her hands. Her fingers—like claws digging against her scalp—gripped and pulled at the roots of her hair.

She reared back, and a long and agonizing cry tore forth from her lungs, the shrill sound of her voice echoing off every wall in the kingdom.

* * *

Ticahrla marched through the ruins of what used to be Athus. Her eyes were still tinted red from crying, but the tears were gone, replaced with a look of pure rage that was fixed to her face. She continued out the city gates and across the open hills to a farming village called Westharvest. There, she found the survivors who had evacuated Athus during the attack.

There were thousands of people all crammed into the small town. Most of the people were huddled in tents and makeshift huts, but none of that interested her. She marched right past the stares of her defeated people. She knew what she was looking for, and it didn't take long to find it.

There was only one building with the queen's royal guards standing at attention outside of it. Seeing them, Ticahrla burst into a quick stride. She hurried up to one of the guards at the front gate and grabbed him by the collar of his armor.

"Who was it?!" she demanded, "Who bought you off?!"

The guard didn't try to stop her. He held his position and looked down at her with a snide grin.

"I swear, I'll beat the answers out of you if I have to. I'll—"

"What is going on out there?!" shouted a man's voice.

Ticahrla looked over the guard's shoulder and her eyes narrowed. Apotri emerged from the front door of the house protected by the queen's guards. "I knew it…" she snarled.

"Ah," Apotri said as he walked toward her, stopping a good distance behind the guards. "I should have known it was you, *Ticahrla.*"

Her brow tightened. Apotri had never called her by just her first name before. A councilman would never address royalty in such an undignified manner. *"Apotri…"* she growled through clenched teeth. "What did you do?"

"What did *I* do? I saved these people." He waved his hand out at the masses.

"You didn't save anything! Athus is in ruins thanks to your cowardice. Did you even try to defend our kingdom? Did you even try to fight?"

"You weren't there. You didn't see the horde approaching. The aiko marched on us with such numbers. Their army stretched out to the horizon. And then they came by sea, turning the ocean black."

"When I walked through Athus, I didn't see a valiant last stand. You let the aiko waltz right in and destroy our home."

"I had no choice. There was no glory to be had in standing our ground and dying."

"And what about the queen? Did you even try to protect her?"

"I did what I had to in order to protect these people. What did *you* do? Where were *you* when your people and your queen needed you?"

Ticahrla winced at the stabbing pain his words inflicted, but she didn't reply. She couldn't. He was right, and it tore away at her. She had not been there for her people when they needed her the most. She wasn't there to protect her mother. Her lips pressed together, and her fingers curled into tight fists.

"What's the matter? Nothing clever to say?"

Ticahrla lunged forward, but two guards grappled her around the waist and shoulders to restrain her. Stretching out her arms, she clawed at the air in front of Apotri's face. She knew better than to think she could ever get past the guards, but her rage drove her to press forward.

Apotri took one step back and laughed. "Oh, you always where a hotheaded one." The guards pulled Ticahrla's arms behind her back and kicked her feet out from under her. She fell hard onto her knees. Struggling to wrestle free, but unable to move, her head slumped forward as she panted heavily.

Apotri squatted down in front of her. With a gentle hand, he lifted her chin. As her head tilted upward, she glared furiously through her brow, and a green flame began lapping at the sides of her eyes.

Apotri's voice was quiet as he looked down at her with a maniacal and victorious grin. "There's that fiery spirit I love about you." He continued in an upbeat tone. "You know, many people say I should have you killed for treason. For abandoning your duties, your people, and your queen. I can't say I blame them. Maybe I should have you executed so the people of Athus can be given some relief. Then the legend of Princess Ticahrla will go down in history as the selfish girl who destroyed her kingdom and died, young and pathetic at the hands of the people she betrayed."

Apotri waited. She knew what he wanted. He wanted to see the fear in her eyes. He wanted to see her beg. She wouldn't give him the satisfaction. All she gave him was the same, unwavering glare.

He went on. "But, then again, I suppose your story doesn't have to end this way. You are still young, and very beautiful. Perhaps I could convince the people you are ready to turn over a new leaf. Why, you may even sit on Athus' throne someday. Just think about it. We could rebuild the city, me as king and you as queen by my side."

As Apotri spoke, Ticahrla's glare slowly began to fade.

Apotri grinned triumphantly, apparently having achieved the expression he wanted from her. "What do you say? Will you be my queen?"

Ticahrla didn't reply. She knelt there, shocked—almost numb to the reality of what was happening.

Apotri smiled as the dread spilled over her face. "I'll take that as a yes," he said. Then, closing his eyes, Apotri pulled Ticahrla's chin up and leaned in to kiss her.

As the man's lips drew close to hers, her face turned into a fierce scowl. With a whip of her head, Ticahrla bashed her forehead against the bridge of Apotri's nose. A loud crunch rang through the air.

Apotri cried out as he fell back onto the ground, clasping his face. The guards wrenched Ticahrla back as she glared intently at him from behind flaming green eyes. A gash had opened across her forehead, and a single line of blood ran down across her scowl.

Apotri touched his fingers to his nose a few times and examined the blood on his hands. The bridge of his nose now sat crooked on his face, blood streaming from his nostrils.

"I'm going to kill you, Apotri!" She snarled, her feet digging away at the ground as she struggled to clamber forward from within the guards' grasps. "I'm going to peal the meat from your body and show everyone what a spineless slug you really are!"

Apotri scoffed and pulled himself back to his feet. Standing tall over her, clasping his broken nose, he asserted, "Don't you dare threaten me, girl." He staggered a bit as he started to walk away. "I was willing to be kind. I was willing to forgive. But maybe that was too good for the likes you. Yes, a quick death is too merciful for a traitor like yourself. I think I'll enjoy watching you die…nice…and…*slow*." With a wave of his hand, Apotri signaled for the guards to take her away.

28

New Clarity

Jokahn was pacing back and forth across the deck of the *Nahktaio*. He didn't like not knowing where Ticahrla was for so long.

His ears caught the sound of footsteps on the dock, and his brow perked up. He hurried over to the ship's railing, expecting to see Ticahrla, but was surprised to see a girl in a purple coat and a thin, robed man walking down the dock.

"Is the princess available?" the man asked.

"Who are you supposed to be?" Bakta asked, rudely jutting out his chin.

Jokahn's head tilted to one side. The girl looked remarkably familiar, but he couldn't place where from. She rocked nervously back and forth on the balls of her feet as she stared solely back at him, a bright smile shining from behind her dark curls.

"It's you…" he said quietly as his eyes lit up and he sprinted down the ramp.

"Hey, where are you going?" asked Bakta as Jokahn rushed past him.

Jokahn came to a stop in front of the girl, his eyes scanning her up and down, not able to believe what he was seeing.

"Hello, Jokahn…" she said, blushing as she ran her fingers through her hair.

"It's you," he repeated, still stunned in disbelief. His brow tightened a bit as he struggled to remember her name, but then it came to him. He smiled brightly at her. "Sihera."

Sihera looked up at him, almost in tears. Biting happily down on her lower lip, she nodded in excitement. The elation spread over her face, so much so that she started to cry and laugh at the same time.

In one bound, she threw her arms up and wrapped herself around him. Jokahn stood frozen for a moment as Sihera hugged him tightly, rocking him from side to side.

"I've waited so long for this day," she said quietly to him. "A part of me thought it would never come."

Jokahn looked nervously back at Bakta and Drahig, a little embarrassed.

Bakta leaned over to Drahig. "Did I miss something?"

* * *

While Sihera and Jokahn embraced, Ticahrla sat in a prison cell in the middle of town. It was a small jailhouse with a few guards placed out front.

With chains around her ankles, Ticahrla sat hunched over and distraught on the bed, her face buried in her hands. Her mind raced with a thousand agonizing thoughts, but one in particular kept playing in her mind. It was the look of grief on her mother's face as she dragged Jokahn out of the palace bedroom. *Mother, I'm never going to be your "little princess," all right?! So just stop it! The faster you can get that through that thick skull of yours, the faster I can get on with my life!*

Her words echoed through her memory, haunting her, tormenting her. That was the last thing she had said to her mother. Ticahrla's face crumpled in agony. How could she have been so stupid? Her mother hadn't deserved that, and she hated herself for not being able to realize it sooner.

But what did it matter now? It was too late. Her mother was dead. Athus was destroyed. Everything was lost. Just like that, everything she had ever wanted—everything she had ever cared for—was gone. What did she have left to live for? Finding the Origin? What was the point? What good was becoming an Arcane Bearer if there was no Athus? In the end, it looked like Apotri had won.

"Really? *Apotri?*" She scoffed in quiet amazement to herself. *How did a filthy scum sucker like that manage to come out on top?* No, that couldn't be right. She wasn't going to let someone like Apotri get the best of her.

She knew what she had to do. She had to keep going. She had to find the Origin, become an Arcane Bearer, and hunt down the royal council—Apotri in particular—and kill off her mother's traitorous guards.

Yes, the thought alone began to give her renewed life. She could already imagine the sweet taste of vengeance, and once again found purpose. She would smile at them as they wriggled and cried out their last dying breath in slow, beautiful agony. Her lips quivered and pulled back into a smile with eager anticipation.

A rustling sound outside her cell pulled Ticahrla from the fantasy playing out in her mind. There was a struggle, followed by some men grunting.

Outside, a hushed voice demanded, "Drop it. On the ground. I said get on the ground!"

Ticahrla cocked her head to the side and stared at the door in confusion. Someone was fiddling with the keys. The lock turned over with a clunk and the door creaked open. Standing outside her prison cell stood a dozen men, all crowding the door to peer inside.

"Princess?" one man called.

Ticahrla rose from the bed and asked in a firm tone, "What do you want?"

The men funneled in through the door and threw themselves onto their knees before her feet, bowing with the utmost humility. "My princess. We are here to help you escape. Your people need you."

Her brow pressed down over her eyes and her head reared back in confusion. "What? What are you talking about?" she demanded, bending over to help the men to their feet. "Stop with the pathetic formalities and start making sense."

One of the men made his way over to the chains that were clamped around Ticahrla's ankles. "Forgive me, my princess," he said quietly as he took the keys and unshackled her.

Free from her restraints, Ticahrla pulled the last man to his feet. "What do you mean, 'they need me?'"

"It's the council. Apotri, he is trying to assume the throne."

She snorted a laugh. "Yes, well, it appears he isn't trying to be subtle about his coup."

"You must stop him. You must take your rightful place as queen. You are the one true heir to the throne."

Ticahrla sighed and looked at the man with a somber expression. "The last queen Athus will ever have died with her kingdom. Athus is a ruin now. There is no more king or queen, and I'm not your princess anymore."

The men appeared dumbfounded. "How can you say that? If you do not lead us, the aiko will kill us all. Your people are ready to fight, Princess. And we are ready to die to save what we have left. To save our families. To save Athus."

She placed a firm but comforting hand on the man's shoulder. "Take your families and flee. Find a safe place to take refuge. There is no protection from the aiko here. Let Apotri have his kingdom of rubble for now. But don't worry, it won't be for long. I'll be back to avenge the death of our queen. Then, maybe, we will finally find some peace."

The men exchanged worried glances, not knowing what to say. Ticahrla nodded and smiled sympathetically. Then she headed for the door.

"My princess!" a man called out in desperation. Ticahrla stopped and turned to look back at them. The man fidgeted in place, rubbing his hands together. He tried several times to form words but repeatedly stopped himself. Finally, he managed to say, "Whatever you think is best, we will remain loyal. Just remember, your people are waiting for you."

Ticahrla gave a grateful nod, and then headed off into the night.

* * *

Back at the docks, Sihera and Laval had been invited aboard the ship. While they waited for Ticahrla to return, Sihera and Jokahn paced around the deck together.

Sihera lavished every moment she spent with Jokahn. He was just as she'd dreamt he would be—warm and kind, and his hair smelled of the ocean air.

"I can't believe it," Jokahn said with a smile. "I didn't know you were actually real. I thought it was all just a dream."

Sihera grinned back at him. "I know what you mean. I've been dreaming about you for so long." Her body suddenly constricted, and her heart lurched up into her throat. *What did I just say?!* But Jokahn didn't seem to think anything of it.

"Wow, so you are a Dreamer too?" asked Jokahn.

She swallowed her embarrassment, attempting to act calm and unaffected. "Yup."

"So, do you know magic?"

"Of course. We're dreamers. I mean, don't you know magic?"

Jokahn lowered his gaze to the floor and shook his head. "No. Ticahrla tried to teach me, though."

She nodded and said casually, "It's hard at first. I'll show you how to control your energy sometime."

Jokahn stopped dead in his tracks. The smile began to fade from his face, replaced by a grave expression. His voice was quiet. "What did you say?"

Sihera stopped to look back at him. She was surprised to find Jokahn glaring at her. "I mean, if you want me to, of course," she answered quickly, but Jokahn didn't reply. Why was he looking at her that way. What did she do wrong? "Sorry, I should have minded my own business. I won't bother you—"

"No, wait." Jokahn lurched forward, grabbing her hand.

She flinched. His skin was so warm. She hadn't expected him to reach out to her like that. Her heart sped as Jokahn's hand wrapped around hers. Carefully, she turned back to face him.

"You can teach me that?" he continued with an awe-stricken stare.

"Oh." Sihera's worry began to seep away as she realized he

wasn't upset with her. "Well—uh, sure I can. If you want me to."

Jokahn moved in close to her and smiled brightly. "Definitely!" He stood there, still gripping her hand, with that ridiculously large smile stretching across his face.

"*Now?*" she asked.

"Yes," said Jokahn, taking another step closer. "I can do it. I know I can. Will you teach me?"

Her face was beginning to warm from how close he was. "All right, well, first I'm going to need my hand back."

"Oh, right. Sorry." Jokahn chuckled, releasing his grip.

* * *

Jokahn spent the next hour with Sihera going over basic magic techniques and breathing exercises that would help him control his energy. Working with Sihera was so much easier than it was working with Ticahrla. With Ticahrla, everything was a challenge, but with Sihera, things just felt easy—peaceful.

"Now, if you keep a constant flow of energy, you can sustain the flame," Sihera demonstrated, cupping her hands around the tiny fire. "That way it is more of a steady burn, instead of an explosion."

Jokahn watched carefully as he studied her movements. It was amazing how easy she made it look.

He closed his eyes, took a deep breath in through his nose, and exhaled slowly through his mouth, just as she had shown him. His brow tightened and he pressed his palms together. The warmth churned in his chest. His face puckered and strained as he tried to push that energy out into his arms, but it just sat bubbling in his center as always.

Why won't you move?! He scolded the stagnant fire inside him.

He knew he would never be able to do it, not even with Sihera's help. Why couldn't he be more like her, or Ticahrla?

Ticahrla… That glorious smile of hers that always warmed his heart.

Without warning, the fire inside him erupted. Jokahn's eyes shot open as he felt the scorching heat of the magma filling his chest. Jokahn's jaw shook as it fell open and air surged inward. The lava poured down his arms and legs, overflowing up into his skull. As it spilled over into his eyes, he felt the heat venting into the atmosphere around him. A tint of blue began to cloud his vision.

His entire body shook, overwhelmed with energy. He glanced down at his hands and could already see the sparks arcing between his grasps. A wide, quivering smile stretched across his face.

"That's it, Jokahn!" Sihera's voice cheered him on. "You've got it!"

She was right. He was doing it!

He pulled his palms apart from each other, a little faster than he had intended, and the electricity exploded into a tremendous fireball, knocking him onto his back.

"Jokahn!" cried Sihera as she hurried over to him. With the lengths of her robe, she knelt beside him and beat out the few singeing flames dotted across his clothing. "Jokahn, are you all right?"

Coughing, he struggled to sit upright, his breathing was labored and his body trembling. His skin was hot and tight, as if lightly charred. Sihera braced an arm around him as her eyes frantically scanned him up and down.

His voice was small and coarse, but he managed to wince a smile up at her. "I did it."

Sihera shook her head and chuckled as he lay weak in her arms.

"What was that?!" exclaimed Bakta.

"Are you all right, Sihera?" asked the robed man in a concerned voice.

"We're fine, Laval. I was just showing Jokahn some magic."

"It worked well." Jokahn grinned at them.

Bakta looked anxiously down at him. "*That* was 'working well'? I'm afraid to ask what would have happened if it had gone badly."

Laval turned to Drahig. "Get the boy some water. It will help him recover."

Drahig nodded and disappeared below deck.

"It's too bad Ticahrla wasn't here to see it," Jokahn said, struggling to sit upright again. "She would have been so jealous."

Sihera scooted around so she could sit facing him, a somber expression on her face. "You wanted her to see, didn't you?"

He nodded. Of course, he did. Then his shoulders shuddered, and a chill rushed over his body. "Oh, it's cold all of a sudden."

Sihera nodded slowly, still looking despaired. "It always feels cold afterward."

He could see something was bothering Sihera. "What's wrong?" he said, reaching his hand out to her. As he rested his palm on the back of her hand, Sihera's face scrunched up, almost appearing pained.

"It's nothing," she said, shaking her head.

"Come on, you can tell me," he insisted.

Sihera looked up at him with large, tender eyes. "You—you like her…don't you?"

A laugh belched out of his chest. "What?! What are you talking about?"

"Ticahrla. I know you like her. In your dreams, I can sense the way you feel about her."

He was so confused. Why would this bother her? "Sihera, I don't understand. What brought this up?"

But now that she had started, Sihera appeared helpless to stop the outpour of emotions. "She's not as great as you think she is. In fact, sometimes I question if there is any good in her at all."

That one stung him a little. "What's that supposed to mean?"

Sihera continued obliviously. "She's going to kill you, Jokahn."

"What?"

"She wants to sacrifice you so she can become an Arcane Bearer."

"Sacrifice me? Sihera, you're not making any sense."

"Nothing good ever comes from her."

"Ticahrla doesn't even want to become an Arcane Bearer anymore. She told me herself."

"She only ever thinks of herself."

"Hey, that's not true."

"She destroys everything around her."

"Sihera, stop. You don't know her like I do."

"All she ever does is corrupt people. And now she's even getting to you. She's like a plague, infecting everything she touches, and there's nothing anyone can do to slow her."

"I said *stop it!*" Jokahn shouted furiously.

Sihera flinched and fell silent. Her eyes were wide as they stared at the floor, and her head slowly retreated between her shoulders.

He didn't understand why, but his heart was racing; his breathing was heavy, and the blood was pulsing through his veins as he stared Sihera down. Slowly, he managed to calm himself, but there was an aggressiveness behind his words that he couldn't mask.

"She took me in, all right? She saved me. Before her, I was nothing, you got that? *Nothing.*"

Sihera looked up at him and began to quickly shake her head back and forth as her eyes grew even wider. "No, Jokahn, don't say that! You're so much better than she is, so much more!"

"Stop talking about her like that."

"She's just using you. Don't you see that?"

"Stop it, Sihera."

"She's going to kill you, Jokahn. Why don't you believe me? You're nothing to her but some—"

Jokahn clamped his eyes shut and held his hands out in frustration. "I said *shut up!*"

Sihera fell silent again. She didn't make a sound, but tears began to run down her face. As he watched her cry, the aggravation inside him became almost too much to bear. *What? Are you crying now?!* He was startled to hear his own thoughts. It was Ticahrla's words echoing in his own voice through his mind.

After a moment, Jokahn managed to calm himself. Looking over at Sihera's saddened expression, he realized he had gone too far and let his anger get the best of him. With a long sigh, he brushed his hand over his face to wipe away the frustration.

He was so bad at this. Ticahrla was so much better with words. He rarely knew what to say, and he had never had to comfort someone who was crying before. He thought to himself for a bit, and then turned to looked back at Sihera.

Pushing himself across the deck, he rested his shoulder against hers and said in a low, empathetic tone, "I'm sorry. I—I didn't mean to…I mean, I didn't—" He paused. Then he let out a chuckle as he found himself struggling to form words.

Sihera turned to look at him with a confused and aggravated glare, apparently not finding anything about the situation funny at all.

"You're right, you know," he continued with a gentle voice and a subtle grin. Sihera raised an eyebrow at him. "Ticahrla isn't a nice person, but she…well…she's *my* person."

Sihera's eyes widened a bit with empathy as she stared at him.

"She's always been there for me when I needed her, and…" He paused for a moment. His eyes were beginning to water. "And, well, that's more than I can say about anyone else."

Jokahn did the best he could to describe how he felt, but he wasn't sure if Sihera would understand. He glanced cautiously at her from the corner of his eye. She didn't say anything, but her glare slowly faded. To his surprise, Sihera's eyes were filled with tears as well, but they held a look of comfort within them.

Not long ago, Jokahn would have been terrified to cry in front of another person. But as he looked warmly over at Sihera, he didn't try to hide his tears from her. He loved Ticahrla more than any man could ever love a woman, and he wanted Sihera to see that. He wanted her to see that Ticahrla was something much more to him. She was his protector, his teacher, and his strength. She was his life in its entirety. Undeniably, irreversibly, and eternally the girl he cared for and worshipped on every level he could imagine.

Sihera stared back helplessly, compassion filling her face, and Jokahn knew she understood. He smiled and nodded, as if to signify his appreciation for her understanding. Then he stood up and walked away.

As Jokahn made his way across the deck, he heard Bakta's voice call out, "Ticahrla!"

A surge of life rushed back into Jokahn. He ran over to the ships railing. Leaning his body over the edge, he saw a lone figure walking with long, intentional strides down the dock. It was Ticahrla. Without a second thought, he raced down the ramp.

* * *

Ticahrla marched steadily across the wooden planks, her eyes fixated on the floor in front of her. Her mind was still racing with vengeful thoughts when a body unexpectedly threw itself at her. She came to a jolting stop as Jokahn collided with her and fastened his arms around her back.

Ticahrla grunted at the force of the impact. "Easy now, boy," she said looking at him with a curious stare. Jokahn clung to her dearly, resting his head on her shoulder. Eventually, she let her arms tie gently around the back of him and chuckled warmly to herself.

Bakta, Drahig, and two others—a skinny man and a girl, both dressed in Archmagi robes—walked down onto the docks to greet her.

"Where did you run off to?" exclaimed Bakta.

Ticahrla's eyes were fixated on the two strangers who had been on *her* ship. Then she recognized them. *Sihera*...the name slithered through her mind. "What are *they* doing here?" She glared at them, gently moving Jokahn to her side.

"We want to work together," said the Archmagi man as he stepped forward to address her. "My name is Laval, if you recall, and this is Sihera. We—"

"Yeah, I remember you," Ticahrla interjected in a harsh tone. "You're the scum that worked with Apotri to turn my own sailors against me."

"We aren't with Apotri anymore. It seems the chairman has forgotten all about the Archmagi after he got what he wanted from us."

"Sounds like poetic justice to me."

"Perhaps. None the less, it puts us both in a position where we can help each other."

"Why would I ever help you?"

A devious grin stretched across Laval's face. "Because we know where the Origin is."

A twinge shot up Ticahrla's spine that straightened her up tall. Inside, she felt the sheer panic running through her, but she masked it well. "Bullshit," she snarled. "How do you know where the Origin is?"

"Sihera has seen it clearly in a dream," Laval said, gesturing his hand toward the girl.

Ticahrla turned a hard eye toward Sihera, and the girl ducked her head between her shoulders, directing her eyes to the floor.

"We've been able to map its exact location," continued Laval. "I figured, instead of fighting each other over it, why not work together? That way, everyone gets what they want."

Ticahrla clenched her jaw shut, trying not to appear as desperate as she felt. She knew the Archmagi didn't want to work together to find the Origin. They were just trying to scheme up some way of snatching it out from under her.

She had no idea the Archmagi already knew where the Origin was. As if by instinct, her feet moved slightly, wanting to hurry back to her ship—to just grab the boy and go. But what was she supposed to do? Race the Archmagi through the Northern Pass to the Origin? No, she had to think. She had to come up with a way to disrupt their plan.

"Jokahn, help Bakta and Drahig get the ship ready to sail," she said, giving the boy a gentle nudge, but her eyes were fixed on the Archmagi.

As Jokahn made his way back to the *Nahktaio*, Ticahrla looked down at Sihera with a stern glare. "I don't understand, why are you helping this man? Why would you willing hand over the power of the Arcane Bearer?"

Sihera gave her a confused stare. For a moment, the girl glanced up at Laval, but then turned back to Ticahrla. Her words were so unsure, they almost came out as a question. "I...*I'm* supposed to become an Arcane Bearer."

Ticahrla's eyes lit up and an evil grin stretched across her face. That was it; she had found the weak point in the Archmagi's armor. They had not been truthful with the girl. "You think *you* are going to be an Arcane Bearer?"

Sihera didn't seem to know how to reply.

Ticahrla chuckled and shook her head. "You are so naive. Haven't you realized? The Archmagi are just using you. They only want the power for themselves."

Laval scoffed. "What rubbish. I've raised Sihera since she was a child. I would never—"

Ticahrla cut him off, her eyes focused only on the girl. "He's going to kill you," she said assertively.

Sihera's eyes grew wide, and her body froze, but Ticahrla could tell from the expression on her face that Sihera was beginning to realize the truth.

"That's right." Ticahrla grinned wickedly down at her. "You've seen it, haven't you? In your dreams. You've had visions of dying, but you disregarded it." As Ticahrla spoke, she could see the dread seeping deeper and deeper into Sihera's heart. "You kept telling yourself you must be mistaken, that it couldn't be true. But it is true, and he will kill you."

Appearing awestruck, Sihera turned to Laval and said in a confident, almost heated tone, "She's telling the truth, isn't she?"

Anguish overtook Laval's expression as he looked down at the girl. His brow pulled together into a high point at the center of his forehead. His mouth gaped open, trying to find the words to explain himself.

The girl's voice was livid. "I don't believe it!" Sihera took a step back from the man. "You said I was like a daughter to you!" Sihera's brow tightened, her fists clenched at her sides, and a rich red flame began pouring from her eyes.

"Sihera, please." Laval dropped to his knees and crawled over to Sihera's feet. Clasping at the lengths of her robe, he cried, "Sihera, I beg you. Let me explain. I'll tell you everything. No more secrets, I swear."

Ticahrla grinned victoriously and hurried aboard her ship. "Let's go," she ordered, and the *Nahktaio* set sail, leaving Sihera and Laval stranded alone on the dock.

Ticahrla peered over the ship's railing as Sihera continued to glare furiously down at the pleading man. Laval turned his head to see Ticahrla sailing away. Rage overtook his face as he watched her pulling away from the dock.

"This isn't going to work out the way you think it is!" Laval shouted at her. Ticahrla gave a snide smile back at him.

Finally, Sihera tuned to look at the *Nahktaio* as it drifted out to sea, the girl's eyes still roaring in flames.

Ticahrla cupped her hands over her mouth. "I'm willing to do whatever it takes!" she yelled back at them. "Are you?!"

Laval didn't reply, and neither did Sihera.

"Just wait!" Ticahrla continued. "You'll see…" Then, as she and Sihera locked eyes, Ticahrla whispered into the girl's mind, *…I always get what I want.*

29

A Turn for the Worse

Darting across the water, at full sail toward the Northern Pass, the *Nahktaio* was in a race for the Origin. Ticahrla had won the jump off the starting line, but she knew the Archmagi wouldn't be far behind her.

By early morning, she could make out a large ship in the distance behind her. The ship was too far away, but she was certain it was an Archmagi vessel. On the second morning, the ship had gained on her enough for its sails to be clearly visible—it was the Archmagi, and they were jockeying for position.

For the past few days, Ticahrla had hardly slept. She wasn't sure if her smaller ship could uphold her lead long enough to reach the Origin first, but she pushed herself and her ship with everything she had to do so. She wasn't about to give the Origin up without a fight, especially not to the Archmagi.

On the night of the third day, the *Nahktaio* finally reached its destination before the Archmagi could. Ticahrla didn't waste any time laying anchor. She ran her ship aground, plowing the bow full speed onto the beach. The *Nahktaio* reared up out of the water—creaking and groaning as it strained, sending mounds of sand shooting out the sides—and then stopped.

She looked out at the shore and felt a sense of victory—a sense of relief. Finally, she could let her muscles relax a bit. She peered back at the ocean behind her. She couldn't see the Archmagi ship in the darkness of the night, but she knew they were out there.

Bakta and Drahig were already standing on the deck.

"This is it," she said, eagerly heading downstairs from the helm.

"Go wake the boy and let's get moving."

Bakta stepped out in front of her with his hand up. His voice was intentionally calm. "Hold on, Ticahrla. I need to talk to you about something."

Ticahrla's brow came together as she stopped and stared at him, irritated and confused by the man blocking her path. She looked him up and down and placed her hands on her hips, waiting for him to speak.

Bakta brought his hands together in front of him and began nervously wringing his palms. He opened his mouth to speak, but then reconsidered and turned his eyes toward the floor.

"What? Speak up," she said impatiently.

"It's about Jokahn. Are you absolutely sure killing him is the right thing to do?"

She tilted her head slightly, not fully understanding what he was trying to say. She was more annoyed by the delay he was causing at first, but then she began to realize what Bakta was trying to do.

Ticahrla's body went rigid. The anger was quickly boiling up inside her. Her breathing and heartrate became elevated, but she tried to retain her composure by assuring herself that she must have misunderstood him. "You're joking with me, right?"

Bakta didn't answer. He just stared at the floor.

Her blood pressure spiked. The rage in her expression jumped up a full notch. With a deep breath in, she took one large step closer to him. She turned her head slightly to one side, as if to help her hear better, and glared at Bakta from the corner of her eye.

"I don't have time for jokes right now, Bakta. But you *must* be joking, because only a *moron* would think it was a good idea to wait this long—to wait until this very moment, when I've got the Archmagi hot on my ass—to start having second thoughts about what we are doing."

Bakta cringed, but then forced himself to bring his eyes up to meet Ticahrla's. She stared back at him, fierce and unwavering, with her hands balled up into fists.

"I've been trying to tell you for a while," Bakta finally managed to say.

Her body arched backward in frustration, and her fists shook beside the strained expression on her face.

Bakta continued, "What we are going to do to him—killing Jokahn—it just isn't right."

Her entire body wriggled in furious anger. She wanted to strangle the man to stop him from speaking further. Her mouth hissed as she pulled air inward through her clenched teeth. "Damn it, Bakta! Are you shitting me?! You had to pull something like this *now?!*"

"I can't do it," Bakta said, shaking his head. "I can't murder Jokahn just so you can become an Arcane Bearer. And I know you can't do it either. I see the way you've been struggling with it. I see how conflicted you are. It's eating away at you from the inside. You don't have to do it."

Fed up with his defiant nonsense, she shot a rage-filled glare over at Bakta. Her claw-shaped hands yearned to cinch around his throat. "I will rip that boy's heart from his chest and devour it if it gets me even one step closer to becoming an Arcane Bearer! I've come too far to stop now, and no one—not you, or the Archmagi, or that cowardly, worthless, piece-of-shit boy—is going to get in my way!"

The faint sound of footsteps in the stairwell behind her caused Ticahrla to turn and glance out the corner of her eye. She scanned the shadowed doorway, but there was nothing there.

"You can lie to yourself, but we both know that's not true," Bakta continued, turning her attention back to him. "I know you too well. You're a good person, Ticahrla. No matter how tough and unfeeling you pretend to be."

"Bakta is right," Drahig chimed in. "You don't want to do this."

Ticahrla's mouth gaped open as she stared up at her ergman, astonished that even Drahig—her closest and most loyal friend— would betray her in her most desperate hour. She clenched her eyes shut and rubbed her fingers over her eyes, trying to reason past the rage, trying to bury the ache that was growing in her chest.

"Ticahrla..." Bakta said in a gentle tone, placing a hand on her shoulder. His gesture was undoubtably meant to be soothing, but it only caused the frustration inside her to bubble even hotter. He said warmly, "You saved my life. You gave my wife and son peace. There is nothing I can do that will ever repay you for that. I've stood by you, and I've supported you because I believe what you do is just and right. Don't hurt the kid. He doesn't deserve it."

Her voice started out low, almost a growl, as she looked at him through a tense brow, "Do you have any idea what I've gone through to get to this point?" Then her voice rose. "What I've sacrificed?! You think I'm doing this for me? I'm doing this for Athus—for my people. I'm doing this for my mother and father."

Bakta shook his head, obviously not buying into her tale. "If it were my son you had to sacrifice, would you go through with it?"

Of course, I would, you moron! Ticahrla's voice cried out inside her head, but as she spoke, her words were soft. "Bakta, you know I could never—"

"Then you understand why we can't now," interjected Bakta. "You need to talk to him. Either you tell Jokahn what we've been planning all along, or—or I will."

Her hands slowly closed into tight fists. Where did Bakta find the gall to threaten her with such an ultimatum? The strangest sense of rage began to grow inside her as she stared back at him. It was a feeling stuck somewhere between anger and pride, as if the two emotions were battling against one another, and she couldn't figure out which was winning.

Her shoulders reared back as she and Bakta stared each other down. But to her surprise, Bakta held his gaze, confident and steadfast. Panting through her nose, she managed to calm herself, and her fists slowly relaxed.

"All right," she said, with a slight nod of her head. "You're right. I'll go talk to the boy."

Bakta let his stern face ease just enough to smile in his relief. Drahig came and placed a grateful hand on her shoulder, and she patted his arm to show her appreciation.

She scanned the deck, anxiously massaging her jaw as she thought to herself. "This isn't going to be easy," she said with a chuckle.

"I know," Bakta said, placing a hand on her back. "The right thing rarely is."

Ticahrla shook her head and snickered at how he had managed to use her own words against her. "You're an asshole, you know that?"

Bakta smiled. "Yeah, I'm aware of that, too."

Taking a deep breath and rolling out her shoulders, she attempted to prepare herself for what was ahead. She turned to Bakta and Drahig. "Can you give me some time with the boy?"

"Sure thing," said Bakta. "We'll wait at the bow to let you two be alone for a while."

She nodded gratefully and smiled back at them. As Drahig and Bakta walked out of view, her smile quickly fell. She took a deep breath in and exhaled.

What was she going to do now? Was she actually going to abandon becoming an Arcane Bearer when she was this close? How insane would that be? Just hand the Origin over to the Archmagi on a silver platter? Let Apotri get away with everything?

No! That's ridiculous! she thought to herself. *I deserve to be an Arcane Bearer, not the Archmagi!*

But, then again, what about Jokahn? She truly had grown to care for him, and he certainly didn't deserve to die. It was exhausting the way her emotions jumped back and forth. She ran her fingers down her face in frustration and let out a long sigh.

What am I going to do?

* * *

Jokahn quietly made his way back down the stairs below deck. As he reached the bottom step, he had to stop and grip the railing to prevent his legs from giving out beneath him. Leaning his back against the wall, he placed a hand on his chest, feeling as though his heart had been torn clean out. Never had he felt such a numbing and hollow pain as when he heard Ticahrla speak those words. *"I will rip that boy's heart from his chest and devour it if it gets me even one step closer to becoming an Arcane Bearer!"*

So, that was why she needed a Dreamer—why she needed *him*. His breathing started to grow heavy. He couldn't believe it. Sihera was right. Ticahrla never cared for him. She was just using him the whole time.

The realization hit hard in his chest. The tears began to swell in his eyes. He couldn't stand another moment of the pain. Jokahn hurried down the hall to his sleeping quarters.

He lay back in his hammock, but his eyes felt as if they were stuck open. His heart sat broken in his chest. After leaving Athus, Ticahrla had never mentioned where they were sailing to, but he could assume they had arrived at the Origin.

He felt so foolish. He should have known better. He should have known no one would ever actually care for him, especially not someone like Ticahrla. She was perfection in every way. Why would *she* ever care for someone like *him?*

Ugh, why am I such an idiot?! He cursed himself as the misery seeped through him, becoming too much for him to bear. That was it; he couldn't stand it any longer. He had to do something. He had to get away. Tossing himself out of his hammock, Jokahn ran toward the doorway.

A figure turned the corner into the room, blocking the exit. Jokahn planted his feet and came to a screeching halt, skidding to a stop and falling back onto his hands and butt. As his eyes turned upward, he saw Ticahrla's suspicious and angered glare staring down at him. His jaw slacked open. She looked like a giant towering over him. The two of them stared at each other for a moment, neither one saying a word—studying each other.

"Going somewhere?" Ticahrla finally said in an unnervingly flat tone. Ticahrla's foot raised up as she took one large step forward. Her boot clunked heavy against the floor, forcing Jokahn to shuffle and backpedal across the room.

"Uh, no." He tried to steady his voice, but he could feel the nervousness shaking throughout him. "I wasn't going anywhere."

As Ticahrla took another step forward, she carefully scanned the room, studying her surroundings. "What were you doing then? You weren't eavesdropping, I'm sure."

His stomach sank. She knew. She knew he had overheard her conversation.

Ticahrla came to a stop, blocking the only exit. The fear was surreal—heavy and unnerving, pinning him to the floor. What was he going to do? There was only one option, really: *run!*

In a burst of speed, Jokahn sprang forward from the ground, pushing Ticahrla up against the doorway as he raced out into the hall. She was taken by surprise and stumbled back to retain her footing.

Jokahn sprinted up the stairs as fast as he could and out onto the deck. He made a beeline for the side of the ship. In an instant, he hurdled over the railing and landed hard on all fours in the sand. His ankles ached, but he couldn't stop. As he ran, there were no footsteps chasing after him. No one cried out his name. He wasn't sure if Ticahrla had let him go or not, but he didn't wait around to find out. He had no idea where he was, but there was a dense forest ahead of him. Jokahn sprinted up the beach and pushed his way into the thick shrubbery.

The speed of his stride whipped branches and leaves that stung against his face and limbs, but he drove forward without regard, deeper into the wilderness. Panting heavily, he quickly waded through the dark forest.

He ran farther than he had run in a long time, pushing his body to the point where his lungs ached, and his legs were loose and filled with acid. He came to a stop at a clearing in the middle of the forest where a river wound past a large cave opening. Confident he had created enough distance between him and Ticahrla, he sat down to catch his breath.

Jokahn looked around. The forest was quiet. There wasn't a sound to be heard other than his own labored breathing. But in that silence, a sensation began to fall upon him. The feeling of being desperately alone.

How could it be? How was he already missing her? His face scrunched up into a sour pucker, and his hands ran back through his hair, hating himself for the way he still longed for her. He knew she didn't care for him. He knew she had just been using him the entire time. But, *ugh!* It hurt so bad just to think of her.

Ticahrla was everything to him. She had taught him how to be strong and to stand up for himself. But, yet again, he found himself running from his fears.

A part of him knew what he had to do. He had to stop running. He had to turn back and face her. And as he thought about it, he finally realized what she had been trying to teach him all this time. She had been trying to teach him how to grow up, how to be confident and face his fears.

Why was that so hard for him to do? Just the thought of confronting her sent waves of doubt and fear washing over his body. He knew he didn't *have* to face Ticahrla. He could run away and never return. It would be so much easier that way. Just keep running. Keep being scared and alone. A part of him really wanted to. The lure was so tempting to give in—to give up trying and stay scared and alone forever.

Jokahn sat at a literal crossroad in his life, one path leading away from Ticahrla—down a dark and lonely road, which he was all too familiar with—and the other leading back toward her—a path where he would be forced to face his fears head on. He debated with himself for a while, but he knew what he had to do. The choice was obvious. Now that he thought about it, there really wasn't even an option anymore. There was only one way forward. He couldn't go on running, alone and afraid forever. No matter how hard it would be, he had to go back and face her.

Jokahn let out a long sigh, not looking forward to the challenge ahead, but feeling confident about his decision.

As he stood and turned to head back to the ship, a hand clasped over his mouth and pulled him back down into the brush. He could tell from the feel of her skin and the smell of her hair that it was Ticahrla.

Still pressing her palm tightly over his mouth, Ticahrla knelt down and hugged Jokahn's back close to her chest. Jokahn squirmed to break free, but she pressed a finger to her lips and hushed him. She whispered in his ear, "Aiko."

He ceased struggling, and he followed her gaze out to where three aiko were creeping into the cave across the river. As the creatures cautiously disappeared into the darkness and out of view, Ticahrla freed Jokahn from her grasp.

"What are the aiko doing here?" he asked.

A concerned expression was pressed upon her face. "I don't know," she said.

As Jokahn turned to face her, he noticed something strange hovering about her neck. He looked curiously at the small, floating object. "Ticahrla," he said, pointing at her necklace.

Ticahrla looked down at her father's jewel hovering out in front of her. Tethered around her neck, the jewel wavered and swayed, suspended in the air, as if being drawn by a magnet. "What the…" Ticahrla started. Her eyes followed the direction her necklace was pointing. It led directly toward the cave the aiko had entered. "That's it," Ticahrla gasped. "That's the Origin."

As if acting in confirmation, the tie of her necklace wriggled loose, and the jewel darted through the air, disappearing into the river with a small splash.

"No!" she cried, reaching out, but the jewel was gone.

"How did the aiko know where to find the Origin if they didn't have your father's compass?" asked Jokahn.

Ticahrla thought to herself for a moment. Then the blood drained from her face. "Oh, dammit, I'm such an idiot," she said with dread in her voice. "That's why they didn't attack us on the docks. They never wanted to kill us. They were following us."

"Following us to the Origin? But why?"

"I have no idea, but whatever the reason is, we have to stop them." Ticahrla thought to herself for a moment, then she turned to Jokahn with haste. "Listen to me," she said, grabbing him by the shoulders and looking him straight in the eye. "Go back to the ship. Get Drahig and Bakta. I'm going in after the aiko."

"What? No, you can't! You can't fight three aiko by yourself!"

"Someone has to stop them from getting to the Origin. I'll take the first one by surprise. Then I'll lure the other two back out here where I can meet up with the three of you so we can finish them off. When you get back here, if I'm not at this exact spot, don't come looking for me. Understand? I want you, Drahig, and Bakta to take the *Nahktaio* and get out of here as fast as you can."

Jokahn's brow came together. He glared at her as he realized what she was saying. She was still protecting him. "Why are you doing this?" he asked in a concerned voice.

She smiled and placed a comforting hand on his shoulder, but tears were forming in her eyes. "Because I care about you, you little shit."

Jokahn's heart sank, and he looked up at her with dread in his eyes. He was suddenly overcome by a terrible fear, a fear that he might never see her again. "Ticahrla…" Her name became lodged in his throat.

"I know," she said, pulling him in close and hugging him tightly. He sat there numb in her embrace. Then she pressed her lips firmly to his forehead. Slowly, he wrapped his arms around her as the tears began to run down his face. Despite everything she had said, she was still looking out for him.

Jokahn sat there holding her in his arms, wanting to never let her go. Finally, she pulled away from him to study his expression. A watery haze blurred his vision, but they both understood what had to be done.

With a nod of her head, Ticahrla gestured to him. "Now go." Ticahrla gave him a gentle nudge back towards the *Nahktaio*.

Jokahn started out slow at first, not able to take his eyes off her. He wanted to keep the image of her forever in his mind. She stood there in the silver moonlight, more beautiful than ever. She must have been terrified, but she didn't show it. Ticahrla stood tall and confident, a subtle but warm smile on her face.

He couldn't believe what he was about to do; he couldn't believe he was actually going to leave Ticahrla to fight three aiko by herself. He clamped his eyes shut and grimaced a reluctant sigh. Then he turned and started sprinting back toward the *Nahktaio* as fast as he could.

* * *

As Jokahn vanished into the forest, Ticahrla could finally relax her charade, releasing the air from her lungs and letting the worry show through her expression a bit. She turned to face the cave. Drawing one of her swords, she took a deep breath. "Here we go."

30

Fear's Embrace

Ticahrla crept through the cave, gripping her sword tightly with both hands. She stepped carefully, rolling her foot from heel to toe so as not to make a sound.

The cave was dark and damp. Moonlight streamed through small, irregular cracks in the ceiling. At times it was hard to see a few steps in front of her, but she could hear the subtle rustling of the aiko reverberating off the walls. Before long, she had caught up to them.

The aiko scanned and felt their way deeper into the cave. Ticahrla tightened her grip around the hilt of her sword and snuck up close behind the trailing aiko. Her heart pounded as she slowly reared back her sword.

Her foot slipped, skidding off a small rock; her metal boot clattered against the stone floor. All three aiko paused mid stride.

She held her breath in the sudden silence. As the aiko began to let out a low hiss and turn, Ticahrla thrust her sword forward. A crunch and sloshing sound echoed as her blade pierced deep into the aiko's back.

Loud, piercing shrieks rang through the cave as she wrestled her blade free. The wounded aiko spun around, swinging its claws wildly at her. She parried and hammered her sword down, straight through the creature's elbow. The aiko and its severed arm fell to the floor, motionless, thick, black goo pulsing from its body. Quickly, she readied herself for the other two aiko.

Standing alert and in a low, fighting stance, her eyes searched desperately for the remaining creatures, but they were nowhere to be found. As the echo of their shrieks died out, the damp cave became eerily silent and still, punctuated only by her heavy breathing and the subtle drip of water against stone. Before, she was the hunter, but now the aiko stalked her.

"Shit…" she said under her breath.

* * *

Jokahn sprinted as fast as his legs could carry him back to the *Nahktaio*. He knew Ticahrla didn't have much time. He had to get back to the ship, retrieve Drahig and Bakta, and then lead them to the cave in time to save her.

He gritted his teeth as he ran. *What is Ticahrla thinking? There isn't enough time for me to run all the way to the ship and make it back in time to help. This is crazy. Why would she—*

A blood-curdling scream rang out through the forest air. His feet plowed into the dirt as he came to an abrupt stop. It was Ticahrla's voice, he was sure of it. He looked back over his shoulder with panic in his eyes. Suddenly, Ticahrla's plan made perfect sense. She never expected him to make it back in time.

His voice quivered. "No, Ticahrla…" Without a second thought, he turned and raced back the way he'd come. He charged out into the opening and trudged across the shallow river, only slowing once he reached the entrance to the cave.

Peering inside, he searched the darkness, but saw nothing. The cave entrance stood open like the jaws of some great monster.

"Ticahrla?!" His voice echoed off the stone walls, but there was no response, just the dreadfully eerie howl of a damp wind exhaling out from the mouth of the cave. He swallowed hard. Clenching his fists, he took one careful step inside and proceeded down the gullet of the cave.

Inside was a dark, twisted maze of tunnels. For a long while, he didn't hear or see anything, until something caught his eye—a color: red—blood red. Patches of crimson and black were painted across the stone floor and walls.

"Ticahrla!" Jokahn cried out to her again, but still there was no answer. Then he spotted the glint of something resting on the floor. It was one of Ticahrla's swords. He hurried over and picked it up. The blade was coated with black goo.

His heart twisted in his chest. She would never leave her sword behind. Something terrible must have happened.

An odd scratching sound—as if something heavy was being dragged across a hard surface—came from behind him. Jokahn hugged Ticahrla's sword to his chest as he turned. His jaw fell open and the damp, stale air rushed into his lungs.

A dismembered aiko pulled itself along the ground with its one good arm. Jokahn stood there petrified, clinging tensely to Ticahrla's sword.

Slowly, the aiko pulled itself up onto its feet. Lumbering forward, the aiko focused solely on Jokahn. His first thought was to run, but he stopped and remembered what Ticahrla had taught him.

His arms shaking, Jokahn raised Ticahrla's sword and squared off, readying himself to fight. The aiko cocked its head curiously.

"Come on!" Jokahn shouted. The aiko let out a hiss and lurched forward, its talons wielded out in front as it charged. Jokahn deflected the aiko's hand with his blade and sliced a gash across the base of the aiko's abdomen as it passed him.

The aiko stumbled to a stop, peering down at the fresh wound across its stomach, almost seeming taken aback by surprise.

Jokahn turned and squared up again, confident. He could do it. He could defeat this aiko; he could stand up for himself. He didn't have to run anymore. All fear was instantly washed free of him. The aiko glowered as it turned and shot a scornful glare at him. Then it lunged again.

Jokahn deflected the attack again and jab the blade into the creature's chest, but the weight of the aiko's momentum continued forward. The aiko's body plowed into him, sandwiching his hands and hilt between the aiko and his chest. Jokahn stumbled back and slammed against the cave wall with the full weight of the aiko on top of him. The impact left him dazed. He struggled to clear the fog from his mind, but he couldn't realign his senses.

A sharp and searing pain shot through his right shoulder, quickly pulling him from his stupor. Jokahn cried out in agony. He looked down to see the aiko's talons buried deep into his chest, just under his right collarbone. Jokahn had never felt a pain like this before. He could feel the creature's knife-like fingers digging and twisting into his muscle, sending spikes of pain shooting through him with each subtle movement of the aiko's hand.

Jokahn's jaw quivered as he turned to look up at the aiko. The creature drew its face in close to his and snarled a deep, low, growl. Jokahn tried to wriggle his hands free, but the blade was lodged deep in the aiko's chest, and he couldn't find room to move his arms, nor did he have the strength to maneuver out from under the aiko's weight.

The aiko twisted its claws again. He let out a reeling cry in agony as the aiko's talons pealed back and tore free from his flesh. Through tear-filled eyes, he could see the aiko rearing back its arm. Jokahn struggled to break free from underneath the aiko's weight, but he couldn't move. He winced his eyes shut, helpless to do anything else as the aiko's claws once again drove forward.

This was the end, he realized. This was how he would die. The pain in his chest began to numb, and his muscles began to relax. His lasts thoughts were of Ticahrla, and despite everything that had happened, he felt content. He was grateful she had been in his life, and he was happy that the last image in his mind was of her glorious smile shining down on him.

The final strike was jolting. His entire body shook from the impact, but there was no pain, just the gush of warm blood splattering across his face.

He eased open his eyes to a perplexing sight. In front of him was the tip of a metal blade pointing at him through the base of the aiko's skull. He stared at it curiously for a moment. Then a familiar voice spoke through gritted teeth.

"Get your claws off my boy."

Ticahrla's blade arched upward, severing the aiko's skull from its body and raining a thick black gunk through the air. The creature's body collapsed lifeless to the floor.

Jokahn felt weak, but the life came surging back into him as he saw her standing in front of him.

Ticahrla's face was dirty and covered in blood. Her breathing was labored, and her expression was drained to the point of exhaustion, but she still managed to crack a half smile at him. Her voice was weak, but full of pride. "Not bad, Jokahn," she said. "Not bad at all."

She hobbled forward, favoring her right leg, as her weight fell on top him. With her sword still in hand, Ticahrla wrapped an arm around him and hugged him close to her.

He relished the warmth of her embrace. Jokahn's shoulders relaxed again as he let out a long sigh of relief. His forehead fell forward, resting against her shoulder. As he looked down at her, he saw a bloodied bandage wrapped around her arm. His brow pulled together with concern.

He stepped back to get a better look at her. What he saw terrified him. Ticahrla's left arm hung loose at her side and was wrapped tightly in cloth. Deep gashes were torn through her abdomen. Her gown had been shredded and ripped away, partly by the aiko and partly by herself to be used as bandages. A makeshift tourniquet was tied off high around her right thigh, which was drenched in blood.

"Ticahrla…" Jokahn said with dread in his voice. He couldn't believe she was still standing in her condition. "Look at you. You're hurt."

"I'm fine," she said dismissively.

Ticahrla groaned, her strength giving out as she slumped forward into his arms. Worry stretched across his face as he helped her carefully sit down on the floor.

"All right, I'll admit I've felt better." She gave a weak chuckle.

He was amazed she was able to find humor in her situation, as injured as she was. Even resting beside the body of a dead aiko, she managed to beam her heavenly smile at him.

A dreadful thought entered his mind. "The other two aiko!" he exclaimed.

"They're gone," she assured him with a calming voice. "I took care of them."

Relief spread through him, and tears of joy filled his eyes. He was helpless to do anything but smile back at her and weep. Ticahrla patted the side of his face with her palm.

A terrible guilt began to fall over him. It was his fault Ticahrla was injured like this. If only he'd done as he was told and gone back to the *Nahktaio* for help. His voice was weak as the tears streamed down his face. "Ticahrla, I'm sorry. I didn't make it back to the *Nahktaio*. I heard you scream, and I panicked and ran back here. And then there was an aiko, and—"

Ticahrla shook her head to silence him. "It's all right. It's all right. You did well. You didn't run from your fears. Even when attacked by an aiko, you faced them head on. I'm proud of you, Jokahn."

He didn't know what to say. He couldn't get over the feeling that he had failed her in some way. His head fell forward with shame.

"Here, let me dress your wound," she said. She set her sword down and tore off some length from her gown. Then she shuffled over to the front of him and—using her one good arm—began wrapping the fabric around his chest.

He still felt bad, but the way she tugged and pulled the cloth tightly around him was oddly comforting. Knowing fully well he should have been in pain, he looked over at her glorious face—her expression stern and intently focused as she diligently dressed his wounds—and realized he had never felt more cared for and loved than when he was with her.

Ticahrla glanced up at him through her brow. It was only for a moment, but she smiled. "You're looking at me that way again," she said as she turned her eyes back down to continue fidgeting with his bandages.

"What way?" he asked, not shying away.

"I don't know. Your look," she said. "That stupid grin of yours. No one but you looks at me that way."

He had no idea what she was talking about, but his heart filled with a warmth and comfort that only Ticahrla could give him.

"There, all done," she said, tying off the bandage. She nodded her head in satisfaction. Then, slowly, the smile faded from her face. "Jokahn…" Ticahrla started to say. He looked at her with a strained expression, taken aback by her suddenly anxious tone. Her eyes had turned down. "Whatever you heard me say…back on the ship. I—"

Jokahn stopped her, holding up a hand and shaking his head. She looked up at him with sorrowful eyes. "It doesn't matter," he said.

He wasn't sure if Ticahrla would understand or not, but no matter what Ticahrla had said, no matter what she did, she would always have his heart. She had done so much for him that he would have given anything to see her happy. He wasn't sure if he would ever be able to express that to her, but then she smiled at him. That's when he knew, at least on some level, she understood.

"Come on," Ticahrla said. "Let's get out of here."

He struggled to help Ticahrla to her feet. As she picked up and sheathed one of her swords, Jokahn extended his arm, offering back the weapon he had used. She stared at it for a moment, then she looked back at him. He couldn't make sense of the expression that had overtaken her face. It seemed to be a mixture joy and confusion.

Without saying a word—him still holding her weapon out for her to take—Ticahrla reached down and unfastened the empty sheath tied at her waist. A light tug pulled it free, and she held it in front of her. "Why don't you keep it from now on?" she said proudly. "You've earned it."

His mouth opened slightly, awestruck, and at a complete loss for words. He slowly reached out and retrieved the sheath from her hand. With a large smile engulfing his entire face, he fastened it to his waistband and sheathed the sword at his side. The weight felt good and solid on his hip, like it was meant to be. He looked back at her with a ridiculously large grin on his face, and Ticahrla chuckled as she smiled back.

Wrapping her good arm around his shoulder, Ticahrla gave a grunt—favoring one leg—and rested her weight on him. "Now help me back to the ship already."

Jokahn walked slowly along, happily sharing her weight. As they made their way through the winding cave, something caught his eye, something glistening on the ceiling.

He stopped. "What's that?"

"What's what?" she asked, following his gaze.

Through a weathered archway lay a pool of dark, bubbling liquid. Ticahrla stared at it in silence, until her chest began to rise and fall with heavy breaths.

The words escaped her mouth as a whisper. "The Origin…"

31

Into Darkness

Ticahrla hobbled through the archway with Jokahn's help, still resting her weight on his shoulder. The arch opened to a large chamber with worn and faded carvings etched into the walls. In the center was a natural spring of black water. Streaks of moonlight shined in through cracks that had weathered away in the ceiling, creating curtains of white that draped across the stone walls. It was a beautiful sight to behold, but for her—in that moment—it was terrifying.

She had finally found what she had been searching for all those years. Ticahrla stared wide-eyed down at the dark water. For a long while, her mind couldn't process what she was seeing; it was hard for her to believe this wasn't a dream.

Her breathing was becoming increasingly labored. She had fought and killed and bled and struggled for so long. Her entire life seemed to have been building up to this point. She had dreamt and longed of this moment.

"This place looks amazing," Jokahn said, as he walked in front of her to the edge of the pool.

"Amazing… Yes…" Her mind raced, but she could barely form words.

As Jokahn looked down into the dark, churning waters, she—almost instinctively—walked up behind him. She stared at the boy, and gently hugged his back to her chest. The movement felt natural, as if she had done it a dozen times before. She could see the boy peering back over his shoulder. He smiled at her. She didn't react. Her eyes were fixed out in the distance, lost in thought, not looking at any one thing in particular.

She knew what she was supposed to do. She'd run through this exact moment countless times in her mind. All she had to do was reach behind her and unsheathe her dagger.

No...I can't... she told herself.

Her heart stopped, and the dread seeped over her face as she looked down, startled to find her dagger already gripped tightly in her hand.

No...

But her thoughts began to wander; her mind began to degrade. Slowly at first, but steadily growing in intensity. Bakta and Drahig's betrayal. Her father's death. Athus burning. Her mother's bloodied corpse. Apotri grinning victoriously over her. The look of disdain on her people's faces as she failed them. The crippling doubt of whether she was strong enough. The weight of it tore away at her. All of it could be rectified; all the wrongs in her life could be made right again with just a simple extension of her arm.

Her heart was suddenly pounding. Her arm had drawn back without even realizing it. She had to do it. She couldn't stop. Not now. She had come too far to fail. She—

"Ticahrla?" Jokahn's voice called out.

She gasped, wrenched free from that dreadful mental spiral. Her muscles tightened, locking her arm in place, ensuring it dared not move. She hadn't noticed the tears already streaking down her face. In a trembling voice, she whispered, "I'm sorry."

* * *

"I'm sorry"? Jokahn thought to himself. What was she sorry about? His brow pulled together. Something wasn't right. Her voice was quivering. He could feel her arms shaking. "What's wrong?" he asked, concern enveloping his face.

"I'm so sorry…" Ticahrla repeated in a weak voice. "I—I'm not strong enough."

What is she talk-ungh—

A small gasp escaped him as a twinge of pain shot through his center. He grimaced, trying to reach behind him, but Ticahrla held him tighter, pinning him to her body.

Jokahn looked down at his chest and, to his surprise, saw the tip of a blade protruding from his shirt. His chest started to heave, struggling to pull air into his lungs.

He watched the blade retract inside him, and felt it exit as it was pulled from his back.

Ticahrla released her grip on him, and Jokahn was free to turn around. He pressed his hand lightly against his heart as the blood began to flow. He turned and looked over at Ticahrla with a perplexed expression upon his face. Her face was distraught and filled with remorse. Her eyes were swollen red as she stared at him, tears streaming down her face. A bloody dagger rested in her hand. "You don't understand…" she pleaded with him. "The things I've done to get here. I—I couldn't… I had to…"

Jokahn's vision blurred as he grew dizzy. His legs began to waver. He stumbled back a step, struggling to keep his footing, but his knees buckled and gave out from underneath him. As he fell back, Ticahrla caught him—supporting him gently around his back and waist—and lowered him softly to the ground. She rested him across her thighs as he looked up at her in bewilderment, but he couldn't bring himself to say anything.

"It—it will be quick," she said assuredly in between her sobs.

She was right. It was amazing how fast the blood drained from his body, how quickly his limbs became heavy and impossible to move. His body began to feel cold. His mind was foggy, swirling with emotion, but as he looked up and saw Ticahrla's face engulfed in tears and misery, all he wanted to do was to reach up and comfort her.

"Don't cry…" he managed to say in a weak but empathetic voice. "Don't…" His heavy eyelids began to droop and close. *No, Ticahrla…* He didn't want to leave her that way. He was desperate to see her smile again, but he struggled to even keep his eyes open. Just one last time, he wished he could bask in the warmth of her glorious smile and know she was happy.

* * *

Jokahn's eyes closed, and his head fell back heavy in Ticahrla's arms.

Ticahrla stared dreadfully down at the boy. "Jokahn?" she said, her voice barely above a whisper. He didn't respond. "Jokahn." She tried to add some volume to her voice as she shook him, but the boy's head swayed lifelessly. The guilt twisted around her heart like a vice. "No…what have I done?" she whimpered. *Oh shit. I really am evil,* she thought to herself.

Ticahrla's eyes clamped shut as the pain in her chest finally became too much for her to bear. She slumped forward, pressing her forehead to his, tears pouring from her eyes.

"I'm s—sorry," she managed to say between sobs. "I'm so sorry."

She sat there holding Jokahn's body for a long while, grieving the terrible mistake she had made—wallowing in the agony of the monster she had become.

She pulled her head away and dared to face what she had done. She opened her eyes and—through a watery haze—saw Jokahn's cold, pale face. There was nothing she could do to help him now. There was only one thing left to be done.

Ticahrla crept her way to the water's edge and gently lowered Jokahn's body into the pool. She watched as his body floated out toward the middle.

As he finally sank and disappeared beneath the surface, she crumpled over from the weight of her emotions. On her knees, she collapsed and clasped her hands over her eyes. Like claws, she dragged her fingers down her face, trying to free herself from the agony.

The water in front of her started to churn and bubble. Soon the entire cave had begun to reverberate.

This is it. This was the moment she had been waiting for, and now that it was finally here, she doubted if it was worth the cost.

The water continued to boil. She let out an anguished cry. "Just do it already! Give it to me! Give me what is mine!"

The water in the pool erupted like a volcano. Ticahrla braced herself as an immense wave came gushing forward. The impact forced a grunt from her lungs as she was thrown backward, crashing against the engraved walls, and slamming her head.

She sat there, dazed, and disoriented, nearly knocked unconscious as she coughed up the rustic water from her lungs.

Glancing around the room, she tried to reestablish her surroundings. The black liquid dripped from her face and poured down from every surface, but it was beginning to settle and slowly run back into the emptied pool.

She looked down to examine her arms and pressed her fingers to her face. Was that it? Was she an Arcane Bearer now? She searched her senses, probing for the answer, but the sound of rocks rustling drew her attention.

Ticahrla slowly turned her eyes toward the pool in dismay. What was that? Another rustle clattered, echoing through the cave.

"No…" Ticahrla growled angrily beneath her breath. As a hand reached up out of the hole and clasped onto the edge, her face crumpled in rage and agony. "*No!*"

* * *

Jokahn was completely disoriented. Slowly, he pulled himself up and over the lip of the pool. Something was different. He viewed the world through strange new eyes, seeing everything through the rich blue flames that lapped effortlessly from his eyes. He could feel the energy coursing through his veins. Somehow, all his senses seemed the same, and yet…different. It was as if he was witnessing for the first time a new range of color. There was a wealth of smells, tastes, and sounds that had never existed before.

He looked down at his arms and studied the odd new sensation he felt as he opened and closed his hands into fists. It was bizarre. He could feel every muscle and fiber moving in his body. He could sense the energy flowing through every nerve. Jokahn looked down at his chest. His wounds were healed. Then he realized what had happened.

"How could you?!" Ticahrla's voice echoed and bounced dizzyingly against every wall surrounding him.

Ticahrla? It was difficult to see where she was. He wasn't used to the thick, blue flames that distorted his vision, and his mind struggled to process the flood of new information pouring in through his senses.

Her voice cried out from a dozen different directions. "How could you take this away from me?!" He couldn't make out where it was coming from. Then he saw a distorted figure through the flames engulfing his sight. The figure rushed toward him, their sword drawn, and Jokahn's training instinctively took over.

He managed to rip his sword from its sheath just in time to deflect the attack. As steel clashed against steel, Jokahn pivoted to parry the blow with ease. It was like a reflex. He turned to see the distorted figure in front of him and waited.

* * *

Ticahrla staggered as she tried to catch her balance on her wounded leg. The pain tore through her feeble body. She was quickly reminded of how diminished her fight with the aiko had left her. She grimaced at the pain, barely able to support her own weight. How had the boy become so fast? How was he so strong? But her rage forced her to press forward and attack.

Her eyes were roaring a bright, fiery green. She lunged at him, swinging her sword wildly through the air. As the boy parried her attack again, she noticed a small shift in the position of his body. Ticahrla's heart stopped, and time seemed to slow down.

From behind a wall of green flame that lapped at the sides of her face like slow and pulsing waves, she watched Jokahn's blue eyes ablaze and staring intently back at her. Ticahrla's expression was strained and filled with rage; her mouth agape, lips stretched tight over her bared teeth, and her brow pulled down angrily over her hate-filled eyes. Jokahn appeared calm, almost detached. He slowly dropped the edge of his blade on top of hers and pulled it toward him.

Her face turned to confusion as a force jerked her body unwillingly forward. What was happening? Ticahrla recognized the same technique she had taught the boy, but somehow it didn't seem real. It couldn't be.

As Jokahn's blade came steadily grinding up the length of her sword towards her collar bone—sparks jumping from the metal and floating up into the air—Ticahrla's expression shifted from confusion to worry.

She couldn't believe it. As she realized the mistake she had made, Jokahn's weapon came to rest against her skin. She winced, and her eyes narrowed. She knew all too well what would come next, but was powerless to stop it.

Watching the cutting edge of his sword as the blade began to draw back, Ticahrla clenched her eyes shut and gritted her teeth. She could feel the steel carving its way into her shoulder, first tearing away at flesh, then digging deeper into muscle and bone. Her jaw fell open, and the air began rushing out from her lungs, but there was no sound, for in that single moment—a moment that seemed to drag on forever in a whirlwind of emotions—the sound of her cry had not yet had time to carry.

In an instant, time came rushing back. Ticahrla cried out in agony as she collapsed to the ground.

* * *

The sound of Ticahrla's cry quickly extinguished the flames in Jokahn's eyes. He looked down at her with a panicked expression as she collapsed and crumpled to the ground before him.

Jokahn's heart felt tight in his chest. He gawked down at Ticahrla in disbelief, not fully understanding what had happened. He stared in horror at the gaping wound drawn across her shoulder down to the base of her neckline. His eyes turned to the bloodied sword he held tightly in his hand. Jokahn gasped and dropped the weapon to the floor. The metal clanged against the hard surface, the sound echoing against the stone walls.

Panic overtaking him, he rushed to kneel in front of her.

"Ticahrla! I—I didn't know!" He reached his hands out, desperate to help but not knowing what to do. Blood was pouring from the fresh gash across her collarbone. "No—I—" The words stuttered out of his mouth.

"It's all right, Jokahn," she said in a weak voice. She waved him down with her good arm, trying to calm him. "It's all right." Ticahrla's words were soft and gentle, but Jokahn couldn't accept what he was seeing. "It's better this way," she continued. Jokahn's heart was nearly torn from his chest by her words.

Ticahrla gestured for him to give her his hand. He reached out and clasped their palms together tightly. The tears swelled in his eyes as he soaked in this simple touch from her; just the warmth of her hand gave him such comfort, and yet he realized he was losing her. His arms were trembling.

Ticahrla smiled—albeit weakly—her heavenly smile up at him. "Forgive me, Jokahn—" She coughed, spitting up blood. "I truly am sorry." Jokahn's eyes widened with fear. "Please…" continued Ticahrla. "Forgive me."

He had had enough of this. "Stop talking like that," he insisted, shaking his head and moving in close to pick her up. "Ticahrla, you have to stand up. I'll carry you back to the ship if you—" Ticahrla lightly pressed his arm away from her. Jokahn clenched his eyes shut, trying to hold back the tears, not wanting to accept what Ticahrla was trying to tell him.

She took his hand and placed it on the hilt of her sword.

"Just make it quick and get it over with."

Opening his eyes, Jokahn saw the sword resting beneath his palm. Instantly, he lurched his hand back and stood up to his feet, appalled at what she was suggesting.

His defiance seemed to aggravate Ticahrla. Despite her injuries, rage filled her eyes. "I said finish me, boy!" she said fiercely, and for a moment he was happy to see Ticahrla acting herself again. But he couldn't bring himself to kill her.

"No…" he whimpered in a shaky voice.

With a long sigh, Ticahrla let her good arm fall to her side. "I suppose you're right. I don't deserve a quick death. I deserve to suffer after everything I've done."

Jokahn bit down hard on his lower lip. He couldn't stand to hear her say such a thing.

"Jokahn…" she started. Then she paused for a moment. "When people tell stories about me, do you think I will be the hero…or the villain?" He didn't know how to respond. With a disheartened expression, Ticahrla nodded and turned her eyes to the floor. "Just leave me, boy," she said weakly.

Jokahn was growing tired of her talking like that. He stood up tall and pulled his shoulders back. "No," he stated in a firmer tone.

"What?" Ticahrla growled as glared up at him, but her expression was quickly shifted, cringing in pain as she attempted to sit upright. She came to rest on her knees, half leaning forward on her good arm, and looked up at Jokahn with furious eyes. "What do you mean, *no*? What else do you want? What more could you take away from me? How could you possibly add to my suffering?!"

Jokahn winced. "I…" He couldn't find the words. "I—I don't want you to suffer." That was as close as he could come to explaining himself.

"Then damn it, Jokahn, put me out of my misery!"

"No…" he said again, his body trembling at the thought. He looked down at his sword on the ground, blood still coating the blade, and clamped his eyes shut at the sight. "I can't… I—I'm sorry. I just can't."

"Do it!"

Jokahn bit his lip and peered down again at that terrible bloody weapon.

"Do it, boy! Give me some peace!"

With a quick dip, Jokahn snatched up the sword and raised it high over his head. Jokahn couldn't believe what he was about to do, but he couldn't stand to see Ticahrla suffer any longer. She let out a grateful sigh and lowered her head, exposing the back of her neck. A blood-curdling scream escaped him as he reared back his sword.

His eyes bulged and his body shook, breathing heavily as he stared down at the back of her neck; her perfect skin waiting for the blade that trembled in his hands.

I can't. I can't do it.

The sword fell from his grasp and clanged against the floor. Jokahn dropped to his knees in front of her. Cupping Ticahrla's face between his hands, he lifted her head so their eyes could meet. She looked aggravated yet disappointed as she glared up at him through her brow. He didn't want to imagine how he must have looked in that moment. He didn't care anymore.

"I can't." His lower lip quivered. Then he pulled her face in close to his. "I can't because I—I love you too damn much."

Ticahrla's eyes shot frightfully wide. She took in a deep breath and her body went rigid as Jokahn leaned forward. He clamped his tear-filled eyes shut and pressed his lips firmly to hers, holding her tightly, never wanting to let go.

Jokahn had fantasized about what it would be like to kiss Ticahrla. Somehow, he had always imagined that her lips would be soft and warm, but they weren't. They were dry and cold to the touch. Still, he held her pressed to him for as long as he could.

Finally, he pulled away and slowly opened his eyes. Ticahrla sat frozen and wide-eyed in front of him, her body trembling. He had never seen her look so terrified before.

"Ticahrla, I—" he started to say, but then her eyelids began to droop, and her body went limp in his arms. "Ticahrla!" Jokahn cried, supporting her weight, and pulling her upper half onto his lap.

He cradled her as he watched the blood from her wound slowing to a stop. She was dying. Tears ran down his cheeks. He had to do something. He couldn't let her die. He cradled her body and rocked her back and forth on the cave floor, sobbing.

A rustling noise echoed from the cavernous hallway. *Footsteps,* he realized. The aiko must have survived somehow.

He grabbed Ticahrla's sword and held the blade out in front of him as he clutched her body to his chest with his other arm. He shuffled desperately backward, never releasing his grip on her. Blue flames erupted from his eyes as the footsteps drew closer.

"Stay away!" he shouted.

The footsteps echoed louder as they neared the entrance to the room.

A startled but gentle voice reverberated off the cave walls. "Jokahn?!"

* * *

Sihera stood in the archway to the room with Laval and other members of the Archmagi by her side. She gawked at the appalling sight of blood as Jokahn sat on the stone floor, clinging desperately onto Ticahrla's lifeless form. She saw the blue flames pouring from his eyes and instantly knew what had transpired. He was an Arcane Bearer. The fiery blue extinguished from Jokahn's eyes, and the sword fell limp at his side.

She rushed over to Jokahn's side. His breathing was heavy, but as his eyes connected with hers, his muscles relaxed. His head lolled forward, staring at the ground with unblinking eyes.

Sihera placed a comforting hand on his shoulder, but he didn't seem to notice. "Jokahn, are you all right?" she asked, examining him for injuries, but Jokahn appeared numb to the world. There were several gashes torn through his shirt, but he didn't appear injured. It seemed that Laval had finally told her the truth.

After Ticahrla left her and Laval on the docks of Athus, Laval confessed to what he had been hiding from her. In order to become an Arcane Bearer, a Dreamer had to be sacrificed and lowered into the Origin's sacred waters. It was only in death that a Dreamer could be reborn as an Arcane Bearer. When Laval first told her this, she wasn't sure if she believed him. He claimed he was trying to protect her from the violent nature of this world. She had her doubts, especially as she sailed with Laval, following Ticahrla's ship as the princess led them straight to the Origin. But now, seeing Jokahn sitting before her—his wounds healed from whatever had torn through his clothing, the intense energy radiating from him—she knew Laval was telling the truth.

Laval's men tried to pry Ticahrla's body from Jokahn's grasp, but his vice-like grip bound her to him.

"Jokahn," Sihera said gently to him again.

Jokahn looked up at her with dead and watery eyes. She knew what was upsetting him. Sihera turned to look down at Ticahrla's lifeless body. For the briefest of moments, she shifted her glance toward the sacred water nearby, but quickly turned back to face Jokahn as to not draw his attention to Ticahrla and the Origin.

Biting down on her lower lip, Sihera carefully contemplated her next words. "It's all right, Jokahn. She can't hurt you anymore. She's gone now." One of Laval's men tried again to take Ticahrla's body away, but Jokahn still wouldn't give her up. "Jokahn," Sihera intervened, moving close to him so their eyes could meet, "you have to let her go now."

Jokahn's eyes desperately searched Sihera's, as if hoping to find some flaw in what she said, but of course, she was right. Ticahrla was gone. The pain and the sadness visibly began to overtake him. Tears again streamed down his face. His chest heaved as he cried and turned to look down at Ticahrla.

Slowly, the men were able to pull Ticahrla out from Jokahn's arms and rested her gently on the ground. As they did, Laval came over to help console him by resting a hand on Jokahn's back.

"I know it's hard right now," Sihera tried to comfort him, "but you can come live with me. The Archmagi will take care of us."

"Come, my son," said Laval. "You are an Arcane Bearer now."

"No," whimpered Jokahn.

"But you belong with us," asserted Laval.

Rage overtook him. Jokahn forced himself to his feet as he tore himself away from her and Laval. Sihera was shocked to see him so suddenly infuriated. His jaw hardened as he took several paces away from her.

"No, I don't need you!" shouted Jokahn. "And I don't need to be any kind of *Arcane Bearer* either! I can take care of myself! Ticahrla showed me that. She gave me everything! She was always there for me, and then…and then I—" Jokahn choked on his words.

Sihera's lips pressed together, and her brow raised as she felt the pain he was going through. But more than that, her heart ached as she realized nothing—not even death—could shake Jokahn's love for Ticahrla.

"Jokahn…" Sihera said in a stale voice.

Jokahn shook his head and held up an aggravated hand to silence her. He stood there for a moment, clamping his eyes shut, trying to hold back the tears, but he couldn't. As a whimper forced itself out from inside him, Jokahn turned, sprinted down the cavernous hall, and vanished into the darkness.

A few of Laval's men started to follow him, but Sihera held up a hand. "No!" she demanded. Then in a softer tone, she said, "Let him go."

The men stopped dead in their tracks. "But he's an Arcane Bearer now! We can't just let him leave!"

"There's only one thing he cares about," Sihera said confidently. She walked over to Ticahrla's body and sighed as she looked down at her. "If we want Jokahn, then I know what we have to do."

* * *

Ticahrla felt hands grip tightly around her arms and then toss her body to the floor. She hit the ground with a thud, gasping as the life surged back into her body. Her entire body was dripping wet. Face down on the rocks, her eyes opened wide, and an immense green flame expelled outward.

The world felt like it was spinning. Her head throbbed from a constant barrage of noise and sound and color that she couldn't seem to filter. She had no idea what had happened to her, but somehow, she was alive.

Ticahrla was panting as she turned her head to the side. The green fire in her eyes steadily burnt out and then went away. Next to her was a small circle of men all dressed in robes, and in the center was a girl with dark, curly hair. The men removed a ceremonial gown from Sihera's shoulders. One man chanted quietly in front of her as he held the tip of a dagger up to the girl's heart.

"Well, I guess you were right, Ticahrla," Sihera said, looking down at her with a defeated expression. "It looks like you do get everything you want after all." Then the man pierced the blade through the girl's heart. Sihera gasped and her eyes shot wide from the pain. As the men gently lowered her body down into the water, Ticahrla slipped into unconsciousness.

32

The Echo of His Name

Ticahrla sat on a translucent cliffside trying to force the thought of *him* from her mind, but everything she dreamt about reminded her of Jokahn. No matter how hard she tried to replace him with something—anything, even nothingness would have been better— she could not force his name from her mind.

A heat slithered up Ticahrla's spine, and her brow pulled together ever so slightly.

"I thought I'd find you here," Sihera called out from behind her.

Ticahrla's voice was small and feeble. "Leave me alone," she whispered, but she knew—even across the distance separating them—her words would echo clearly into Sihera's ears.

Sihera shook her head in disgust and chuckled. "The *Great* Princess Ticahrla. So, this is what you've been reduced to."

Ticahrla didn't reply. She just cupped her face in her hands.

"Why, Ticahrla? Of all the people in the world, why did he have to choose you?"

Ticahrla didn't care to offer a rebuttal. She wanted no part of whatever Sihera was trying to say. She decided not to stay any longer.

As Sihera continued speaking in the background, her voice gradually grew softer. "You, who has everything, and yet appreciates nothing. You should have—" As the world around Ticahrla faded from existence, Sihera's voice trailed off and disappeared.

A new world materialized around her. Ticahrla sat cross-legged and floating upon the surface of the ocean. She bobbed up and down as the waves rolled beneath her.

"What are you trying to hide from, Ticahrla?!" Sihera shouted out across the sea, her voice turning hard.

Ticahrla let out a soft sigh. She should have known she wouldn't be able to escape Sihera for long. The girl always managed to track her down in her dreams. "Please," Ticahrla pleaded. "Just leave me alone,"

"Why? You've got the power you so desperately wanted! Aren't you happy now?! Or are you finally starting to realize there are more important things in this world besides yourself?!"

The anger boiled over inside Ticahrla, and her eyes erupted in a blazing inferno. "I said *go away!*" In a rage, Ticahrla rose to face Sihera and skimmed across the ocean surface in an instant—nothing but her toes dragging along the water.

An enormous wake kicked up behind Ticahrla as she came to an abrupt stop, face to face with Sihera, but Sihera didn't flinch. The giant cloud of water Ticahrla had created dispersed into a heavy mist that rained down upon them as they glared at each other. Ticahrla's breathing was heavy, and the fire poured from her eyes.

Sihera cracked a wicked smile as she looked Ticahrla up and down. "Don't you see? You have nothing left to threaten me with."

As the two stared each other down, Ticahrla noticed a hint of sadness behind Sihera's confident expression. Ticahrla began to reel in her temper, and the fire in her eyes slowly dissipated.

Sihera's voice turned unexpectedly somber. "Believe it or not, I didn't come here to watch you wallow in misery," Sihera said. "I came here to help you."

Ticahrla couldn't stop herself from snickering. "Why would *you* help me?"

"Because there is a boy I care about. A boy who, despite my best attempts, will never look at me the way he looks at you."

Ticahrla's expression fell, and Sihera ducked her head, as if to hide how much it hurt to say it. "You have everything, Ticahrla. Wealth, power, beauty. You are the envy of every woman, and the love of every man...and every *boy*, as well." That last part seemed to pain Sihera the most. "You will never be able to make up for the hurt you've caused, and I want you to know you don't deserve him. Not in the slightest. Yet he has devoted himself to you completely." An almost pained chuckle escaped Sihera as she realized she was crying, and she stopped to brush away a tear.

Ticahrla stared on in shock.

"He needs you," Sihera continued. "And as much as I hate to admit it, you need each other." She paused for a moment to collect herself. "It's ironic, isn't it? Jokahn has found the one thing you've truly yearned for all along."

Ticahrla frowned. "And what is that?" she asked.

Sihera looked up at her and smiled warmly. "The ability to love *you*...just for being you."

Ticahrla's face went blank at the realization; the air slowly escaped her lungs as her gaze steadily turned toward the ground. She had struggled with this question all of her life, yet it seemed so obvious to her now. Why had she not been able to figure that out on her own? Perhaps she had been too distracted trying to prove herself to everyone—even to herself—to notice.

"Make him happy," Sierra concluded, saying the words with a confidence that surprised Ticahrla. "Treat him better than you would treat yourself." Then Sihera faded from the dream, leaving Ticahrla alone with her thoughts.

Ticahrla's eyes blinked open, and she gradually began to wake from her dream.

It was dark as she woke. The moonlight had all but gone as she slowly pushed herself up from a shallow puddle of water on the cave floor. Glancing around the quiet and empty cave, she realized she was all alone.

Ticahrla grunted and massaged the stiffness out of her muscles. As she did, she felt a strange new sensation. She could somehow feel the energy coursing through her body. She examined her wounds, looking down and pressing her fingertips to her body. Her arm, her chest, her leg. They were all healed.

A faint memory of Sihera's voice suddenly echoed through her mind. *"It looks like you do get everything you want after all."*

Ticahrla stared down curiously at her open palms. Could it be? Was she an Arcane Bearer?

Rising to her feet, she focused her energy. With ease, the heat poured down her arms. A gust of wind followed, like a small shockwave, and a flame ignited between her palms. She gave a gasp that was closer to a laugh as she stared down at the brilliant inferno she held within her grasp. She couldn't believe it. The line of a single tear streaked down her cheek.

Ticahrla flexed her arms, pouring her energy into the fire, creating an enormous fireball that illuminated her surroundings. Something that would have been impossible for her was suddenly accomplished with ease. Ticahrla collapsed her hands and extinguished the flames, then all was quiet again, and the room became dark.

She stared at the floor. She had done it—she was an Arcane Bearer. She should have been elated. This was supposed to be her defining moment, this should have been the highlight of her entirety, but as she stood there by herself in that damp cave—the burden of her last memory with Jokahn still weighing heavy on her heart—all she felt was cold and alone. Ticahrla let out a long and disheartened sigh.

As she exited the cave, the light of dawn was barely cresting over the trees. She trudged back to the beach and saw Sihera and the Archmagi waiting on the sand. Their eyes were fixated outward toward the ocean. Ticahrla followed their gaze.

The *Nahktaio* sat perched awkwardly on the beach, right where she had left it, but marching up the sandy shore in formation was a battalion of Athus' soldiers.

Out on the water, Ticahrla saw the Archmagi's ship anchored in the bay, and beyond that rested a vast armada of Athus' warships already encircling the beach.

Ticahrla came to a stop at Sihera's side. Two Arcane Bearers, fresh and rich with power.

"They've taken him. They've taken Jokahn," Sihera said to Ticahrla, neither one looking at the other, but instead staring out at the ocean before them.

"We'll get him back," Ticahrla said confidently.

Sihera didn't reply, but she nodded in agreement. They stood there staring out at the army that marched forward.

"Is it everything you wanted it to be?" Sihera eventually asked. "Being an Arcane Bearer, I mean."

Ticahrla chuckled, shaking her head, and sighed. "No. It is so much worse."

Two figures were sprinting up the beach. "Ticahrla!" cried the smaller one. It was Drahig and Bakta. "Ticahrla!"

Drahig and Bakta came to a stop in front of her, panting and out of breath. Bakta rested his hands on his knees, "Ticahrla, there's an army coming!" He paused and glared at her, scanning her up and down. "Ticahrla, what happened to you?!"

She shrugged. "I died."

Bakta and Drahig looked at her with a confused expression as the battalion of Athus' soldiers marched toward them.

"I'll explain later," she said.

Bakta's voice was low. "Where's Jokahn?"

"They've taken him," Laval answered, shaking his head. "I don't get it. What is Apotri doing? Why would he send an army here?"

"Isn't it obvious?" Ticahrla replied. "You don't send an entire battalion as a greeting party. Apotri wants us dead. And he's gathered more than enough soldiers to do it."

A group of four men started approaching on horseback.

"Looks like a negotiating party," Ticahrla said.

"What do they want?" asked Sihera.

"I don't know. Let's go find out."

Ticahrla marched over to the men where she was met by an Athus general and some high-ranking officers.

"My Princess. It is you," greeted the general as he and his soldiers quickly dismounted to kneel before her. Ticahrla signaled for them to rise. The general stood and gawked at her torn attire. "My word. What happened to you, Princess?"

"It's a long story," she sighed. "What are you doing here?"

"We were sent by Apotri. His orders were clear. You and the

Archmagi are charged with treason. We were to hunt you down and kill you on sight."

"Well, why aren't you getting on with it then?" she had asked bluntly.

The general pulled back his shoulders, appearing offended. "My loyalty is to you and your family alone, Princess. I would die before carrying out such an order."

"There—there was a secondary order," one of the lower-ranking officers hesitated to admit. "We were instructed to locate a boy named Jokahn and bring him back alive."

Ticahrla took in a deep breath and glared at the general. "What did you do with Jokahn?"

The general cleared his throat. "What we were ordered, Princess. He is on a ship back to Athus as we speak."

Ticahrla looked out at the open ocean. "Order your men back on to your ships, General, and bring the Archmagi back to Athus with us."

A soldier marched over and grabbed Sihera around the bicep, but Ticahrla snatched the man by the wrist. The soldier looked over at her with surprise.

She shook her head at him. "The Archmagi are our guests, not prisoners, understand?"

The soldier nodded and released Sihera. Ticahrla let go of the soldier and looked down at Sihera with a smile. Sihera grinned warmly back at her.

"What are you going to do, Princess?" asked the general.

Ticahrla turned to glare at the horizon in front of her. "Take me to Apotri. I'll deal with him myself."

33

Bearing the Arcane

Jokahn hadn't slept for the past…however many days it had taken the soldiers to sail him back to Athus. His broken heart wouldn't let him. He couldn't come to terms with what he'd done. Now back in Athus in a dark prison cell, Jokahn sat with his face down in his palms.

The sound of footsteps stopped outside his cell.

"Where's the boy?" a man's voice asked. "Where is Jokahn?"

Jokahn's head rose at the sound of his name. Through the bars, he could make out the silhouette of an overweight man.

"He's inside, your majesty," said the guard stationed outside his door.

Your majesty? Who would have that title?

"What of the princess?" asked the man.

"Dead, sir," replied the guard. Jokahn's chest tightened, and his eyes clenched shut from behind his hands. "The boy claims to have killed her himself."

"Hmm," the man grunted. "How long before the rest of the fleet returns?"

"I'm not sure, your majesty. We haven't received word from them yet, but I would suspect any day now. Would you like to speak with the boy?"

"No. Keep him there for now."

Then the man walked away, and Jokahn knew he was justified in doing so. He deserved to be locked away in a prison cell. No, he deserved so much worse. He would never be able to forgive himself for what he had done to Ticahrla. Jokahn's heart was numb—dead—

inside him. He lowered his head back into his hands and wept.

* * *

Not far from Jokahn's prison cell, the bodies of two guards lay dead on the floor. Ticahrla wiped her blade clean on her fresh new gown and opened the door the guards had been protecting. It swung open, revealing a large room filled with guards and men in robes. She recognized them immediately. It was just the group she was looking for: the queen's royal guards and Athus' councilmen. She stood silhouetted in the doorway, her sword still in hand, as she scanned the faces of each man. One person was notably missing from the crowd: Apotri.

What had once been lighthearted chatter now quieted to a murmur as her presence became known. All the men turned their gaze toward her.

"Princess," said one of the councilmembers with surprise in his voice. "You're back?"

Taking one large stride in through the doorway, Ticahrla stepped into the light. The men gasped as they finally noticed the dead bodies on the ground behind her.

"Where is Apotri?" she asked bluntly.

No one answered.

"You know," Ticahrla began, shifting her gaze to the floor. "I've been waiting for this day for so long now." She sighed. "I've imagined it over and over in my mind. I had prepared such elegant speeches; beautiful verses of how I would gut each one of you and watch you suffer for all your wrongdoings. Truly, it was poetry. Yet, as I stand here before you now, I seem to have lost my appetite for such vengeance. So, I offer you this." She looked up through her brow and glared at them. "Flee. Leave now and never return to Athus' borders. Do that and I will grant you my pardon. But stay, and I will kill you all."

As if to answer her, the queen's guards one by one drew their swords. Slowly, they closed in, forming a half circle in front of her.

One of the councilmen in the back let out a chuckle. "Princess, please. You are but one girl against over a dozen royal guards. This is hardly what I would call a fair fight."

Ticahrla snickered. "You're right," she said, shaking her head with a one-sided smile. "You should have brought more guards."

A fiery green vapor erupted from her eyes as the heat poured over her body. The energy flowed from her center down into her left arm, igniting a fireball that she held in her claw-like grip. In her other hand, she clasped the hilt of her sword. She could feel the static arching across her entire body. Her long braid had started to fray and come loose as it danced behind her with the eb and flow of electricity, eventually falling apart all together. As she stood in the doorway, her hair fanned out into a large halo around her as it waved and pulsed through the air, as if underwater.

The once confident expressions on the men's faces steadily turned to dread as their jaws slacked open.

"I don't believe it," a councilman gasped. "She found the Origin."

She smiled a satisfyingly wicked grin as steam came spewing out from between her bared teeth. Her voice reverberated in a low, demonic growl. "Damn right I did."

The closest guard attacked first. Ticahrla parried, toppling the man forward. Rearing her left arm back, she pressed the fireball down on top of the back of the guard's head, blasting a small crater where his skull had once been.

Her mouth fell open as a sharp breath of joyful surprise escaped her. Her eyes were filled with elation at the sight of her new power. Before the next guard could attack, her heightened senses detected the subtle ripples radiating from the blade as it sliced through the air. A second guard was charging in from her other side. She moved out of the path of one blade and cut her sword across the midsection of the other guard.

Dragging her nails across the tile, electricity arced between her palm and the ground. She whipped a bolt of lightning up at the guard who had missed her. The bolt let out an ear-shattering crack—the shockwave reverberating back into her chest—as it sent the man flying into the opposite wall.

"Yes!" she exclaimed. She was growing drunk with her new power, to the point of ecstasy. *This!* This was the power she had been waiting for. Like an elated child with a new toy, she turned—smiling ear to ear—as three more guards charged toward her. "Oh, *please,* give me more."

Ticahrla reared back her left hand—her fingers like talons—as lightning began to coil up and down her arm. She lunged, jutting her claw-like hand forward as a shockwave burst forth from her palm. The blast wave blew a hole the size of her fist through the guard in front of her and sent the two adjacent men flying outward off their feet. As the blast radiated out in a circle around her, the entire building strained and shook.

The remaining guards and councilmen were frozen in silence—awestruck. She stood up tall and reared back her shoulders. As she spoke, she intended to sound stern, but she couldn't hide the overwhelming glee from her voice. "The fear of cowardly men is so palpable in this room." She closed her eyes and took a deep breath in through her mouth. "Oh, the taste is even sweeter than I imagined."

Opening her eyes, Ticahrla turned a stern gaze toward the remaining men. The guards stutter-stepped backward as they brandished their weapons defensively. Ticahrla held her sword low and in front of her, bracing her palm against the back of her blade. Slowly dragging her hand from the hilt all the way down to the tip of the blade, she heated the metal, turning it hot red and eventually causing it to catch fire as embers sparked from her weapon.

She grabbed the hilt of her now flaming sword with both hands and lowered herself into a fighting stance. "Now…" she said, taking a moment to scan their faces. "Who wants to die next?"

The remaining guards threw down their weapons and ran for the back exit. Soon after, the councilmen followed. As the last, heavier-set councilman was waddling as quickly as he could toward the back door, Ticahrla snatched him by the scruff of his collar.

"Eh, eh, eh. Not so fast," she said. The man jittered and squirmed as she turned him around to face her. "Now, I'm only going to ask this one more time. Where is Apotri?"

The man looked up at her, his eyes bulging out of their sockets with fear, as he pointed a trembling finger out the window. "H—he—he's in the bah—bah—bathhouse."

Ticahrla glanced out the pane of glass to her side and saw a lone building sitting high atop a hill in the distance.

* * *

Steam filled the room, blurring the white stone tiles lining the walls. Ticahrla sat quietly in the corner as Apotri entered and made his way towards the tub in the center.

The overweight man took in a deep breath and smiled. "At least someone in this armpit of a town was smart enough to build themselves a spa."

Removing his towel and tossing it to the side, Apotri gingerly crept his way into the hot pool. As he nestled himself in, letting his shoulders seep beneath the water, Apotri laid his head back, closed his eyes, and let out a long, comforting breath.

Reaching over to his side, Apotri's hand felt around for a wine glass that had been left for him. His fingers found the tall drink and, raising it to his lips, he took a swig. "That's more like it," he said with a grin. "Now if only I had some decent company in this tub, things would be complete."

"Ask and you shall receive." Ticahrla's voice echoed quietly throughout the steam filled room.

Apotri's body went rigid as he let out a short gasp. "Who's there?!" He scanned his surroundings, but he didn't seem to see her through the steam. When Ticahrla didn't reply he set down his glass. He quickly reached for his towel, but found it was missing.

"Looking for something?" she asked, holding Apotri's towel in one hand and her sword in the other. With her blade, she drew small circles on the floor, the tip cutting through the condensation on the tile.

Apotri's eyes finally spotted her. "Princess Ticahrla!" he cried as his body leaned back out of the tub. "Wah—what are you doing here?"

She didn't answer. She wanted to give him time for the fear to set in.

"Guards!" Apotri cried. He waited in silence for a moment, but no one came. *"Guards!"*

Ticahrla looked at him through her brow. Panic jittered through his gelatinous body as he stared back at her with dread in his eyes. "What's the matter, Apotri? You look like you've just seen a ghost."

"This is the men's bathhouse. You can't—"

"I can't what?" Ticahrla interrupted, quickly rising to her feet and stabbing the tip of her blade toward him. Apotri reared back, cringing, visibly terrified. The fear shook his entire body, but he didn't respond. Ticahrla gave him a wicked smile—thoroughly pleased with the reaction she had gotten out of the fat man—and retracted her blade.

"H—how did you get here?" Apotri managed to say.

"You mean, how am I still alive after you sent an entire battalion to kill me?"

Apotri swallowed hard.

"Unfortunately for you, coin can only buy you so much loyalty." Ticahrla paced in small circles beside the trembling, naked man. She smiled wickedly down at him. "There is something about a bathhouse that is rather…humiliating, don't you think?"

Again, Apotri didn't respond. He ducked his head between his shoulders as he sat halfway in the tub.

"Just imagine it," she continued. "Your glutinous body, naked, strung to a pillar, stripped of all dignity, oozing blood across the pristine tile. How long do you think it will be before someone comes looking for you? How long will the fluids slowly drain from your body before your heart finally gives out?"

"Wah—what do you want from me?" cried Apotri.

"This isn't a matter of want, Apotri. This is a matter of redemption."

"Redemption for what?"

"For the murder of the queen, and for the destruction of Athus."

"Ha!" Apotri belched out a laugh, suddenly appearing more confident in his position. "Don't preach your hypocrisy to me, *Princess*. Point that blade where it truly belongs, against your heart. You could have been there to protect the queen, to protect Athus, but you only cared about one thing. *Yourself.*"

Ticahrla's eyes suddenly burst into flame, pure rage engulfing her face.

Apotri appeared unfazed. "Go ahead, kill me if you want, but it won't subdue your hate! We both know who is really feeling the guilt of their actions!"

Ticahrla let out a horrid scream as she pulled back her sword. Holding up an arm in defense, Apotri clenched his eyes shut. Her blade careened downward over the top of him, but she stopped with the cutting edge of her sword just inches from his neck.

Her breathing was heavy, and her eyes were filled with rage. She wanted more than anything to kill him—he didn't deserve to live—but something was stopping her. It didn't take long for her to understand. It was the heart-wrenching realization that Apotri was right.

A somber ache began to rise in her chest. Her stern expression started to fade, and her grip loosened around the hilt of her sword.

A loud clang echoed through the room as her sword slipped through her fingers and fell to the floor.

Apotri let out a startled scream, but realized she had laid down her weapon. He looked up at her with caution in his eyes as she made her way around the back of him and knelt down. She hugged her arms gently over Apotri's shoulders and rested her hands on his chest.

"You're right," she whispered to him in a solemn tone. Tears began running down the side of her face. "I have done terrible things in my life."

"Admit it," said Apotri with an attempt at confidence in his voice. "You don't care for anyone but yourself. Not even that boy of yours.

You were just using him the whole time."

"You're wrong about that," Ticahrla said softly, her lower lip quivering. "I adore him."

With that, she took a deep breath and extended her arm out far in front of Apotri. The man gasped as he saw Ticahrla's dagger held in her hand. She pulled the blade back toward her, plunging it deep into his chest with a thud, and the air rushed out from Apotri's lungs.

Desperately, he tried to pull at the dagger, but she held her arms firmly around him. For a while, Apotri's body kicked and squirmed, thrashing water in every direction throughout the bathhouse, until, finally, he was still.

The muscles in her arms relaxed, and she wrenched the dagger free from his chest. Standing up tall, Ticahrla watched as Apotri's lifeless, fear-stricken body drifted slowly out to the center of the tub, and the water began to shift from clear to red.

Exiting the bathhouse, Ticahrla walked past the bodies of the Apotri's guards that lay dead and bleeding on the ground.

* * *

Alone in his prison cell, Jokahn sat with tears still streaming down his face. His entire body ached. The days he had spent alone had been brutal on him. He couldn't eat. He couldn't sleep. How could he live with himself knowing Ticahrla was dead, and that *he* had killed her?

Jokahn collapsed his face into his palms and wept. The pain in his chest was so strong. Even the sound of the key turning to unlock the door of his cell could not distract him.

He heard someone sigh, and—in a familiar, velvety voice—say, "What are you crying about this time?"

Air rushed into his lungs with a gasp, and his head lurched up. Through a watery gaze, he saw her standing there, whole and beautiful in the doorway. He couldn't believe his eyes. Was he dreaming?

Jokahn wasted no time. He leapt from his bed and ran to her.

Throwing himself at her and wrapping his arms tightly around her shoulders, he sobbed uncontrollably. Ticahrla hugged him back even tighter as they both fell to their knees, still clinging to each other.

"I'm sorry" Her voice quivered. "I'm so sorry."

For a long while, they sat their holding each other, until finally Ticahrla untied her arms and leaned back to get a look at him. He must have looked terrible, covered in snot and tears, his eyes swollen red, but she smiled brightly at him anyway. A tear-felt but joyful chuckle escaped from behind her grinning teeth.

He looked at her in amazement. "How?" he struggled to say.

Ticahrla shrugged. "I'm an Arcane Bearer now, just like you."

A sense of relief fell over him, and he smiled brightly at her.

With a chuckle, she pushed the hair from his eyes and wiped the tears from his cheek. "You are such a mess. Come on, let's get you out of this cell."

As they exited the room, Bakta and Drahig were waiting nearby. Bakta smiled happily at Jokahn, and Drahig rested a friendly hand on his shoulder.

"Drahig! Bakta!" he said gleefully. "You're back."

"Actually," Bakta said, with a slightly solemn expression, "Drahig and I are about to head out. We just wanted to make sure you were all right before we left." Jokahn looked at Bakta with a confused stare. Bakta turned to Ticahrla and Drahig, and said, "We've been discussing it for the past few days, and I think it's about time I went back to my hometown. I'm getting a little old for a life at sea. I think I'm going to find a nice place to plant myself and see if I can start over again."

"And where are you going?" Jokahn asked Drahig.

"With Nalia and her clan. I've decided to take her up on her offer."

Jokahn nodded, realizing it was the right thing for them to do. But none the less, he was going to miss them.

Bakta must have seen the sadness in Jokahn's eyes. "Hey, it's going to be all right, kid." He walked over and hugged Jokahn with one arm around his shoulder. "The truth is, we have you to thank for all this, Jokahn. None of this would have happened if you hadn't stumbled into our life. And I mean that in a good way."

Jokahn laughed. Then he turned to Ticahrla and looked over at her with a cautious expression. "What about you? You—you aren't leaving, are you?"

"No," Ticahrla said with a warm smile. "I'm not leaving." Jokahn beamed brightly back at her. "Honestly, I have no idea what I'm going to do now."

As Ticahrla said that, a scout—panting for breath—rushed to her side and kneeled. "Princess Ticahrla! A huge army is approaching from the South."

"Aiko?" she asked sternly.

"No, they're human."

"Who is it? What kingdom do they hail from?"

"Well, it's…it's all of them, I believe."

34

The Last Stand

Ticahrla stared out over the hillside as the massive army marched steadily closer. She couldn't believe it, flags of all seven nations—practically the entire human race—had unified to march against her. What were they planning?

Mounting a horse, she quickly rode to address them. In front were the carriages of kings and leaders from each nation. She knew each man in every one of those carriages, and she despised the lot of them. As she neared the approaching force, it was surprising to find not only soldiers, but also families—men, women, and children clinging to what few belongings they could carry. A few of the kings and nobles exited their carriages and approached her.

"Princess Ticahrla, we seek refuge from the aiko's onslaught. Will Athus grant us stay?" one of the kings asked desperately.

A bitter laugh burst from Ticahrla's lips as she shook her head in disbelief. "There is no refuge for you here. Not even Athus is safe from the aiko's wrath."

Another king stepped forward. "There must be something you can do. The aiko have already ravaged our kingdoms, and now they hunt us down like wild game."

"We have to do something," a man pleaded. "The aiko are only days behind us."

Ticahrla's eyes grew large as she stared furiously down at the men. "Let me get this straight," she said through gritted teeth, taking a few steps forward on horseback. "You *great men*, with all your power, decide to turn tail and run, abandoning anyone who can't keep up, leading the aiko directly to *my* doorstep, and now you plead to me for *salvation?!*" She glared at each of them, waiting for an answer, but they stood silently as they hung their heads in shame. Ticahrla muttered under her breath, "Fucking cowards," and reared her horse around to lead them into city.

* * *

Jokahn stood beside Ticahrla on a low parapet overlooking the droves of refugees as they funneled through Athus' walls. The atmosphere was unusually quiet for such a large crowd, with nothing more than the echoed shuffle of their feet to break the silence.

"There's so many of them," he said, his heart aching.

A sigh escaped Ticahrla. "They must really be desperate if a ruin like Athus is their only hope."

Jokahn's eyes blinked as he leaned back, astonished to see people from Broich—with their short, stocky builds—lumbering into Athus. He couldn't believe it; they had travelled all this way just to find Athus reduced to nothing but a husk of its former glory.

Shortly after, he recognized people from the Olthar kingdom, their once lively spirit completely stripped from their faces. Just as Jokahn was thinking back on his time in Prixia, his breath became lodged in his chest. Jokahn's eyes locked on one man walking amongst the crowd; it was the same man that had bullied him in the tavern. The man's once elegant clothing was now torn and dirty. The man hobbled past, and his fear-stricken eyes turned up to meet Jokahn's. Their gaze met for the briefest of moments, but to Jokahn, it felt much longer.

As the man turned his eyes to the floor and walked past, the breath eased out of Jokahn's body. Jokahn watched the man pass by, not with hatred, but with compassion, realizing what the man must have endured in recent days. He wouldn't wish that on anyone.

* * *

Ticahrla walked through the sea of bodies that now littered the floor of her kingdom. It was surreal, almost dreamlike. She had never seen a more dejected and miserable people. It made having Jokahn by her side all the more important—a small reminder that not everything was completely lost. Still, the decrepit sight of humanity's last remnants sat heavy on her chest.

A hand reached up and clung to her wrist. Ticahrla reacted by trying to pull away and glaring down at the woman who had latched onto her, but Ticahrla's eyes softened as she saw the look on the woman's face.

"Please," the woman begged. "We haven't eaten in days."

Ticahrla's brow tightened, and her lips pressed together. All of Athus' reserves wouldn't feed these people for more than a day. But, then again, the aiko were only about one day away. What good were reserves if there was no one to eat them. She leaned forward, placing a strong yet comforting hand on the woman's shoulder. "No one is going hungry today."

The woman smiled wearily and released Ticahrla's arm.

Across the way, the sound of a scuffle caught Ticahrla's attention. A look of disappoint weighed on her face as two men argued and wrestled each other to the ground. Not surprisingly, they were the kings of Olthar and Celara. It wasn't long before their personal guards assisted in breaking up the pathetic squabble and separated the two rulers.

Ticahrla shook her head as she walked away. "Morons."

"My Princess!" a voice called out from behind her.

She stopped and turned. A group of four men were running up behind her. As they fell to their hands and knees, groveling before her, she recognized them as the men who had rescued her from prison.

"Please, Princess, let us fight for you," pleaded one man. "If you can avenge our queen as you did, then you can lead us against the aiko."

She turned an empathetic gaze toward the man and sighed. "Slaughtering a few fat pigs is not the same as defeating the aiko."

Six of Athus' high-ranking generals stepped forward from the crowd. "Only you can unite us, Princess. If you lead, our soldiers will follow."

"We beg you, Princess. We will fight to protect what little we still have, but you must show us the way."

Ticahrla grimaced, struggling to find the right words to say. "I'm not sure this is a fight we can win."

One general stood up tall. "Someone is going to lead us in our last stand against the aiko. If not you, then who?"

Ticahrla's head slumped. She wasn't sure.

* * *

In the ruins of the palace—in Athus' once great hall—the kings, councilmen, and noble elite of each nation gathered. A dozen chairs had been arranged in a large circle to provide those in power with a means to address one another, while people from every civilization filled the back of the room. Just outside the circle sat two empty chairs, the thrones previously reserved for the king and queen of Athus.

Ticahrla was allotted one chair in the circle—signifying her status—while Jokahn, Drahig, Bakta, and a few generals stood behind her representing Athus in the ring of nations.

The meeting was arranged to discuss a strategy for the survival of the human race, but the conversation quickly degraded into a meaningless debate for power. As the men argued with each other over who should lead humanity in their last stand, Ticahrla slouched in her chair and pressed her palms against her temples in frustration. She watched as the men shouted and screamed at each other, accomplishing nothing. It was chaos.

Men in every direction bickered with each other, throwing insults and judgments at one person, while demanding respect from others. Only Ticahrla remained silent.

This is it, she thought to herself. *This is how the human race dies. In a pointless bid for control.*

"I have won more battles than you can count," shouted the high ruler of Broich as he stood up tall, "and I have lost more than most of you have ever fought. There is no one here more suited to lead this army then me."

"The only way you win battles is by betraying those closest to you." Olthar's king jabbed an accusatory finger. "Only a fool would trust you on the battlefield. You are more likely to offer the rest of us up as a sacrifice to the aiko to prove your loyalty to them."

"That is some gall you have speaking of loyalty. How many affairs is your house known for having?"

"Don't forget, my heritage and right to the throne traces back far before any of your bloodlines."

"Not all of us could be born into royalty. You have been handed everything to you on a silver platter. Do you know the tribulations I've endured to achieve my status? I have fought for and earned my right to lead more than anyone else in this room!"

Ticahrla's face tightened and contorted as her frustration grew from listening to the incompetence of these men. Her head slowly retracted between her shoulders as her body began to sink deeper into her chair. Her fingers dug like claws into the armrests until finally she could take no more of it.

"SHUT UP!" Ticahrla's voice roared over the crowd as she thrust herself up from her chair. The men's voices grew steadily quieter and then fell silent as they turned toward her. She stood there, her fists quivering with rage. "Are you self-centered morons really this incapable of making a decision? Your people's lives depend on you, and you sit here quarrelling like a bunch of children over what *you* want, what *you* deserve, what *you* have the right to. What about *them?*" Ticahrla jabbed a finger behind her at the audience and scanned the face of each man in the circle. "Who is speaking up for them?"

No one answered.

Ticahrla let out a sigh as she tried to calm herself. "You know, the truth is I don't give a shit who leads this army or sits on that throne, because at the end of the day, it doesn't matter. Our people want to fight. They want to survive. And I'm going out there to help them. The rest of you can sit here and rot, for all I care." With that, she kicked over her chair and stormed out of the room with Jokahn, Drahig, Bakta, and a following of people close behind her.

The kings and councilmen stared at each other in silence for a while. No one said another word after that, yet they all knew and understood their decision was unanimous. Ticahrla would be chosen to rule.

* * *

Sihera watched as Ticahrla stomped angrily out of the meeting and exited through the palace corridors.

"Come, Sihera," Laval beckoned her, grabbing her by the wrist. "Quickly now."

Sihera hurried to keep pace with Laval as he chased after the princess.

"Ticahrla!" Laval shouted. He hurried through the crowd to intercept her path, pulling Sihera in tow behind him. Ticahrla stopped and looked Laval up and down with a stern expression as he tried to catch his breath. "Er, I mean, Princess," Laval corrected himself with a polite bow. Then he paused to question himself again. "Oh, uh, well…actually, I'm not quite sure how to properly address you at the moment. I suppose 'Last hope of the human race' might be a little presumptuous?" Laval gave a light chuckle.

Ticahrla stared impatiently back at him. "Spit it out already. What do you want?"

"Right," Laval continued. "With the aiko marching on us in a matter of days, I know you are going to need all of the help you can get. I thought I could be of some use to you."

"What good can you do?" she asked bluntly.

"Well, I control an Arcane Bearer. That could be of great use to you, could it not?"

Sihera's expression turned to confusion as she felt a twinge of pain in her chest. *What did he say?* "You what?" Sihera interrupted.

Laval looked back over his shoulder at her, appearing surprised by Sihera's unexpected outburst. He tried to laugh off the uneasy interruption and continued addressing Ticahrla. Ticahrla looked curiously down at Sihera, and then turned back to Laval, unimpressed. "Pay no attention," Laval said, trying to move the conversation along. "Anyway, as I was saying—"

"Hold on," Sihera said sternly, her blood pressure rising. This time, she stepped forward between Ticahrla and Laval and turned to face him. "Say that again," she demanded. "What do you control?"

Laval looked down at Sihera, then back up at Ticahrla, and chuckled nervously, "Sihera, please, don't get hung up on semantics. It was a poor choice of words. Be reasonable. Come, stand beside me." Laval reached his hand toward her, but Sihera took one large step back. She came to a stop at Ticahrla's side, just out of Laval's reach, and glared at him.

"No," she said, her voice calm but stern with conviction.

Ticahrla looked over at Sihera and raised a brow.

Sihera was breathing heavily as she glared up at Laval.

"Sihera…" Laval's face had turned pale with shock and disbelief. His jaw hung open. He turned to look up at Ticahrla, but he could no longer form words.

Eventually, Ticahrla responded for him. "You can go now. It's clear you aren't wanted here anymore."

Laval seemed to be trying to say something, but he kept choking on his words. He shot one last baffled expression at Sihera and then turned and left.

Jokahn moved to Sihera's side and placed an arm around her shoulders. "Are you all right?" he asked. Sihera's face was still stuck in that aggravated pucker as she stared down the now empty hall.

Ticahrla chuckled. "Is she all right? I bet she's never felt better in her life."

Sihera's eyes began to blink as the rage slowly faded from her. She looked over at Jokahn and smiled lightly. "Yes, I'm fine," she said in a quiet but grateful tone, finally feeling as though she could breathe again. "I should have done that a long time ago."

Ticahrla patted a hand at the base of Sihera's neck and gave her a wink of assurance. "I think I'm actually starting to like this one."

Ticahrla and her crew, Sihera included, started walking down the hall again. As they did, Ticahrla leaned over to one of her generals. "Assemble as many soldiers as you can. If they can fight, I want them armed and ready by morning. When the aiko get here, we'll be ready."

"Right away, Your Highness."

* * *

Later that night, Ticahrla lay on a cot in the tent that had been assembled for her on the front line. Ticahrla had ordered her generals to position their forces at the base of a ridge that would intercept the approaching aiko forces before they reached the civilian population in Athus. The location she had chosen was perfect for their defense. The ridgeline would force the aiko through a narrow funnel that would slow down their advance and force them to only be able to attack with a small force at a time. Meanwhile archers could release volleys of arrows down into the congested enemy from the flanks. The stage for battle was set. Now all she had to do was wait.

Ticahrla stared over at the ivory-colored plate armor that had been specially crafted for her and set up on display next to her cot. She knew she should get some sleep, but her mind raced with questions. Despite her confidence in her strategy, she couldn't help but wonder, was it good enough? Would it be enough to stop the aiko? Was *she* good enough to save her people?

Ticahrla looked over at Jokahn, lying sound asleep in his cot. How could he sleep so soundly at a time like this? Rising, she walked over and stood beside him in her nightgown. He looked so calm. She wished she could feel that same kind of peace. She debated waking him, but she knew it was better to let him rest. Maybe she could lie down with him for a bit. That would be all right, wouldn't it?

Are you awake? she thought to herself.

Jokahn began rubbing the sleep from his eyes. He turned to look up at her with drowsy surprise. "Ticahrla, what's wrong?"

Without saying a word, she climbed in under the covers beside him and hugged Jokahn's body close to hers. The warmth of his skin soothed her heart. He was smiling his ridiculous smile at her, and she couldn't help but smile back at him.

A warmth inside her began to grow. It started in her chest and slowly spread throughout her body. Eventually, even her cheeks were flushed with heat. She liked holding him close to her. She didn't want to lose this.

With a quiet voice, she asked, "Are you sure I can't convince you to sit out this battle? We have plenty of soldiers."

Jokahn stared curiously at her. "I want to be with you, wherever you are."

She smiled as a calm washed over her. She closed her eyes, and before long, she was fast asleep.

* * *

"Princess Ticahrla," a man called.

Ticahrla lurched upright with a grunt, her hair tousled and eyes squinting at the daylight that now poured inside the tent. She was still beside Jokahn in his cot. One of her generals had pressed open the flap to the tent, and she held her hand up to shield herself from the morning sun.

The general continued, "The aiko are approaching. We are assembling the troops."

As the general stepped aside, two handmaidens and an armorer entered.

"Come, sir," the general called to Jokahn, who was now wide awake beside her. "It is time to suit up."

Jokahn looked over at Ticahrla with a concerned expression.

"It's all right," she assured him. "Go with the general. I'll meet you outside in a few."

Jokahn went outside, and the general closed the flap behind him. The two handmaidens helped Ticahrla undress and bathed her with a bucket of warm water. They dried her off and dressed her in new undergarments. Ready for the armorer, Ticahrla thanked the handmaidens and excused them from the tent.

"My Princess." The two women curtsied as they made their way outside.

The armorer had already laid out Ticahrla's armor in preparation. "Do you like your new armor?" he asked. "I had it specially commissioned for you as a gift."

"A gift?" Ticahrla tilted her head at the man.

"For your birthday," the armorer smiled and stood before her with the first piece in his hands. "Don't you remember? You turn seventeen today."

She had completely forgotten about her birthday. She looked the man up and down with an inquisitive glare. He was an older gentleman with a long white beard.

"Come," the armorer gestured. "Let's begin."

She stepped forward and raised her elbows. He fastened the first piece of armor around her waist. "You look familiar for some reason," she said. "Have we met?"

The man nodded. "I've proudly served your family my entire life. I used to dress your father for battle, and before that, I dressed his father."

Ticahrla chuckled as she recalled the memory. "I remember." She smiled. "Your hair used to be darker."

"Indeed, a lot has changed over the years." The armorer tugged at her hip guard to make sure it was fastened well. Content with his work, he pointed at her left thigh and reached for another piece of armor. Ticahrla presented her leg, but her mind was still lost in her memory.

"Cahldwell," she eventually said, proud of herself for recalling his name.

"At your service," he said, tying the ivory plate around her thigh. Piece by piece, Cahldwell assembled her armor around her. Finally, after tying off the last plate around her wrist, he took one last look over her and announced, "There you are, my Princess. You are ready and suited for battle."

Ticahrla felt a twinge of pain in her chest. Her voice was soft with a hint of regret in her tone as she spoke. "You know, you don't have to call me that anymore."

Cahldwell looked at her with a puzzled expression.

"I failed," she explained. "I've let Athus fall to ruin. I'm not worthy to be a princess of anything anymore."

Cahldwell let out a short breath and expressed a disgruntled frown. Then he turned and pulled her sword off the weapon rack. "With all due respect, may I speak freely?" he asked as he came around and presented her weapon to her.

She nodded, taking her sword and began tying it to her waist.

"I'm reminded of something your father once said: 'The measure of a person is not what they have done to further themself, but what they do every day to better the lives of others.' For as long as I've known you, since you were a small child, you have always fought vehemently for your people. And, as you stand before me today, I see that has not changed. For as long as you continue to do that, *my Princess* you will remain."

Ticahrla found tears swelling in her eyes. She could practically hear her father's voice as Cahldwell spoke to her. She nodded gratefully. "Thank you, Cahldwell."

He took a step back and bowed his head respectfully. "It has been an honor." Then Ticahrla exited the tent.

The campground was bustling as people prepared for battle. Ticahrla made her way to a neighboring tent where she found Jokahn waiting outside, already dressed in full plate. He stood there fidgeting with his new attire.

"Come here," she called to him with a smile. Jokahn stomped his way across the grass toward her, his armor clanking and clattering the entire way. As he stopped in front of her, she knelt to examine him, pulling and tugging on each plate of armor. "Very good," she said, pleased with the quality. "It's a nice fit for you."

"It's heavy." Jokahn grimaced.

Ticahrla nodded. "I wish I would've had time to train with you in full plate, but you will adjust."

As she stood, she realized something peculiar about Jokahn that she hadn't noticed before. Standing in front of her, Jokahn was nearly as tall as she was. She peered curiously at the boy who had unexpectedly grown into a young man before her eyes.

Jokahn apparently saw her puzzled expression. "What?" he asked with a concerned glance of his own.

"Nuh—it's nothing," Ticahrla said, chuckling as she shook her head. "I—I just hadn't noticed how tall you've gotten."

Jokahn smiled warmly.

"Your Highness," a soldier approached with a horse's lead in his hand. "The troops are assembled and ready. They await your command."

"Right." Ticahrla smiled confidently at Jokahn, giving him a gentle pat on the cheek. "Let's go."

The soldier helped her up a small staircase to straddle the horse, followed by Jokahn, who sat behind her. Servants handed her and Jokahn their helmets and bowed.

"To victory, my Princess," the soldier said. Ticahrla nodded and kicked her horse into a full gallop.

* * *

Jokahn clung to Ticahrla's waist as they galloped up the hill to regroup with the rest of the troops. The horse reared to a stop as two soldiers helped Jokahn dismount.

Ticahrla slid gracefully off the horse and marched up the hill. As Jokahn followed her, the sight of an armor-platted ergman caught his attention. It was Drahig, and standing beside him in line was Bakta. Jokahn's eyes lit up to see them both. He ran over to them with a smile. "What are you guys doing here?" he said with excitement.

"We're here to help," a girl's voice called out. Sihera stepped out from behind Drahig wearing her full leather Archmagi armor. Jokahn chuckled, happy to see her. He reached out and hugged her in his bulky armor, squeezing her tight. Sihera grunted at first, but then she wrapped her arms around his back and hugged him warmly.

"It's time," the general signaled to Jokahn.

Jokahn gave Sihera one last grin and then turned to make his way up the hill behind Ticahrla. As he crested the top of the ridge, he saw for the first time the horrors that he knew even Ticahrla had only read about in history books. Athus' emerald hills had turned black, covered by an endless sea of aiko. The horde moved as one—almost flowing like a thick liquid through the narrow channel—a single mass, creeping inevitably closer.

Ticahrla scanned the countless enemies in front of them. "Admiral, how many soldiers do we have with us today?"

"A little over 40,000 strong, Princess."

Ticahrla's composure never faltered, but Jokahn knew they were drastically outnumbered.

As Jokahn looked out at the unimaginable size of the enemy, he should have been terrified; he should have been running in fear. That would've been the natural response to what he was witnessing, but as he stood by Ticahrla's side, he wasn't afraid. On the contrary, he was joyous. He looked at Ticahrla standing beside him, and he was grateful just to be, even if it was only for that moment.

Ticahrla sighed. "Are you sure you want to be here, Jokahn?" she asked wearily. "I can have a rider take you back where you will be safe." He looked at her in confusion as Ticahrla turned to face him. "Are you sure this is what you want?" she clarified.

She was trying to mask her worry as best she could, but Jokahn could see the concern in her eyes. He knew what he wanted. The truth was there was nowhere else he would rather be than by her side. He smiled and nodded confidently. "I'm positive."

His confidence seemed to surprise her at first, but then she smiled.

"Princess Ticahrla," a man called out. It was the admiral. "Are you ready to proceed?"

Ticahrla looked out again at the invading army and sighed. Then she lifted her helmet over her head and locked it in place. Raising the visor, she nodded and drew her sword. "Follow my lead, Admiral."

The admiral signaled one of his officers with a gesture of his hand.

"Soldiers!" an officer shouted. *"March!"*

In complete unison, the human army gave one clash of their weapons against their shields, causing a thunderous echo to fill the air, and chanted, *"Oohra!"* The soldiers started their advance, the clatter of metal echoing through the air, each step sent synchronized shockwaves through the ground beneath them. Jokahn had never felt anything like it.

He fastened his helmet and raised the visor so he could see. As Ticahrla marched one step in front of him, green flames lapped from the sides of her helmet.

"Ticahrla," Jokahn called. She glanced over her shoulder at him as they continued forward. Jokahn smiled at her and focused his energy. As the magma inside him spilled over, blue vapor poured from his eyes. "You are the best thing that ever happened to me."

Ticahrla grinned her heavenly smile and gave Jokahn a wink.

The end.

THE GIRL WHO LONGED TO FLY
~ A tall tale from the Kingdom of Athus ~

Once upon a time, in the cradle of the valley, lived a sprightly girl named Liahna. Liahna was just like any other girl, full of life and laughter, but there was one thing that set her apart. She had a longing, an innate and insatiable need to fly. She yearned to soar through the liberating vastness of the sky, to feel the roar of the wind rushing past her face, and to watch the world as it streaked by.

Day after day, Liahna would attempt to fly. She sewed together wings from feathers, flapped her arms in wide circles until her muscles screamed in regret, and launched herself from tree branches. All this only to fail each time, leaving her dress stained with soil. Her continued defeat echoed through countless sniggers as she became the laughingstock of the town. On many nights, the ridicule of the outside world snuck into the quiet comfort of her home; even her family would sometimes chuckle at her futile endeavors.

Yet, Liahna remained undeterred. The taunting only strengthened her resolve; the laughter in her ears translated into the mocking wind that she was increasingly determined to conquer. The desire lived inside her, gnawing and growing until her heart was heavy with its weight. Nevertheless, she knew, one day she would soar; she would fulfill her destiny, no matter the cost, even if it meant giving up everything she loved and cared for.

Despite what you might think possible, Liahna's efforts were not in vain. For one day, she journeyed beyond her homeland, trudging to the top of the highest cliff she could find. From there, she gazed out at the sky whose blue vastness had kept her captive for so long. The breeze whistled past her, like a siren's song in her ears, filling her with courage. She stepped out onto the precipice and, without hesitation, she leapt.

She felt the cool rush of the air as the ground pulled away beneath her. Her heart pounded in concert with the ebb and flow of the wind. Her hair danced wildly behind her, her eyes brimming with excitement. The girl who had longed to fly, was flying.

A wide smile stretched across her face as the wind swept away the tears from her eyes. As she descended, she could see the images of her past flicker by—every chuckle, every ridicule, every condescending look. But instead of being marred by insults of folly, these memories were now reborn in vindication. She had proven everyone wrong, proven that soaring through the sky was not just for the privilege of the winged.

No matter how joyous, her flight of freedom was not destined to last forever; the end was imminent. As the ground neared, her flight nearly over, a serene calm washed over her. Her heart was light. She had done it. Liahna, the girl who longed to fly, had at long last flown.

Though Liahna's tale may seem morbid or offensive to some, to many others, it is a story of encouragement. In the face of her tragic outcome is the radiant testament to the determination and resolution of her persistent spirit. In the end, Liahna was not a punchline, but an inspiration, a girl who dared to chase the impossible and, in her own way, achieved it. She remains immortalized, not as the girl who leapt from a cliff to her demise, but as the girl who gave everything she had to achieving her wildest ambitions, breaking all worldly shackles that attempted to restrain her, and flew.

DEAR READER

If you enjoyed this journey and the characters you met along the way, please consider leaving a review. Your feedback means the world to me and helps others discover my stories.

Follow me on social media to stay up to date on my writing.

Website: RyanBartlettBooks.com
Email: contact@raynbartlettbooks.com
Twitter: @ryan.bartlett.author
TikTok: @AuthorRBartlett
facebook.com/RyanBartlettAuthor
instagram.com/AuthorRBartlett

ACKNOWLEDGEMENTS

Thank you to my friends and family, and to all who accompanied me throughout this incredible journey of bringing my story and characters to life.

A heartfelt thank you goes to my wife, Saili, whose glorious smile inspires me to do everything in my power just to see her happy. Thank you for enduring my countless writing hours encroaching on our life. And thank you for being one of my first and biggest fans.

Thank you to my editor, Stephanie Slagle, for taking on the challenge that is my writing. You were able to grasp the heart of my vision, see through the jumbled mess of ideas I had on paper, and help give my story shape. This book would not be what it is without you.

I would be remiss if I did not pay tribute to all my beta readers and ARC reviewers. I'm eternally grateful for the time, love, and energy you provide. Your enduring enthusiasm and feedback helped to polish this book and make it shine. I am grateful for your selfless dedication to the craft and the love of storytelling.

In addition, an enormous thank you goes to Maria Berejan. Writing a book is a challenge, but navigating the intricacies of self-publishing is a whole other beast in itself. Your experience, knowledge, and patient explanations showed me a clear path to achieving my dream of sharing the story and characters I adore with the rest of the world.